SECOND SON

Christy Kenneally

HODDER
HEADLINE
IRELAND

Copyright © 2005 Christy Kenneally

First published in 2005 by Hodder Headline Ireland

The right of Christy Kenneally to be identified as the Author of the
Work has been asserted by him in accordance with the Copyright,
Designs and Patents Act 1988.

2

All rights reserved. No part of this publication may be reproduced,
stored in a retrieval system, or transmitted, in any form or by any
means without the prior written permission of the publisher, nor be
otherwise circulated in any form of binding or cover other than that in
which it is published and without a similar condition being imposed
on the subsequent purchaser.

A CIP catalogue record for this title is available from
the British Library.

ISBN 0340 89620 5

Typeset in Plantin Light by Hodder Headline Ireland
Printed and bound in Great Britain by Clays Ltd, St Ives plc.

Hodder Headline Ireland
8 Castlecourt Centre
Castleknock
Dublin 15
Ireland

A division of Hodder Headline
338 Euston Road
London NW1 3BH

To my wife, Linda, who has been my champion and heart's companion while I worked on Second Son.

To my son, Stephen, who was wise beyond his years in his observations and whose grasp of grammar and syntax compensated for his father's ignorance of either.

To my son, Shane, whose energy and delight in the everyday things kept me anchored to what matters.

To the memory of my beloved brother, Michael Kenneally, who was always my hero.

BIRMINGHAM CITY COUNCIL (CBC)	
H J	16/12/2005
A	£6.99
	SHELDON

1

The Island

THE BEATING WAS a warning. It was also comfortingly crude: a couple of digs, awkward and ill-timed; a few kicks, delivered with no more conviction than an afterthought. There was, of course, a message. He knew there would be.

'Keep out of it, Gabriel.' Dan O'Toole hunkered down to whisper in his ear. 'It won't be us next time.'

Mingled with the smell of stale beer, he detected a note of pleading, and he was chilled. Brady and Leahy he could understand – lazy fishermen who had found permanent anchorage in the factory, straw men – but O'Toole was a genuine water man.

Unbidden, the image of Brady and Leahy, drunkenly righteous, nodding approval at his plight, made Gabriel Flaherty shake with repressed laughter. He bit down hard on his lip. Laughter and drink could make a lethal cocktail.

The footsteps moved away, out of the pool of light from the pub window, and he was alone. His mind wandered as he curled on the cold stones, seeking refuge from the pain. It is long ago and the sun is shining, as it always seemed to do then, minting the beach stones into squinting silver. He is mining the beach for treasure while his brother, Michael, sits cross-legged in a pool of shade, reading. He tires of the hem of high waves and begins to climb a high rock for a wider view of the water. His outstretched hand scrabbles at an outcrop, slick with seaweed – kelp, his brain registers as his hand begins to slide. 'Catch me, Michael!' he screams. 'I'm falling!' The brief exhilaration of flight, the shock as the sand rises up to thump him between the shoulders; then his older brother's face swims into focus and he searches that face for any spark of panic that might ignite his own.

Michael is as impassive as ever. 'Time for a post-flight check, Angel Gabriel. Left leg and foot, raise and twist. A-OK. Right leg and foot, raise and twist. Ditto. Landing gear fully operational. Instrumentation check – head left, head right. All pressures perfect, both flaps free and responsive to the rudder. You'll live, Gabriel; get up.'

The cold of the flagstones pricked Gabriel back to the present. No Michael now, he thought wryly, not since he signed up with the sky pilots. Imagine? Michael, a priest. He went through the ritual anyway.

'Right undercarriage, as sore as bloody hell. Left side of cockpit beginning to swell. Check the flight log. Departed Finnegan's pub 23.00 hours to dump excess fuel against outhouse wall. Executing manoeuvre when bandits appeared at six, twelve and three o'clock. Brief dogfight. Downed but not destroyed.'

A full moon peered cautiously from the rim of a racing cloud; stars trembled back into view. Then he remembered. 'Oh, excuse me,' he muttered absently, tucking his penis back inside his pants.

For two days Gabriel lay on his bed, simulating flu sounds to quell his sister's anxious queries through the locked door. The cracked mirror over the basin recorded the progression of his bruises from red through purple to jaundiced yellow, his left eye's deflation to something approaching normal proportions.

All the time his brain formed and re-formed a plan. The beating had been a warning. It had also been a confirmation that what he suspected was true. 'The truth will set you free,' he said, smiling wryly at the mirror, his split reflection smiling lopsidedly back.

2

Home of Major Devane

MAJOR RED DEVANE, US Army (retired), preferred the dark. He stood at the tall window and nodded affirmation of this fact, his lips parting slightly as his ghost smiled back from the glass. "'If a man be afraid of the shadow, how may he ever walk in the light?'" he quoted softly, and sipped the neat Glenfiddich.

Deliberately, he turned the tumblers of a locked vault in a memory bank most men would have worked to forget, and selected a favourite sequence from one of the many nameless wars he had fought for his country. As the images flickered in his mind, his eyes glazed, his breathing slowed.

There were six of them in a cell designed for two, sitting on the floor with their backs to the walls. Only Devane had room to stretch – the mantle of myth he wore ensured that none of the others would risk even a casual contact. For twenty-four fetid hours they slow-cooked in their own sweat, moving restlessly to distribute the numbness in their limbs. Devane slept, but none of the others could be certain of that. One by one they were dragged out for interrogation. The ones taken never returned, but the screams pulsed through the walls and the stench of fear intensified in the tiny cell. Devane knew he would be last.

They took him, blindfolded, deep into the cellars to a sound-proofed room. He coughed once, to satisfy himself that it was state of the art; the sound was absorbed almost as quickly as it left his mouth. Someone moved to his left and he registered the creak of leather. Holster, he thought. One man armed. How many others? In the corridor he had stumbled against his two captors, who had laughed at his awkwardness and jostled him roughly, just long enough for him to be certain neither was armed. The one cutting his clothes away from him wasn't armed either. There are four of them and only Holster is armed, he concluded. He felt anklets and bracelets of a soft material looped on his feet and wrists. The slight heaviness of each bond and the rasp of a rope completed the picture forming in his mind. The weights were metal loops; the rope would be threaded through and he would be hoisted and suspended from a pulley.

He was half-right. It was only when they attached the face mask that the picture became complete, and he shivered. Sensory deprivation was a popular technique in this part of the world. He should have been flattered. It was expensive and time-consuming, and usually reserved for someone whom they considered had a song worth hearing but who, even after enduring the less subtle methods, stubbornly refused to sing. Go straight to jail, Devane thought wryly as the ropes tightened and his feet left the floor. Do not pass Go. Do not collect two hundred dollars.

The water in the tank was maintained at body temperature. By the time his ears equalised to the change in pressure, Devane felt nothing at all. He had been on the dry side of the tank on more than one occasion; he knew the drill. Without a reference point for any of his senses, he would inevitably lapse into a detached, almost catatonic state, and they would wring him dry of all he knew.

Immediately he began to regulate his breathing, visualising the hot spot of hate he kept in reserve for such eventualities. The air he was taking in through his mask seemed to solidify to the mould of his father's face. The resulting surge of hatred washed over it and grew in clarity, like a photographic plate.

They must have been confident when the limp body dripped from the tank, an eternity later. They must have taken some satisfaction from the wide-eyed stare as they removed the face mask and helped him to the chair. They had been confident and satisfied – and stupid enough to appoint Holster as one of his bearers.

The one who went to plug in the tape recorder was the last to die. He was still turning in surprise at the gunfire when his captain took a bullet that vaporised his lower jaw, spotting the tunic of the tape man with bone-flecked blood. The survivor stood on twitching legs, the recorder held out before him like a votive offering. His shocked gaze fastened on the eyes of the naked, bloody demon as it approached; he tried to scream, but his mouth opened and closed mechanically without uttering a sound. The sudden rush of warmth on his legs pushed his panic to such a level that it was almost a relief when the revolver touched his forehead in benediction.

Slowly, Devane's eyes refocused. He was back at the dark window, backlit by the faint warmth of two lamps. Far below, the sea moved and stretched like a waking cat, its surface banded yellow by a feral moon.

A square of light appeared and disappeared in the window. Devane sensed a presence behind his right shoulder.

'Sergeant Skald.'

'Major.' He wondered how Skald's voice could remain so stubbornly atonal. It had resisted all the inflections with which nature and nurture and every normal human emotion imprint human speech.

Ah, but Skald was special.

Devane, the man who preferred the dark, was rarely seduced by appearance. He had long since blinded himself to the masks of young, old, male or female. He preferred to listen to the music of the human voice as it balanced its burden of passion. He had discovered through long, patient hours that, whether they spoke Arabic or Aramaic, Farsi or Mandarin, under the threat of implacable pain they all eventually flatlined into truth.

'Has our message been relayed?'

'Yes, Major.'

'Is this the kind of man who listens, Sergeant?'

'No, Major.'

'Men who don't listen prefer to talk, Sergeant. But to whom does this man talk?' He touched the glass to his chin. 'When the hermit finds illumination, who can he tell? No, Gabriel Flaherty is a scholar and scholars write. They always do, Sergeant. Speer, Bonhoeffer, Frank, even our erstwhile employer Nixon, all had this insatiable urge to record, to give some independent life to what they knew. Where the words are, there will the man be also. Find them, Sergeant.'

3

The Flaherty House

THROUGHOUT THE SECOND night, Gabriel's sister, Fiona, tossed uneasily, the mouse pecking of his typewriter nibbling at the edges of her sleep. As the light from the east swamped the bulb, he pulled the last sheet from the roller. His body felt leaden and the unruly bed beckoned, but a hot core of anxiety fuelled his focus. He counted the carbons twice and locked them in the lower drawer, then stretched above the desk to the bookshelf, dropping the key into the headless statue of the Infant of Prague. On impulse, he lifted the spools from the machine and tucked them into his pocket. Quivering, he pushed two copies of the document into brown manila envelopes. He scrawled the name and address of a journalist friend in *The Irish Times* on one; the other he left blank. Then he tucked both inside his windbreaker and pulled up the zip with a gesture of finality.

A wave of leg-trembling tiredness washed over him and he leaned his forehead against the cool windowpane. Before him, a patchwork of small fields draped upwards to a headland limned with early light. The backdrop beyond was all Atlantic, hazed and calm. He never liked to be out of sight of the sea. When he had studied science in Trinity College, a borrowed bicycle had taken him regularly to Bray Head. He had chosen the University of San Diego in California for his doctoral studies in oceanography, humping his books and charts to the white sands, sitting incongruously among the bronzed bodies, hunched under a straw hat, his red beard pearled with perspiration. Initially, the 'beautiful people' had given a wide berth to the freckled hobo, so markedly uncool in his 'Kiss me, I'm Irish' T-shirt. In time, his intense focus had drawn them, like children, to sidle closer and peer over his shoulder at the rippling lines and whorls on the charts pegged with shells against the wind.

'You're into maps, right?'

'Right.'

'Where is this place?'

'Well, as a fella at home would say, if I were you I wouldn't start from here at all. It's about six thousand miles back over my shoulder. Basically it's a knuckle of limestone jutting out of the Atlantic. Here, have a look. D'ye see that there...' His consuming passion for the world underwater had mesmerised the bikini-clad youngsters who pooled round him. These unofficial seminars had added two months to his thesis but, as soon as it was delivered, he had disappeared. He had slept soundly in the window seat of the plane, oblivious to the Rockies, the prairies and the endless geometry of Kansas wheat fields. He had awoken, refreshed and expectant, when the aircraft banked at Newfoundland and headed for the open sea.

Gabriel's head bumped him awake against the window. The room, mirrored in the glass, reflected his passion. Dolphins arced across the wall from one poster to another; islands of paper were anchored by pieces of coral, forming untidy archipelagos that stretched lazily across the carpet and under the bed. A shingle of fossils flecked the worktops, and the bedside lamp gleamed from the smile of a rose-lipped conch. The small, warm light beckoned him. Only for a few minutes, he thought, pushing away from the support of the window.

A few minutes. Gabriel Flaherty slept.

4

Finnegan's Pub

FOR AS LONG as she could remember, Sarah Dolan had felt invisible. Her parents, hobbled to a bad marriage by their only child, acted as if she wasn't there, punctuating their long silent troughs with squalls of anger that raged over her small head. I'm invisible, she said to herself, connecting the spills of porter on the kitchen table with a patient finger. Her magic followed her to school, where a succession of teachers, tired of dragging her into focus, elided her from the normality of questions and expectations. Only the Master, lapsing further and further into his own unreality, took time with the shabby, overweight little girl.

'Butterflies come from unlikely places when the sun shines,' he would admonish his assistants.

'True for you, Master,' they would concur dutifully, but they were less sanguine behind his back. 'She's the Bermuda Triangle,' one of them scoffed in the sanctuary of the small tea room. 'Stuff goes in and never comes out.'

Whether her father had jumped or had fallen dominated Island conversation for two whole days. He was found bobbing with the plastic bags near the pier, spared the attentions of fish and crabs and the cruelty of the rocks. The bereaved were also spared the long search, the bloated belly and the closed coffin. 'The sea was kind to her,' the islanders nodded; and, 'Hadn't he drowned in the bottle anyway?' Whether or which, it was an answer to her mother's prayers and an excuse for Sarah to make permanent her invisibility at school.

It was the Master who suggested to Finnegan that Mrs Dolan was a willing worker who would scrub his premises twice weekly. Finnegan considered acting affronted by the suggestion that his premises needed scrubbing, but thought better of it.

'I'll give her a start, Master,' he said magnanimously.

'I knew I could depend on you, Mr Finnegan,' the Master said. He lowered his glass thoughtfully to the counter and added, almost as an after-thought, 'I hear the daughter is a good-mannered girl – a bit quiet in herself, but very respectful all the same. I was wondering…'

'God, I don't know. Things is shocking slow, Master, so they are.'

'Things will pick up for the summer, Mr Finnegan, and it would be a kindness.'

Finnegan considered saying that kindness never paid the rent, but he bit it back. He saw himself in his mind's eye: an overweight and unco-ordinated boy, the butt of casual cruelty until the Master had intervened. It was hard to refuse the Master. The Master read his silence as consent and raised his glass in thanks.

Sarah started her apprenticeship, clearing the tables and washing the glasses under Finnegan's critical eye. He approved of her self-effacement and she graduated to pulling pints behind the bar. But nature conspired against her invisibility. The older men often left their small change on the bar; the younger ones tarried a bit longer than usual. She liked that. Leo couldn't take his eyes off her, and she liked that a lot. Leo was a few years older than herself. He had difficulty holding his drink and keeping a job, but he had a gamey eye, and that eye roved ever more frequently over the ample shape of Sarah Dolan.

The only shadow on their fun today was the man sitting alone in the far corner, his back to the wall, his body angled towards the window which gave a clear view of all who entered or exited the bar.

'He's one of them Yanks,' Sarah confided, leaning across the bar to whisper. Her breath tickled Leo's ear, sending a hot flush to his cheeks, and his eyes strayed to the promise beneath the straining buttons of her blouse. He dragged his eyes to the figure in the corner and his ardour cooled. The man was straight out of the war comics Leo had studied under the desk in school. His head was square and bristled with gunmetal-grey spikes. If he had a neck, it was lost in the swell of his massive shoulders. To the waist, he was a solid block. He had the biggest hands Leo had ever seen, but it was the eyes that attracted and repelled him. Leo had seen eyes like these once before, in a giant squid beached after a storm. Even in death there had been a cold malevolence in them, and his skin crawled again at the memory.

'Frank O'Stein,' Sarah giggled in his ear. When he dared to look again, the chair was empty.

'Jaysus, the ghost who walks.' Now that the shadow had passed, Leo was back to himself. 'I'm the phantom,' he laughed, tugging his pullover up over his head.

'The wind will change and you'll be left that way,' she said, flicking the damp cloth at him in mock exasperation.

Skald's passage through the bar cleaved the swell of conversation and left a satisfying silence in his wake. As he reached the door, the talk resumed, but at a lower register. Gooks, he thought, letting his eyes adjust to the sunlight outside. He didn't understand a word of their language.

Theodore Roosevelt Skald, his immigrant mother had christened her tow-headed son, hoping that the name would act as a thermal to lift him out of the East Side neighbourhood and float him up there among the 'real Americans'. He would 'learn the English good', find an indoor job and maybe an American wife and have the kind of home she scrubbed twice weekly for the doctor on Riverside Drive. Then, maybe, there would be a room for Mutti, and grandchildren with straight white teeth, and… It was her mantra as she knelt before the icon of the Virgin in the spartan apartment she shared with her silent son.

Instead, at seventeen, he found a war and lost his name. In a cramped recruitment booth in Lower Manhattan, he became Ted Skald and a soldier in just six minutes, under the bored gaze of a Marine sergeant who saw enough potential in the opaque eyes and muscular frame to waive the particulars.

'Just put your X here, sonny, to be a part of this man's army.'

'I can write,' Skald said quietly, his steady gaze pushing the sergeant to break eye contact.

So you can, thought the sergeant, pecking the details two-fingered on the army-issue typewriter and filing in his brain the name, rank and serial number of one Caucasian male – Skald, Ted – under 'ass to be kicked'. He smiled mirthlessly as he jerked the form from the roller. A brief call to his old friend Casey Baines in boot camp and Skald, Ted would be speaking with a little more respect and in a higher register than hitherfuckingto, yessir. And in that brief moment of malice, the sergeant ensured that Casey Baines would retire prematurely from the forces, with a wired jawbone that never set quite right and gave him a curious click in his speech as a constant reminder to leave some recruits alone.

It took Skald just two bloody tours to work his way out of the Marines and into the elite Special Forces who operated without a codebook on the fringes of a dirty war. These were men who wore no identifiable insignia and ignored the fresh-faced officers from West Point, who babbled of vectors and surgical strikes and believed that a modern war could actually be won. For Skald and his ilk, war was an end in itself. It was what they excelled at, and they knew their terrible talents would be neither needed nor appreciated in peace-time. They lived day to day and hand to mouth, with the constant companionship of foot rot and dysentery. Death by shit-smeared punji stick and slow starvation in a bamboo cage were the norm that moved the Corps to coin the motto, 'Do Unto Others…' War was the refiner's fire that consumed the dross in its white intensity, casting the survivors as unlikely saints or serial sinners. It refined Skald to his essential animal nature, expanding the range of his senses to register the slightest nuance of threat, tempering him to endure the unendurable and then a little further still, honing him to a cold blade.

It was the bloodiest of all wars and the very best time of his life. But then it ended. The goons and gooks conspired to sign it into history over coffee in Geneva, and the stockades began filling up with people like Skald, and the talk was of atrocities, hearings and inquiries. It was at this point in his life that Skald needed, and found, a saviour.

He already had a simple plan constructed. It involved the certainty of killing his three cellmates, the probability of taking out the two military policemen on the block, and the possibility of random civilian casualties over a three-mile radius in the Leavenworth area. It also took as a given that Skald himself would die, but his hand was rock steady as he palmed the spoon from the cafeteria. He honed it against the coarse-block wall of his cell with careful strokes, humming tunelessly to mask the sound. His demeanour was composed, almost meditative, as he waited for time, place and opportunity to synchronise.

If he was surprised at the sudden turn of events, he showed no sign of it. His acute hearing captured the strengthening sound of footsteps he didn't recognise. Males, he concluded, one older, with more authority. The younger one speaks more often. The home-made shiv vanished seconds before the visitors halted at the cell door.

The older man was a study in composure; the younger one, outmanoeuvred and outranked, was fighting a rearguard action to salvage some shred of self-importance.

'Major, I must insist.'

'The lock, if you please, Lieutenant.'

'Goddammit, Major, you must go through the proper—'

The Major turned and took a step closer to the young officer. It was only a single step, but the man

flinched as if he had been struck. Skald closed his
eyes to better hear the whisper.

'Lieutenant Bow.' The voice was without
inflection, a blunt instrument, all the more
frightening for being matter of fact. 'You have a
choice. You may oblige me, in which case I will
speedily complete my business and just as speedily
depart from your jurisdiction. Or you may seek to
delay me, in which case I will have you charged
with whatever offence I can manufacture at short
notice and you will be incarcerated, pending
inquiry, in this very cell and among its present
occupants. They will, no doubt, take cognisance of
the fact that, while they were involved in bloody
conflict for a country that now arraigns them, you
were tending paper cuts with a styptic pencil in an
air-conditioned office.'

The key skated across the metal plate before
finding the lock.

'You three gentlemen, outside. Sergeant Skald,
as you were.' It was a lion-tamer's voice, totally
confident in the compliance of others, with just
enough snap in it to intimate consequences.

'That will be all, Lieutenant.'

The young officer tasted his protest and
decided to swallow it.

'At ease, Sergeant Skald. You may sit.'

Skald settled on the bench set into the wall and

was mildly surprised when the Major sat beside
him. He was genuinely surprised to feel the hard,
round mouth of a pistol pressed firmly to his side.

'Let us dispense with the small talk, Sergeant.
You will unburden yourself of the shiv, thereby
guaranteeing the integrity of your liver. In return, I
will make you an offer.'

Using his left hand, Skald slowly withdrew the
hidden weapon and dropped it on the floor
between his feet. Equally slowly, the Major placed
the pistol between his. A Mauser, Skald noticed
with a hint of admiration, a stopping piece that
would have vaporised his liver and decorated the
cell wall with most of the left side of his body.

'Thank you, Sergeant. I will be brief. I am
Major Devane.'

Skald stiffened slightly.

'I see you have heard of me,' the Major continued, as evenly as before. 'However inflated
barrack-gossip tends to be, in my case anything
you have heard is probably true.' He paused,
weighing his words and his silent companion. 'I am
in the process of recruiting a unit to operate in
Colombia. Our mission is to influence certain
persons involved in the drug trade. Upon comple-
tion of our mission, each member will receive an
honourable discharge and a remuneration package to guarantee a long and happy retirement.

Should you agree to this offer, you will accompany me now to our temporary head-quarters in Quantico and thence to the theatre of operations. You have two minutes to consider.'

The Major glanced at his watch and then stared impassively ahead.

'Yes,' Skald said simply. He felt something he had never felt before. It was a feeling beyond admiration; a feeling he had no vocabulary to describe.

It was a feeling that would focus in the months ahead, as he watched the Major mould a disparate group into an effective fighting unit without ever raising his voice or pulling rank. The operation further convinced him that the Major was one of a kind.

Dropped from a Dakota flying below the sweep of radar, they systematically interrogated and assassinated. Sometimes they garrotted the extended family, one by one, until the subject divulged names and locations; they were always careful to leave witnesses alive, to carry and expand the nightmare. It was textbook terrorism. A subject turned the ignition key of a jeep and watched in horror as his home exploded. A subject lifted a mobile phone beside a swimming pool and heard the dying screams of his children. The pattern was to have no pattern – to strike and disappear, to blast a bloody swathe of destruction from A through B to C and reappear at Z to crucify a subject in an Armani suit to the cedarwood doors of his expensive villa. And when they stopped, the carnage continued. In the absence of hard fact and concrete evidence, rumour thrived and spawned suspicions that, in turn, generated vendettas, decimating the leading families in the cartel.

The debriefing was perfunctory, the congratulations understated, the Major no less imposing in a well-cut civilian suit. The others sat uneasily out of uniform, except Skald, who would be a soldier in any garb.

Outside the window of the airless Quonset hut, the unmarked plane was already completing pre-flight checks, engines humming on the frosted tarmac. Without the focus of the operation, the squad were strangers obliged to share a flight, already working at distancing themselves from one another.

'That's it, men, and bon voyage. Sergeant Skald – a word.'

He was to remain. Automatically, he took a position just behind the Major's right shoulder. Impassively they watched the others embark, the huge, brooding Hercules turning a wide circle as it nosed for the wind.

The Major spoke over the drone. 'The persons I referred to in our previous conversation are pleased. They would like me to remain in their service in a consultative capacity. I have recommended that the offer extend to you, and they have accepted. You have two minutes to consider.'

It was the first time Skald had seen him smile.

As they rode in a chauffeured limousine to the civilian airport, the Major checked his watch and used the remote control in his armrest to activate the television. The newscaster's inane smile and cheery manner never faltered through the details of the recent air crash. Helicopter footage lovingly detailed the swathe of litter strewn over the half-mile scar on the forested slopes.

The anchor had adjusted his expression of concern when the studio camera brought him back to the screen. 'There are no survivors of the fireball that so tragically lit up the evening sky,' he intoned. 'And now, today's financial news. Cheryl.'

For Skald, it was an epiphany – a sublime, liberating moment. For the first time in his life, he felt accepted by someone whose regard actually mattered. He allowed himself to relax in the presence of another human being. Theodore Roosevelt Skald had found his father.

5

The Post Office

THE FACE THAT peered from the Island beret was aged. Keen winds and sea spray had pared the flesh from her cheekbones so that the tired, light blue eyes were salt-sore pools in deltas of lined skin; the depths of desperation in those eyes owed more to her unruly brood, who had sought and found trouble at home and abroad. Noreen Joyce did not like the post office. It smelled of officialdom and bad news. She felt threatened by the posters pinned all about, threatening dire punishments and fines. But the focus of her fear was Lena – Lena the postmistress, with her slow walk and knowing eyes. Lena, who now held the precious envelope between thumb and fingertip before dropping it like a soiled dressing in a kidney dish.

Noreen tightened her coat to bolster her courage. I will not let this bitch best me, she thought.

'That'll be one pound fifty for the United States, missus.'

'A bargain, Lena.' It was out of her mouth before she could think better of it.

'Ah, yes. Very droll, Mrs Joyce, very droll indeed.'

But Lena's hard eyes held no spark of humour, and Noreen already regretted her quick tongue. Lena smiled, that lazy half-smile she affected to mask her anger. 'Tom will be delighted to get it, so he will.'

Noreen flinched. She had deliberately left the envelope blank. Lena registered the reaction, her smile widening to a rictus of false sympathy.

'I have to be going now,' Noreen said desperately, fumbling for her money, but Lena was not to be denied.

'Ah yes, poor Tom – God help him. But then, who are we to judge, I always say.'

Noreen dropped her money on the counter and snatched her envelope and stamps, tucking them inside her coat as if for comfort. She was away out the door and walking blindly down the road before the last of the coins, tired of circling, rattled down to rest. Lena scooped the money into the open drawer, butting it closed with her ample stomach.

'Foolish bloody woman,' she whispered fiercely. 'More money for that work-shy waster of a son beyond in Boston. Biscuits to a bear,' she snorted, returning to the high stool by the window and the open letter trembling in the draught from Noreen's hasty departure.

Lena Muldowney was almost as broad as she was tall, her round body topped by a small, round head. The bottle that came from the chemist in Galway kept the thin wisps of her hair impossibly black, and she tied it so tightly in a bun at the nape of her neck that it stretched the pale skin of her face into an expressionless mask. Only the eyes gave access to the emotions that churned inside, and they gloated over the letter before her. It was still damp from the steam that had liberated it from the sealed envelope in the dingy back kitchen. She read, her lips moving soundlessly, her spectacles perched on the tip of her quivering nose.

'"I'll be staying on in London for another while, Mam,"' she mouthed, and lifted her eyes. 'Indeed you will, my fine lady,' she murmured with satisfaction, 'until you're delivered of Tom Rourke's bastard.'

Some of the islanders were careful to write in code. Some of the younger ones abroad, those who had nothing to hide, often added the postscript, 'And best wishes to you, Lena.'

'Will you stamp that for me, Lena, and shove it in the bag?'

She had been so engrossed in the sad·blue letter, she hadn't heard him enter. Flustered, she knocked the letter to the floor and glanced quickly at her surprise customer. She breathed a sigh of relief when she recognised him. *This one was so wrapped up in his thoughts, he wouldn't notice if she were bare-arse naked, thanks be to God.*

'Oh, certainly, Gabriel. Two pounds fifty,' she said, squinting at the scale and taking the time to check the seal. 'Isn't that a fright for such a small thing? Sure, 'tis like papers or something?'

'The boat goes at five?'

'Oh, aye, five it is, and the gentleman in Fleet Street will have it the day after tomorrow.'

She shot him a glance from under her brows to see if he had registered her slip of the tongue, but Gabriel Flaherty was gazing out the window. She wondered if it was a trick of the light in the dim office that made his face look suddenly older. Her curiosity piqued, Lena swivelled her head to follow his gaze and saw the squat man sitting on the stone wall opposite. He's like a stone himself, she thought suddenly.

The sound of the back door slapping brought her out of her reverie. Gabriel Flaherty was gone. 'All that education and no manners,' she muttered.

She turned from the sound, her hand stretching for the forlorn letter, and almost screamed. The stone man stood silently at the counter – not leaning an elbow or drumming his fingers, not doing anything at all. Just standing.

As if he had grown there, Lena thought wildly, hearing the blood drum in her ears the way it did when she forgot the nurse's warning and lifted a heavy parcel from the floor. 'God almighty, but you took the heart out of me,' she croaked, hearing the crack in her voice.

'Mr Flaherty made a mistake,' he said evenly.

'A mistake? But, sure, isn't he after...' She wasn't sure how to end her sentence, and she found she hadn't enough breath for it anyway. Her throat closed.

'A mistake,' he said again, without emphasis. 'He would want you to give the envelope to me.'

Lena's conscious mind raced to formulate objections, but her tongue responded to something much more primitive and visceral.

'He would,' she murmured wanly.

The man laid his right hand palm up on the

counter. There was something obscene about the gesture, as if he was exposing himself. Lena backed away from it until she felt the rough comfort of the postbag against her legs. She edged around it and delved frantically for the manila envelope, her fingers suddenly awkward and unresponsive, heavy drops of sweat running from her scalp. She could feel his eyes boring through the top of her head and, just when she thought her brain would burst, she had the envelope in her hand and was holding it aloft, breathless as a child who has dipped her head in the basin for a coin. Walking back towards him was the hardest part, as if she was walking on sucking sand. She held the envelope out before her. Wordlessly, he left the post office.

She didn't raise her eyes until his footsteps had faded and the ordinary noises of the day crept back into her consciousness. Standing in her cooling sweat, willing her heartbeat to slow, Lena knew that her kingdom had been violated. A force such as she had never encountered before had stormed, ravaged and discarded her world, and she had been powerless before it. Her high throne beside the window would now become her watchtower; the counter where she had granted favours and dispensed slights had been soiled forever by that flat, demanding hand. She also realised that something else had happened to her, something that hadn't happened since she was a very small girl, lying lonely in the loft at home and terrified of the dark. With a snort of self-disgust, she hurried to the bathroom.

6

The Pier

THE BOY PERCHED on a bollard, his knees and spine a steady tripod for his swivelling head as he panned along the quay. The trawlers bobbed companionably, two and three abreast, rubbing against their fenders. His eyes locked on the old man sitting on an upturned crate, his spent pipe clenched for comfort in his jaw. Lar Begley sieved a net through callused fingers, half-listening to the banter of the two young men in the hold. He judged by the laughter in their voices that they would soon finish the hosing down and were already anticipating the first swallow in Finnegan's.

He looked up from his work when their heavy boots rattled the ladder.

'We'll be off, so, Lar.'

He nodded absently, the pipe bobbing his permission.

'Hey, Lar,' the older one called from the pier, 'the albatross is back.'

He lifted his eyes slowly to the bollard and its passenger. He must be about twelve years old now, he thought, and as wild as ever. Slowly, he eased himself off the crate and plucked a mackerel by the tail, two-fingered, from one of the ice-packed plastic cartons. Without a word, he flipped it in the boy's direction and watched him uncoil to catch it deftly before it hit the quay. Then the boy was away, over the quay wall and across the flat rocks towards the cliffs, sure-footed as a goat over kelp and sea moss, until the old man lost sight of him and returned to his task.

Always the same, he thought, and what does he need it for? The nurse keeps him well enough, God knows, and she a good woman hawsered to a bad man. The pipe was suddenly sour in his mouth. Irritably, he plucked it out and knocked the bowl against the heel of his rubber boot. ''Tis the innocent suffer,' he said aloud, putting the pipe into his waistcoat pocket. Maybe he'd have a pint himself. It might take the taste out of his mouth.

7

Home of the English Couple

Brothers, be sober, be watchful. For your enemy, like a roaring lion, goeth about, seeking whom he may devour. Him let you resist, steadfast in the faith.

DAPHNE CLOSED THE Bible, carefully checking that the marker was in place. Equally carefully, she placed it back on the shelf in its niche between *The Collected Works of William Shakespeare* and *The Stone Forts of Ireland*. The latter wouldn't have been her choice as a constant shelf companion for the Good Book – but then again, she mused, who would have matched her and Ron?

Daphne Bentham had always thought of herself as a sensible woman. The only child of an astute banker and a profligate mother, she had weighed the odds in her early teens and had modelled herself on her father. Thomas Marcham was the perfect gentleman; a man who rose automatically, and with the same courtliness, whether a lady entered the room or his carriage on the Tube. He was also a valued partner in Leopold, Brown & Marcham, valued for his solid competence rather than for his flair. 'Marcham the nut-counter,' Leopold and Brown were apt to snigger into their cups. 'Solid fellow, though. Good egg.'

The Metropolitan policemen had been awkward and apologetic at the door. 'Your mother in, Miss?'

'She's in the drawing room. Resting,' Daphne had added hastily, interposing her slight frame between them and the door behind which her mother was indulging her taste for old sherry.

She was eased aside by a large hand. 'A little word with her, Miss, if you please.'

For the first time in her short life, she compromised her principles by putting her ear to the crack between the oak-panelled doors. She listened to the antiphonal music of the policeman's bass voice and her mother's measured contralto – until, that is, her mother started screaming. Then

Daphne moved quietly to an upright chair in the hallway, where she sat, her hands folded in her lap, as the policemen departed.

She soon put together the jigsaw of whispers and silences and the incoherent shouting of Mr Leopold on the telephone. At the end of that first dreadful day, when the last of the visitors had crept gratefully away and Mamma had lapsed into a stupor on the chaise longue, she went quietly to her room and locked the door. Taking down her diary, she wrote: 'Papa found dead in a brothel. A large sum of money unaccounted for at the bank.' It was a telegrammatic epitaph for a man she had never known. 'The end,' she printed carefully underneath.

The subsequent inquest and court case were a prelude to the further disintegration of her world. 'We shall have to comport ourselves as best we may, my dear,' her mother stated, slurring her words despite her best efforts. 'We shall also have to be more frugal.' She pronounced the adjective as if it were a foreign word, as indeed it was to her. 'Thomas is so good at that sort of thing,' she had always said vaguely, whenever the subject of money intruded into the conversation. 'Frugal' meant poor, Daphne thought correctly.

She was twenty-five when her mother's liver tired suddenly of the punishment she had still managed to inflict on it, despite their reduced circumstances. Daphne was offered a position as a junior clerk at the Ministry of Defence in Whitehall – a position she owed to the influence of a relative, an MP, who had been unavoidably out of the country for the funeral.

Ron Bentham was intrigued by the young clerk who never wore make-up or made eye contact, and who seemed intent on fading into the drab surroundings of the Whitehall office. A chameleon, he thought, not unkindly, merging for protection with the available backdrop. But Daphne owed her dowdy image to the heavy burden of guilt she carried within her. She had loved too much, she concluded, and her love had been an expectation beyond the capabilities of her parents. In some way that she couldn't quite fathom, it had brought about their ruin.

As a courier from the Guards Regiment, Bentham was a regular caller on Miss Marcham. He grew to admire her quiet efficiency, and found an odd comfort in the fact that she never once focused on his artificial leg or raised her voice, as others did, to mask the sound it made on the unforgiving office floor. She obliged him by accompanying him to the opera: 'Yes, it's a pity your sister has flu, and it would be unthinkable to waste the tickets.'

He was a man who talked easily, and Daphne was a good, if guarded, listener. Ron's fictitious sister lapsed and relapsed through plays, poetry readings and an entire season of *lieder* recitals. After that, she had become an extra in their personal drama and could be tacitly dropped from the programme. He proposed at a performance of *Othello* in the Barbican, during the interval. Anticipation had deafened both of them to the dialogue, or they might have been struck by the lines Othello speaks of his wife Desdemona: 'She loved me for the dangers I had known, and I loved her that she did pity them.'

Whatever the basis of their attraction, their friendship developed into a warm companionship. Ron was constantly surprised and delighted by Daphne's unexpected flashes of lightness, in those rare moments when she was lulled into unselfconsciousness and something of her real self emerged. She found him dependable – she often smiled wryly at her choice of adjective: it was hardly a word that conjured up passion, but it was a quality she valued and needed. He was considerate and kindly, an undemanding and gentle lover, a man singularly without masks.

'What you see is what you get, my dear,' he had added, as an unrehearsed rider to his over-rehearsed proposal, and he was amazed to see how much that off-hand remark had meant to her.

She could deny him nothing, and when his disability pension came through and he revealed his wish to live on some island off the west coast of Ireland, she did not demur. Daphne knew at first sight that the cottage wasn't worth the money, but she balanced her caution against Ron's pleasure and decided it was a bargain at the price. The islanders were a different story.

'I find them rather distant,' she had confided one evening as he pored over the old maps that were his passion, the BBC World Service purring away comfortably in the background.

His sudden explosion of laughter had startled her. 'Oh, my dear,' he had said finally, polishing his glasses one-handed on the tuck of his shirt, 'that is richer than you know.'

'Perhaps, Mr Bentham would like to explain,' she had said sweetly.

'Imagine this scenario,' he had said, replacing his spectacles and tilting back in his chair. 'Two Scotsmen, two Welshmen, two Irishmen and two Englishmen are marooned together on an island. Well, my dear girl, the Scots would get drunk together, the Welsh would form a choir, the Irish would argue, and the English would not speak because they hadn't been properly introduced.'

'So the fault is mine?'

'Oh, no fault, dear. Maybe it's just a matter of opportunity. We are a little self-contained, after all.'

'You mean I am.'

'Well…'

'Well, indeed, Mr Bentham. You go to the pub occasionally and seem to know everyone by name. Strangers salute you on the road and we have had sacks of peat mysteriously appear at our gate. The problem seems to be Mrs Bentham.'

Ron had sighed and then brightened. 'Daphne, my love, let me tell you another story.'

'Why, Ron, how very Irish of you.'

'When the Pilgrim Fathers settled in America, they knew there were Indians in the forests, but they never saw them. They had a choice. They could build a stockade and live within the walls, or…'

'Or?'

'Or put food in the forest.'

'I don't quite follow you, dear.'

'They put food in the forest and it disappeared,' he had said patiently. 'Gradually they moved it closer to the settlement until, one day, the Indians let them see them take it.'

'So the sacks of peat…'

'Are food in the forest,' he had said happily, returning to his maps.

Today, Mrs Daphne Bentham will make an appearance, she decided later. Ron was somewhere behind the house, pondering the deaths of his English roses, which had been scalded by salt winds from the Atlantic. Daphne checked herself in the wardrobe mirror. She wore sensible brogues, a tweed skirt and a rollneck sweater, under a waxed jacket. The entire ensemble was topped off with an Island knitted beret.

'Sainsbury's catalogue meets the Celtic twilight,' she murmured. 'Whatever will the Indians make of this?'

Her resolve faltered a little at the turn of the road when the high walls shut off the comforting view of their cottage, but she took a deep breath and pressed on towards the village. Should I try a greeting in Gaelic? she wondered, awkwardly mouthing some of the words Ron had gleaned in the pub and carried home triumphantly, like trophies from a safari.

The man startled her with his speed. People on the Island moved slowly, leaning backwards as if walking against a strong wind; this man was hunched over and running. He shot her a startled glance, paused indecisively, then vaulted the drystone wall. Daphne stood looking at the site of his disappearance, gradually regaining control of her breathing, before walking on to where the mazy road forked for no apparent reason. Ron delighted in the haphazard nature of Island paths. Daphne tended to view them as unnecessary embroidery on the landscape.

The second man was not running but walking, steadily and without effort, his eyes on the path before him as if he were following a spoor. A hunter, she thought suddenly. She gathered her wits to make the supreme effort.

'*Dia dhuit*,' she managed.

His eyes held no surprise as he raised them to hers.

'You are the English lady,' he said after a pause long enough to be disconcerting. 'Perhaps you have seen someone – a man?'

Daphne did not like to lie – as the child of two consummate liars, she had first-hand experience of the damage caused by deceit – but some instinct shook her head.

'You have not seen this person?' he asked again, stepping closer. It was only a single step but her skin cooled as if a stray cloud had leached the sunlight around her.

'No,' she said firmly, and he was past her on the road, his head raised and scanning as if he was sniffing the wind.

'You're back early, love. I thought you… Is there something the matter, dear? Why, you're shaking. Come inside.'

The warmth of her own kitchen brought tears to Daphne's eyes, so that Ron swam out of focus across the table.

'I believe I should like a glass of port,' she said slowly.

Wordlessly, he fetched the bottle from the press, pressing the cork free with his thumb and snaring a glass with his little finger. Despite her emotional turmoil, she admired the grace of his movement.

8

The Island

GABRIEL'S SCHOLARSHIP WAS a two-edged sword. In the world of academia, his analytical bent had always been a strength. While other students launched themselves into a project or thesis, he tended to dally at the starting line, parsing and planning. His tutor called it 'the paralysis of analysis', but it worked for him and, though he rarely tendered flashes of brilliance, his work was solid and comprehensive. Outside the world of academia, however, he had found that his talent for instinctive action was as atrophied as an unused muscle. He was surprised, therefore, at the

suddenness of his flight from Lena's; but something in the menace of the man on the stone wall
had short-circuited his conditioning, and now he
was in free flight.

The exhilaration of that first unthinking dash
was soon replaced by his normal thought pro-
cesses, and he began to slow down. Years before,
this had been his downfall in school sports: when
he found himself unexpectedly in front, he
would rationalise himself into losing the race. *You
shouldn't be here*, his head reminded his feet, and
they obligingly tripped or tangled; he realised his
image of himself and felt unaccountably content
again. He knew, deep down, that he could not
outpace his hunter, and part of him longed for
capture.

The woman startled him into brief hope –
perhaps she could give him refuge… As quickly as
the thought entered his mind, he dismissed it. He
would not bring this darkness into the lives of the
innocent. Best to move on somewhere, anywhere.
When he vaulted the wall, he was unaware that he
had turned instinctively towards the sea.

Rose O'Toole stood with her back to the cottage,
one hand resting lightly on the stone wall that

bordered her small, neat garden. She had a stillness about her that was almost trance-like, as if she were unaware of the freshening wind that lifted her brown hair from the nape of her neck and teased the flowers through the gaps between the stones. The islanders would have said she was *ag féachaint amach uaithi* – looking out from herself – and they would have been right. Her thoughts wandered as far as Boston and Brisbane, moving like a slow caress from one emigrant face to another, travelling across the dizzying distances with all the ease of the untravelled. As her free hand rose to her swelling belly, a tiny pulse of movement reeled her back to the present. Her conscious mind registered again the scent of her own turf fire and the murmur of the radio through the open door.

Maybe this little one will be off as well? she thought, and sighed. Sure, what would keep them, apart from the fish factory? Aye, there's some hope there, all right.

At the thought of the factory, she turned her gaze to the east, watching for Dan. Now she could watch with ease. With every single day that had passed since he had left the fishing for the factory, Rose felt the old knot of anxiety loosen a little more. She would never again have to watch the colour of the sky or the lie of the grass before the wind; she'd never again have to sit wishing for the scrape of the gate, straining her ears for that small threnody of hope amid the screaming strings and thunderous percussion of a westerly gale. When there was tragedy now, she could sit in another woman's house, ashamed at the elation in her own heart, her eyes downcast for fear they would see the relief that it wasn't her man they had carried cold from the water. Thanks be to God, and the good word from Father Mack, her Dan was finished with the sea.

She shuddered slightly and drew her shawl more tightly for comfort. Inexplicably, her heart sank. She saw Dan rounding the bend in the lane, and something of her own mood seemed reflected in the slope of his shoulders and the mechanical way he placed his feet on the path.

There's part of him lost to the sea after all, a small voice said inside her, and she could not gainsay it. Yes, they had the regular hours and the steady money and the new Aga cooker and the possibility of putting a few pounds aside, and all the little things they'd done without – the small comforts that would neither flow nor ebb should the winds change or the shoals move. For the first time in their lives, they were not dependent on chance. Then why, she thought, in the names of Jesus and Mary, are we not happier?

The man materialising with every step of the

path had changed. She had weathered his temper before and could tack a course that would help them sail out the worst of it without major damage; but it was different now. Now he blew squally and stinging at the smallest thing, and then lay becalmed in sullenness till she was fit to scream. Where once he would hold a briar in his jaw for comfort, bending to the radio for the long-range forecast, or sit with a week-old newspaper spread before him on the table as if it was a meal and he was famished, now he alternated between bursts of energy and longer periods of lassitude. He went to the pub more often, and usually with two men he wouldn't have crossed the lane with before. And the night before last, when he had come home, there had been a darkness about him that precluded all talk. He had stridden straight by her to the kitchen and washed his hands in the sink. 'I cut my hand on broken glass,' he had said when he returned, and she had felt frightened because she hadn't remarked on his grazed knuckles.

The little pulse came again to her palm, and she took courage from it. She forced a smile to her face as he reached the gate. 'A good day, Dan?'

'Aye, a good day enough.' He lifted the cap from his head and ran a hand through his hair. The failing sun glinted on the fish scales trapped between his knuckles. 'There's a big order in for

Paris. If things keep going the way they—What is it, Rose?'

'I thought I saw something over there.'

He turned and shielded his eyes to follow where she was pointing.

'There, beyond by the hump in Twomey's field. Do you see it?' 'Tis like someone running.'

Dan O'Toole could see the figure now, stumbling towards the sea, clambering over dry-stone walls. His face hardened. 'We'll go inside now, so,' he said, turning for the door.

'But who is it, Dan?'

'What is it to us who they are or what they're doing?' he said harshly. 'Why can't people mind their damned business in this God-blasted island?'

The suddenness of his outburst rooted her where she stood.

'It's no one,' he said more softly. 'Come into the house.'

'I'd swear it was the young Flaherty. Did you notice the red head of him?'

He swung her by the elbow so that she was looking into his face. 'Listen to me, Rose. We saw no one. It was a trick of the light – nothing more.' He squeezed her tightly so that the bulge of her belly pressed against him. 'It was no one, Rose,' he whispered, 'no one at all.'

Gabriel felt no pain as he rolled over the wall and tumbled into Twomey's field. In the sudden stillness, he could hear his heart drumming a mad tattoo, pumping the high octane of panic that fuelled his legs to move, move, move. But not yet. His lungs were still fighting for oxygen. Time and place had become peripheral, shaded into irrelevance by the bright fear that pulsed behind his eyes.

Desperately he pushed away from the clinging earth and stumbled forwards. Through a haze of sweat, his eyes looked for the sea, but they fastened instead on a cairn of stones standing in a small stone circle. The simplicity of the Bronze Age tomb brought him back to a level of rationality.

Twomey would have picked his field of stones from dawn to dusk and never touched this little pile, mounded up by some other islander long before Christ was born. He fumbled the envelope, stained a deeper brown now by his sweat, from inside his jacket and fell to his knees before the cairn.

''S beart de réir ár mbriathar,' he whispered fiercely, echoing the code of the ancient Irish Fianna, 'and a commitment to our word.' Shielded by this mantra, he stretched his hands forward to the sacred stones.

The boy lay full-length on a lip of rock, his head
hanging out over the water. He watched the kelp
stream back and forth with the ebb and flow and
felt the rhythmic beat of the breakers on the stones
below. When, at last, the seabirds lost interest and
found a thermal farther out, the regular sounds
returned: the rolling of surf and breaker, the long,
slow sigh of sea-bound water over stones. The boy
raised his head, opened his mouth and made a
sharp barking sound that ricocheted among the
rocks. He stretched his neck and bent upwards to
his knees in one fluid movement as the seal broke
the surface before him. He flipped the silver
mackerel high into the air, his arms outstretched in
exultation, and the seal mimicked his rise, taking
the fish almost shyly before it hit the water. It
settled in contemplation of the boy, who sat back
on his heels like a priest who has made his offering
and is loathe to leave the holy place. Then the water
swirled and eddied, and the seal was gone.

Instinctively, the boy rolled and coiled into the
shade of the overhang behind him. The seal had no
predator save man, and one of these was moving in
the field above. It was the frantic nature of the
movement that had repelled the seal, and the boy's
stomach tightened at the tension that flowed from
the figure clawing at the cairn of stones. He
watched through a lattice of yellow grass as the

man rose from his crouch and stumbled to the path, weaving unsteadily towards the beach. He saw him halt and rear back as if struck, then turn and run in the direction of the high cliffs and the tower that dominated their crest.

The boy knew him as the seaman, who often spent hours watching the waves, giving no sign of knowing he was being watched. When the seaman stretched and turned reluctantly for home, he always left something as salvage: a pencil, a notebook, sometimes a toffee wrapped in paper, still warm from the nest of his pocket. Instinctively the boy moulded his body to the rock, moving his head in a slow arc to source the man's terror.

There. Another might have missed him, so complete was his stillness, so perfectly had he chosen his lair amid a tangle of rocks where light and shadow camouflaged all form. There was something reptilian about the shape and the boy watched in a mixture of horror and fascination as the blunt figure stirred and moved with ease towards the path, gliding over the rough surfaces with a hungry lope. He waited until the man had disappeared, high up on the cliff path, before venturing out of his cover and moving with purpose to Twomey's field.

The old lighthouse tower stared blindly out over
the Atlantic, standing on the site where a cairn of
stones had held up a bonfire a millennium before.
As the centuries passed, the cairn had been
fashioned and refashioned into round, squat
towers, growing ever higher. There was never any
shortage of stone. This tower was the last in that
long line of beacons, and it had been the last to
be inhabited. Slightly lower down the cliff, the
automatic lighthouse gleamed whitely against the
evening sky, its swinging beam growing in
strength.

The plank nailed across the door was a token
deterrent to tourists who might climb the rickety
stairs for 'one hell of a picture' and end up lying
concussed or broken in the belly of a currach
grudgingly rowed to the mainland.

Gabriel hit the plank at a run and was pitched
into the fetid darkness of the ground floor. A beer
can rolled away noisily, coming to rest against the
rubble mounded at the far wall; before the sound
had ceased, he was back on his feet, searching for
some avenue of escape. As his eyes adjusted to the
gloom, the spidery stairs beckoned, and he
clambered up to the first floor.

This had been the living area of the last keeper's
family, a curly-headed brood with the singsong
accent of Wexford. Gabriel remembered them as a

wild bunch who had scampered over the cliffs like
goats and amazed the islanders by surviving intact
until their father was relocated to the Old Head of
Kinsale and the entire Island had breathed a
collective sigh of relief. Their mother had been a
vaguely distracted woman who coped with the
confinement of the lighthouse by becoming a
voracious reader. She had shipped the first
playpen to the Island by currach, prompting the
locals to remark, 'That'll put a stop to their
gallop.' Gabriel's most vivid memory was of the
mother seated serenely in the playpen, book in
hand, safe from the children who rampaged round
her kitchen.

The memories faded and the darkness and the
fear returned, even deeper than before. The creak
of a board pushed him back until the windowsill
butted the small of his back. The darkness before
him seemed to coalesce, and he knew instinctively
that his hunter had arrived. The footsteps drew
nearer, crunching over debris on the floor, no
longer making any attempt at stealth.

Gabriel turned and dropped his hands on the
sill; then, using the last reserves of his strength, he
propelled himself backwards, his right foot
extended behind him. Skald grunted in surprise.
The blow to his hip caught him off balance and he
fell to the floor, arms flailing. Gabriel broke for the

stairs, but an iron hand gripped his ankle and he was flying. His head filled with pure white light as it struck the concrete floor.

Despite a bursting bladder, Leo kept to the cover of the gorse. It had been his only refuge on the bare cliff top when the rapid, stumbling steps had roused him from his reverie. He waited a whole minute, dancing from one foot to the other, until the footsteps had faded, and then he dove back again when the second figure appeared on the path.

Jaysus, he thought angrily, so much for a quiet court. He fumbled frantically with his fly. Why the hell had he worn the bloody Levis his brother Mick had forgotten to pack before heading back to the States? *No wonder the Yanks have pale faces; sure, the damned things would cut off your circulation. Come on, come on... Oh, Saint Anthony, the blessed relief*

He was doing up the unfamiliar metal buttons when Sarah Dolan rounded the headland.

'I needn't have bothered,' he muttered philosophically.

'Is it you, Leo?'

'Who else, woman? For the love of God, stop

talking so loud. The world and his mother are abroad tonight.'

There was a hollow behind the gorse, springy with heather, and she lay back with a theatrical sigh. 'Leo…' She crooked a finger at him.

He was crouched in the middle of the hollow, his knees bent inwards, holding his breath and wrestling yet again with the buttons of the Yankee pants, when they heard the scream.

'What was that?'

'Ah, Leo, aren't you the scaredy-cat? Sure, it was probably an owl in the tower. The place is full of them. I've often heard them before.'

Leo wondered briefly what Sarah might have been doing there before and with whom, but she was unbuttoning her blouse languorously and his breathing shortened with every revelation. Finally she peeled it from her shoulders and lay back, her arms extended.

'Will you be dancing on your own all night, or what?'

'I'm coming. Will you have a bit of patience?'

He duck-walked across the hollow, the jeans refusing to go beyond his ankles, and was lowering himself when he started up to his knees again.

'What's that?'

'Cripes almighty, Leo Crosby, have you never seen a woman's chest before?'

'It was a light, out there west of the point. But who'd be out on the water at this hour?'

She was already up and moving, tucking her blouse into her skirt. He tried to catch her elbow, but she caught him with a glancing blow and sent him cartwheeling into the heather.

'I'd be a right eejit to be baring my bosom for a fool like you,' she snapped.

Gingerly he picked himself up, tugging the trousers up around his waist. Feeling around, he encountered the trailing threads where the fly buttons had formerly defied his best efforts. Only Leo heard the second scream; and, owls or no, he was running full tilt when he passed Sarah on the path.

An insistent ringing sound woke Gabriel. It took a long moment for him to comprehend that the sound was coming from inside his head, the left side of which felt oddly inflated. He moved to ease the pain, and the chair creaked. The man sitting opposite looked up.

He smells of gunpowder, Gabriel thought, watching the pale eyes flick expertly over the bonds that held him. Satisfied with his scrutiny, the man leaned forward on his knees. His voice, accentless and cold, seemed to come from a metallic voice box.

'The document, Mr Flaherty. Where is it?'

The silence stretched between them.

'You are a writer, Mr Flaherty. With which hand do you write?'

Gabriel's reflexes tightened his right hand into a fist. The man reached forward. Swiftly, he prised open the fist and snapped the little finger backwards with his thumb. Gabriel screamed and spasmed in the chair, tears spurting from his eyes.

'I will ask again presently,' the man said calmly, elbows resting on his knees, his square chin nestling on his closed fists. 'You have two minutes, Mr Flaherty.'

Skald's cryptic telephone message had brought the Major to the old lighthouse. He stood immobile on the littered floor, oblivious of the acid stink of old urine that tainted the air. The other man, D'Arcy, prowled restlessly, his heavy feet crushing small pieces of fallen plaster. The only time he paused was when Gabriel screamed from above. Then he would tilt back his head and angle his face to the ceiling as though inhaling. Just like a dog, the Major thought contemptuously, but then again dogs were biddable. The sound of a footstep on the stairs halted his reverie.

'Has he spoken?'

'No, Major.' The reply was not exactly accurate, and Skald expanded. Gabriel Flaherty had spoken, laughed, screamed and sung for over four hours in a delirium of agony, until Skald ran out of fingers. But he had never once mentioned the document.

'Let me try,' D'Arcy asked eagerly. 'I could make him sing like a fucking canary.'

The hunger in his voice made the Major twitch with distaste.

'Mr D'Arcy,' he said evenly, 'I may need your services a little later.'

He turned to Skald.

'True believers are a rare breed.' He dipped his hand inside his black jacket and produced a flat case, not much bigger than a wallet. 'Have you ever read a poem called "The Lotos-Eaters", Sergeant? No. Well, as I recall it is one of the earliest anti-drug poems. Quite spellbinding and soporific, with long vowel sounds to lull the reader. I think Mr Flaherty might be appreciative of the work.'

He flipped the black case open to reveal a neat array of phials and a hypodermic syringe.

I am Gabriel!

The recognition of his own name sent a shock arcing through his body. For a moment he strained against the tape that sealed him to the chair, his head whipping from side to side, fanning the floor with blood. He was as unaware of the blood as he was of the glistening, shapeless bags that had been his hands, or of the smell of the urine he was sitting in. The cold sting in his upper arm had numbed his pain and all memory of the beating.

I am Gabriel, he thought again, the messenger of God. He moved to flex his wings, but something held him to the chair, restraining his flight.

'My earthly body,' he confided to the motes gleaming in the anaemic light that leaked from a crease in the cardboard blacking out the window. 'Soon,' he whispered; 'my time has not yet come.' His head fell forward and he slipped into unconsciousness.

His eyes opened to the dark. He was afraid of the dark, always needing to surface gently through the shallows of sleep – not like Michael, who came fully awake and tossed the last of the sleep away with the flick of a swimmer coming up for air. He was alone in the dark, without the comfort of his brother's warmth.

'Is it time?' he whispered, his words moving hesitantly around a litter of broken teeth. The dark solidified before him; he felt hands moving gently on his arms and feet. 'Is it time?'

The light came painfully, washing from the open door behind him. The figure before him flinched, then straightened to look him in the face.

'It is time.'

Gabriel felt a wave of relief spread from the pit of his stomach, so that, when he spoke again, his voice was sibilant with tears. 'I am Gabriel.'

'No,' the man with the empty eyes replied. 'You are Icarus, and you have flown too high.'

Other hands turned him to the light. He scarcely felt the rough path against his bare feet, automatically rolling from heel to toe as they had throughout his childhood, thwarting the vengeful teeth of scallops marooned in the dunes. The path wound through a haze of heather humped with scrub grass, shawled with webs against the morning chill. Although the air was still, every stalk angled away from the muffled, rhythmic roar, which grew in volume as he strained against the steep rise in the path.

At last the gradient tired, relaxing into level ground again. They stopped him and turned him to the east.

The world is blood, he thought as he struggled through the slit of his right eye to focus on the rising sun. There was a figure beside him, a servant of the voice.

For a moment Gabriel was overcome by sadness. He tasted his own tears. Then he bellowed at the top of his lungs, 'I am Gabriel. I am the messenger of God.'

He rejoiced to see the man start in surprise, to hear his cry echo in the cliffs, to see the spume of gulls rise as his shout crashed against its face. Then it was gone and the silence stole back, and the servant of the voice was at his side.

'So fucking fly.'

Gabriel fell towards a green, heaving sea that rose to take him down to darkness. His final thought was, Catch me, Michael, I'm falling.

9

The Donnellys' Apartment,
The Bronx, New York

THE SILENCE STRETCHED, tautened and
jerked the cat awake. Reflexively she arched, fangs
bared, claws extended. Then, as the man resumed
breathing, Pooka flowed from the bed across the
floor to the sanctuary of the desk. She knew this
was a forbidden perch. Michael would have swept
her to the floor, automatically and without malice;
but he was somewhere else, moaning in a tangle of
bed sheets. The cat settled to her vigil, her tail, a
black antenna, twitching to the bursts of nightmare
from the bed.

'Liam, *dúirt* Daddy… no, no, Daddy said… *agus* fuck you too… Liam, look at the light, *a Chríost* – the sky is green… Cut the lines – bloody fish, to hell with them. No. Take the beat… row… row… nose to the wave. Daddy says. *Jesus!*'

Pooka lowered her snout to her forepaws, slitting her eyes against the shout.

'Liam… Liam, I have you… Cold… Sing, ye lanky bastard, sing… *Báidín Fheidhlimid*… Louder, I can't hear you… Liam… Liam!'

The cat sped through the door and along the narrow passage to the safe haven of the lighted kitchen. Mal sat in his usual place, chair angled to the wall, his lips moving soundlessly as he pretended to read his newspaper. Hanny turned from the sink, her apron balled in her hands. Pooka called softly to her from the doorway.

'I know, cat,' she nodded wearily, and the cat flickered away.

'They'll come for you with a net one day, Hanny,' Mal murmured. His tone gave the lie to his words, and she sighed.

'It'll get worse, and then it'll get better,' he said in the same tone, and in an accent that had resisted the sandpaper of the Bronx for forty years. She looked across the table at the butt of a man with his lived-in face. Mal was as broad as she was tall, and the eyes that looked at her over the half-glasses were as innocent in that battered face as they had been all those years before. It was the eyes that had held her, she remembered. Well, the uniform of New York's finest hadn't hurt either.

'Maybe, if you were to—?'

'No.'

It was their regular script. His big fingers quested over the table to hers.

'Hanny, he held his brother for four hours in the Atlantic. When they came in the currachs, Liam was gone and Michael was swimming away out to sea.'

She tried to lean back from him, but he pressed her fingers. 'They had to beat him senseless with an oar before they could get him into the boat.'

She rocked, her eyes closed, but his fingers would not release her.

'But it's been years, Mal.'

'I know, *a chailín*, I know,' he crooned comfortingly, but his heart wasn't in it. *No man should ever have to carry such a cross. He should have gone to one of them doctors years ago; but, sure, he's a Flaherty, and how could they live without tragedy? Water would as easily run uphill.*

The old couple sat in silence, their hearts tuned to the drowning cries of the son they had never had.

Michael woke, wondering if he had screamed when the face before him in the water had changed, telling his breathing to slow… slow. He swung his feet to the floor, grateful for its solidity, and hunkered with his elbows on his knees while the overhead fan cooled the sweat on his shoulders. The cat looked at him from her new perch on the bookshelf, between a faded photograph of three solemn boys and a larger one of forty young men stacked on benches, dressed in clerical black, frozen in a formal fraternity.

'You don't fool me, cat,' Michael growled, almost smiling. The cat gazed back in a mixture of hurt innocence and relief. He was back.

He balled the sheets, stripped the pillow and carried the load to the basket in the bathroom.

'Morning,' he murmured to the two in the kitchen, Mal studiously prodding the paper, Hanny irritating sausages on the pan.

'Jesus!' The shower stream was coming all the way from Canada, but it tautened his body and cleared his head. Above the hiss of the water he could hear the city music – the train, stitched with graffiti, rattled and groaned from the catacombs of New York towards the solace of the next tunnel; car horns registered the blood pressure of impatient drivers; a siren's high cadence of urgency above the grumbling arterial pipes of the apartment building and the syncopation of loud voices.

Hanny blotted the bacon on kitchen paper and dealt it onto his plate with all the grace of a Vegas croupier. 'Gracie's nephew is out for the summer,' she said, by way of explanation. The prerequisite for a visitor's visa, he thought ruefully: a passport, the promise of a job and a ton of bacon.

'Easy there, Hanny. One blimp is enough around here.'

'Muscle, my boy, pure muscle,' the blimp muttered from behind the sports section. 'Hanny's crowd all came from west of the Shannon. They still remember the Famine.'

'Remember it or caused it?'

'Eat your breakfast.'

'Yes, Hanny.'

'So am I the only one working on this lovely morning?' Michael asked.

'Sure, there's a game on the box, and the word is out that no one comes looking for the super.'

On his retirement, Mal had moved seamlessly from being a cop to becoming superintendent of their building. When a problem arose, he made the call and signed the chit. Sometimes, he made the call, watched the work and never had to make that call again.

'How about you, Hanny?'

'Oh, Hanny's Jew boyfriend is making his bar mitzvah or something, so she's a lady of leisure. No cooking the books today.'

'I plead the Fifth,' Hanny growled. Hanny had worked as a book-keeper for a garment factory in Brooklyn ever since stepping off the boat. She was semi-retired now, which meant that she cast an eagle eye over the computer hotshot nephews whom old Bernstein employed to balance his books. 'And you?' She nudged some more brown bread within Michael's reach.

'Big meeting downtown.'

'Collar job?'

'Yeah.'

'There's a clean collar in the second drawer. It's the only one cause it's the only one you got, and it's always clean cause you seldom wear it.'

When Michael came back to the kitchen, he was dressed in a black clerical suit that hung loosely on his spare six-foot frame. He had the ivory pallor of the Spanish traders who had plied more than their wares up and down the western seaboard of Ireland. The jet-black eyebrows and long lashes were Iberian, but the blue eyes and the hint of melancholy were unmistakably Irish.

'Will I do?'

'Not bad,' Hanny said grudgingly, 'but your dog collar is a bit crooked.'

10

The Prison Ship, New York

'COME RIGHT ON through, Your Holiness.' Elroy V Gillespie, Jr – black, Baptist and, according to his world view, beautiful – pressed the buzzer and admitted Father Michael Flaherty to the floating prison moored in New York Harbour.

'Remember, it's only my ring you'll have to kiss.'

'Naughty. How you ever going to make pope with that kind of dirty talk?'

For the first few weeks of Michael's tenure as prison chaplain, he had been subjected to a slew of lewd stories at the officers' mess table. His

comments about the baseball league, and his
general disinterest in saddling a high horse, had
seemed only to provoke his dining companions
to greater salacious effort – until Elroy had
spoken up.

'I got a wife and daughter. Next man who talk
that kind of fuck talk in my presence's going to be
shitting from two places and wearing a goddamn
wee-wee bag. Saving your presence, Padre.'

The pair often met for a beer after work to
chew the rag. Michael knew all about Irene's job in
the Manhattan bank, about Calvin, the son Elroy
thought might be gay, and about the daughter who
was a medic in Bellevue. Elroy knew that Michael
Flaherty was a priest from an island off the west
coast of Ireland, period. But he was working on
cracking the enigma.

'Head honchos all aboard for the meeting,'
Elroy said on the way to the gate. 'Rabbi Isaac and
the not-so-very-Reverend Lomax already in the
Oval Office, and the good Lord herself is dee-
scending. Chico here is your altar boy for today.'
He made a mock bow in the direction of the young
Hispanic officer. 'Spic, Mick. Mick, Spic,' he
introduced them with a flourish.

'Ay, that hombre,' Chico smiled, riffling his key
ring for the interminable unlock-lock procedure
ahead.

'¿*Cómo está tu madre,* Chico?'

'Ay, Padre…' Chico launched into turbo-drive Spanish. Michael could barely follow, but he managed to grunt at the right places. Prisoners passed in regulation pyjamas – some staring straight ahead, marching to some coke-fuelled drummer; others nodding, hesitantly or deferentially; a few calling out a muted greeting. Chico studiously ignored them, as officers tended to do. Michael was finding it hard to strike a balance between getting involved and keeping his distance. He smiled at the memory of the final piece of advice bequeathed by his predecessor as he helped him pack: 'I grew up on a sheep farm in Wicklow, Mike, so listen to what I'm going to tell you. Shear 'em high – d'you follow?'

At every junction and level, gates and more gates. 'Padre coming through.' Near the gym, they passed a large bored cop and a nervous female rookie riding shotgun; a big red-haired guy slumped between them, his chin resting on his massive chest.

Finally, they reached the engine room, at the heart of the behemoth. As Chico swung the door wide, Michael gasped, '*Dios,* Chico, somebody stole the engine.'

Chico grappled with this for a while; then, the slow grin. 'Ay, Padre.'

The space where the engine should have been was honeycombed with offices. This was the nerve-centre of a ship that had never sailed under her own steam. She had been built, neutered in New Orleans and towed to her docking, never going anywhere but here. Like most of her occupants, Michael mused. Like you, a small voice in his head echoed back.

'*Boker Tov*, Isaac,' he nodded to the rabbi, who was, as usual, hunched into a chair as far from the table as he could manage while still being at the meeting. Isaac was a thin wisp in a black suit, with a fuzz of baby beard struggling to assert squatter's rights on a negligible chin. He suffered from claustrophobia, and already he was working on a fine sheen of sweat, despite the chill air-conditioning.

For me it's the sea; for him it's small spaces below decks, and we're all working on a boat. God has the weirdest sense of humour, Michael thought.

Reverend Lomax, by contrast, had been born without a humorous cell in his body. He was already seated and working on a righteous ex-pression. As far as the Reverend Lomax was concerned, 'What these boys need is a goose with the juice, yessiree' – and if they saved the state some dollars by inserting three fingers into the wall socket some morning, well, Hallelujah and pass the basket. Michael knew from Elroy that the reverend moonlighted as a car salesman somewhere out in Yonkers, and this gave him hope for his eventual salvation.

His train of thought was abruptly derailed by the arrival of the warden. Carmencita Maria Esteban was Ecuadorian and all of five feet tall, café au lait poured into a tiny tumbler. Reverend Lomax went into extreme unction in voice and body, attempting a bow from a seated position, which brought him nose to fabric with his own tie. The rabbi shifted even farther back from the table. The warden was aware of the effect she was having on the assembled males – except, of course, the sky pilot, who was already laying out sheets and pencils.

A klaxon blared from a loudspeaker set high in the wall, shocking the group into immobility. It was replaced almost immediately by a tense voice. 'Warden, we got a hostage situation in the gym.'

The first sound after the initial hush was the rabbi's breathing, accelerating from nervous to frantic. 'Remember, you guys,' the warden said quietly, 'I've got a gun over here.' As the siren whooped, her lilting tone flattened to steel. 'You gentlemen will remain in this room and lock the door when I leave.'

They heard her chair scrape and she was momentarily framed in the doorway, before disappearing. Michael saw the rabbi swaying feverishly and the quizzical look on Lomax's broad face. 'If he's praying, join him. If he's hyper-ventilating, put a bag over his nose and mouth,' he said as he made for the door.

'But she ordered us to stay,' the reverend protested with more than a tinge of relief in his voice.

'I didn't know that Jesus was born in Quito,' Michael shot over his shoulder.

The popping of small-arms fire was coming from the direction of the gym on the next level. Elroy was already hunched into the stairwell outside the gym, barking into his radio, 'Officer down and hostage situation. Medics and shrink, on the double.'

He listened to the answering static and rolled his eyes. 'Shit, Dr Loeb's at a conference in Manhattan.'

'What will the warden do, Elroy?'

Elroy tugged at his aquiline nose before replying. 'That Carmencita is one feisty lady. I think if she can't parlay, then she gonna fillet.'

Michael retreated into a corner as the stairwell began filling with flak jackets. There was a hush, and the warden began speaking.

'Listen up, people. As they say in the movies, we got us a situation here.'

A small ripple of laughter pulsed through the group of officers, and Michael sensed an easing in their tension. Nice move, Carmencita, he thought.

'Rap sheet says the perp's name is O'Brien, twenty-seven-year-old Caucasian male, currently on remand for an arrest following a saloon brawl. So far this sweetheart has to his credit two dislocated jaws, one internal bleeding and one very large barkeep who may or may not walk again. Now he's added to that tally an NYPD officer, who has been shot in the shoulder with his own gun, and a trainee female officer who has now got that very same gun jammed under her chin. SWAT and the boys in blue are on their way.'

There was a wave of groaning from the group; her clear, precise voice easily overrode it. 'Remember, people, we contain. In every sense of the phrase. It's what we're paid for. OK, let's get organised.'

'Warden.'

She was angry at the interruption, but too much of a pro to show it before the ranks. 'Padre.'

Michael didn't know how any person could pack so many inflections into a two-syllable word, but she could, and none of them boded well.

'You said his name was O'Brien.'

'Padre, we got work to do here, if you don't mind.'

Michael felt the blood tingle in his temples, but he matched her neutral tone. 'O'Brien is an Irish name; chances are that—'

She was in his face, as much as her height would permit and biting off her words. '*Chances* are something we do not take with a hostage at gunpoint, and I distinctly remember ordering you to stay below.'

'I have all the orders I need, Warden.'

There was an audible intake of breath from the huddle of officers. Elroy rolled his eyes heavenwards. Carmencita held Michael in a fierce gaze, but she knew from his face that she would be the first to blink.

'We already have one man down,' she said, turning as if to leave.

Michael was at her elbow, spinning her to face him. 'And a rookie cop, and a young man on remand in our care, and any one of these men here could go down if we let SWAT come barging in.'

'Stick to your prayers, Padre,' she spat, dragging her arm out of his grasp.

'I don't have enough prayers to cover that many casualties, Warden.' He took a deep breath and exhaled. 'Begging your pardon, ma'am, for speaking out of turn, but I think I can talk this man out.'

Carmencita kept her back turned and fired the question over her shoulder. 'You have done this before?'

'No – and, to save time, no to all your other questions as well. But if he's Irish, he may even speak Irish and so do I. That gives us an edge.'

She hesitated, and he pressed ahead. 'What's a worst-case scenario? He ends up with two hostages, a woman and a priest – not very shootable options, for your average Irishman.'

He watched the warden struggle for control of her anger. Finally, she turned and jabbed a finger sharply into his chest. 'I'll make a bargain with you, Padre. You get the perp, and I'll change my mind about letting SWAT have you.'

Again the stairwell swelled with muted laughter.

'OK, Warden – and thank you.'

'Wear a vest.' She prodded him once again, more gently, and turned to go.

'No, ma'am. If he sees a vest, he'll think cop; then he'll shoot first and say an act of contrition later.'

She muttered something in Spanish and left. Michael couldn't quite follow it, but he knew it had 'stubborn' and 'mother' in it, and it hadn't been a compliment.

Elroy was suddenly all business. 'You sure about the vest?'

'Yeah. I want him to see the suit and collar.'

Elroy grabbed Michael's arm and walked him to the gym door. 'Keep your arms extended from your body at all times, and no sudden moves. This is not the time to get an irresistible nose itch. And don't let the damn furniture get between you and him. Leave him a clear line of fire.'

'Thanks.'

'You're welcome. Go get him, Barry Fitzgerald.'

Michael leaned his frame against one half of the gym's double door, and it creaked open.

'Anyone walks in here gets shot, d'you hear me?'

'I hear you.' Michael kept his voice calm and clear. 'This is Father Michael Flaherty. I'm the Catholic priest here, OK? I want to come in for a chat – only me. I'll come in, walking nice and easy where you can see me. Only me, OK?'

After what seemed an age, the voice echoed back, less belligerent than before. 'Just you, Father?'

'Just me.'

'OK.'

As soon as he stepped through the door, Michael felt the urge to hold his hands defensively across his body. His stomach tightened and sweat prickled on his shoulders, but he kept his arms extended.

'O'Brien, I'm over here. Watch me coming. Can you see me?'

'I see you, Father.'

'You see where my hands are?'

'I see them.'

Michael had gradually dropped his voice through the sequence of questions and noted with satisfaction that O'Brien was matching him tone for tone. As he neared the hump of the dais, the rookie's pale, round face appeared like a full moon, locked in the hairy aureole of O'Brien's arm. The gun was angled under her jaw. Michael was too far away yet to read her eyes, but he could feel their gaze locked on him. Don't talk, he prayed, please don't say anything to spook this guy any further.

'Miss,' Michael said gently, never taking his eyes from the man, 'you just rest easy now, Mr O'Brien and I are going to have a talk.'

The tearful eyes blinked slowly, but she made no sound. Good girl, he thought gratefully; one voice, just one voice.

O'Brien's head shifted into view from behind the hostage. 'That's near enough.'

'OK, I'm stopping right here. Can I lower my arms?'

'Yes.'

Slowly he let them drift to his sides. 'My name is Michael. What's yours?'

The head jerked sideways to check the gym. 'Eamonn.'

Michael rifled through his mental file of accents. Galway, he thought, West Galway. Please, God, let me be right.

'*A bhfuil Gaeilge agat?* Do you speak Irish?'

'*Tá.*'

Slowly, Michael introduced himself again, this time just in Irish.

'I'm an Island Flaherty,' he added. 'Would you be from the Spiddal direction?'

'I would.'

'I know your place well. I suppose that robber Murphy is still running the petrol station?'

'He is,' more softly now.

'And by what name are your mother's people known?

'She's dead. A long time ago.'

Strike one, Michael thought as he watched the man stiffen. Painful memories. Bring him back. 'Was there someone there who would speak well of you – a teacher, perhaps?'

'Teachers?' The word was a spark in the darkness. O'Brien tightened his arm, his shaggy head moving towards eclipse behind the rookie's shocking white face.

Lost that one. All or nothing.

'There was a priest in Spiddal – I knew him

years ago. A great man for the football, but I'm damned if I can remember his name...'

'That'll be Father O'Connor.'

'Did you play yourself?'

'Aye, a bit. But, sure, there was no work, so I came here. Bad luck to the day I did. Nothing but trouble since.'

'Would Father O'Connor speak for you?'

'Aye, he would.'

'I'm a priest. Would you have me speak for you, Eamonn?'

'They'll shoot me, Father. I think I killed one of them. He made a drive for me when I got his gun away from him, and—'

'Eamonn, listen to me. He'll live; you only wounded him. You're a lousy shot. Are you listening to me, Eamonn?'

'Aye.'

'Give them back a life now, Eamonn, and I'll protect yours with my own.'

'Promise me, Father.'

'I promise you, on the soul of my mother.'

The man's arm loosened and fell away.

'Miss,' Michael said, in English, 'will you go out and tell them that Father Flaherty and Eamonn O'Brien will be along in a while?' Don't run, he thought, for the love of God, don't run.

He needn't have worried; the young woman

stepped down from the dais and moved slowly towards the exit. Michael waited for the creak of the door before moving to the place she had relinquished. He sat sideways to the man, not touching him, and looked away into the darkness. It was the way men sat together at home.

'Eamonn,' he whispered quietly, as if they might be overheard, 'slide the gun away from you.'

He heard the metal scratch the wooden floor in protest. The young man's head was slumped on his chest. 'I'm in terrible trouble now, Father, so I am.'

'You're not alone, *a mhic*,' Michael replied tenderly.

Even in his short time in New York, Michael had met his fair share of Eamonns; lads who had made the futile visit to the local factory, then taken the bus to Dublin to repeat the pilgrimage, without an answer to their prayers. America was still the dream – a dream promoted in letters from uncles in the Bronx and Brooklyn, who assuaged their own reality with the fiction they wrote home. For a very few, it was a chance to make something of themselves. For the majority, it was a furtive life spent in the limbo of illegality, working the Irish network for a job pouring concrete in temperatures below zero for wages below minimum. Our own living off our own, Michael thought bitterly. It was the ghetto pub and

the ghetto songs and an apartment shared with six
others, redolent of old socks and spoiling dreams,
thanks to the venality of the Irish landlord. And
when the payoff came, as it nearly always did, they
were fish out of water, prey to the sharks that could
smell blood a block away. In a few minutes,
Eamonn O'Brien, greener than any of the forty
shades, would be processed into a yellow jumpsuit
and introduced to the first level of a penal system
that Dante had never even dreamed of.

Without thinking, Michael lifted his head and
started into an old Island air, a lament for a boy
lost at sea. It was slow and sad, with all the grace
notes the traditional singers employed to com-
pensate for the lack of an accompanying
instrument. He had an easy, unaffected baritone
that swelled out and pushed the shadows back
before it. As he sang, he closed his eyes and extended his right hand; and, in the traditional
manner, Eamonn clasped it, to earth the singer
lest the sadness of his song consume him.

As the last notes ebbed away, Michael heard
the squeak of the door and felt the tremor through
his hand. 'Padre, if you and Mr O'Brien would like
to come to my office, we can get things sorted out.'
The warden's voice was pitched respectfully low,
as if she had stepped inside a church and found a
service in progress.

Michael tightened his grip. 'Keep your courage now, Eamonn O'Brien,' he whispered fiercely.

Elroy dropped four cubes of sugar into the coffee and pushed it under Michael's nose. 'OK,' he said breezily as Michael grimaced at the taste, 'Lay it on me. What the hell was that all about?'

Michael smiled tiredly. 'At ho— on the Island, we call it *sean nós* singing. It means the ancient way.'

The eyes opposite registered the term and filed it for further review. '*Shan nose*... hah. You learn that shit as a boy, right?'

'Only the words, Elroy. The music... well, the music sort of comes from yourself. I can't really explain it very well.'

Elroy leaned closer. 'Hey, my friend, I come from a long line of shan-nosers. Hell, yeah; where you think we get the blues?'

The radio crackled in his belt, interrupting his laugh.

'Gillespie... Yeah, roger that.

'Time for your autopsy, my friend,' he sighed. 'The warden wishes to see your pretty face.'

The warden's office was spartan: a functional city-issue desk, wearing only a spotless blotter for modesty, hemmed about with swivel chairs; bare walls, an unusual feature in a culture that favoured vanity walls, heavy with framed testimonials and mugshots of the incumbent with some politician. Michael took all this in at a glance, but his attention was riveted immediately to the figure overflowing a chair. Mal looked incongruous and uncomfortable in a baggy suit and spotted tie. The walls pulsed and seemed to bend in a little.

'Sit down, Padre,' the warden said.

For once, Michael didn't argue; his eyes never left the averted face of his old friend. 'Mal?'

The old man remained impassive, eyes downcast.

'Mr Donnelly has received a message from your home, Michael.'

The knot in his stomach dissolved into something wet and bitter that threatened to flood his throat. The warden never used his name. He breathed deeply through his mouth and brought himself under control. 'Mal, is it him?'

Finally the old man raised his puzzled eyes. 'It's your brother, Gabriel... He's missing, Michael.'

The part of Michael's brain that still functioned registered that Hanny had packed his bag and that Mal had booked him a ticket and pocketed his passport. Mal wove the Taurus one-handed through the downtown traffic; the Manhattan skyline moved like a graph across Michael's window. He came out of his reverie as the car slowed and stopped. A cacophony of horns worried the corpse of a truck stretched across their lane, twenty vehicles ahead.

'Ah well,' Mal sighed resignedly. He leaned under the dash and fished out a red dome light tethered to an extendable cord. Cranking down the window, he leaned out and set it snugly on the roof. Obligingly it began to revolve, blinking red beams in all directions.

'Leave the talking to me,' Mal said calmly, swinging onto the verge and barrelling up the inside. As they neared the blockage, a uniform peeled away from a knot of officers at the rear of the truck, paddling his hand. Surprisingly quickly for a big man, Mal was out of the car and in the cop's face.

Detachedly, Michael watched the old pro strut his stuff in the dumb show through the windshield. Mal walked right by the cop, beckoning over his shoulder for him to follow. Thrown by this, the cop lost some of his swagger and reversed to Mal's shoulder. Now he was getting a microsecond flash of a badge that materialised from Mal's inner pocket; there was a glance about to check for eavesdroppers, and a conspiratorial leaning in close. A nod, a brisk slap on the shoulder and Mal was back in the driving seat – thirty seconds, tops – and the cop was waving them through with big arm movements.

'Don't look at him,' Mal mouthed as they swept by into the traffic-free highway.

Over the next rise, Mal leaned out and retrieved his pet, snuggling it carefully back under the dash.

'Well?' Michael said.

'Well what?'

'Start with the dome.'

'Oh, that. Just a little token I took with me from a grateful police department on my retirement. You never know,' Mal added innocently, his eyes never straying from the road.

'And the badge?'

'Ah, yes – that too.'

'So what did you tell the guy?' Once a cop, always a cop, Michael thought, watching Mal check all his mirrors as if there might be someone from the department crouched on the trunk recording their conversation.

'Informant Relocation Program.' He switched his eyes from the road to Michael's blank expression. 'Remember that bomb factory in Brooklyn? Ah, it was all over the news. Well, you're the snitch. You heard it in the confessional and the Vatican wants you relocated to Ireland.'

'He believed that?'

Mal switched his indicator to follow the airport sign. 'If you're going to tell a lie, Michael, make it a big one. Adolf Hitler said that – or maybe it was Eichmann, I can't remember now.'

It was as near as either of them came to smiling.

The check-in lady readied her smile for the priest and quickly took refuge in efficiency instead. Trouble, she thought; drive 'em through. Awkward at the gate, they shuffled around with the bag between them.

'Thanks, Mal.'

'Ah, for nothing. Look, Michael, I could come over if...'

'No, thanks. Let me see what's happening and I'll call you, OK?'

'Right. Well... Hanny said you're to mind yourself over there. She says it's not the same.'

'Bye, Mal,' Michael said quickly, shouldering his bag through the gate.

Suddenly, the old man felt very tired. 'Bye, son,' he said, too softly to be heard. He contemplated an overpriced beer, then thought of Hanny alone in the apartment and her last question to him as he left for the prison, 'Will he come back, Mal?'

11

Flight EI103, New York to Dublin

WEDGED IN A window seat, Michael barely registered the geometry of urban life angling beneath him as the 747 leaned out over Long Island and nosed northeast for Newfoundland. Some part of his consciousness registered the voice of the captain. 'Hi, folks, and welcome aboard. We are currently cantering up the Eastern seaboard at twenty thousand feet. When we get to St John's, I'll rein her right and saddle up on the Atlantic air-stream all the way to the Emerald Isle.'

'Yeehaw!' chorused a group of guys in Stetsons who were sitting, sprawling and standing in the midsection.

'Father?'

Resignedly, Michael turned from the window to the elderly man in the middle seat. He had the spare frame and unfinished hands of a carpenter; a hawk-nose jutted under washed-denim eyes.

'Jake O'Leary. How Irish is that, huh?'

'It qualifies. You going over on vacation, Jake?'

'Naw, not really.'

Jake drummed his fingers on the fold-down table. He took a swift gulp from his glass and continued. 'I've never been in Ireland before. Now Norma, my wife, boy, she was over and back like a cross saw, before she… Well, she got a lump on her, eh… breast, Father.'

Michael nodded encouragement.

'Yeah, well, I'm on her case all the time. Go see the doctor, we got insurance, what's the problem? You got something you shouldn't have, it's better in a bucket, know what I mean? I didn't say that exactly, but I just kept pushing. Then she gets up her courage and goes and this young guy with a shiny shingle outside the door and more letters after his name than a whole fucking dictionary, excuse my French, Father. He says things like "primary tumour" and "secondaries" and shit like that, like he's got some problem with the word cancer. And that's what it comes down to, Father, a whole load of guys in white coats and a shitload

of dollars later. So I go and see the head honcho.
Maybe three, four cancelled appointments and he
gives me five minutes tops. "Too far gone, nothing
we can do", wham bam thank you ma'am, and I'm
back outside. "What did he say?" she asks when I
get home to the apartment. "He says you're pregnant," I say. Boy, that cracked her up good. She
laughs and laughs till she can't get her breath.
"Jake," she says, "you are full of it." That's as close
as she ever came to saying anything off-colour.
Classy lady, my Norma. Me? I'm what you see.
Never could figure what she saw in me. But you
know what they say, Father – for every shoe there's
a sock. Anyways, she takes my hand and says, "I'm
not going to get any better, honey." I'm crying like
I never done in forty years. "Jake O'Leary," she
says, "you dry your eyes. We got things to do. I
want you to do just one thing for me." I tell her
straight up that I won't talk to her asshole nephew.
"Take me home," she says, "one last time. Can we
do that?" So I get the tickets from this Irish travel
agent in Brooklyn in a fancy folder and I come
home early from the job, and she's sitting right
beside the window. I knew she was gone. I sat
down beside her, holding her hand and I say, "I
love you, Norma." Never said that all the years we
were married. She knew I did but I never said it,
Father.'

'You'd got quite a lady there, Jake.'

'I sure did.'

'And I think Norma got a good man.'

'Well, kind of you to say so, Father.'

'So where will you go?'

'I thought maybe I'd go see her brother in Galway and maybe some of the nieces, just for Norma's sake. After that, I don't know.'

Jake said this in such a lost voice that Michael leaned over and took the paper napkin from the table. He scribbled directions and a rough map on the napkin and handed it to Jake. 'It's not far from Galway and it's quiet.'

'The Island. Hell, I might do just that. This your place, Father?'

'Not any more,' Michael replied, and there was something in his tone that caused Jake to give him an appraising look.

'Maybe you should try and grab some sleep, Father,' he said kindly. 'And thanks. OK?'

Michael returned to the sanctuary of the window, letting the last of America's sunlight bloom inside his closed eyelids. Somewhere in a dusty recess of his heart, an old projector sparked, whirred and flickered faces in the dark. Gabriel, as fair as he himself was dark, 'the living image' of Eileen – Eileen, their mother, a teacher of Irish from Donegal. 'From Ireland,' the islanders sniffed, 'a blow-in', bringing her pupils to polish their book-Irish on the rough tongues of a people who would speak no other language if they could choose. An outsider who had met and married Michael Flaherty, a teacher like herself. But there the resemblance ended. She was day to his night, words and laughter to his silence; a woman attuned to touch and hold, married to a solitary. In quick succession, she had shocked the Island teacher with three sons: Liam, the eldest and wildest; Gabriel, the dreamer; and, between their force fields, Michael, the mirror-image of the Master, careful and controlled.

And then, another ebb in her monthly flow, and complications: bleeding and pain that frustrated the abilities of the Island nurse. The story was well known, and often told by those who were oblivious to small ears: the man with the haunted face placing his stricken wife in a currach and turning to the little knot of islanders on the beach. He never spoke, they said; just looked from face to face until there was none could stand his gaze, and they left him there and went back to the comfort of their own or the absolution of the bottle. All gone, but for the priest; he was more a hindrance than a help, but he climbed into the currach and held the woman through a gale spawned three thousand miles away in frozen Canada, a roaring wind that

screamed across the Atlantic to boil the sea
between the Island and the mainland. And later,
the slow journey home on the ferry, with the coffin
under canvas, the empty currach tethered out
behind, the priest hunched at the rail watching the
now-quiet sea and the Master sitting in the cabin,
absently holding the bundle of blue blankets.
Fiona, Michael's sister.

For a long time after that, Michael's world was
devoid of colour, ordinary things demanding extra-
ordinary effort, as he worked slowly towards a new
normality. His father grew dimmer and more
distant by the day, only occasionally lured to a
semblance of life and interest by the beguiling
Gabriel. Liam, without the sea-anchor of Eileen,
was like a lodger in the echoing house, working
the boats with his friends and putting a down
payment on alcoholism in the evenings. Fiona
had Michael to worship, and Michael had Father
Mack, the ascetic, bookish Island priest who had
held Eileen in his arms through the gale, crooning
old songs in her ear to comfort her terror. Father
Mack trained him in the Latin and fed him books
to devour by candlelight: 'They're your passport
out of here.'

Time passed. A grudging detente developed
between Michael and his father, founded on the
fragile stepping stones of books, a demilitarised

zone they could both enter to share the odd insight on some dead writer's style and build a causeway underneath the waves of their reserve. It might have developed into something stronger, something like the 'normal' Michael read of in books, if it hadn't been for Liam. Liam, drunk and scary, launching the currach on a day when even his pals held back, a day when the gulls clung to the cliffs and islanders anchored their thatch with ropes and stones. Liam, trying to kick Michael's fingers from the stern as he waited for a wave to belly him up and in.

In Jake's dream, Norma sat looking out the apartment window. A large bird fluttered to the sill outside and pecked at her reflection in the glass. It had the long mangy neck and scabrous head of a vulture and its eyes gleamed with hunger. Jake smashed his fists through the glass and the bird wheeled away to circle beyond his reach. When he stepped back, he saw that he had destroyed Norma's image. She called to him. 'Jake. It's dark here, Jake. I'm afraid.' He tried to take her in his arms but his arms passed right through her. He could see his blood dripping on the empty chair. As Jake woke, eyes starting, his quivering hands held up before his face. He wiped the sweat from his forehead and breathed deeply, putting his hand on the empty chair beside him. 'Oh sweetheart,' he whispered.

The priest beside him groaned. He was trembling like a man with malaria, one word struggling over and over through chattering teeth. 'Liam.'

Awkwardly, Jake patted the hand that drummed the armrest, and winced as he was caught in a death grip.

'I have you. I have you. I won't let you go. I promise…'

The voice trailed off into some gibberish that Jake couldn't figure out.

Jesus, son, he thought, I wouldn't be where you are for the world.

Gradually the grip relaxed, and the young priest curled for comfort to the dark window.

12

Dublin Airport

FATHER JAMES O'REILLY looked like a man who had held his breath for a very long time. On closer inspection, his florid cheeks and slightly bulbous nose revealed their plumbing of purple veins. His eyes, behind the slightly tinted glasses, always gave him the look of someone who had been crying, or who wanted to. He had a carefully pressed off-the-rack black suit and a bright white Roman collar that added to his general appearance of imminent asphyxiation. He stood at the door leading into the terminal building so that the stream of people from the plane had to flow either side of him.

'Father Flaherty?'

'I'm Michael Flaherty.'

'Ah, good man yourself,' the priest said enthusiastically, as if Michael had answered a particularly difficult question.

'I wasn't expecting to be met, Father…?'

'O'Reilly, James. Well now, you see, your bishop called from New York.' He took Michael's arm. 'Ah, yes, a lovely man – Irish-born, of course. Never lost a trace of the accent at all. "Am I waking you?" he said. Sure, it was three o'clock in the morning, but then, what are we here for?'

He dropped his voice to a conspiratorial hush. 'He said the cardinal would appreciate a little fraternal courtesy under the, eh, circumstances.'

It had Mal's prints all over it, but Michael kept his counsel. 'I'm very obliged to you, Father.'

'Ah, not at all – and call me James, won't you? Give me up the bag and we'll be off.'

Michael quickly gathered that Father O'Reilly was the airport chaplain. Passport Control and Customs were a matter of 'How are you, Tommy?' and 'Grand day, Mick.'

'I have the car beyond in the car park by the church, and we'll be in Spiddal in good time for the evening boat.'

Michael stopped dead in his tracks. 'Now look, Father—'

'James.'

'James. I'm really very grateful to you but I can get a bus from Dublin.'

'Indeed and you will not,' his guardian angel spluttered, going from red to a threatening puce. 'I was over there myself last year in New York, and I never got to put my hand in my pocket at all. Turn about is fair play, isn't that right?'

Michael raised his hands in mock surrender. 'Right. I hope you don't mind if I doze off along the way.'

'Not at all. It'll be a relief to you – God knows, I'm a terrible talker.'

Michael sensed that this self-accusation craved denial. 'Indeed you are not, James.'

It was the right response. James's hand tightened appreciatively on Michael's arm. 'You just let the seat back for yourself whenever it suits you. I'll put the bag in the boot.'

In the car, James grunted out of his shoes and sighed into the black fleece-lined slippers nesting by the pedals. 'I'm a martyr to my feet.' The dash sported a thin metal crucifix on a stand and a magnetised cameo of Padre Pio waving reluctantly with a bandaged hand. Michael began to wonder what sort of driver needed such strong intercession.

'I guess we drive through Dublin to get to the western road?'

'Not at all. Sure, we have this new ring road now that avoids the city completely. No harm at all: there's parts of that place that aren't safe night or day.'

All the religious objects suddenly made perfect sense as James scraped the gearshift into reverse and shot blindly backwards, with hardly a glance over his shoulder. Two teenage girls screamed and dragged their trolley of duty-free to safety. Michael just had time to notice that the single finger had become an international salutation before James wove happily out of the car park, hunched myopically over the wheel.

'Ah, yes, changed times,' James continued. 'When I was in the seminary, you could walk abroad in the city day or night. Not now,' he sighed, absently edging in front of an enormous truck full of the national beverage. The blast of the air horn shuddered through the car. 'Bless you,' James murmured absently, waving an informal benediction in the rear-view mirror with his left hand. Michael realised that he had stopped breathing, and started again with a gasp.

'Ah, yes,' James continued happily, 'where would you get fresh air the like of that? But, of course, everything is changing – and not for the better.' He swung his head away from the road to make eye contact with his passenger. 'Drugs,' he said ominously. 'The country's awash with drugs.'

Desperately, Michael racked his brain for a subject that might ride the fine line between passion and politeness. 'Do you know any of the lads down West?'

'Ah, yes. I was ordained with three of them.'

'I was wondering if you knew the Island priest, Father Mack.'

Clergy on clergy could sometimes qualify as a blood sport, but Michael was desperate and exhausted. If he could encourage James to an intensive burst of conversation, it might sate his need and sense of duty. Otherwise, Michael was faced with the endless attrition of polite, meaningless words.

James pursed his lips. 'Ah, yes – poor Mack.'

'Is he sick?'

'Ah, no; not that we've heard, anyway. No, no, it's just that he tends to… draw fire, if you follow me.'

Terrified that James would turn to him for confirmation, Michael said quickly, 'I'm not sure.'

'Well, he had all these visions for the Island, you know. Eco-friendly industry to put a stop to emigration, and self-sufficiency to end the dole culture. It was all in the papers. Ah, Mack was a visionary all right – and not a bit shy about it.' He chuckled conspiratorially.

'How did it go for him?'

'Badly,' James said, with the slightest inflection of satisfaction. 'He criticised the government of the day. They diverted his funding and dropped a quiet word in the usual quarters, so he got a little rap of the crozier from the archbishop. He went quiet for a long time after that, but I hear tell he has a co-op and all sorts of enterprises up and running now. Foreign money, they say.'

His tone implied that this was hardly legal tender. Michael had a sudden vision of James's parents. They would be pumped-up versions of James, appropriately red-faced and proper. They would have a shop in an upmarket suburb, but would always refer to themselves as being 'in business'. They would have a ready smile for people whom they recognised as equals, and a carefully ruled notebook under the counter for the owings of 'that crowd' from the council houses. He was on a roll, surfing along on an uncharitable stream of consciousness. They would refer to their son as 'Father James' and keep a finger on the scales to maintain his lifestyle... Nice one, Flaherty, he thought. This poor dope is duped out of his warm bed to drive your arse across the breadth of the country, and you psycho-bubble-wrap him for his pains.

'Would you know him well yourself, Michael?'

'I did,' Michael replied after a slight hesitation.

The florid priest felt deflated and irritated, for no reason that he could fathom. Hadn't he tried for prudence in his portrayal of Mack, the Island priest? The same Mack who had told him that prudence would be the death of him at the last meeting of the National Council of Priests, just because James had tried to put a little gentle brake on some of his more outlandish notions. 'If you took your head out of your arse for one half-hour, James, you might actually see something.'

Oh, they had laughed at that; all of them, even that newly ordained pup he had gone out of his way to befriend. James' fingers whitened on the wheel at the memory of his humiliation. He overtook a lorry on a bend and felt a little better. Well, James, the little voice said in his head, maybe you are inclined to run with the hare and hunt with the hounds, if you follow me. 'Fuck off, you,' he muttered savagely over the steering wheel and by some miracle of telepathy, the elderly lady up front swung recklessly into the grass verge out of his way. 'Maybe,' he mouthed again, his heart thumping the drums in his temples, 'maybe I should have told that Yankee bishop to fuck off at three o'fucking clock in the morning. I did not spend seven years in seminary to drive a clerical taxi, my lord, so kiss my arse and

good night. Oh yes, maybe. And maybe I should
tell this languid young fella in the passenger seat
that his shagging Island priest is a mad and bad
bastard.' In this manner James streaked
westwards, slaying the smart-mouthed shitheads
that bedevilled him, with the limp sword of
'maybe'.

Michael put his head back and stretched his
legs. Slowly his eyes closed.

The silence and stillness roused him. For a
moment, he was disoriented. His forehead and
nose were cold from smudging the passenger
window. His mouth felt stale, his lips gummed and
he had no feeling in his legs.

'Ah, the dead arose.' James the ebullient, the
master of the well-honed cliché, was back.

Get a grip, Flaherty, Michael thought savagely,
rubbing his calves vigorously.

James was all business. 'There's your ticket,
now. No, get away with you; it was the least I could
do. You have a good hour, now, before the ferry
goes.'

Michael shook the last wisps of sleep from his
brain. 'Look, Father—'

'James.'

'James. Could I stand you a night in the Galway
Corrib Hotel? I don't like the idea of you just
turning around and heading back.'

'Arrah, man dear, I've a classmate up the road I haven't seen for an age.'

'He's expecting you?'

'Expecting me?' James shut his eyes, leaned his head back and turned redder still. 'Indeed and he's not,' he spluttered when he had control of himself. 'The same fella is over and back to Lourdes twice a year, and always looking for a bed going and coming. I'll put a dent in his duty-free now, so I will.'

He pulled some inner master switch and went suddenly from hilarity to solicitude. 'And I'll remember your intentions at mass in the morning.'

13

The Pier, Spiddal, County Galway

MICHAEL COUNTED FOUR men with cloth caps leaning crooked elbows on the rim of the pier wall. They rocked, almost imperceptibly but in perfect unison, to the thud of water on the invisible seaward side. Islandmen, he thought. He passed behind them, without sparking a ripple of interest on their part, and sat on a bollard, watching the water, waiting. In the tame waters of the small harbour, a white plastic shopping bag floated by, its belly swollen obscenely with trapped air. Mercifully, his thoughts were distracted as one of the men peeled away from his perch and ambled to his shoulder.

'Is it Father Michael?'

Michael stood to acknowledge the greeting in Irish. The face beneath the cap's rim was permanently weather-cured to a light brown. The old man looked back and nodded to the others; immediately they doffed their caps in Michael's direction.

'I said it was yourself,' the islandman said with quiet satisfaction. 'You won't remember me. I'm Tim Pat Cronin from west of the Point.'

'I know you well, Mr Cronin. My father always said you were the only man worth his salt for reading the weather.'

Impossibly, a few extra lines cracked the old face as the man smiled. 'Aye, maybe so. You have trouble,' he added gently. Michael nodded.

'Well, maybe there'll be good news waiting for you beyond.'

He turned to go, but Michael's question stayed him. 'He didn't take the boat, Mr Cronin?'

'No, then, he did not,' the old man sighed regretfully.

The tradition for emigrants was to leave without goodbyes. Michael had done it himself. Up to that point, he had managed to keep reality at bay. Now, a cold feeling started in his stomach and spread to numb his legs. He sat down abruptly on the bollard.

'They'll be looking for a body then?'

The silence stretched between them.

'You'd better be getting a scat in the cabin,' Tim Pat suggested kindly. 'There's a gang of Yankee students in Moran's bar; they're for beyond as well.'

Brian Quinn was having a bad day. Like most of his bad days, it had started the night before in Finnegan's, the only pub on the Island. He'd been flush with dole money and he'd kept old Finnegan hopping behind the bar, drawing pints and muttering like the old woman he was, 'Will you go easy, Brian, and leave some for another day?'

'Isn't my money good enough for you?' he'd growled back truculently, loud enough for the benefit of the knot of cronies in the corner; loud enough to draw a wince from Finnegan. He loved the sudden fright in the small eyes, darting in the flabby folds of his pig face.

'There's no need for that class of talk, so there isn't.'

'Me arse,' Brian had spat back. 'You set up and I'll pay up.'

More drink for himself and the lads, more drink than he could handle. Swaying onto the dance floor, the head still nimble to the tune, the legs a few beats behind. Couples drifting apart to avoid colliding with the big, shambling man. Then grabbing Kathleen Tuohy by the waist and swinging her round and round till the room blurred and the cheers melded into one long roar as Kathleen's feet left the floor and she began to scream; her brother Paddy folding her neatly in his arms and setting her securely among her friends. Then Paddy and Seamus, the other brother, in his face, pushing him towards the door; the pals suddenly oblivious to his plight, staying well away from a tangle with the champion oarsmen. Outside and alone, the night air had cooled his temper; he had thrown a few last shouts at the closed door to salvage a sliver of pride.

Ah Jesus, the morning. Stumbling in from the bed to a bare table and that cold bitch letting the daylight flood the kitchen as she hemmed new curtains. The slap of her back to him as she stepped on the chair to measure the drop.

'Money is scarce enough without wasting it on bloody curtains.'

'It's no thanks to you that we can have the likes of this… and other things.'

The pause was all the firing he needed, and soon they were hacking away. It was a ritual bloodletting, the slitting of old veins along familiar

lines; it eased the madness of a long-dead
marriage. Usually it would peter out into longer
pauses, until he banged the door behind him and
she sat in a foam of net curtain, smoking and
coldly examining the reflection of the madwoman
in the window. But, this time, they lost the script
and floundered for telling lines; she was more able
than he at improvisation until, enraged at his tardy
tongue, he stepped outside the rules.

'There were no loonies in my family, Kate
Logan.'

She winced as if struck and sagged into the
chair.

'Except yourself, Brian Quinn,' she managed to
reply. But the venom was leached from it. The boy
had always been off-limits. In their terrible war of
daily attrition, the boy had represented something
better than either of them, something unsullied by
their sordid reality. Until today.

Brian was surfing on a crest of adrenaline and
nausea as he reached the boat.

'If you're late again, Quinn, I'll leave you.'

Tess bloody Duggan, a farmer's whelp, up to
her lilywhite arse in grants, talking down to a
man who had taken his first steps in the belly of a
currach under oars, who could smell his way in a
fog through Creggan Rocks. A man who could
have had his own bloody boat if it wasn't for the

begrudgers. He wanted to tell her where to shove her pissy little job, but the money was off the books and supplemented the dole.

But by Jesus, his day would come. Though not this day. Not this cursed bright-blue day, when the sea ran fine and there was a warmth where the sun pooled aft of the wheelhouse. No, there had to be the ritual degradation before the four dry gannets on the pier wall in Spiddal. The beady eyes of them watching the moneylender harry him like a tern, out on the pier. 'It's three thousand pounds, Mr Quinn.' Mr Quinn, by Christ. It was Brian – Brian – when he had first gone to him. 'No bother, Brian. Sure your name is enough.' Now it was 'Three thousand pounds, Mr Quinn', and 'Court would be the last thing any of us would want, Mr Quinn' and 'Sure there was no need to be involving any interested parties, Mr Quinn.'

And now, the perfect end to Brian's day – a priest. Brian had had a deep well of universal hatred and then a sub-well for priests, ever since that whore's melt Father Mack had down-faced him on the beatings and the boy. 'Fuck all these geldings to hell and back,' he swore to himself.

'Grand day, Father,' he nodded.

Michael noticed the slightly spread feet of an islander. We come that way from the womb, he thought, poised for balance on land or water. His gaze travelled upwards, over the nondescript

trousers badged with oil smears and the Island
sweater impregnated with oil to resist the rain. The
clothes couldn't hide the solid bulk of the man
beneath, the overall impression of strength only
slightly marred by a bulge in the middle. As he
passed, the man's breath confirmed Michael's
suspicion that the bulge was courtesy of a brewery.
But it was his face that captivated Michael. It was
the wreck of what had once been handsome. There
was a quality in it that reminded Michael of a
deserted Island cottage, the hearth long dead, the
walls mouldering from within. The mouth had
given up the fight with gravity and had settled to a
permanent sneer. He wondered if the anger there
was reserved for him, or available to the world at
large: for both, the eyes confirmed.

'You'll find a nice warm seat in the cabin,
Father.'

Wordlessly, Michael took the stub from the
calloused hand and made his way across the deck,
sensing the eyes boring into the small of his back.
With a sense of relief, he let the door bang behind
him. The cabin was large and well-lit by picture
windows. The walls were bordered by benches
screwed into the floor; a small bar snuggled into a
corner at the bow end.

His reconnaissance was interrupted by raucous
laughter from the quay. Six pairs of sneakers
jogged by the window and tramped hollowly

across the gangplank. Two husky young men and four young women exploded into the cabin.

'Wow. Is he Charon or what?'

'More like Cerberus.'

They had met Brian Quinn.

They were slightly muted by the sight of the priest; they found a table and bent their heads to the brochure spread flat between them.

'OK, so what's this place called?'

'Dunno. It just says "The Island" here. Cryptic or what?'

'That's the big one, right? So the other two are what?'

Michael noticed that most of the queries were addressed to the guy who looked a little long in the tooth for his Notre Dame sweatshirt. He was about six two and lean. He was also the only one who hadn't dumped his haversack on the floor, secreting it instead under the bench he was sitting on. He was no student, Michael thought, and certainly no linguist: he managed to mangle the Irish names of all three islands.

The others laughed good-naturedly at his efforts, and he looked around with feigned hurt. 'So I'm Italian, OK?'

'Hey, Father?' One of the girls was looking Michael's way. 'Can you tell us what these places are called?'

'Sure. The smallest one is the East Island, the middle one is the Middle Island and the big one is just the Island.'

'I could've told you that,' the big guy protested, and hunched under a barrage of mock blows.

The gangplank scraped; the engines coughed once and startled the screws into life. Michael sensed through his feet when they left the placid waters in the lee of the pier and faced into the Atlantic. It was a still day, and the green water moved in a steady swell. Whoever was at the wheel knew his trade and held a course that would swing the boat in a broad arc, lengthening the journey but guaranteeing a smoother passage. After the initial excitement, the young Americans' banter tapered off and they were lured out of the cabin one by one to contemplate the majesty of the water on either side and the three short brushstrokes of grey-blue that seemed to hover just above the horizon.

'You from hereabouts, Father?'

He was surprised to find himself alone with the map-mangler.

'Yes, I'm from the Island. I've been working in the States for some time.'

'Vacation, huh?'

'No, not exactly.'

Michael didn't elaborate, and the young man didn't pursue it.

'Maybe you could advise me, Father. I was kind of hoping to rent, like, a cottage or something on the Island.'

'There's a pretty good hostel, I believe.'

'Nah. Hostels are convenient, but they always end up like a frat house. I'd like to get a bit closer to the real life of the place.'

'Why don't you ask at Finnegan's when we land? The people in the pub know everything and everybody.'

'OK. Thanks.'

Michael stretched his legs and flexed his toes.

Now is as good a time to face it as any, he thought.

Mario Luigi Ricci watched the priest push himself away from the wall and walk resolutely to the door. Alone now, he allowed his leg to drift away from the haversack and thought about the priest: walks like a Newfie, talks like the Bronx Irish, as open as a New England farmer talking to a tax inspector and eyes like a highway patrolman. Jesus, if they're all like him on the Island, maybe I should just walk into the bar and declare my name, rank and serial number. Mario relaxed his shoulders and leaned his leg against the reassuring bulk of his haversack.

It wasn't the roll of the swell that glued Michael's back to the cabin door. It was the sounds and smells, the very things that had still brought him gasping into wakefulness even when he was over three thousand miles away, that threatened to overcome him and drive him back inside. So Sarah Leibowitz – shrink extraordinaire, with her Manhattan high-rise office and her monthly high-rise bill to the archdiocese – had been right after all. 'Shit happens; and shit travels, Reverend.' 'Father' was a bit of a problem for Miss Leibowitz. Good defence strategy, Flaherty: psyche the psychologist.

With a supreme effort, he peeled his back from the rough warmth of the door and moved forwards to the rail before the wheelhouse. For the first time in twelve years, he looked out over the ocean at the islands, coming up ever clearer, like a photographic print, with every wash of the waves. His eyes stroked the familiar outline of the Island, and snagged on the sea stack. The Devil's Finger, as the islanders called it, stood slightly apart from the land and, even from that distance, Michael could see the white tormented water that writhed in the channel between.

Brian Quinn backed through the wheelhouse door, already gulping from one of the tea mugs in his hands. He placed the other before the skipper with a barely concealed sneer.

'There you are, now; all aboard and shipshape.'

Tess Duggan grunted and let one hand drop from the wheel to hunt the mug handle, her eyes never leaving the sea. Quinn lifted his own mug and sighted on the priest standing at the for'ard rail. 'Who's your man?' he asked, slurping noisily.

She eased back a notch on the throttle. 'Whoever he is, he's one of our own.'

'Islander?'

'Aye.'

'I don't recognise him,' Quinn said in an aggrieved tone, as if the priest had held back information he had a right to know.

Tess registered the tone, but her face remained expressionless. Pretty soon, her oldest brother would be finished with schooling and she could bid a grateful goodbye to Brian Quinn. 'Take the wheel for a while, and hold her steady by the needle.'

Michael turned from the rail to acknowledge the greeting and found himself face to face with a pixie-faced woman about his own age, her slim figure bulked out by an anorak, her bleached hair defying the confines of her hood to soften the sharpness of her features.

'I know you,' she said bluntly.

'And I know you, Tess Duggan,' he smiled back. 'You were in my class in school, when you weren't running off in anything that would float.'

'Aye.' She smiled despite herself. 'I didn't know you were keeping such a close eye on me, Michael Flaherty.'

Her slightly mocking emphasis on the 'me' brought him up short; he felt the colour rising in his face. To salve the moment, she pressed on more seriously 'We're all searching for Gabriel.'

Tess was a woman of few words, but he sensed that she was anxious to say a few more, so he held his silence.

'You'll find a lot of changes beyond, and not all of them for the better. Gabriel was outspoken, like.'

'I always thought that was one of his finer qualities,' Michael said softly. He watched Tess struggle with a thought and subdue it before it could escape her lips.

'You've been gone a while, Michael,' she said, almost sadly.

The sound of powerful engines swung them towards the launch that was fast approaching

astern. A thirty-footer, Michael guessed, with twin
Merlin engines that were swallowing the distance
between them at half-throttle. The cabin roof
sported a revolving dish and an array of antennae.
A squat, powerfully built man, bolstered in a navy
wind-cheater, mirrored Michael's own position in
the prow; as the gleaming craft powered by, he
glimpsed another man in the wheelhouse. A
woman stood in the stern, half her face masked in
wraparound sunglasses, her ash-blonde hair
straining in the slipstream, pulling her face into
sharp profile. Armani does the Islands, Michael
thought caustically, and raised his hand in a
sardonic wave that was not returned.

'*Stroinséiri,*' Tess grunted, in a tone islanders
reserved for strangers. 'They own the fish factory
beyond; old Danny Pat sold them the land near
the harbour.' Her face darkened with disapproval.
'Never worked a day in his life, the old bastard.
Now he's the toast of every waster in Galway. And
themselves' – she nodded in the wake of the other
boat – 'the answer to all our prayers.' She mimed
a dry spit to the side – no islander would ever spit
on the boat that carried them or into the sea that
fed them.

A sheet of spray burst over the bow and sent
her striding to the wheelhouse. 'You're two points
off the heading and riding the swell,' she snapped,

shouldering Brian unceremoniously away from the wheel.

'Sure, it'll be a bit of excitement for the passengers,' he laughed uneasily.

'Save your excitement for your own boat,' she gritted, straining to bring the bow back to true.

To cover his anger, Brian asked innocently, 'Did you figure your man beyond?'

'He's Michael Flaherty, the Master's son,' she said grudgingly.

A cruel glow crept into his dull eyes. 'Is he indeed? Then he'll be the one that drowned his brother.'

Tess's fingers whitened at the wheel. 'There's no islander worthy of the name, or with a knowledge of the water, that ever blamed him,' she said evenly. 'I'll thank you to check the bumpers for landing, Mr Quinn.'

'But we're a good half-hour out yet.'

Brian went anyway, letting the door slap peevishly behind him. He moved to the side rail, watching the stern of the powerboat recede into the distance, the anger in his eyes replaced with longing.

14

The Island

'SEE YOU ROUND, Father.' Mario hoisted his bag with a practised swing and ambled after his companions.

Alone, Michael hunched forward, leaning on his knees, watching a Coke can roll on the cabin floor in sympathy with the slight swell in the Island harbour.

'I could make a drive for Boston if you like,' Tess smiled from the door.

'You'd make it, too, Tess,' he smiled back, easing himself upright and stretching the kinks out of his spine.

'There's someone waiting for you.' She inclined her head towards the dock. A tractor, drawing a trailer for passengers and their baggage, was already piled high with the students and their rucksacks. Changed times, Michael thought. Time was when the donkey would have panniered visitors over the optional roads to their digs. The tractor moved off, revealing a young woman staring at him. He took in her baggy Island sweater and faded Levis at a glance, but his eyes were drawn back to her hair. It was a riot of red, a burning halo that surrounded a pale face. The eyes that scanned him were green tidal pools, the sharp cheekbones beneath shingled with freckles.

'Michael?'

He nodded.

'It's Fiona, Michael.'

His heart swelled and threatened his breathing.

'Fiona,' he said stupidly. 'You grew.'

There was a moment when they could have embraced, but it passed. To cover its wake, she said with forced irony, 'That happens.' In a way that didn't invite protest, she swung his bag over her shoulder and threaded her arm through his. 'Come on. We'll talk on the way.'

Like a parish priest shepherding a distracted bishop through his flock, she whispered names as she nudged him past a knot of locals. 'That's

Paddy the Point, May Finnegan from the pub…
uh-oh, brace yourself: here comes Lena the Phone.
She'll know you.'

She did. 'Is it yourself, Father Michael?'

He was tempted to reply with an Island
proverb: 'There is no answer to the question that
needn't be put.'

'After all the years,' Lena pressed on, her sharp
eyes cataloguing the black suit and the small bag.
'And how are you at all?'

'He's the way anybody would be after a long
journey, Lena,' Fiona said strongly, steering
Michael around the crag of her nose. 'Nosey old
bitch,' she whispered when they were out of
earshot. 'She'd live in your ear.'

They wound their way up the paved narrow
road until they were walking on sand and stones
between the filigree of Island walls. Every step
jolted the lid Michael had pressed down so firmly
on memory, and suddenly he felt weak from the
overload of sights and smells.

'Can we stop for a moment?'

Fiona sat with her back to the dry-stone wall,
her shoulder dappled by the sunlight sieving
through.

'How's…?'

Fiona eventually took pity on his struggle.
Blowing out a long breath, she leaned forward to

pluck a stem of haresfoot. 'He's failed a lot in the last while.' Absently, her fingers plucked the seeds from the plant. 'After Liam... and you, I thought he was pining.' Her voice shook a little on the word and she turned away, her fingers shredding the innocent grass stalk.

I am numbered among the dead, Michael thought dully. That was no surprise. That was why he had left – well, a large part of the reason, anyway. Someone saved from the sea could not stay: he had foiled the water, and someone else would be taken in his stead. It was the way of things.

Fiona was speaking again. 'Well, the weight fell off him and I was worried.' She forced herself on. 'I asked the nurse if she'd have a look at him – on the sly, because you know what he's like. She said he might be in the early stages of Alzheimer's.'

The word dropped like a heavy weight between them, and Fiona was released of her burden.

'Some days, he's like his old self – you know, cranky and moody.' She tried to laugh, but tears leaked from her eyes. 'Oh, Michael, if anything's happened to Gabriel...'

He held a finger to her lips. 'Shh, Fi,' he said softly. 'Hush, *a chailín*.' He stroked the top of her head awkwardly.

The pet name dissolved her, and he held her

against his crumpled black coat. They sat that way, listening to the wind sighing through the stones like a long-lost soul calling from the sea.

The house was as Michael remembered it: built from rough stones cut from the foreshore at low tide and shaped into place by a craftsman using only a hammer. Like its neighbours, dotted about like sheep in a meadow, it had walls of blinding white, but the modern slate roof made it stand apart from the thatch of the others.

He let his eye coast down the hill behind, to the squat schoolhouse. 'Is he still teaching?'

'No, we've had a new Master for the last few years.'

'Do I know him?'

'Her.'

'Her. Do I know her?'

'You're looking at her.'

'Fiona Flaherty, you're full of surprises.'

'Would you listen to the mystery man talking?' She laughed and prodded him inside.

Inside, the house was the same and not the same, like a retouched photograph where the colour seemed to seep beyond the limits of the forms. It was more than the new Aga cooker or the bright curtains, or the fridge that hummed companionably beside the worktop. His eyes skidded over these intruders, finding no purchase, and focused gratefully on the bookshelf, still leaning crazily to the left. He let it fill his eyes, as a seasick seaman locks his gaze on the steady line of the horizon. No, it wasn't the place that caused his ache, but the absence of someone. Eileen. Some old familiar phantom pushed against a well-locked door deep inside him. Down, he thought fiercely, not now.

Not ever, Michael? the phantom questioned sadly, in his mother's voice.

He must have groaned, because he felt his sister's palm between his shoulder blades.

'Are you coming or going, Michael?'

'A bit of both, Fi,' he said wearily. He took a deep breath. 'Where's…?'

The pause lengthened.

'You're going to have to call him something, Michael,' she said without reproach.

He riffled through the words he knew for something appropriate. *Father? No, way too formal. Pop? God, no; too bizarre and American.* Stalling for time, he turned to face her. 'And what do you call him?'

'I call him Daddy,' she said simply, and he was overcome by something like envy.

'Suppose I say "Himself"?'

'"Himself" will do just grand,' she said, giving him a small smile of absolution. 'We'll have the tea and then get you sorted.' She moved briskly to the sink.

Typical Irish solution, Michael thought. Have the tea.

'What's so funny all of a sudden?' Fiona asked.

'I was just thinking that when the world ends and the Day of Judgment dawns and the graves give up their dead and all are called to answer, the Irish will miss that part because they'll be having the tea.'

'And what would be wrong with that?'

'So where's Himself, Fi?'

'He's probably beyond in Father Mack's. He goes there a lot and they play chess, when he's able.' Her voice faltered and gathered again. 'Most of the time they just sit and read. You remember what the two of them are like for the books?'

He remembered.

'The phone's beyond on the desk there. You might want to ring someone?'

Michael was tempted to remark that American phones don't ring; they buzz, like a drill through the constant roar of the trains and the honking horns and what passes for conversation, until the nuisance can no longer be ignored and someone snatches it up.

Hanny picked up on the first buzz.

'You're sitting on it, Hanny. He'll get suspicious.'

'Nah. I knew it was you. The toy boy calls on the cellphone. You OK?'

'Yeah.'

Hanny had a range of harumphs. This one betokened disbelief, with an underlay of concern.

'Is the blimp sober?'

'Near as dammit. Mal!' she yelled.

Too late, Michael held the receiver away from his ear. If Hanny ever had lessons in voice projection, the phone would become superfluous. When he put it back to his ear, Mal was breathing heavily at the other end.

'Maybe you put that beer down a little quickly, old man.'

'Come right over, Doc, and bring the restraints. She's bitten me twice already.'

Over three thousand miles of ether, Michael heard Hanny's harumph.

'Any news, Michael?'

'No.'

'OK, so let me bring you up to speed.'

He heard Mal fumble for spectacles and riffle the notepad. Once a cop... he thought, and smiled.

'Mr Eamonn O'Brien is now the client of one Richard Downey, attorney-at-law.'

'Is he good?'

'Good? This guy is Milo O'Shea in a seersucker. He can toora-loora better than Bing. And you ask if he's good?'

'Mal…'

'Keep your shirt on, Michael. He's a Patrick's Day Irishman, but yeah, he's good.'

'Thanks, Mal.' The shootist from Spiddal might have a chance after all.

'So, on to lesser matters.' More riffling pages and heavy breathing. 'Right. I made three calls to the Chancellor of the Archdiocese of New York before the prick picked up the phone. Quote, "highly irregular", unquote. Quote, "could adversely affect standing in the archdiocese", unquote, et cetera, et cetera. I told him to shove it up his butt.'

'You didn't!'

'I nearly. Really pissed me off. Anyways, I called my good friend and golf handicap, Monsignor Riley. Consider that circle squared. Oh, yeah, the warden called – says she hope's all's well. Sexy lady… Ouch! Your days are numbered, Hanny.'

'You're a saint, Mal.'

'He says I'm a martyr.'

Hanny yelling in the background, 'Don't forget to take out the garbage.'

'You cooked it, you take it out… Mike?'

'Yeah.'

'How's it going?'

'I'm here.'

'OK. Well, take it easy.'

'Thanks, Mal.'

When Michael had hung up, he looked up to see Fiona standing in the centre of the kitchen, the bedsheets folded over her crossed arms and dropping to her knees in a neat square.

'What?' she smiled uncertainly.

'You look like a Carmelite nun.'

The smile evaporated and her head drooped forward over the sheets. He moved to her and took her gently by the shoulders.

'What is it, Fi?'

The coldness in her eyes shocked him. 'God has taken more than His fair share of the Flahertys, Michael.'

'Is that how you feel?'

'It is.'

'Fair enough, so,' he said softly. 'No more bad jokes from the clerical brother.'

She nodded, breathed deeply, and came erect again. 'Right. You'll bunk down in Gabriel's room for the time being.'

Again her head faltered. This time he took her in his arms, smelling the faint must of the sheets between them, searching for some words of comfort that might soothe her pain. As if she had divined his thoughts, she tightened her grip on him. 'Promise me something, Michael,' she whispered fiercely into his chest.

'What?'

'Promise me that you won't say anything about God's holy will or carrying our cross bravely or any of that old shit. I couldn't bear it and I might hate you for it, and I don't want to lose you too.'

He placed his forefinger over her lips and tilted her chin with his thumb until their eyes met. 'I promise never to say any such useless, cruel thing to you, Fi. None of that old shit… ever.'

She almost smiled and laid her head gently on his chest, sagging against him.

'They were my blood too, Fi,' he whispered into her flaming hair, too softly to be heard. A pounding deep inside shook him from head to toe, as the phantom of a desolate boy rose up to rage at the raw empty place in his heart. He put his hand to his forehead, rubbing ineffectually at the crevices between his eyes.

'I'll make up the bed,' Fiona said, moving to the door.

Her gasp brought him out of his stupor, moving him quickly to her side. 'What is it, Fi?'

Her mouth moved, but no sound escaped her. He shifted his gaze to the room beyond and felt his chest balloon and grow rigid.

'Oh, Jesus.'

Michael stretched out his arm and grasped the doorjamb of his brother's room with all the desperation of a drowning man.

For a moment he hung there, suspended in shock, his fingers white against the wood. Then, as if an automatic switch had clicked in his mind, his training reasserted itself and he became cold and functional. Fiona sensed the transformation and, despite her reluctance, turned her head to watch her brother enter the devastation of the room. Some part of her brain noted and marvelled at the way he moved, his feet sliding between the debris, his upper body coiled and ready. Like a cat, she thought; a very large and dangerous cat. She shivered involuntarily and hugged the sheets tighter for comfort.

Michael scanned the room perfunctorily, already knowing that whatever force had wreaked the havoc was long gone. Satisfied, he began to pick his way between the debris, quartering the space in search of a trail. Everywhere there were papers, bunched and tossed in corners or torn to shreds in frustration as they failed the test of the intruder. Something fragile cracked quietly underfoot; without lowering his eyes, he bent and hooked his fingers under his shoe, bringing the translucent sliver of a seashell into his range of vision.

More than all the scattered fragments, the ravaged posters and tipped drawers, more even than the ultimate violation of the mattress tumbled naked on the floor, this frail broken shard of what had once been perfect and complete confirmed for him the truth his energy had kept at bay: Gabriel was dead. And the monster who had defiled his room had played some part in his dying. Instinctively, Michael tightened his fist on the shell fragment, willing the pain to stop him from howling his rage. Blood dripped shockingly red on half a dolphin leaping through a fragment of a wall poster in search of its companions.

The statue of the Infant of Prague riveted his gaze, funnelling his anger into hard focus. In all the devastation, it stood intact – apart from the head, which he sensed had been long gone. It drew him like a magnet across the room, deaf to the crunching beneath his feet and the sharp pain in his fingers. Slowly he stretched out his hand, took the hollow plaster figure from its perch and turned it upside down. Nothing.

His brain was racing, conjuring memories of Gabriel's idiosyncrasies. Gabriel who always slept nearest the window to hear the sea; Gabriel who always left his shoes overturned at night to dissuade nesting spiders; Gabriel who always pulled out the chair to stand on so he... Yes. Michael's own body mimicked his brother's movements as he reached up to replace the statue on the shelf. Gabriel always put his things in the hollow sanctuary for safekeeping.

It was empty. Feverishly Michael dropped to the floor, scanning the area underneath the shelf, running his fingers over the Braille of items beneath the desk, scooping them out into the light. A glass marble, opaque and milky, and a fishhook muzzled by a small cork lay on the carpet and, beside them, evidence of the intruder – an uncapped pen and the butt of a cigarette. Someone else had discovered Gabriel's cache; someone else had sieved the contents through his fingers, letting the chaff drop to the floor and holding on to... what?

He took a step back from the desk to get a wider picture, certain that the answer lay before him, forcing his conscious mind to relax and allow his instinct full rein. In the past, this seeming trance had saved his life more than once on Asian jungle trails, when the faint ridge of earth around the

claymore mine or the merest tip of the punji stick
became suddenly apparent, as if the light had
shifted to paint them a giveaway shadow.

He wondered how he had missed it before. The
bottom drawer of the desk was neatly closed, a
paradox among the chaos all around. Carefully he
drew it open, and his eyes went immediately to the
tiny fish fossil, wrapped in ancient sediment, lying
neatly on a shoal of papers. It was a message and
he understood it. Gabriel was dead.

Michael turned and looked at Fiona, who
returned his gaze, like a rabbit before a weasel.
Gradually her eyes widened and her mouth
formed a scream. He moved quickly to stand
before her, his arms reaching.

'Fi.'

But she was gabbling, curses streaming from
her mouth in Irish, spittle mixing with the mucus
from her nose so that her face was a glistening,
contorted mask. He shook her shoulders until her
teeth snapped together. 'Fi, listen to me.'

The urgency in his voice brought her back
from the brink of hysteria.

'He's dead, Michael, isn't he?' she whimpered,
her eyes beseeching him to lie. Then her face
crumpled and she began to shake. He tightened his
grip on her shoulders, forcing her head up to face
him.

'Fi, whoever did this wants us to know and be afraid. Hold your anger now; feel it inside you. No one can take it from you unless you give it to them. We will not give them that power over us. Do you hear me, Fi?'

She nodded slowly.

'We'll tell no one and act as normally as we can. Whoever it is will know that we know. They'll watch us for signs of weakness and feed on it. That's the nature of the animal. I know.'

She looked at him as she might at a stranger. How could her brother, Michael, the dreamer, the priest, know such things? But his eyes brooked no disbelief, and she was filled with a sensation of almost savage satisfaction.

'Find them, Michael,' she whispered fiercely. 'Find them.'

15

O'Reilly's Bar, Clifden, County Galway

AT THE SAME moment as the truth about Gabriel became clear to Michael and Fiona, Jake O'Leary was saying goodbye to the last of the mourners after the wake, leaving just Norma's family at his side.

Norma had been good to them, Jake thought. She had always remembered their birthdays, sometimes secretly sending a few dollars to help them along. Jake had pretended not to notice; it was another little thing that had brought them closer, so that he was never quite sure where she stopped and he started. Now that she was gone, he felt something he had never in his life felt before. He felt afraid.

The wake was hosted in the local pub. Where else? Jake thought wryly. He sat flanked by two solicitous nieces who whispered names and connections in his ear, 'That's Michael Smith, a second cousin to Auntie Norma on the mother's side. He has a farm outside Athenry, so he has.'

Yet another big-boned man, uneasy in his good suit, dwarfed Jake's hand in consolation. He was amazed and touched at the turnout, and at the amount of drink that these people could pack away. Around 4 p.m. he asked one of the nieces' husband if there was a closing time.

'Oh aye, but not for something like this, you know.'

'Uncle Jake.'

It took him a minute to realise that the young man was talking to him.

'Oh, yeah – sorry, son. It's Rory, isn't it?'

'It is. Now, Uncle Jake, I've been meaning to have a word with you, and this might be as good a time as any, if you don't mind.'

'Not at all, son. Shoot.'

The young man leaned closer.

'Well, we were talking among ourselves, like, and we were thinking that, seeing as you and Auntie Norma had no, eh, family...' He paused awkwardly, running his finger under his shirt collar until Jake took pity on the kid.

'It's OK, son. That's something we kind of got used to a long time ago. So no sweat. But I guess seeing all you guys with your parents tonight sort of brought it all back.' He paused and cleared his throat. 'Sorry, son,' he said, eventually, 'you were saying?'

'Well, we were thinking that you mightn't want to go back to the States on your own. So the father told me to tell you that he has a site on the farm, and 'tis yours if you want to build on it.'

The astonishment on Jake's face brought Rory up short. Again, the finger reamed the collar, and he pressed on.

'The father said to tell you that you'll always be welcome here, anyway, as part of the family, like. Auntie Norma and yourself were awful good to us growing up, and the father says we'd have had some bad times if it wasn't for yourselves.' He sat back perspiring, his duty done.

Jake slowly removed his spectacles and wiped them thoughtfully.

'Son,' he said, so softly that Rory had to lean forward again, 'you tell your dad that I said thanks, for everything – specially for organising this wake and everything. Me and Norma, we planned to travel around a bit and, seeing as I've

never been to your country before, I think maybe
Norma would like me to do that anyways. So I'd
like to take a little whiles to consider your dad's
kind offer. OK?'

'That's grand, Uncle Jake. I'll tell him that...
and your glass is empty!'

16

The Island

MICHAEL DOUSED HIS face in the kitchen sink, holding the cold spring water in his cupped hands until it leaked through his fingers. As he towelled his eyes, Fiona appeared in the corner of the mirror. He was relieved that she seemed calm and in control again.

'Are you all right, so?' he said, and held her gaze until she nodded.

Priests' houses were traditionally built near the church, and, because the church usually bordered

on the graveyard, the Island priest dwelt in a kind
of limbo between the living and the dead. Michael
recalled an islander giving directions to a visitor:
'It's away from here, like.' Then, observing that his
message wasn't getting through, he had added,
'And there'll be nothing on the washing line.' He
and Fi navigated the rough lane, wrapped in their
individual thoughts, oblivious to the sun frag-
menting behind the walls.

Already, the porch light was burning above
the door. It had always been a weak light, barely
illuminating a modest patch. Michael remembered
their conversation.

'Father Mack?'

'Yes, Michael?'

'Why don't you get a stronger bulb for the
outside?'

'People coming to the priest's door will find it
anyway, *a mhic.* But they won't want to be found
at it.'

Even then, he had understood and would drift
unbidden to the kitchen whenever a knock
sounded after dark.

Over their heads moths beat frantically at the
glass globe as Fi, with the ease of long practise,
fished the key from above the door. Michael
followed her along the dim hallway to the rim of
light from under the living-room door.

The room seemed to have contracted with the years. There were even more books than he recalled, slopping out of the shelves to puddle on the floor so that he and Fi had to pick an erratic path across the bald carpet. The fire silhouetted two figures hunched over a chessboard set on a coffee table.

'Would you look at the grandmasters?' Fiona said with forced good humour.

The taller figure rose from his chair, and Michael found himself scanning the face of his old mentor. The unruly thatch of hair was bleached white; the cheekbones rose to prominence on either side of a sharp nose. The rest of the face was a mass of fissures, dragging the expression towards despondency. Only the eyes held some faint flicker of the Father Mack he remembered, and they were locked on Michael's face.

The silence stretched until it was broken by the soft voice of the other man. 'You'll concede, so?'

'Concede? Blast and damn it to hell, I will not. Sure, I could beat you with one pawn.'

'That's what you'll have after the next move.'

Michael's father turned to them from the chessboard.

The Master's clothes hung loosely on his skeletal shoulders. His hands, almost delicate, were mottled with liver spots, the left hand twitching

gently like a dreaming dog. His eyes, shy and
quizzical, held no sign of recognition.

'You'd better come away home now, Daddy,' Fi
interposed quickly, 'before this old reprobate starts
cheating.'

The old man laughed ruefully as she bundled
him into his coat. 'Don't take notice of her, Father
Mack. Eileen always had a desperate tongue.'

The tableau of characters froze at his words.
Michael felt the old priest grip his arm painfully,
and then the moment passed.

'Go on home with you, so,' Father Mack said
lightly. 'Another grape has come to the vineyard of
the Lord for crushing.'

Fiona, in the act of looping a scarf round her
father's neck, glanced at her brother.

'The Father will stay with me,' Father Mack
said quickly.

'Well, maybe we'll see you in the morning,
then… Father,' she said awkwardly.

Michael could only trust himself to nod as they
left.

Mack plucked a bottle from the press. 'Your
father…' he began, cradling the whiskey to his
chest, 'sometimes he's with us, and then again…'

'Fiona told me.'

He hadn't meant it to sound so abrupt, but the
older man's expression never changed.

'Hard on the girl,' Father Mack concluded mildly. He twisted the cap and tossed it on the fire. It was the ultimate gesture of hospitality, an invitation to drink the bottle dry. Michael groaned inwardly; it boded a long night and his body ached for rest.

'She's tough as old boots, that one. Too tough too young. That and the brains make for a wicked tongue; frightens off the fellas.'

The amber splashed in solid tumblers.

'Water?'

'No, thanks.'

'Ah, thank God. Adultery is a serious sin. *Sláinte.*'

The whiskey smelled of turf smoke and had the same effect. By the time Michael had got his breath back, Mack was standing *tóin le tine*, rear to the fire, one hand thrust deep in a trouser pocket, the other rotating the glass under his gaze. Michael recognised the pose and the implications. He remembered his father saying dryly that Father Mack was the only man he knew who could drown conversation with talk. Resignedly, he adjusted his back to the chair and sipped more respectfully from his glass. And then, despite – or perhaps because of – the lethargy of his body, his mind paged back the years.

Him, a youngster in short trousers, sitting on

the mat in a pool of firelight while Father Mack prowls the bookshelves, finally swooping to pluck a tight-packed volume from its anonymity.

'Heinrich Böll, Michael. The one poor bastard German who insisted on remembering in a nation of amnesiacs. Listen up, boy!' He lowers his half-glasses like gunsights to the page, ranging for the relevant line. '"He had the eyes of a cardinal who had lost the faith." What d'you think of that, hah?'

'But, Father, how could he stay a cardinal then?'

'Good lad. A question is a key, Michael, but a good question is a skeleton key. Why so?'

Michael pauses. 'A skeleton key can open more doors.'

'You're not as thick as you look, Michael Flaherty,' the priest trumpets with satisfaction, hammering the thin volume back to obscurity. 'Beware the easy answer, boy. Now, who have we here?'

The long fingers tap the spine accusingly.

'Ah, Yeats – W. B. himself. Sit up straight, boy, we're in the presence of greatness. Or so he thought,' he concludes, a wicked half-smile folding his mouth. 'One of the stranded gentry, God love them, left high and awfully dry when the Empire ran out. Pomposity, Michael – a thorn in the flesh of the gifted man. He used his sisters like skivvies while he paraded Dublin, a "dignified procession of one", looking "as if he was about to evict imaginary tenants". Sources, boy?'

'P. G. Wodehouse for the first. I don't know the other one.'

'Gogarty,' Father Mack exults, the joy of the sorcerer on finding a lack in the apprentice. 'Oliver St John Gogarty, a surgeon with a tongue as keen as a scalpel. He cut wee Willie down to size, though, oh yes.'

Flipping suspiciously through the Yeats volume, he stops. 'Old goat,' he murmurs disapprovingly, seemingly unaware of his audience. 'Mooning after a woman half his age. There's a great safety in infatuation, boy. Iseult and the Celtic Twilight... Bloody old fool, in love with the abstract.' Slamming Yeats back into his place, he stretches his back and draws from the glass.

'D'you know what a French writer said about the clergy in the seventeenth century?'

Michael is old enough to recognise a rhetorical question and stays silent.

'"Because they love no one, they think they love God."' Father Mack pauses for a long time, lost again in the swirls of his glass. 'All the same, you could forgive a man anything who can say so much in so few words, like Haiku, Michael.'

'Japanese poem, made up of only seventeen syllables.'

'Yes, boy, paring it down to the core. For the love of God, is that the time? Go away home, Michael Flaherty; you've kept me up half the night.'

'Good night and God bless, Father Mack.'

'And you too, *a mhic*,' he answers reflexively, his hand already reaching for the bottle.

At home Michael is unsurprised to find his mother reading before a fire already banked and smoored with turf dust for the morning kettle.

'Ah, the wanderer returns.'

'Sorry, Mam.'

'More books, I see. What will you do with all this knowledge, Michael Flaherty?' she asks, her fingers questing in his hair, her eyes looking deep inside his own. 'Remember, Michael, there are more things in Heaven and Earth than are dreamed of in Father Mack's philosophy.'

'A fresh drop?'

The old priest loomed over him, the bottle poised.

'I'm not sure I should.'

'Ah, you haven't far to fall.' Father Mack poured relentlessly, ignoring Michael's feeble protestations. 'You'll see changes.' He parked the bottle on the mantelpiece and nudged a cairn of turf into sparks of indignation with the toe of his slipper.

'Well, I haven't had much of a chance to see, but, yeah, Dublin looks different – more prosperous, for sure.'

'Ah yes, the economic miracle. It is the best of times and the worst of times. Here's a Chinese curse for you, Michael: "May you live in interesting times." Great people, the Chinese: a developed civilisation, civil service based on merit, art, poetry and calligraphy – when we were still scrawling lines on standing stones. Until, of course, they were beheaded by old Mao and his gang. Imagine that, boy, beheading a nation and sending the intellectuals out to grub in the paddy fields. *Sic transit gloria mundi.* No one has a smidgen of Latin these days, Michael. Not taught in the schools, you know. As for the seminaries, they're trawling for vocations in the shallow end of the gene pool.'

'Ah well,' Michael said, rubbing the heel of his hand across his eyes, 'the Latin wasn't exactly holy, was it? Just old.'

Father Mack measured his steps to the armchair and settled back, his face shrouded in shadow. His voice held a tinge of wonder. 'We woke up one morning to find it all gone. And, like most aphorisms, that's much too simple to be true.'

He laughed, a sharp bark that had more hurt than humour in it. Another long pull at the glass.

'We were the last of the Lotos-Eaters – "Let us alone. What is it that will last?" But it did last. Oh, the ostrich element muttered about fads and enthusiasms. It won't last, they said definitively, at the cosy card games up and down the country; it can't last. God in heaven, if Noah had been Irish, he'd have said that after three days of rain. So we waited for our world to right itself; after all, we had the ballast of history. But it didn't, and we had been so confident in the unsinkability of Peter's barque that we never thought to have lifeboats.'

Father Mack shook his head, whether in puzzlement or anger, Michael couldn't tell. He refreshed his drink, waving the bottle vaguely in Michael's direction and continued with his rambling speech.

'For generations, we had Adam and Eve trapped in the Garden of Eden, two happy vegetables. Then, when they discovered they had a choice, they took it and there was no going back. The Church educated young minds and then muttered damnation when they used them. You can't damp a forest fire with holy water; you just let it burn itself out and hope something fresh buds from the ashes. We kept them in their place,

Michael, poor and uneducated. Oh, the nuns and Brothers went about bearing gifts of maths and physics, and all the other stuff – but theology? No, that was our patch, and we were damned if the laity would enter the exclusive club. And we *were* damned. A people in poverty have no problem with the concept of the hereafter. Why would they? It can't be worse than the here and now, and it's free. But bread in the belly and a few bob in the bank demand a different theology altogether.'

'Surely there were priests who could see how things were going?' Michael said, trying to make sense of Father Mack's disconnected thoughts.

'Of course there were prophets,' Mack answered vehemently. 'There were men and women in every diocese striking the hollow horse outside the walls, and what happened to them?'

'Laocoön the priest and his two sons were devoured by serpents when he spoke against the horse of Troy.'

'Yes, serpents. They came slithering out from under their comfortable stones to demonise anyone who had the temerity to question the status quo. Good people threatened with silence.'

Again, the pause stretched, punctuated by the soft shifting of the dying fire. Father Mack drummed the rim of his glass for a few moments, then seized it suddenly, taking a long swig before placing it on the table with deliberation. 'It's kind of you not to ask the obvious question, Michael, but I'll answer it anyway.'

He got to his feet slowly, using the arm of the chair for leverage, and Michael saw the toll of the years in the effort. He leaned into the fire so that Michael had to strain to hear him.

'And what was Father Mack of the Island doing when all this was happening? Well, in the early days, I said as I saw; and then the letter arrived. God, how Lena must have loved reading that one. Terse and to the point. "The archbishop requests you to attend for interview at the archbishop's house, et cetera, et cetera..." Signed by the secretary, as I recall. His Grace was affability itself. "Well done, thou good and faithful servant. A long, hard labour in the vineyard of the Lord. Troubled times for all of us, Father; time to pull together, Father; keep the head down and tend to the flock, Father." And then the barb, "We are the servants of the servants of God, Father; we do not seek admiratio." Why does the sucker punch always come in Latin, Michael? Like opera, I suppose – you can sing any old shite once it's in Italian. I should have seen the next one coming, but I was consumed with keeping my temper. "Perhaps a

rest, Father; time to watch the flowers grow –
maybe even some quiet chaplaincy on the
mainland, Father?"'

Father Mack's voice dropped almost to a
whisper. 'I'm seventy-two, Michael. I came to the
Island in a currach almost fifty years ago and have
grudged every minute I've spent away from it
since. How hard it is for those who have riches to
enter the kingdom of God.' He laughed harshly.
'So Father Mack came home and brought a
factory to the Island, and will be remembered as
the man who brought the steady jobs that wouldn't
drown them and all the comforts that go with a
steady wage. I learned to play the game, Michael.'

'I think you're being too hard on—'

'Hush.' The raised palm stopped Michael in
mid-sentence. There was a reflection of the old
humour in the tired eyes. 'Remember, I am an
Irish Catholic priest. Don't you dare remove my
cross.'

Michael nodded. 'And what about Gabriel,
Mack?'

The last of the light ebbed from the old man's
eyes as he slumped back in his chair, scrubbing his
face savagely with both hands. 'Gabriel. He was
yourself to the life. Couldn't keep him in books.
When his eyes weren't running down a page, they
were out on the water. Day and night soaking up

ideas. Coming here, as you did, always asking why, to the point where I was Sancho Panza to his Quixote, trying to earth him into reality, trying to make him aware of the danger.'

'The danger?'

'Yes. You remember the story "Eyeless in Gaza"?'

'You told it to me when I was fourteen.'

'Did I? Well, in the city of the blind only one man sees. The people begin to resent his visions, and eventually… they…' His voice cracked.

'They blinded him to make him like themselves,' Michael finished. 'Who are *they*?'

Father Mack raised a face that was haggard and haunted. 'Listen to me now, boy.'

'Who are they, Mack?'

'Listen.' He held Michael with his gaze. 'Find Gabriel's body and bury him beside your mother and Liam.'

'No.'

'For the love of Christ, Michael.' Father Mack's gnarled hands brushed absently at Michael's lapels, then came to rest on his shoulders. 'When you've done your duty by them, go back to America and make a life for yourself. There's nothing for you here.'

With a final squeeze of his shoulders, Father Mack walked unsteadily from the room. Michael curled up on the old sofa, dragging the rug over him. His temples pulsed with a combination of whiskey and perplexity, until sleep drifted him away to the familiar green water where, inevitably, the white face of his brother surfaced and disappeared.

17

Finnegan's Pub

MARIO RICCI WAS beginning to think that the pub wasn't such a swell idea after all, but Erin had been persuasive. 'They've got this great pub; it says it right here in the guidebook. Real old world, with guys playing banjos and stuff.'

He trailed the excited students through the door and saw them concertina against the sudden silence. 'Uh-oh, American werewolf time,' Timmy whispered, and the girls giggled. Mario scanned the crowded room. Some old heads flicked up in welcome; others flicked sideways in derision or hunched exaggeratedly over their drinks, forming impenetrable cloisters with their companions.

The murmur of talk resumed as the group approached the bar. Mario watched the fat barkeep flick his eyes nervously to a trio on the high stools at the far end, then turn to the cash register, loudly fingering coins to and from the till. Fat guy takes his cue from big guys, he thought wryly. His charges, as he now thought of them, puddled uncertainly until a girl with a round face presented herself at the bar. He saw her eyes roam over the tanned faces and perfect teeth, her lips narrowing with disapproval or envy, he wasn't sure.

'Oh, hi,' Erin had recovered her poise. 'I'll have a Bacardi and Coke.' The round face remained impassive. 'You know, like, rum?'

Oh, shit – Erin would be miming a bottle pour for the slow native any minute now.

'We have no rum.'

'OK.' Erin shifted into sweet reasonableness mode, pitching her voice a little higher. 'Well, gin and tonic would be just *great*.' The 'great' had an enthusiasm only a dedicated cheerleader could achieve.

'We have no gin.'

'I hear the Guinness is really good here,' Mario cut in. 'On me,' he added.

'Whatever,' Erin said lightly, her perfect smile back at full wattage.

The music came as a shock, erupting without
warning from the corner by the window.

'Wow, violins and a tambourine.'

'Actually, those are fiddles and that's a
bodhrán.' He affected a mock-professorial voice to
soften the correction.

'A what?'

'It's made from goatskin stretched over a
wooden frame. It means "the deaf drum".'

'Wow.'

The musicians hunched into their instruments,
fingers flying, toes tapping, locked in that strange
cone of concentration that made them seem to
play only for themselves. The bodhrán player
stood upright, his head inclined to the instrument,
his knuckles riffing across the skin from the bass
notes in the centre to the higher notes nearer the
rim, sometimes switching to a stubby stick held like
a pen to rattle high, staccato rhythms from the
wood. Mario was only slightly surprised to feel his
own foot tapping as if it had a will of its own. An
elderly man ambled quietly between the tables to
the clear space before the bar and began to dance,
body upright, arms hanging straight at his sides, a
soft, unfocused expression on his face. As his feet
tapped the wooden floor with gathering urgency,
all eyes locked on his slight figure and their focus
seemed to imbue him with an energy that belied

his years, as his old, black shoes stuttered puffs of
dust from the boards.

Mario tried not to breathe and break the spell
until, with a final virtuoso clicking of heels, the old
man stamped and stopped. Before Mario's eyes,
he relaxed into being a little old man again, picking
his way through the hot silence of the room,
nodding absently at tiny gestures of appreciation –
a glass half-raised, an inclination of the head.

The talk resumed. Mario's companions were
ecstatic. 'Is that, like, Zorba or what?' He tasted his
pint and found it flat and stale.

The boy materialised at the door, limned in
darkness for a moment before he glided through
the room and stopped behind the trio at the far
end of the bar. The talk faltered and faded.

'What?'

The big man turned abruptly, and the single
word was charged with drink. Mario watched the
boy raise his hand and extend it towards the man.
Did he want money? Wrong guy to touch, son.

'What?' The tone was softer, almost pained.
'What is it?'

Slowly, the young fingers unfolded like petals
from the out-stretched palm. Something glittered
dully in his palm, something coiled and still. There
are no snakes in Ireland, Mario thought, and then
the man's arm snapped up and the object sailed

from the boy's hand, winding in a slow spiral to the floor.

'What're ye looking at?' the man shouted. 'Drink your drinks.' He swung back to his companions.

It was a length of ribbon, like videotape. Mario picked it up gently with thumb and forefinger. No, it was a typing ribbon – or a piece of one, at least – still hatched with the hieroglyphs of an old manual typewriter. God, a collector's item. He raised his eyes to the face before him. It was the face of a child, but the eyes, under the thatch of raven hair, were wondrous; his grandmother would have said they were the eyes of an old soul. The pupils were light grey, with just a fleck of amber floating in their light. The boy held his gaze, his hand outstretched.

'I think this is yours, son.' Mario dropped the tape gently in the pale palm, watching the fingers close into a brown fist. Then the light ebbed from the nurse's boy's eyes and Mario was conscious of the silence. Almost with regret, he felt all his old instincts flood back. He was immediately aware of the man behind his left shoulder; aware, too, of the sharp smell of menace.

'What did you call him?'

He straightened slowly without turning, his feet instinctively splaying, looking for purchase.

'Aw, the kid just lost his toy.' He dropped his shoulders as he spoke – 'making like a schmuck', as his partner said. Most guys read it like a dog rolling on his back and huffed off. But not this guy.

'You called him "son". He's not your son.'

'Yeah, well, it's just a figure of sp—'

Shit. He saw it coming in the shift of the man's feet, and swivelled automatically as his training took over. *Shit, shit.* The big fist of Brian Quinn arced in his peripheral vision. Only in the movies, Mario thought; real punches come straight.

Almost nonchalantly he nestled into the big man's shoulder, his left arm snaring the elbow as his right forearm swung up and forward, blocking the blow. A slight hitch of his hips and the man was cartwheeling into a table and over in a spray of spilled drinks and oaths. Some people, Mario thought resignedly as the man raged upright from the mess of drinks and broken glasses.

He went for Mario directly, hands held out before him like claws, lips stretched back over yellowed teeth. Mario spun on his right foot, his left hand delicately aiding the man's momentum so that he went sprawling over the bar. He draped his left arm over the massive shoulders, hunching his head close to the suffused face, his body covering his right hand, which grasped the splayed fingers, whipping them up and back. The man

grunted and tried to shake him off, grunting again
as the pain coursed through his body from the vice
grip on his fingers.

Mario whispered, no effort in his voice, 'You
keep jerking like that, buddy, and you'll bust your
own fingers. OK?' He flexed his hand a millimetre
for emphasis. 'OK?'

The body beneath him went slack. He felt a sick
feeling in his gut. Stay with the programme, Ricci,
a hard voice warned in his head. 'OK?' He relaxed
his grip, and, as the man turned woozily towards
him, shook the hand up and down. 'A misunder-
standing, right? No hard feelings?'

In one swift movement, he snatched his bag
from the floor and headed for the door. He knew
the guy would try to salvage something – had to,
before his own people – but it would be a token
gesture. Sure enough, chairs scraped behind him.
He heard the collision of bodies, the urgency of
soothing voices 'Easy now, Quinn. He's not
worth it.'

He was outside, breathing in the salt night air.
He heard the faint click of the door and tensed.

'Hey, Yank!'

'Yes, Miss.'

'You're after making an enemy there,' the
barmaid said. He detected a taint of satisfaction in
her voice.

'Do you know if there's some place I can stay around here?'

'Miss O'Connor would put you up. To the end of the road there, the second house beyond the church. It's whitewashed; you can't miss it.'

So helpful already?

He walked shoulder-deep in the shadow of dry-stone walls, the moon a low mosaic to his left. He became aware of a vast sky frosted with stars, and immediately experienced a rush of vertigo. He was a child of New York's canyons; the only slivers of night sky he had ever seen had been ochred with the wash of city lights, the only twinkling had been 747s stacked for JFK. The church loomed out of the shadows, squat and aloof from the straggle of single-storey houses all whitewashed into anonymity. This one, he decided. The faint light against the curtains heartened him.

'Who is it?' A woman's voice, no trace of anxiety at the late-night knock.

'Mario Ricci, ma'am. I'm an American,' he added lamely. 'The lady at the pub said you took guests.'

There was a pause and then a fumbling of locks and bolts before the door swung back. She was taller than her voice had sounded, and younger. In the half-light, Mario saw a spare frame bulked out by an Island sweater. She looked at him, head cocked. 'That Sarah has a quaint sense of humour,' she said dryly.

Mario's heart sank, and the bag on his shoulder seemed to gain a few pounds. He entertained murderous thoughts about the round-faced barmaid.

'You'd better come in, so, Mario Ricci of New York City.'

The small, windowed porch led into a spacious sitting room. The only light – a turf fire glowing behind a screen – illuminated two armchairs flanking the hearth. A low coffee table hunched between them supported a sprawled book, splayed and deserted at his knock. Miss O'Connor was moving towards what he guessed was a small kitchen at the rear of the house. 'Coffee?' she called over her shoulder. 'It's American. I could destroy it with something stronger if you'd like?'

'Just coffee will be fine, ma'am.' He eased the bag to the floor, unzipping his jacket and folding it on a straight-backed chair. As he stood upright, his eyes widened. Seascapes bracketed the white walls wherever he looked – wild, savage water straining at the frames. Powerful rather than perfect, he thought; definitely not the clichéd sea, sand and sky.

'I like your paintings, ma'am. Quite a collection.'

'Thanks. Cream and sugar?'

'Yeah – uh, yes, please, Miss O'Connor.'

He cocked his head to read the title of the upturned book but couldn't decipher it in the firelight. Again, his eyes were snared by the waves on the walls; they seemed to undulate in the flicker from the grate.

'If you'd be good enough to shift the book...' She was standing with a tiny tray. Hastily he fumbled the book from the coffee table, trying not to lose her page. Her foot jarred the table slightly and then she lowered the tray, correcting it to the surface. She sat back in the armchair, one trousered leg tucked up, her face angled to the fire. She had a firm chin and high, wind-tanned cheekbones, pale laughter lines webbing around her eyes. The eyes themselves held a distant look, as if she had been called from reverie and would return to it gratefully as soon as her duty was done.

Realising that he was staring, Mario dropped his eyes to the mug in his hand. It was a chunky blue ceramic, with Celtic whorls rippling up from the base, and the coffee was real. He sniffed appreciatively before sipping.

'You miss it, of course?'

'Pardon?'

'The coffee. The Irish are a great people for tea. My grandmother often said that if we had tea for dinner, we'd have to have tea after, but coffee is another country altogether.'

'Yeah, it's wonderful.'

The silence stretched.

'How come you know I'm from New York?' he asked lightly.

'Oh, that,' she smiled. 'I lived there for a time. I guess I have a good ear for accents.'

She replaced her mug carefully on the tray. 'So what brings you here? You sound a wee bit... mature to be doing Ireland on ten dollars a day, or to have rich parents funding you while you find yourself.'

He coughed into his coffee.

'You mustn't think I'm abrupt,' she added, 'but I like to know who's under my roof.'

'No, no,' he stammered, 'not at all.' He took a deep breath. 'You could say I'm a photojournalist, ma'am. Freelance. So it's a magazine assignment, you know. The far-flung isles kind of feature.'

She nodded, a pucker of concentration between her eyes. 'And what impressions of the far-flung isles have you gathered so far?' Her quizzical smile softened the parody.

Mario was tired; at least, that was how he rationalised it later. Halfway through his practised spiel, he began to hear himself spouting clichés like 'the wild Atlantic', 'windswept island'

and 'enigmatic islanders'. But in the presence of
this quiet, attentive woman, he found he didn't
have the heart for it, and he ground to a halt.
Again, the silence settled as she seemed to weigh
his words.

At last she leaned forward and smiled. 'What a
crock,' she said quietly, and they were laughing
and, God, how he loved what laughter did for her.
Finally, she rubbed her eyes with the heels of her
hands and settled more comfortably in the chair.

'Well, that's a relief,' she sighed contentedly. 'I
think if you're really going to tell me your
impressions, you should call me Anne.'

He told her, some of it. The fire dwindled to a
fine white ash as he described the priest on the
ferry.

'That'll be Michael Flaherty,' she said quietly.

'You know him?'

'I did, one time.'

He tested her tone for nuance but drew a blank.

'That will be Quinn,' she said when he
described the fracas in the pub. She wrapped her
arms about her as if she was chilled.

'Trouble?'

'Trouble,' she responded. She paused, weighing
her words. 'You're not the cause, Mario. None of
that was about you, but be careful.'

He felt a curious mix of cold and warmth. 'And

you?' he asked with forced levity, trying to lighten the mood.

'Me?'

'What brought you here?'

Her long fingers stroked the armrest meditatively and then moved to her lap. 'In a nutshell, I had a mother dying here and I had run out of reasons to be over there.'

'I'm sorry.'

'Thank you,' she said softly, then brightened again. 'So I belong to that interesting subspecies known as the returned Yank. We're neither flesh nor fish; we're the ones who pine for a place that ceased to exist – except in nostalgia, of course – the day we left it.' She laughed softly, shaking her head. 'That's probably the most I've said to a human being in a very long time.'

'You don't really keep guests, do you, Anne?'

'No.' The humour had fled her face and he regretted his question. 'Ach,' she continued, 'Sarah meant no harm. It's just... well, unhappiness can cause people to be cruel. I left and came back, Mario, and that's a big no-no. Vacations are no problem – you do the rounds, press the flesh, drink endless cups of strong tea.' She grimaced wryly. 'But don't stay. Guests should go, otherwise they might... So,' she resumed, 'I try to pick up a few threads worth picking, and I paint.'

'These are yours? I mean, you painted them?' he said, shaking his head in admiration.

'Yes. It's how I earn my living.'

'Well you're definitely not an amateur,' he said.

'And you're no photojournalist, Mario Ricci,' she replied tartly, rising to her feet.

'Excuse me?' He was standing too, facing her across the small table.

She walked round it, extending her right hand until it touched his chest. 'And did your mother never tell you not to lie to a blind lady?'

She smiled, tapping his cheek lightly with her palm. 'You're first on the right. Sleep well.' And she was gone.

Her door had already closed before he realised he had spilled coffee on his jeans. Great, Sherlock, he thought. You felt the dots on the book, saw her nudge the table and wondered why she made coffee in the dark. Nothing. And now, the *pièce de résistance*, you've gone and spilled coffee on your best jeans.

Still grinning, he rinsed the mugs and went to bed.

18

The Major's House

THE MAJOR PERCHED, a praying mantis, on the chair. His head nodded a metronomic beat to his flickering fingers on the computer keyboard. Finally, he spoke, without turning. 'My daughter has arrived?'

'Yes, sir.'

He nodded. 'Daughter', he accepted, denoted a blood link, not a relationship. Deirdre was a kite soaring on some current mysterious to him, the only tangible connection a twine that twitched through his fingers, lengthening with each passing day. Wilful, he thought, like her mother; but that was the quality that had attracted him,

the earthbound longing for some sensation of
freedom and flight. There had been a time, too
brief to calibrate, when he had contemplated
risking becoming something other than he was,
surrendering to someone he could not subdue. His
toes curled in his sturdy brogues, gripping the
floor. It had been an interlude, a brief whimsy
before the curtain rose again on the next solid
scene of his career. The army, he knew, was akin to
the fit-ups of travelling theatre: a series of set-ups,
performances and dismantlings before moving on.
Always moving on. The constant shifting from
base to base, from one box-like billet to its clone a
thousand miles away, had leached her light,
brought her in ever-decreasing circles down to
earth. He had hoped the child would give her some
focus, to keep at bay the vacancy that threatened
her. It had worked, for a time.

He remembered the posting to Germany –
walks in the mountains, the baby warm against his
chest, his wife striding out with new-found vigour,
raising her face to the sun. 'I can breathe up here,'
she had said. And then had come his chance at
command. A twenty-four-hour, need-to-know
operation. As required, he had disappeared
without explanation; when he reappeared three
months later, he found a stranger, pacing the
neglected house like a caged animal.

The army had taken care of it, providing the very best medical practitioners, consultants, psychiatrists and, as her light had dimmed further, his helplessness had turned to rage. Was there nothing they or she could do to fix her? That was the word he had used, and he had raged again at the incredulity in the doctor's face. She had brief furloughs home from the institutions; she sat at the window gazing vacantly at the cube houses in serried rows, the come and go of dun-coloured vehicles and uniformed people. The Major did what he did best – making order out of chaos: feeding and cleaning the child, working tirelessly to create some semblance of normality.

That she had found his hidden service revolver, and had been lucid enough to angle it to the roof of her mouth, filled him with a cold fury. It coursed through his veins, thrumming dully to every part of his body. He imagined it seeping from his pores, congealing on his skin into a carapace. It would weld him tight against cowardly dissolution, armour him against the weakness of vulnerability.

His daughter had the best the army could offer, and shook the army from her shoes as soon as she came of age, scornful of everything he cherished. She had returned from time to time, to lick her self-inflicted wounds, and he had been dutiful. It was never enough. She craved something, someone, and he recoiled before her need. A thankless child she most certainly was, but she was his daughter. He felt an obligation to her, as he might to a subordinate. He would do his duty.

'Sir.'

Skald's flat voice called the Major back to the present.

'Did she say anything?'

'She said there were two bags, sir.'

The Major permitted himself a brief smile. His daughter might be down, yet again, but she was not out. 'Observations, Sergeant?'

'Your daughter disembarked at 07.00 hours, unaccompanied. Two pieces of luggage containing an assortment of clothes, cosmetics and one pair of walking shoes, not waterproofed.' In flight but not frantic, the Major thought. 'There was also a writing pad, unused, with no indentations on the top page, and a book.'

'Yes?'

'A life of Francis Bacon, sir.'

The Major snorted and shook his head dismissively. 'Shakespeare wrote the plays, period,' he pronounced. The book was a provocation. 'Drugs, Sergeant?'

'Prescription drugs for hay fever and insomnia, and a small tube of arnica cream.'

'Continue.'

'No other indications, sir. No tracks, marks or any other signs.'

'Very good, Sergeant. You have been thorough.'

'Sir.'

'I thought there might be more.'

'She wore a headscarf and aviator sunglasses at all times. She also wore heavy make-up.'

'Conclusions?'

'I believe she may have some facial abrasions or contusions, sir.'

'Hence the arnica.'

'Yes. The headscarf may conceal further injuries to the forehead. This is conjecture on my part, Major.'

Was there the slightest change of tone in Skald's voice – had the flat graph quirked, even infinitesimally, into the range of anger or concern? Was it possible that this Caliban harboured feelings for Prospero's daughter? The Major filed it under 'later'.

'Her husband, Sergeant,' he said tonelessly. 'I suspect Carlo Vespucci has reverted to type, despite our counsel on previous occasions. It may be time for remedial action.'

Skald stiffened, his big hands bunching instinctively.

'No, I need you here. This calls for creative intervention. I recall a young desk-bound officer lecturing on the subject in Virginia. The room was full of Special Ops, probably shanghaied from rest and recreation to make up the numbers. My fellow pupils, Sergeant, were veterans of various conflicts, virtuosos of creative interventions of the most unimaginable kind. I suspect their amusement distracted the callow lecturer somewhat. We will offer this... intervention to Siren.'

He nodded a dismissal and waited until the door clicked closed before lifting the phone. The call completed, he swung to the glowing screen and pressed a button. The light shrank to a pinpoint and winked out.

19

The Priest's House

MICHAEL WAS DREAMING. It wasn't the usual nightmare of waves and wind and his brother slipping from the grasp, but a nightmare nevertheless.

The matte black aircraft bumped its way through tropical clouds, monumental with rain. 'On the light,' shouted the drop-master, above the roaring in its belly. Seven heads bobbed in silent acknowledgement; seven pairs of eyes fixed on the yawning black hole in the floor. 'Go.'

The plane bucked with relief as the last of its human cargo stepped into the void. It roared away in a tight angle, burrowing into the clouds for shelter, its deadly spores drifting to the drop zone. All except Kowalski, who dropped into a tree, as usual. 'I swear, if we came down in the frigging Sahara, that bastard Kowalski would find a tree,' muttered Lieutenant Bryson, watching his charges stow their chutes in the dense foliage. 'Flaherty, Mendez, pluck that fruit.'

The nominated shadows disappeared and returned a trio.

'Meet any relatives up there, Kowalski?'

Kowalski grinned good-naturedly, his teeth a flash in his camouflaged face.

'OK, listen up. I'm on point. Mendez, Philips, Wilder, Brown, Kowalski, in that order. Flaherty takes the rear position. Three clicks, double-time.'

The Lieutenant led at a trot, the conga strung behind him, settling into a ground-eating lope. The monotony freed their minds to ponder the briefing delivered before the drop.

'Rogues, gentlemen,' Bryson had said. 'We got us a bunch of good ol' boys waging a private war in this here area.' Bryson liked to affect a Southern drawl in the field, though he was Washington born and bred, a third-generation WASP West Pointer. The squad had exchanged glances.

'Intelligence reports a spate of killings in this particular area.' He smacked the pointer at the map behind his head. 'The victims are some of the most notorious drug lords in the region; genuine pure-cut bastards and no great loss to humanity. But Washington has not authorised this little foray and in its wisdom has decreed that we should search them out as swiftly and silently as possible with extreme prejudice. Yes, gentlemen, you are required to engage with American soldiers on foreign soil and kill every damned one of them.'

All eyes had been locked on a point just over his crew-cut head. Bryson had faced his group in silence until each pair of eyes climbed down to lock with his. 'If there be any man here who has reason to exclude himself from this little soirée, rack your weapon and go in peace.'

All eyes had swung back to the point over the Lieutenant's head. They were professionals culled from the various services, a crack squad. They had been honed for the kind of missions that would never be acknowledged should they succeed, and would be most emphatically denied should they fail.

Ours is not to reason why, Michael thought grimly, and pushed it to the back of his consciousness as the terrain flashed beneath. The sharp hand signal, mimicked from front to rear, froze the line. Sharp chops to left and right, and they were fanning into cover. He felt the rush of adrenaline as, all around him, he heard the muted cricket-chirp of safety catches sliding free and noted with mild surprise that his own thumb had automatically done the same. In his heightened state, the jungle smells assaulted his senses: the high, sweet tang of crushed vegetation beneath his prone body, the salty, fetid smell of himself. A single drop of sweat slid to the tip of his nose, but he made no attempt to wipe it clear. He channelled his focus to his ears. Silence. Nothing. The faint sibilance of insect sound, a constant song punctuated by the squad's soft footfalls along the trail, had stilled. He swung his head slowly from side to side, to enhance his night vision, and saw the signal to proceed.

Had Bryson missed it? The Lieutenant had a bloodhound's instinct… Belatedly, Michael was rising into a half-crouch as Bryson and the others moved forwards.

He had only a heartbeat to register the sphere that materialised chest-high before the Lieutenant. The mine was a sunburst. Blinded, but unhurt, Michael rolled reflexively into cover as the shockwave of screaming shrapnel scythed through flesh and foliage.

Slowly, sight and hearing returned. The familiar sound of automatic fire sent him burrowing deeper into cover, scanning for its source, ready to engage.

High-velocity rounds whipped the air above his head. Operating on an instinct more animal than human, his body found a hollow and moulded to its contours.

Silence.

His brain had just registered the lull when a patch of darkness shifted to his right. A shape squirmed away from the killing ground, a man-shape that emitted whimpering gasps as it moved. Reaching out, he pulled, folding the man in his embrace, feeling the gusts of breath warm on his face, the slickness wherever his hands touched. Kowalski's moonface swam into focus, a mask of surprise. His gasps were replaced by bubbling as he fought to inflate shredded lungs, his lower jaw already black with blood. Reflexively Michael rolled him onto his back, hooking an arm across his chest and stretching backwards to tug him into a stand of cane, reaching and dragging like a swimmer in a weed-clogged sea. An eternity later, he sensed the safety of the reeds and flipped Kowalski face down as he fumbled for sulfa in his webbing.

Turning on his knees, he found himself face to face with his squad-mate. 'Mike,' Kowalski gasped; then suddenly he arched his back, his arms extended in supplication, before flopping lifelessly into Michael's arms, pinning him to the ground.

Michael vaguely registered the hot numbness in his left shoulder before the ground surged up to drown him.

When he floated back to consciousness, the sky was lighter, the jungle gathering colour from the dawn. He became aware of Kowalski's lifeless body draped like a blanket over his own, his round head nestled beneath his chin.

Voices – American voices – and the swish of feet. It took all Michael's reserves to stifle a cry for help; he focused instead on the dull throbbing in his shoulder where the shot that had killed Kowalski had gone through him too.

'Like lambs to the slaughter,' laughed a high Hispanic voice.

'Hey, guys, get the Lieutenant. You got a choice – front or back end.' More laughter.

A third voice quelled the merriment. 'Weapons and dog tags. No souvenirs.' A strange voice, Michael thought absently, flat and toneless, could be from anywhere. But undoubtedly the leader. Michael risked a quick glance and imprinted a bullet head and broad shoulders on his memory. 'Evac in five minutes,' the voice continued. 'Check the bodies; the friends will clear the mess.'

Footsteps approached beyond the horizon of Kowalski's head. Michael closed his eyes. 'We got two sleeping beauties here, Sarge – large and little.'

A hand on his dog tags, yanking the medallions. Overhead, a Huey was coming in fast.

'Move, move.' The leader again.

Michael felt the downdraught of air breaking over him and then the gradual ebbing of rotor noise as the helicopter winked in his peripheral vision, disappearing over the trees.

When he next regained consciousness, it was to the smart of strong sunlight and the hiss of a thousand insect sounds. He gasped at the fire in his shoulder. In dazed slow motion, he eased Kowalski aside and staggered to his feet, the luminous green world heaving and threatening to swamp him back to unconsciousness. He concentrated on standing until the world righted itself.

The wound was mercifully clean. Relief flooded him as he probed the entry and exit with trembling fingers. A flesh wound, from a regular round, not a dum-dum. There was a minute of agony as he tamped sulfa at either end, slipping pads in place to staunch the bleeding. Then, reluctantly, he stumbled into the clearing, automatically counting the corpses twisted in the exaggerated poses of violent death. The Lieutenant lay farthest away, cut in two by the mine, a look of surprise etched on his cooling face. Numbly, Michael detached a small black box from the officer's webbing and clipped it to his own. Finally

he stood in the clearing, his head bowed for a
moment, honouring the men who had been the
closest thing he had to friends.

As the sun rose, he backtracked erratically,
instinctively hunting for shade, rationing sips from
the bottle, until, in a delirium, he stumbled into a
clearing. In the merciful shade, he thumbed a
button on the little black box and slumped down,
oblivious to the impact or the scream in his
shoulder.

Hands tugged his webbing. A voice shouted,
'Soldier, soldier.' A flat palm-crack on his cheek
stirred him to wakefulness.

'Soldier, where are the others?'

In a frenzy, he gripped the face before him.
'Dead, all dead,' he shouted.

The medic's face changed into the frightened
face of Father Mack. 'Michael,' the priest said, with
infinite sadness, 'what have they done to you?'

'All dead, all dead,' Michael muttered again and
closed his eyes. Tenderly, Father Mack tucked the
rumpled blanket around Michael's shoulders and
padded away.

Father Mack's hand was six inches from his
shoulder when he snapped awake.

'It's ten o'clock, Michael. The mass for Gabriel is at eleven.' The morning light showed Mack haggard and unshaven, as if he hadn't slept.

Michael washed perfunctorily in the bachelor bathroom. Mack 'did' for himself, and it showed in the threadbare towel and balding shaving brush. Gratefully Michael pulled on the black slacks and clean shirt Hanny had folded into the small suitcase. He glanced in the freckled mirror to straighten his Roman collar, and finally zipped himself into a black windcheater.

Father Mack nodded as he emerged. 'I sent out word that we'd be searching after mass.' Without waiting for an answer, the old priest lifted the front-door latch.

20

New York and the Island

FIVE HOURS BEHIND, on the nearest landfall for three thousand Atlantic miles, the pre-dawn light goaded the Manhattan traffic from a hum to a roar. Carlo Vespucci kicked at the strangling sheets and swung his feet to the floor, padded naked through the detritus of the night before, tugged robotically by the drilling phone. 'What?'

'You know who this is?'

'Frankie, for Chrissake, you know what time it is?'

'No names, no names,' the tinny voice whined in his ear. 'Remember the rules.'

'Fuck the rules and fuck you. What the hell you calling for?'

'Your uncle—'

Vespucci, suddenly sobered, changed his tone. 'Hey, it's early, man, OK? I'm not feeling the best, you know?'

'Sure, kid, sure. Your uncle says meet him in the usual place. About one hour.'

'OK, OK. And Frankie—'

'No names.'

The receiver clicked and buzzed in Carlo's ear. *Frankie and his fucking games.* Carlo shook his head and regretted it immediately, pressing his fingers to his throbbing temples. *All that code shit – give me a break...* He swept the apartment: no bugs in the pictures, the sockets, the bulbs. *Too many movies, Frankie.*

The shower stream made him gasp, but he turned it all the way down to the blue and raised his face to the icy jet. No point in pissing off Uncle Al. Any sign of slack and the old tart went ape-shit.

Michael blinked and stared at the two boys in the sacristy. Twin faces met his gaze.

'Would you look at what the tide washed in?' Mack laughed gruffly. 'Scylla and Charybdis, Michael. The rock and the whirlpool. Tough men.'

The identical brown heads flicked up at the description. It was an old routine.

'Meet the O'Dowds, Michael,' Mack continued, bowing into the pooled alb on the vesting bench, flicking his upper body with practised ease so that the long white garment cascaded to his ankles. 'Mark and Matthew, no less. Named for evangelists but switched at birth for demons.'

He twisted the cincture about his waist, looping it at either hip, and stood with his hands hanging loose, like a gunslinger. 'Don't turn your back on them desperadoes,' he drawled.

Four hazel eyes lifted and lowered in the two impassive faces.

'I'm Michael Flaherty,' he said.

'We know,' they chorused with one voice.

Automatically, Michael vested for mass, lining up behind the twins at the door to the sacristy. Ritually, he dabbed the middle finger of his right hand in the font by the door and offered the holy water to Father Mack.

'*Procedamus in pace,*' the old priest muttered as he accepted. His fingers were icy.

Frankie was straight from Central Casting. He had
heavy jowls and a sagging belly, as if he had been
melted and reformed. His round face was topped
with a fringe of fine hair, dyed an improbable
black. He was looking back at fifty and still second-
string. 'Fetchit Frankie' the hard-eyed youngsters
called him to his face. The eyes that held his own
were in a different league altogether.

'OK, so the call's made,' Frankie said, smearing
the sheen on his forehead with a hot palm,
wincing at the break in his voice. 'C'mon,' he
added desperately, dropping his eyes to the terrible
mouth of the silencer. His gaze slid along the
handgun, rising unwillingly to those eyes. 'So
what happens now? I did like you said.' But he
knew. He was trying to dredge up some long-
forgotten prayer when the back of his skull
exploded.

'We remember our brothers and sisters who have
gone to their rest in the hope of rising again.'

Mack said mass like many older priests Michael
knew, rattling through the phrases without
emphasis or inflection, as if afraid to interpose
himself between the ritual and the receivers.
Michael allowed his eyes to wander among the

faces, mentally subtracting the years, planing them with memory in an attempt at recognition. He scanned all the way to the back row before he found Fi, sitting rigid and remote. A man and woman entered cautiously, halting self-consciously just inside the door; the man seemed to start and doffed his cap belatedly. Michael switched his gaze to a short, stocky figure adding a white candle to the shrine in the corner. There was something familiar about him. Recognition was rising to the surface when the door sighed open again.

Domenico's, always Domenico's. The place was a fucking time warp, Carlo thought – old mom-and-pop joint with chequered tablecloths in the booths and the usual cast of characters: the young guys loitering outside, making like in the movies, all swagger and bullshit; a brace of made men just inside the door, frisking all-comers, ready to intercept any geek who ventured towards the Holy of Holies at the back and risked disturbing the high priest, Uncle Al. Carlo snorted, hammering the horn at a young guy in a convertible who pulled over slowly, raising one finger in a nonchalant salute. Carlo cocked his left hand like a pistol, popped it out of the side window.

'Christ!' The red taillights were burning into his front fender by the time his brakes kicked in. Mouth working savagely, he was out of the car and striding forwards to the little shit-bucket blocking his lane. 'What the fuck you doing?'

His anger distilled into a more pleasurable emotion as the driver's window opened.

'Remember, nephew, a man has only enough blood for his brain or his prick' – one of Uncle Al's sayings surfaced briefly in Carlo's mind and submerged without trace. His head was most definitely empty as he stared at the young woman. She was a slope, all almond eyes and high cheek-bones – but, man, if the lower deck was anything like the superstructure… And it was. As she stepped out of the car, his eyes roamed up, down and all over.

'Gee, I'm so sorry,' she said, 'the damn thing just cut out. Maybe I flooded the engine or something. Could you…?'

'Yeah, sure; no problem.'

He was in the bucket seat, reaching for the ignition, when the passenger door opened and she eased in beside him. His brain was suddenly transfused with blood as the silencer jabbed his kidneys.

'Drive,' she said sweetly.

'And forgive us our trespasses, as we forgive those who trespass against us.'

It was Kate. So many years on, and shadowed by the sagging balcony, but he was still certain. It was a recognition that exploded in his stomach and rose upwards so that he could hardly breathe.

'Michael, Michael.'

Mack was gesturing at the book. In a daze Michael intoned, 'Deliver us, Lord, from every evil…'

Carlo could smell her perfume as her head rested lightly on his shoulder.

'Hang a left… second right.' Her voice was flatter than yesterday's beer as she directed him through old marshalling yards, the car bumping over grass-whiskered railway ties.

'What is this place?'

'Out here. Hands on your head, spread your feet.'

He could run when she was moving across the driver's seat. But how far, how fast, over all that shit on the ground? A tingle at the base of his spine tethered him to reality.

'There's money in my billfold… and a lot more

in plastic.' He was babbling. 'What the hell happens now, lady? What's going down here?'

'*Dolce non far niente* – sweet doing nothing,' she said softly, up close again, the silencer chafing, the tingle at the base of his spine buzzing all the way up to his brain.

'Slowly, hands behind you.' Click.

'Shit, cuffs?'

Carlo almost laughed with relief. *She's a Fed, a goddamn Fed. Now for the Miranda shit, yabba yabba…* He settled for a smug smile. 'Oh, lady, you just made the mistake of your recent career. Uncle Al's got more lawyers—'

'Move.'

Prodded by the gun, he stumbled into a concrete bunker, vaguely registering the graffiti on the walls and the turd smeared on his expensive loafers. Otherwise, the place was featureless, apart from the yawning hole in the floor, its cast-iron cover angled against the far wall. 'Sit on the rim.'

He lowered himself awkwardly so that his feet were dangling in the darkness. Swiftly, she picked up a length of rope, already fastened at one end to a metal ring in the floor, and snapped the clasp at the free end to the cuff-chain.

'As we wait in joyful hope for the coming of our Saviour, Jesus Christ.'

Michael felt the sweat pearl in his eyebrows. He was aware of the concern in the stance of the old priest beside him. He felt a palm placed comfortingly in the small of his back.

Carlo was falling. His mouth opened in surprise and he screamed as the rope came up taut, almost popping his shoulders. The dark smelled of fried air and generations of dust. He sensed his tormentor squatting above him.

'The Major says you've got two minutes.'

'Lamb of God, who takes away the sins of the world, grant us peace.'

Michael stepped back on rubber legs, trying desperately to anchor his reeling senses. He fastened his gaze on the burning candle, letting the lambent flame fill his vision.

Carlo had almost ceased breathing. His mind focused on one bright, burning thought: the Major. That flat voice on the phone. 'You lay a finger on my daughter again and she won't save your sorry ass.'

The dark was resolving into shapes; a breeze began to build against his face, chilling his sweat. He felt a tremor of sound growing from somewhere ahead. With an agonising effort, he raised his head as the luminescence at the end of the tunnel wavered, with a metallic chattering, into a single point of light. It raced to consume him.

21

The Priest's House

KATE PAUSED BEFORE the door, hitching her shoulder bag a little higher with her thumb. Like a schoolgirl, she thought, memories bubbling up unbidden from her subconscious. With a great effort of will, she capped that sour well. That's not what you're here for, Nurse, she told herself sternly, and raised the latch on the priest's door.

As she entered the book-strewn living room, the capstone shifted in her mind and she was assailed with memories. How many times had she come here, 'to borrow a book', and spent an hour trying to be invisible while Father Mack held forth to the boy sitting on the mat before the fire. The boy had been tall for his age. His hair, with only a nodding acquaintance of a comb, had hung in a black flick over his right eye, a flick he would rake with his fingers when he replied, or tug to a point when he was thinking. God, he was as pale as porcelain – 'Book-reading pale,' Kate's mother would have snorted, adding dismissively, 'like all the Flahertys.'

'Did you find that book, Kate?'

Startled from her reverie, she would pluck the nearest one. 'Yes, Father. Keats.'

'Ah, Keats, is it? All kisses and blisses. You'll be away home to read it, then? Now, Michael.' She would be forgotten before the latch clicked.

Standing under the porch light, she would look angrily at the book. Who in God's earth would read Keats? He would, she would think smugly, folding the book to herself.

'Did you find that book, Kate?'

She took a moment to compose herself before facing him. 'Yes, Father. A long time ago. But, sure, it was all kisses and blisses. I didn't finish it.'

He held her gaze, the ghost of a smile softening his face. 'Pity,' he remarked finally. 'Keats had flint and iron in him in the end. Will you sit, Kate?'

'If you're sitting yourself, Father.'

They were back on level terms.

'Tea?' he offered with a vague wave of his hand.

The Island wisdom held that he could turn water and wine into the body and blood of Christ, but Father Mack couldn't make tea.

'No, thank you. I have other calls.'

'Maybe you'd like a drop of something stronger?' he said with forced energy, dragging the bottle to himself.

'It's a bit early for me,' she said evenly, 'but work away yourself.'

He held her gaze.

'Will I be needing it?'

Kate dropped her eyes. Slowly, he replaced the bottle.

'The results have come through, then, Nurse?'

She matched his formal tone. 'They have, Father.' She pulled the thick envelope from her shoulder bag.

'I think we might cut to the chase,' Father Mack said mildly, but his eyes had a sheen of fear.

She had done this many times before, across kitchen tables to women whose first instinct was to glance at the door that barred the children from the room; once to a man sitting in the shade of an upturned currach, tamping his pipe as she spoke. 'I suppose I might as well enjoy this, then,' he had said bravely, but she had held his cupped hands to keep the match flame steady.

'It's as I thought, Father.'

He seemed to deflate in the chair as he exhaled the breath held in anticipation.

'And?'

'And it's spread.'

The old clock was suddenly loud in the shadowed room. Father Mack smiled briefly, perhaps with a sense of irony.

'Bottom line, Nurse?

She riffled to the final page. 'He says he can go after it if—'

But his hand was waving her to silence. 'No,' he said emphatically. 'There's no point digging out the root when the seeds have spread. No, not that. And I won't take poison to beat bad odds,' he added with finality.

'That's your choice, Father.'

'Is it the right one?'

'I'm no doctor,' Kate said tiredly, pushing the envelope back into her bag.

'You're as good as any doctor; probably better than most.'

She inclined her head in acknowledgement of the compliment. 'In your case, I think surgery would be pointless.'

'Thank you, Kate,' he said softly. 'And what about time?'

Everybody asked the unanswerable question. She shook her head. The clock resumed its cruel song.

'Right,' Father Mack said brightly, 'I think I'll have that drink after all.'

She watched him fumble two glasses from the sideboard and make his way across the room, a distracted expression on his face. Shock, she thought, nature's own anaesthetic. He gestured with the bottle.

'I suppose it's evening somewhere in the world,' she relented.

He smiled at that. It was the most desolate of smiles; the smile of a solitary who is ambushed by casual camaraderie. Kate was suddenly hugely angry at herself for pitying him. Snatching the glass from the table, she downed the measure.

The blaze consumed the oxygen in her lungs, and the blood boiled in her face. She opened her mouth, and a long, choking wheeze tugged at her eyes. Father Mack was standing uncertainly before her, the bottle held before him like a talisman.

'Are you all right, Kate? Will I get you something?'

Oh, Jesus, she thought with mounting hysteria, I'm choking to death on neat whiskey, and he wants to give me more.

She was whooping and gasping, tears spilling down her face. Relief washed over him as he watched her colour dim from puce to pink.

'Lord,' he said shakily, 'I thought we'd lost you there.'

She had a sudden vision of Father Mack attempting the Heimlich manoeuvre, and was whooping again. Please don't hit me on the back, she prayed, as he wavered before her, the bottle held up in a gesture of concern.

'I'm fine,' she said at last. 'It went against my breath.'

She pulled her bag to the table, rummaging in its depths. When she spoke again, formality had levelled her voice. 'I'll leave you these, in case you have any discomfort.'

He raised an eyebrow at the euphemism.

'If needs be, we'll move on to something stronger. We'll have no heroics, Father. Pain is a cruel friend.'

He held her gaze for a moment and then nodded, lowering his glass to the table. 'A cruel friend,' he enunciated clearly. 'And is that how you see me, Kate?'

'What's done is done, Father,' Kate said firmly, snapping the catch and hauling the bag to her shoulder as she rose.

'Perhaps,' he went on, 'but whatever it is, I'd like the chance to undo some of it, while there's still—'

'You'll call me before you need me,' she said, reaching for the latch.

'It's Michael, isn't it?'

She froze at the door, as if at a loss.

'I did my best for him, Kate. He deserved that much.' Her silence tugged him on. 'God in heaven, girl, what could he do here?'

'Nothing, Father,' she answered finally. 'You saw to that.'

'He was gifted, Kate; you know that. This place, this ordinary life would have smothered him.'

'There are other gifts beyond book learning, Father,' she spat, 'but he never existed for you outside of this.' She gestured at the living room. 'Out there, in what you call the ordinary, he was different. He could have had a life.'

'With you, you mean?'

'Yes. Imagine that, Father: with someone as ordinary as me.'

'I spoke out of turn, Kate.'

'No, Father. You spoke out of ignorance. You wanted him to have what you never had. I don't blame you for that, but you deprived him of other things, whether you meant to or not.'

'What do you mean, girl?'

'I mean love, Father. It's what ordinary people find if they're lucky.'

They were both spent. Father Mack sagged back in the chair.

'He was… a gift, Kate. There were others, but

their gift got drowned in this place. Do you hate me, Kate?'

She paused a long time before answering, and he ached at the desolation in her voice. 'No, Father. I pity you. I saw him this morning at mass.' Her voice broke and steadied. 'He's a dead man,' she said sadly.

Father Mack closed his eyes with desperate weariness.

'You'd never tell him, Kate?' he asked hesitantly.

But she was gone.

22

The Island

THE CONGREGATION FILED past. 'Sorry for your trouble.' The traditional mantra, repeated with a firm press of weathered hands, chilled Michael's heart. Gabriel was dead.

'Thank you,' he replied automatically, his emotions in turmoil. He had just said mass for his brother's soul. He focused his gaze on the little man standing before him, registering the air-conditioned pallor and the American taste in clothes, before the name bubbled into his consciousness.

'Jake?'

'Yeah.' His face creased in a smile that didn't quite reach his eyes.

'How did things go in Galway?'

'Norma's folks were real nice, Father, but... well, I didn't want to be a burden, you know. One of her cousins ran me over to Spiddal last night. Hope I'm not...'

Michael put his hand on the American's shoulder. 'You're welcome here, Jake. Got somewhere to stay?'

'Oh yeah,' Jake grunted, back in control again. 'So can I help out with this search?'

Michael directed him to a small man wearing a flat cap, who was already surrounded by a knot of people.

'That's Mr Twomey. He's the boss.'

Deirdre Devane finally braved the mirror. It could be worse, she thought calmly. Her mother's soft Irish voice echoed from far away, *It's just bleeding under the skin, love. It looks dark now, but your light will shine right through it and soon it'll fade away.* She told herself again, sternly: It could be worse. It has been. She donned her aviator glasses, as a knight might lower his visor.

She turned away to the small bedroom. It was

painted a spartan white, its walls bare of any decoration by her own decree, 'I have a window on the ocean, that's more than enough.' And that vista began to soothe her. It reminded her of army billets in far-flung places, and of her mother. Abruptly, she tossed the contents of her suitcase on the bed: Gucci and Armani, the armoury of the trophy wife. Almost tenderly, she salvaged a pair of frayed and faded denim jeans and a combat jacket, complete with home-made peace symbol. How her father had hated those.

When she emerged from her room, she was carrying a bath towel wrapped around a bikini. The Filipino woman didn't hear her approach above the drone of the vacuum. 'Hi, Mama Lybe.'

'Oh, Miss.'

Deirdre registered the fright in the brown eyes before she was enveloped in a huge hug, redolent of furniture wax and cooking. 'Oh, Miss Deirdre, it's so good to see you again.'

Holding Deirdre at arm's length, Lybe scanned her with a critical eye. 'But so thin.'

'Please, Lybe, don't start. So how's Fernando?'

'Same as always, but he can't help it; he's a man.' Lybe giggled infectiously, covering her mouth with her hand like a teenager.

'And Raimundo?'

'My son is well, thank you…' The laughter had leaked from her voice. 'He works on a boat for the Major now.'

'Ah, I see.' Deirdre reached out and raised the woman's chin. 'I'll see you later, Mama Lybe. Love you lots, OK?'

The smile she hoped for failed to surface in Lybe's eyes.

'I think that's everyone sorted, Father.' Mr Twomey pulled his cap more firmly over his eyes. 'You'll take the beach beyond the headland, as far as the old village.'

'But—' Michael started to protest. He knew the water carried most of its load to the opposite end of the island.

'That'll be grand, so,' the old man said. It was a traditional kindness afforded families who should not witness the ravages of the sea before the ministrations of neighbours.

'Thank you, Mr Twomey.'

Deirdre paused on the headland path to look back at the house. It was, she thought, a monument to concrete and bad taste, burrowing into the cliff top and overhanging it. The waxing sunshine burnished the squat building, gleamed on the antennae bristling from the flat roof. The centre of the web, she thought, and she shivered despite the balmy air.

The path wound down through the old village. Port, it was called – the Irish word for harbour; a rather grand name for a straggle of ruined houses above a cobbled beach. The last time Deirdre had fled her life and come to the Island for refuge, she had met Fiona Flaherty here, leading a motley of children through the ancient village, their happy voices accentuating the desolation of the place. Deirdre the journalist had asked all the right questions, and soon Fiona had been in full flight.

'It's mentioned in the Annals of the Four Masters, so it must have been important in its day. But the world changed; maybe a mini Ice Age came along and the people left this place. It's only stone walls and silence now – well, it was silence before this mob arrived.'

Fiona had found an enquiring mind, and Deirdre had found herself a child among children, touched by the casual way they opened their lunchboxes to her as they wiggled for comfort on the smooth stones, chattering to one another in

lilting Irish, but addressing her courteously in
English. It was an English of a richness and texture
she had never encountered before. 'We're the
descendants of illiterates,' Fiona had explained;
'that's why we paint pictures with words. You'll
come up to the school and tell us about America.'
It was the Island style of invitation – an offer she
couldn't refuse, Deirdre had thought wryly.

That phrase broke the spell. Carlo hadn't
called; no telephone tears and pleading and
promises. Well, *que sera, sera*. She spread her
towel on the stones and began to undress. The
man on the hill behind her raised his binoculars
gratefully.

As Michael rounded the headland, he paused.
Some thirty yards to his left, a boy crouched in a
patch of heather and bog-cotton, his hands deep in
the growth before him. Michael judged him to be
about twelve, not yet gangly and self-conscious;
the cast of his body was reverent as he smoothed
the heather to cover the object of his veneration.
The boy rose from a crouch, extending his arms
upwards. Only then was Michael aware of the lark
fluttering above him, seeming to sustain itself on a
thin thread of song. The boy began to mimic the

sound, until the watching priest could no longer distinguish bird from boy. And then the boy started; his head jerked to scan the stranger and he was gone, loping over the rough ground to disappear beyond a rise.

Michael savoured the lark for a few moments more – like an acolyte before the tabernacle, he thought wryly, amused at how he had been drawn into the mood of a nesting boy.

He was being followed. It was a certainty, evidenced by a sensation of cold in his lower back which resonated dully in his left shoulder. As he topped the headland, he stopped and spoke without turning.

'I'd be glad of the company.'

A hillock behind him sprouted two faces, wearing identical sheepish expressions. The O'Dowds drew level.

'They wouldn't let us go on the search, Father.'

'Well, you'd better come with me, then. It's a long time since I was here, and I guess I might get lost.'

The twins inflated with importance. They surged before him on the path and stopped suddenly, in sight of the bay.

'There's something in the water, Father.'

Michael's heart froze in his chest. 'Step back a little, lads, and I'll take a look.' He stumbled down the path on trembling legs to a better vantage point, then sighed with a mixture of disappointment and relief.

Something glinted in his peripheral vision, and he hunkered low. A wave of his hand brought the boys to his elbows, mimicking his crouch in the cover of the heather.

'It's a woman swimming,' he told them in a whisper.

'Maybe it's a mermaid,' breathed one.

'No,' his brother corrected with conviction, 'the water in Port is too cold for them.'

Michael hushed them with a finger to his lips; his flattened palm nudged them deeper into cover, and he began to stalk. It niggled in his head, the realisation that he was still part hunter, but his instincts quelled it. He flowed in an arc until he was crouching above and behind the supine form.

'Fine soft day,' he murmured, and watched with satisfaction as the thickset man started awkwardly to his feet, the field glasses tumbling to the ground.

'What the hell do you think—'

'Hey.' Michael's voice was a sharp crack, and he stepped closer to the tottering stranger. *Use your voice as a weapon*, the instructors had said. *Push the brain before you strike the body*. His right arm tensed, fist bunching for the blow; the man recoiled backwards, lost his footing and rolled all the way to the rim of the beach. He scrambled upright, backing onto the smooth stones as Michael bore down on him.

'The Major will hear about this, you mad Irish bastard.'

'Go,' Michael snapped. The man sidled away, reluctant to expose his back, in the direction of the ruins.

'Just who do you think you are?'

The woman was shawled in a white towel, hands on hips, her hair plastered to the nape of her neck, her eyes armoured in reflective glass. Suddenly, Michael felt tired. He began to turn away.

'Hey, I'm talking to you! What were you going to do – kick his butt for doing his job?'

Nonplussed, Michael could only stare. She leaned closer. 'My father pays that poor schmuck D'Arcy top dollar to keep an eye on me.'

'Well, you can't be too careful in Port,' he said dryly. '*Begorrah*, ma'am, them ruins is fair crawlin' with rapacious islanders, and the water only teemin' with mermen, and them with only one thing on their fishy minds.'

She smiled suddenly – sunlight after a shower, he thought – and she was beautiful. 'You forgot the banshee and the *púca*.'

'No, Sunday is their day off. Sorry,' he added

lamely. 'I just thought the guy was a peeping Tom.'

She tugged the towel a little tighter. 'I think the cavalry are coming.'

A tumble of stones announced the arrival of the twins. 'I thought you were going to clock him!'

'Fellas.'

'But Jaysus, Father—'

'Fellas.'

'Father?' the woman asked.

'I'm Michael Flaherty,' he said.

'Flaherty? I know a Fiona Flaherty. So,' she said appraisingly, enjoying his discomfort, 'Fi's long-lost brother.'

'Not that long,' he murmured.

Her tone softened. 'I'm Deirdre Devane. You'll come up to the house for tea, Father?'

He knew she was playing him at his own game, and struggled for escape. 'Maybe another time.'

'That's a desperate insult, you know,' she told him wickedly, 'only to be satisfied by cocked sods of turf at twenty paces. At dawn, of course,' she added with feigned gravity. 'The invitation includes the enlisted men.'

Without waiting for a reply, she turned back to collect her clothes.

'Who's your woman, Father?'

'She's a mermaid,' Michael informed them. 'There's no escape for us.'

The twins exchanged a look before hurrying after her. 'Meet-and-greet time at the Big House,' he muttered to himself, trailing reluctantly behind them.

At the house, he registered the razor wire and the almost invisible cable stretched at knee-height within the perimeter. Perimeter? Strange choice of words, he thought. Let it go. The antenna on the flat roof suggested otherwise, and he calmed his mind to be alert. When he stepped inside the spacious reception room, Deirdre was already directing the awed twins to chairs at a blackened bog-oak table. A plump woman appeared from somewhere, whispered conspiratorially with Deirdre and disappeared again.

'Please sit here, Father.' She motioned him to the head of the table. The matronly woman appeared again, with two glasses of juice and a china cup and saucer balanced on a silver tray.

'I asked for a mug, but Mama Lybe has strong religious convictions,' Deirdre said mischievously. The older woman smiled sheepishly as she set the delicate ware before him.

Michael spoke softly in a singsong language and Lybe's smile blossomed into a genuine grin. She replied animatedly before self-consciousness kicked in and she began to busy herself with the tray.

'Would you excuse us for a moment?' Deirdre murmured, prodding Lybe into what Michael determined was the kitchen, judging by the state-of-the-art equipment he glimpsed through the swinging door. When they were safely behind the door, Deirdre caught Lybe round the waist.

'Hey, you awful old flirt. What was all that about?'

'He speaks Tagalog,' Lybe giggled happily.

'So what did he say?'

'Oh, nothing much,' she replied archly, skipping out of Deirdre's grasp to scoop scones into a scalloped dish. 'Just "What's a sexy lady like you doing in a—"'

'You are loving this, you mad old woman.'

'Well, he is kind of... hunky,' Lybe giggled. 'For a priest,' she added, trying for composure.

Deirdre scooped the dish from her hands. 'Hunky,' she snorted derisively.

'Better dim those eyes, girl,' Lybe said coyly.

Deirdre swung through the door, her animated features immediately slipping into neutral. The Major had arrived, and with his coming much of the light seemed to have drained from the room. She stood frozen inside the door, remembering the effect he had on people:

messengers and subordinates stiffening to automatons, one or two hopeful swains of her own lapsing into awkwardness and incoherence until they made their stammering excuses and fled. Even the twins seemed to hunch lower at the table. Nesting chicks, she thought, with a fox about. The priest, she noted approvingly, was just as languid as she'd left him, one elbow angled back over the chair, his knees crossed comfortably, giving the Major an attentive profile rather than his full face.

'Ah, Deirdre. Father Flaherty has been telling me about his valuable work in the New York correctional system.'

She had long ago developed a Richter Scale for the Major's seismic mood shifts. At the moment, it registered seven on sardonic.

'Actually, I said I worked as a prison chaplain,' Michael said evenly, to her.

'Sounds like a challenging job, Father—'

'Sounds like a hell of a waste of time,' the Major said, raising his voice to drown the end of her sentence, his jocular tone a thin sheath on the steel of contempt. 'Those men are dross, Father,' he continued, warming to his theme. 'Irredeemable, recidivist jetsam. Surely,' he pressed on, grotesquely sweet and reasonable, 'the saviours of the damned must have come up with some drug that could keep their collective little demons pharmaceutically subdued?'

Deirdre moved protectively to the boys, who seemed too scared to chew. Michael Flaherty stretched his long legs and seemed to find his shoes of immense interest.

'I believe Aldous Huxley beat you to that one, Major,' he said calmly. 'No. We saviours of the damned are working on the utilitarian model.'

Something like indecision flickered across the Major's face; it lost its sheen of false bonhomie, exposing the flint beneath. Deirdre stifled an urge to warn Michael, but he continued. 'At the moment, we're working on the flange-bottomed sewage barge project. You know: fill her up with prisoners, tow her out a mile and just haul on the damn lever.' Then he turned his head from the Major, caught her eye, and winked. She smiled admiringly.

A door opened noiselessly behind the priest, and Skald entered. Instinctively, Deirdre wrapped her arms around herself. She was struck by the priest's reaction: he straightened suddenly in the chair, his feet flat on the floor, his hands knotting into fists on his knees.

'A call for you, sir.' *That horrible metallic voice.* She saw the priest flinch and roll his shoulder, as if easing a bruised joint. She moved towards him, but he was already on his feet.

'Thank you for your hospitality.' The hand he offered her shook slightly, but his face was inscrutable.

'So soon, Father?' The Major was back in the ring, sensing a falter. 'This hardly reflects the famed Island regard for strangers.'

The priest's voice sounded weary. 'Our history teaches us to be wary of strangers, Major. We have found, to our cost, that most visitors come to us looking for something.'

The Major smiled and raised his eyebrows. 'Now what could you have, Father, that we would want?'

'Well,' Michael Flaherty replied softly, 'that's what puzzles me, Major. Boys!'

The twins glanced longingly at the scones, but his tone brooked no discussion.

'Deirdre.' The sharp crack of the Major's voice made her waver, but she followed the priest out to the hallway.

'Father Flaherty?' she called.

He turned at the door.

'Look, Father, I'm sorry about the—'

'That man?'

'Who? Oh, Sergeant Skald. He's…' She was at a loss for words.

'Thank you, Deirdre.' Michael Flaherty was smiling again, and she felt ridiculously pleased that he had used her name.

'Yeah, well, watch out for mermaids,' she managed lamely. She watched him stride back to his world, the boys already yapping and scampering before him like collies let loose from a pen. She shivered and closed the door.

23

New York

IT WAS ONE of those September days when New York, tired of playing the brassy, raddled, old bag lady, scrubbed itself young and fresh-smelling with sunlight. The air still held the smell of snow, but the trees were opening up.

Mal was thinking of Michael, which brought Hanny to mind, and with that thought came a twinge of guilt. She'd been broody since the boy left, filling the time after work with absent-minded housekeeping.

'OK, old woman,' he conceded in exasperation when she called in sick and moped within pouncing distance of the phone, 'you get to make one call.'

Amazingly, it rang, right on cue, and they both lunged for the receiver. Hanny just shaded it. She cradled the receiver under her chin and Mal watched her face go slack with disappointment.

'Some guy who thinks he's Clint Eastwood,' she said, and he ached at the emptiness in her voice.

'Hey, Mal, we got us a situation here. You want to haul ass to the corral and help out the *hombres*?'

Mal made a mental note to tell Hanny that Tony Tan was a Chinese-American cop, about five feet nothing and addicted to cowboy talk, but she had wandered off. 'Saddling up right now, *compadre*,' he sighed.

He took the downtown bus from White Plains, merging anonymously with a handful of commuters, enjoying the colourful splurge of the Bronx Park Zoo before the view wintered to the glittery broken-glass playgrounds of Harlem. The Church of Saint Athanasius lay somewhere between shabby brownstones spliced upright with graffiti and the ostentation of Fifth Avenue. With its cool white marble columns and onion-topped towers, it looked as if it had upped from Istanbul and relocated in Manhattan without processing through Ellis Island. A sign slung across the bronze doors read 'Closed for repairs'.

Mal stooped nimbly under the sign and fumbled a key from his pocket. Inside the door, he found himself staring at six foot something of the perfect security guard – visor shading his face, one hand outstretched palm up for ID, the other hanging nonchalantly near his holster.

'Phil,' Mal greeted him, flipping his wallet.

'Sir,' Phil barked. Holding the ID to the light, he scanned the picture.

Jeez, Mal thought, three years on and still the same routine? 'So how's the family, Phil?'

'All in order, sir. You may proceed.'

The family or the card? Mal itched to ask, but Phil had been elsewhere when humour was divvied up. 'Second floor, third door on the left, sir,' he barked.

As the elevator door closed, Mal watched his reflection in the glass window. What would Hanny say if she discovered his alter ego, he wondered. She knew he had retired from the force as a Detective Inspector, but didn't know about the summons to Washington and the special army medical facility and the ghost of Michael Flaherty behind the one-way glass. And the deal he had made for Michael's freedom.

The doors hissed open and he stepped into the vestibule. He was now a member of an elite law-enforcement unit set up by the New York Metropolitan Police Force and charged with sifting

information on major crimes, with special reference to drugs and organised crime. Mal was the
only member of the group who searched for a
particular criminal, and who reported to a much
more elite group in Washington. He was also the
only one who knew that. It bothered him that he
couldn't tell Hanny or Tony but it was 'need to
know', and sometimes even a little knowledge could
be a dangerous thing.

The ops room was a mixture of icons and
engineering that never failed to amaze him. Serried
rows of metal desks squatted off into the gloom,
flicker-lit with computer wash. Along the alcoved
walls, full-sized plaster saints gazed reproachfully
at the knot of men in yanked ties and shirtsleeves
at the powwow table in the middle.

'Hey, Mal.' Tony rolled away from the group to
grip his hand. 'Feeling lucky today, punk?'

'Make my day,' Mal rejoined, tossing his hat
and coat on a chair.

'Guys, listen up.' Tony led him by the elbow to
the table. 'Mohammed has come to the mountain.'

One or two of the older guys flapped a hand in
Mal's direction. Some of the younger ones
stiffened, looking at him with a certain awe. Mal
nodded amiably at the group and sat. The others
followed, as if by permission.

'So,' Mal said quietly, 'what we got?'

Tony nodded to a young man in earnest half-

glasses at the end of the table. Mal let his eyes drift
to the windows, wondering at the mosaic of glass
that filtered mysteries into colours, daubing
crimson across the young guy's profile.

'Suspected homicide reported to Brooklyn
Seventh Precinct, at approximately fourteen
hundred hours, Wednesday the—'

'Son!'

'Sir?'

'Do an old man a favour and skip the logistics.
Your own words will be just fine.'

'Sir, yes sir. The driver of the Brooklyn-bound
subway train reported a collision in a tunnel.
When he emerged at the station, there was blood
all over the windshield.'

'Jumper?' one of the younger men interjected.

'Nah,' Tony said dismissively, changing one
cowboy boot for the other on the lip of the table.
'That'd be easier in the station. Jumpers don't do
it in a tunnel, in the dark. No, sir,' – he plucked a
toothpick with amazing delicacy from his shirt
pocket and popped it between his teeth – 'not a
jumper. Go ahead, kid.'

Half-glasses looked as if he'd like to loosen his
tie, but he ploughed on. 'Subway cops found a
rope hanging inside the tunnel about a quarter-
mile from the station.'

'Is there a connection?' one of the younger
acolytes asked eagerly.

'Yeah, like it had a head in it,' quipped an older hand dryly. Half-glasses blushed at the sudden burst of laughter.

'Carry on, son,' Mal urged, staring at the symbol of the Holy Spirit, a dove suspended over rays of light, on the window to his left.

'Yes, sir. We got an ID through Quantico.'

A number of people at the table shifted into more attentive poses. *Shit, Quantico?* their expressions suggested. *Heavy duty.* Only Mal seemed oblivious, tapping his middle finger on the table before him, his eyes distant.

'The victim's name is Carlo Vespucci.'

Mal's finger stopped drumming. 'Come again?'

'Carlo Vespucci, sir. Quantico had him as a small-time perp, juvenile record, not much after.'

'Tony, a word.' Mal rose and nodded towards the corner of the long room. The others stood immediately and withdrew to their desks, leaving Half-glasses stranded with his paper.

'Sir,' he said hesitantly, 'don't you want to know the rest?'

Mal paused. Tony rolled his eyes theatrically.

'The rest?' Tony said. 'Do you want to explain the rest, Mal?'

'Well, let me see. The rope originated in a small room above the tunnel; it probably doubles as an airshaft and a maintenance access route. The other end would have to be tied to something – a heavy piece of machinery would do it, or maybe something embedded in the floor. The victim was most likely conscious beforehand, so he was encouraged to sit on the rim of the shaft.'

'You can't know that.' The young man seemed shocked at his own importunity.

'I think I can, son. See, Vespucci is family. His uncle is Don Alfonso, a man of vast interests – alleged – and short fuse, proven. So either we're looking at internal punishment as a lesson to all within the fold or we're looking at a takeout. Either way, Vespucci would have been alive and handcuffed. Have they found the cuffs?'

'No.'

'Tell them to keep looking. So, to sum up: he was alive, cuffed and sitting on the rim. He was pushed down there just in time to catch his train, if you'll pardon the expression. Is there anything more?'

'Ah... no, sir.'

'There should be. What was he wearing? That'll tell us who he thought he was going to meet. Focus on the room above – scuffs on the floor, prints on the bracket, ring or whatever he was tied to. Look for shoe prints. Now,' he said quietly, 'that's the rest. Maybe you'd see to it.'

Crestfallen, the young man gathered his papers and left.

'Was I too hard on him, Tony?'

'Naw, the guy's a high-flier on computers, never worked a crime scene in his life. So Vespucci is family, and he's whacked. They killed him themselves or another family saved them the trouble. What's it to us?'

'It doesn't figure. The families stash bodies in the subway, but they don't whack them there. So what did this guy do to burn his ticket? Who did he bully, maim, rape or frame to deserve being executed by train? Whose modus operandi is it, Tony? We're dealing with a specialist. Have them run the files for matches.'

'OK.'

'And Tony… how would you like to go to a wake?'

'Irish?'

'Italian.'

24

The Island

FIONA SCANNED MICHAEL'S face as he entered the kitchen.

'Michael?'

'Nothing.'

Her relief mirrored his own, and the guilt came rolling back.

'And the others?'

'Nothing.'

'Will you have tea?'

'No, thanks. I had some at Deirdre Devane's.'

'Oh.' She brightened. 'You met Deirdre, then? I must have her up when…' She faltered, and fought for control.

'Yes, when this is over.' He sat down beside her at the corner of the table. 'What do you know about the Major, Fi?'

She ran her hand through her wild hair, holding a bright red clump upright as she thought. Michael recognised it as a trait of his own, and was warmed.

'It's all a bit sketchy, really,' she said finally. 'Father Mack went to some government department beyond in Dublin, asking for money for the fishing. It was bad and getting worse. People were leaving, Michael – and who could blame them? I had to let a teacher go because the numbers in the school were dropping.'

'That must have been hard on you.'

'Harder on her,' she said firmly. 'Anyway, they put him in touch with this Yank who had money to invest.'

'The Major?'

'Yes.'

'So he's an answer to our prayers, then?'

She glanced up sharply at his tone. 'He brought the packing factory and employment, Michael. Families came back, the school filled up – and he promised to build up the fleet, buy trawlers and so on...'

'But?'

Angry tears started in Fiona's eyes. 'But Gabriel...' Her voice cracked.

'What about Gabriel?'

She was weeping now. 'He couldn't let it be. He said it didn't make sense; we hadn't the fish stocks in the water. He went to meetings, asking questions, and things changed. People we'd known for years began to avoid us. Even the children…'

'What did Gabriel do, Fi?'

'He said…' Her voice spasmed in her throat. 'He said we had brought a Trojan horse inside the walls. Ach, he was all over the place, Michael – out late at night, typing like a madman in his room when he did come home. He wouldn't open the door when I knocked. I knew he was in there, but he wouldn't open the door.'

Michael put his hand gently on her bowed head, automatically holding a clump of her lovely, crazy hair. 'There's something else, isn't there?'

She raised her head.

'I think they beat him, Michael,' she whispered.

She saw the colour leave his face, the cheek-bones pushing through the pallid skin.

'Who beat him, Fi?'

'Michael, I don't know. What are you going to do? Please, Michael, don't—'

'Shh, Fi.' The awful pallor had abated somewhat, and she was soothed. 'I need to make a phone call. I'll have that cup of tea now.'

She ran the heels of her hands over her eyes. 'Give it another five minutes. Lena will be closing up, so the phones will be automatic.'

She attempted a smile, and left.

'Hi, Hanny.'

Michael smiled and settled back in the chair, holding the receiver a little away from his ear as Hanny rattled into overdrive. 'Hey, Hanny – Hanny! Where's the geriatric delinquent?... OK, so get him to call me when... What? Oh, sure; I'll take his cellphone number.' He held the phone away as Hanny gnawed another bone of contention; his right hand groped the table drawer ajar, his fingers questing for a pencil. 'OK, got it. I'll call him, Hanny, and ruin his day... You OK?... Well, I'm fine too. I love you, Hanny.'

Michael didn't know what had prompted that. It was something he'd never said to her before and had never imagined saying but, for once, he was happy that instinct had won over intellect. He was aware of the silence at the other end and knew she was crying. He could visualise her, sitting beneath the wall-mounted phone in the corner of the kitchen, the golf calendar defaced with ballpoint phone numbers behind her head. The rattle of a subway train was growing in volume as he replaced the receiver.

Quickly he dialled Mal's cell, tapping his fingers to its insistent dial tone. *Come on, pick up...*

'What?'

'Articulate as ever. So who pressed the button for you, old man?'

'Michael?'

'The same.'

'Hold it a minute, OK?' Michael heard a door close, and the hubbub in the background abated.

'Lots of echoes there, Mal. You at a prayer meeting?'

'So now you're Father Brown, priest-sleuth extraordinaire.'

'I need some information.'

'Shoot.'

'Major Devane – D-E-V-A-N-E – United States Army, retired. And a certain Sergeant Skald – S-K-A-L-D.'

'That's it?'

'That's it. I'm with Fi, so if anything comes through, you'll call?'

'I'm on it.'

Lena sat close to the fire, her head slumped forward, cruelly exposing the white roots of her hair.

'What?' She started awake, her hands welded to the arms of the chair. Fearfully, she swivelled her head and scanned the room: nothing. Nobody. She gave a great, shuddering sigh of relief.

Every light in the room was burning, and the harsh glare revealed the ravages of fear. Her huge frame had diminished; her clothes hung loosely and carelessly. The hardness of her eyes had been replaced by a flat, dull stare. Her eyes darted furtively to the door that joined her living quarters to the post office. Like someone in a trance, she rose and shuffled slowly to the door, whimpering softly. With terrible reluctance, she turned the handle and, closing her eyes, scrabbled her hand along the wall for the light switch. *Where in the name of Christ is the bloody thing? Where is it? Where is it?* She was keening in terror by the time her hand knocked the switch and the office was bathed in light. She leaned on the jamb of the door, fighting her heartbeat back to some semblance of normal rhythm.

A tiny ruby eye winked at her from beneath the counter, beckoning, and she was drawn to it, kneeling painfully before the blood-red eye. Skald had spoken slowly, every word embedded in her brain by that hammer voice. 'This is the switch. Turn it to this position when you are leaving. If the light blinks when you return, phone and say, "There is a message." Go back to your room; we will collect it. The Major will be grateful.'

With nerveless fingers, she lifted the receiver. The phone rang twice and was picked up at the other end.

'There is a message,' she breathed into the silence, and hung up. Her eyes were drawn upwards, to the grille that separated the office from the public area. Bars, she thought, prison bars.

Lena returned to her light-filled room, anxious to drink herself into oblivion courtesy of the regular supply of bottles from the Major.

25

New York

TONY INCHED HIS car backwards until the fender nudged the two-toned Cadillac, then straightened the wheel.

'Parking by sound these days, Tony?'

'Yeah, well, these *paisanos* are not exactly taxpayers, Mal.'

Mal pulled out his cellphone, stabbing suspiciously at the digits. 'Why not check your trunk, Tony? That Cadillac gave you quite a bump.'

'Oh, yeah… right.' Tony rolled out of the car and waddled to the rear.

'Six, six, six…' Mal said. *The mark of the Beast.* Somebody in the Pentagon has an apocalyptic sense of humour. He listened to the holding music: Sousa. *Subtle.*

'Code, please?'

'Lost Boys.'

'Hold.' Oompah, oompah-pah...

'Mal?'

'Jerry. Two names. Major Devane, Sergeant Skald.'

'I'm on it.'

The young bucks outside Domenico's tossed their smoke butts and began to straighten as the two men approached. They smiled in anticipation as the rolypoly one waddled forwards, but there was something in the other one's gait that gave them pause.

'Don Alfonso is expecting us,' Mal said levelly, and they tried to maintain their strut while getting the hell out of his path. Inside the door, Mal and Tony paused, letting it clack behind them. They raised their arms as the men with hooded eyes frisked them perfunctorily.

'Hi, Sal. How's Betty doing?'

'Ah, you know. Not so good.'

'Sorry to hear that.'

Tailed by the hooded eyes, they made their way to the rear, where a gaunt man was playing solitaire on a table in a side booth. He was alone, his white-capped head wreathed in cigarette smoke.

'Don Alfonso.'

The old man didn't miss a beat with the cards, flicking them into columns with the nonchalance of experience. He bobbed his head and they sat. Only when all the columns were complete and the man sat back, lighting a cigarette from the corpse of its predecessor, did Mal speak.

'Don Alfonso, we offer our sympathies at your loss. May your nephew's soul rest in peace.'

Don Alfonso inclined his head in acceptance. He gestured vaguely with his right hand, and the shadowing centurions disappeared. He looked directly at Mal for the first time, and Mal was struck by the paleness of his eyes.

'We go back a long way,' he said. His voice rasped from the hole in his throat and Mal reminded himself not to look there; never to look there. He was aware of Tony's immobility beside him and relaxed. He knew Tony would do most of the legwork on this one, so he needed to hear things first-hand. 'Good times, bad times,' the voice whistled. 'I'm listening.'

'Your nephew was murdered – cuffed and hung through a shaft in the subway tunnel. We have his head for you to bury.'

Tony flinched in his peripheral vision, but Mal was calm. He knew this man. The face before him remained impassive.

'We have forensics all over the scene, but this is different.'

Don Alfonso nodded for him to continue.

'We think this is a visitor – someone from outside the families.'

'Yes, I have made enquiries.'

'We need your help.' Mal folded his hands in his lap; he had said his piece.

'Why should I do this for you?'

'Not for me,' Mal replied calmly, 'for your nephew.'

There was a burst of air from the hole, and Mal realised the old man was laughing. The noise ceased and the raspy voice resumed. 'My nephew was something I would wipe off my shoe.'

Mal nodded, and appeared to consider. 'It seems like someone else has wiped your shoe, Don Alfonso.'

He rose to leave. Tony, momentarily confused, struggled upright.

'We will make further enquiries,' Don Alfonso whispered. '*Va bene.*'

Back in what he called a car, Tony exhaled noisily. 'The grieving uncle seems a tad upbeat, wouldn't you think? Someone did him a favour, for Christ's sake, so why would he help us?'

'Someone doing him a favour is a burr under his saddle,' Mal replied thoughtfully, 'and in his world that means they have to pay.' His cellphone rang and Tony did his roll-out routine from the car, resignation on his round face.

'Yes?'

Mal nodded once or twice, then thumbed the Off button and dialled.

'Michael? Listen up. Checked out Devane and Skald. Leave well enough alone, OK. What? You know I can't answer that. Hell, kid, this is an open line… all right, OK, both did time south of the border, get my drift? Michael, listen to me, steer clear and wait for the cavalry. I'll do some more checking at thi— Michael? Michael.'

26

The Island

THE SHADOW ENTERED the post office noiselessly, as if cruelly aware that, if one fears the coming of a phantom, it is even more dreadful if the phantom comes unseen. Unerringly, the shape extended a hand to the blind box and paused as it glowed to life. Only when it had blinked to black was it detached and taken.

The Major pressed rewind and play, filling the room with Mal's and Michael's voices. Finally, he stabbed savagely at the stop button. Skald sat to his right, an attentive and silent presence, watching his master's face as it twitched to the tempo of an internal dialogue. Finally, the head nodded almost imperceptibly. A decision had been made; the action would follow, and unconsciously Skald opened his hands in a gesture of acceptance.

'To paraphrase an English king, we have a troublesome priest.'

It was unclear to Skald if he was being addressed, and he maintained his silent vigil. The Major swung to face him.

'Sir.'

'To erase him might prove problematic. After all – to mangle a good line from a queer playwright – to lose one brother might appear to be carelessness; to lose a second... We will strike to the right and the left of him. I detect a weakness in his character, commendable in priests and fatal in soldiers: sentiment, Sergeant. The Nazarene was a pacifist, so dizzy from turning the other cheek that he was vulnerable to guile, sensitive to betrayal. It led him to embrace his cross, and despair. Let us see if Michael Flaherty has a taste for crucifixion.'

The Major had a sensation of flight. The world, framed in the window, was patched with cloud that only enhanced the full moon, the scattering of stars. Even as he watched, the fog welled upwards. Some men hated the meantime, that limbo-time between decision and action. He was not one of them. He was always a little amused at the rituals others employed to while away – no, to file away – the hours between, as if they could control it with random actions. In the belly of a Hercules they would check and recheck weapons, or initiate strained, mindless conversations with equally fraught companions, while he sat comfortably, letting his subconscious process the details of the briefing in preparation for the action to come, aware that he was already in it.

He dialled a number. 'I hear Debussy was a big hit in Chicago,' he said as the woman answered.

Siren laughed, a high, tinkling sound. 'Debussy is what's expected, Major, but in my heart I yearn for Bach.'

'And the concert this evening?'

'They seemed pleased.'

There was no false modesty in her tone, the Major noted approvingly. He didn't doubt that the reviews would be ecstatic; the critics had been waxing from disbelief to astonishment since she had performed at her Julliard graduation concert.

When he had first seen her, she had been a young girl holding her father's severed head in her lap in the madness of Saigon. She had seemed unsurprised as the armed unit materialised in the room.

'Who is the Major, please?' she had asked. 'My father said I was to ask for the Major.'

He had sensed his companions' incredulity at her calm. A flick of his hand, and the unit had dematerialised. They had perhaps four minutes, tops, before Charlie would be knocking on the door, begging an audience that, through sheer weight of numbers, would prove terminal. Adrenaline had buzzed through the Major's body, heightening his senses to note the cheap barrette that held her hair, the metallic odour of what drenched her lower body, the gracefulness with which she held the severed head. She had bowed her head in salutation. 'There were too many of them,' she had said, 'and so…' For a moment her composure had wavered, leaving her eyes huge and vulnerable. Then she had breathed deeply and life had flowed back to her face.

The Major looked at the head in her lap and gritted his teeth. One of his most effective operatives in South Vietnam, dead. He felt he had an obligation to do something for his daughter. 'I came to get him out. I'm sorry. He was a brave man and a friend. We will give him due honour another time. Now you must come with me.'

'Yes,' she had replied simply, placing the head with infinite tenderness on the floor. 'There is nothing for me here.'

He had spirited her out on the last Chinook and secreted her in a Washington school for the select few. She had matured into a spirited, if solitary, being. He recalled their first meeting in the college visitors' room: she had removed the flustered headmistress with the merest inclination of her head. When they were alone, she had held his gaze for a solid minute, and he had known from her eyes that she saw him as an equal. There would be no master and pupil, Svengali and acolyte. Whatever she had would be given, not taken.

'I would like to be of some service,' she had said calmly. 'As my father was.'

The weekend trips to Company facilities had been largely silent and formal affairs. She had answered questions concerning her academic progress, particularly her musical development; by tacit agreement, nothing more personal had been asked or offered. The Major remembered the hesitancy in the voice of her instructor, a man not noted for doubt. 'A natural,' he had confirmed. And, when prompted, the stoic master of all things lethal had shifted uncomfortably, his hand questing over his shaved pate.

'But?'

'Humans are not usually natural killers, sir. You get my drift?'

Oh yes, he got it all right, loud and clear. She was perfect, and she had proved it, most recently in the matter of Carlo Vespucci.

He realised that his musing had extended the silence stretching between the telephones. 'I'm sorry. I have things on my mind.'

'You have instructions, sir?'

The lightness had departed her voice, replaced by a Skald-like tone.

'Yes,' the Major said, gathering his thoughts into focus. When he replaced the handset, he turned briefly to the window. The rising fog had all but obliterated the moon.

27

The English Couple's Cottage

'I THINK WE have said quite enough about your inherent aesthetic beauty and your potential for development, seemingly to no avail. Perhaps we need to be more direct in our communication. For my part, I have dug, mulched, pruned and, God help me, empathised. You, on the other hand, have obdurately refused to bloom. We have reached an impasse. At the risk of appearing insensitive, I should perhaps, at this juncture in our relationship, mention secateurs.'

Captain Ron Bentham, Sapper (retired), straightened painfully from this discussion – so far, thankfully, one-sided – with his roses. He surveyed the fog that rendered his modest garden horizon-less. Well, thank the Lord for that, he thought gratefully. Eccentricity might be admired on this island, but total gaga was quite another matter. A fair man, he had listened carefully as Daphne explained the new concept of talking to plants. Albeit reluctantly, he had done his husbandly duty; and still the little buggers remained stubbornly... little.

Despite the ruin of his roses, Ron was content. Ever since his first visit to the Island... His eyes lost their focus as the scenes replayed in his head. The army surgeon, usually so precise and detached, taking a moment from his rounds to sit gingerly on the side of Ron's hospital bed.

'Married, Captain?'

'No, Doctor.'

'Family?'

'No. Not that you'd notice.'

The patrician in the immaculate white coat had plucked off his half glasses, leaving a welt on the bridge of his nose which accentuated the tired eyes. He had rubbed the spot between thumb and forefinger. 'I understand my registrar has filled you in on what we've done to patch you up, and so forth?'

'Yes, Doctor.'

Something in Ron's tone had prompted the surgeon to continue, almost defensively, 'A good man, you know – very skilful, but… well, a bit young. It's not my field, of course – I'm quite sure the psychologist will be around by and by – but a leg is more than a limb, Captain.'

'Yes, Doctor.'

'What I mean to say is…' He had rubbed frantically at the raw spot for inspiration. 'There are deeper wounds that will take time. For instance, you may feel a certain amount of antipathy, shall we say, towards those who were responsible for your… situation.' He had leaned forward, his eyes fixed on the bare top of the bedside locker. 'Some men find their healing in a partner or family… You might consider going back. Not quite to Belfast,' he had hurried on. 'Good Lord, no – but to Ireland.'

Then he had been upright again, fumbling in his pocket for a pad and pen, scribbling furiously. 'There you go, then. I would ask you just to consider this.'

Abruptly, he had gone, striding down the ward, half-glasses back in regulation position, every inch the army man.

Ron remembered palming the note from the locker and his surprise that the address scrawled across the page was on an island off the west coast of Ireland. He had tossed it aside, distracted by phantom signals from a limb no longer there; but, when at last he was discharged, the note had travelled with him.

His first acquaintance with the Island had hardly been propitious. A rough swell had bucked the ferry as it sidled into the lee of the harbour wall. But – and he nodded at the memory – there had been a healing in the timelessness of the place and the shy courtesy of the people. And yet he had clung to his denial, regarding his trip as a furlough, getting himself up and out, shipshape and, almost frantically, back to normal. But all the rising at dawn, the meticulous making of beds, the fastidious personal habits and the long, swinging marches on his crutches had merely welted his hands and rubbed his armpits raw. It couldn't last, and it had ended simply enough, when he swung over the headland one day in exhaustion, blinded by sweat, and stumbled to a low stone wall, gasping for breath. He had been unaware of the old man forking kelp on the pocket-handkerchief field until he had felt the grip on his elbow.

'Will you slow down, Englishman?' the man had said kindly. 'Or you'll walk off the end of the Island and drown.'

And then had come the tears, so many tears, and the old man had hitched himself up on the wall beside Ron, puffing at a briar in silent solidarity, until the spasms had passed.

'You might come out in the boat with me tomorrow.'

'Fishing?' Ron had enquired blankly.

'Aye, we might do that too.'

For a whole week, the old man had feathered lines and checked lobster pots while Ron sculled him, single-handedly, hither and yon and, by the end of that week, he had been at ease with himself once more. He had known better than to offer payment, but he had attempted thanks. They had been waved away.

'A man can learn to walk well with one bad leg,' his companion had said solemnly, in parting. 'You'll come back to us now!' And when Daphne had not been averse to the notion, Ron had returned eagerly.

Now, things had changed. The Island had changed. It had been as subtle as the shift from sunlight to twilight. There was a tension abroad in the place, and the once-open faces were more covert. Ron knew it was not his imagination – bomb disposal had suppressed that gene, if not removed it from his DNA altogether; and yet the fog felt colder on his face and that long-deceased leg still sent signals. He heaved an exaggerated sigh, shifting his weight to the one real leg as he turned his thoughts to Daphne.

Immediately, his whimsy was swallowed like the moon, to be replaced with anxiety. The fog seemed to press on him, pearling his hair and rough gardening clothes. Perhaps the communication theory would work better indoors, he thought, stamping the clay from his boots in a final biblical admonition to the reluctant blooms.

Daphne was where he had left her, nestled at the corner of the kitchen table, the ever-present book spread-eagled on the checked cloth. Probably on the same page, he thought, hanging his limp cap on the hook behind the door and draping his jacket to steam before the kitchen range.

'Well, I tried your theory with the roses, my dear.'

'Hmm.'

'Gave them a right old talking-to.'

'Mm-hm.'

'One of them had the effrontery to claim it was a Rose of Sharon and enjoyed a better documented lineage than my own, by God.'

'Yes, dear.'

He stood behind her, placing his hand tenderly on her head, and was pained to feel a tremor pulse through his palm. Briskly he pulled up a chair and sat close, taking her unresisting hand.

'You're somewhere else, old girl, and I miss you.'

'Oh, no, my dear; it's just—'

'Daphne.' His firm tone stopped her protestations and filled her eyes. 'Daphne, my darling, hear me out. You are the strongest and most sensible of human beings. You are also the most caring woman it has been my privilege to know – not that I have known many women quite so intimately.'

A small smile softened the abstracted face before him and, heartened, he plunged on. 'These past few days, you haven't been yourself. Bad things sometimes happen to good people, my dear. We both know that. We need to withdraw for a while and think about them. Sometimes, these thoughts frighten us.' The small hand tightened in his. 'And we consider what is our duty as good people, and that too may seem a fearful prospect.' He tightened his grip until her eyes aligned with his.

'I will be with you all the way, *a chroí*,' he concluded huskily.

'What does "*a chroí*" mean?' Daphne asked softly.

'Translating Irish to English,' he said, with mock pomposity, 'is like looking at a tapestry from the back. I think it means "dear heart".'

She dropped her head, and a single tear swung free and splashed his hand. When she looked up, he was encouraged to see the resolution in her eyes. Her voice was tremulous, but her eyes betrayed relief.

'You're quite right, my dear. I can't quite rid my mind of that young priest. He looked so… haunted.'

'Yes, I noticed.'

Straightening in the chair, she looked at him with something akin to determination. 'Perhaps, tomorrow morning, we should attend the service again?'

'Agreed,' he smiled. 'Oh, and by the way, I think they call it mass.'

'Mass, then, *a chroí*.' She smiled back.

28

Anne O'Connor's House

SHE WAS FLOATING some six inches from the
floor, a beatific expression on her face – a face
marred by the black holes where her eyes should
have been. Mario was standing in full medieval
armour, a broken sword in his right hand, and the
pictures on the wall began to leak. As he turned his
head, the waves cascaded down the walls, rising up
to his knees, his armpits. Something itched inside
the chainmail glove. Hell of a place to have a flea,
Mario thought absently, and awoke.

Automatically, he jabbed the alarm button and
swung his feet soundlessly to the floor, padding to

his rucksack. The cellphone's stubby aerial peeped innocently from a rolled sock. In the semi-darkness, his forefinger hesitated over the code. *She does this all day, every day,* he thought.

'Code,' the too-loud voice requested.

'Seal,' he murmured, cupping his left hand over the mouthpiece.

'In situ, Seal?'

'Affirmative.'

'Mule approaching. Rendezvous, ETA 18.00.'

'Instructions?'

'Reconnaissance on mother lode and report.'

'Affirmative.'

He pressed the power button and returned the cellphone to its quarters, tucking it deep in the bag. *Old habits die hard,* he thought, lifting the rest of the contents to the bed. By the light of the pencil torch, he inspected bottles, gauges, hoses and masks, all the trappings that made up the merman. Satisfied, he repacked and padded back to bed.

'Good night, Anne,' he murmured. 'Pleasant dreams.' He did not dream.

Dawn broke over Ireland, lapping as an after-thought over the Island, burning the fog like condensation on a mirror, so that the fretted coastline, houses, fields and stone walls rose into relief.

'Lights up, Mr Photojournalist.'

Mario was already awake; he tumbled out of bed. The smell of coffee and bacon lured him to the little kitchen. 'Let me.'

'Just put everything back in its place, OK?'

'Yes, ma'am.' Carefully, he positioned her plate, pouring coffee into her mug. 'You like it black, right?'

'You're a quick study.'

'Waiter's memory – three summers hustling orders in a Manhattan restaurant.'

'That would be while you were doing photojournalism in Columbia,' Anne said sweetly, raising her coffee mug. 'More bacon? You didn't sleep very well.'

'I slept like a baby.'

She put down her full mug. 'Babies don't talk in their goddamn sleep.' A flush spread to her throat and suffused her cheeks. 'I'm blind, OK? Not deaf, and most decidedly not dumb.'

Mario was silent. After a moment, she heaved a sigh and joined her hands on the tabletop.

'Sorry. I really didn't mean—'

'No, I know you didn't—'

'Look, Mario… By the way, that is your name?'

'Yes.'

'OK, so I'm not your mother or your sister or your… anything, but you're a guest in my house. You've already managed to make a bad enemy in Quinn. Mario, this is not a place for fun and games just now, you could get hurt.'

He stretched out his hands to cover hers. She flinched but didn't withdraw them. 'Thanks, Anne.'

'I hear things,' she said, almost to herself.

He tensed, remembering his phone call during the night. She smiled. 'No, I'm not that good.'

Before he could respond, she tightened her grip on his hand. 'I listen, Mario,' she went on urgently. 'It's the way I map the world. Most people don't. You know what they say – an Irish conversation is two happy monologues.'

He laughed, but the pressure of her hands silenced him again.

'People assume that, because I'm blind, I'm deaf as well. It's like the way adults talk in front of children. Mr Twomey – oh, you don't know him… anyway, he listens to the sea and forecasts storms. He's never wrong, Mario. I listen to voices – to tone more than words, because words come from the head, but tone comes from here.' She held his hand to her heart. 'That's where the truth is. Nobody can twist that.'

'You're amazing.'

'No, I'm not. I'm worried, maybe even frightened. There's something going on, I'm not sure what. But a young man is missing. When people talk about him, there's more than sorrow in their voices.'

She stopped again and lowered her head.

'I listened to you, Mario,' she continued earnestly, 'and I heard two people. One was a warm and sensitive man, the other was… cloaked. This is my home. I have friends here I care about, and—'

'I would never do anything to endanger you or your friends, Anne.'

'Yes, I believe you, because you're such a terrible liar. But I seem to recall a certain Norman Schwarzkopf talking about friendly fire. You know what friendly fire is, Mario, don't you?'

'Yes.'

'I thought so. I want you to meet some people.'

'Yeah, sure.'

'Will you come to mass with me?'

'Sure, I'll go to mass with you. Who are these people?'

'I'd like you to meet Fiona Flaherty; she's a friend of mine. She runs the school. And I think you should meet her brother Michael again.'

'The priest I met on the ferry? He seemed like he had a lot on his mind.'

'He has. It's his brother who's missing.'

'Why do you want me to meet them?'

'I don't know why you're here, Mario. Maybe you could tell me, but then you'd have to shoot me.'

She smiled again, and he wished they could go on sitting like this over cold coffee and congealed bacon, his hand in hers, surrounded by seas all safely back in their frames.

'I don't know,' she repeated. 'It might help you to do whatever it is you do without good people getting hurt in the process.'

'OK, Anne.'

Mario felt a familiar surge of sadness. Some people did get caught in the line of fire. He had seen it, been part of it. It wasn't something he could rationalise away, ever. Some of his colleagues referred to them as John and Jane Doe. It was an attempt at distancing and depersonalising, but it had never worked for him, and that was a burden he would always carry.

As if she sensed his mood, Anne raised her hand and found his cheek. 'You're a good man, Mario,' she said softly. 'Now, take a girl to mass.'

29

New York

THE SUN HAD moved, leaving the Holy Spirit flat and lifeless, rousing the Archangel Michael to vivid action on the other window in the long room. Mal paused to contemplate the heroic figure astride the dragon. Half-glasses was almost obsequiously eager. 'Sir, I have the reports you asked for.'

'Good work, son,' Mal replied briskly, purging his residual guilt. Now roll over and I'll tickle your tummy, he thought wryly.

'As you suggested, sir: ring in the floor, no stains or splashing, so the victim was not

roughed up prior.' Mal nodded encouragement. 'The fibres lab says they got good
samples from the coat and slacks – quality label
stuff. There are footprints, too – size twelves.
However, they're only partials, as if the perp
was… tiptoeing.' Half-glasses looked up in
puzzlement. 'Why would he do that, sir?'

'*He* didn't,' Mal replied.

'Didn't what, sir?'

'Wasn't a "he", son. Gentlemen, I believe we
have a shootiste on our hands, a specialist. Get
them to run it through the computers. There
shouldn't be too many women with such an
interesting modus operandi.'

Mal was already heading for the door, with
Tony in hot pursuit. 'I'll drop you near the
hacienda, *señor*.'

Tony drove to some particular music in his
head, weaving in and out of lanes with
abandon, occasionally taking both hands from
the wheel to hammer the beat on the dash. Mal
was relieved when the car screeched to a halt,
a few hundred yards short of his home, so he
could enjoy his constitutional.

'OK, Tony. Spit it out.'

'What?'

'Tony, take it from an old friend: you will never play successful poker.'

Tony pulled a sheaf of fax paper from the dash pocket. 'Latest from south of the border, Mal, the old powder trail. All the usual about shady pols, yabba yabba...' Tony paused for effect.

'Drum roll all over, Tony.'

'Special Services, my friend.' He grinned as Mal's face went rigid. 'A whole slew of reports detailing the exploits of a gang of guys all mixed up in the hazy crazy days of Big Ronnie's private sorties.'

Suddenly serious, Tony spoke into Mal's silence. 'This is like *Twilight Zone* stuff, Mal. Maybe it's time we called the shades.'

Mal felt a tiny twinge of anxiety, and shifted his feet to the street. Tony was a good agent, one of the best FBI men he had ever worked with, but calls to the CIA could be problematic.

'Let me ponder that one, Tony, OK?'

There was a short pause.

'Whatever you say, Mal. Hey, you gotta trust a guy who says "ponder", right?'

As Mal straightened out of the car, Tony riffled through the papers. 'Hey, Mal, you know

Vespucci had an Irish wife? Yeah, Deirdre Devane – we even got a cellphone number...'

But Mal wasn't listening. Shit, he thought savagely, and looked down to find he had, indeed, stepped in it.

30

Due West of the Island

FIFTY MILES DUE west of the Island, beyond the smother of its enveloping shroud, the *Anne-Marie*, out of Galway, was a most unlikely jewel set in a glass-calm sea.

Bloody rust-bucket, her master thought grimly. Knocking the ash from his savaged black briar, Noel O'Neill stamped forwards to the rim of the hold. 'Jerry, for the love and honour of God...'

It was his third cantankerous pilgrimage in as many minutes, and the voice from below matched his mood. 'Will you go away and not be annoying me, Mr O'Neill? This bloody bastard is as old as yourself and twice as contrary.'

'There's fish waiting to be caught, Jerry.'

'That's your easy job, Mr O'Neill; mine is to bring this whoring engine back from the dead. Now, will you feck off and let me at it?'

O'Neill reined in his temper. Jerry was the original pain in the arse but, when it came to matters mechanical, if it could be done, he'd do it.

'Well, don't take all fecking night,' he snapped, shuffling away to the sanctuary of the wheelhouse. Behind him he heard the squeal of a slipping wrench and a blue stream of profanity. He smiled.

With his hand on the door handle, O'Neill paused, listening. 'What the sweet Jaysus?' The throb of engines came pulsing faintly from away to his right. Swinging from the door, he made his way to the rail.

Weasel Williams was there before him, a small man with a feral face that was canted to the source of the sound.

'You hear it?' O'Neill asked.

'I do.'

Weasel was a man of few words – if there was a lull in the conversation, he'd be in the thick of it – but he was a seaman of the old stock, to the tip of his nose, which was swinging to follow the strengthening sound.

'Coaster?'

'Bigger,' muttered Weasel.

'But why can't we see her?'

'Lights.'

'Where?' O'Neill scanned left and right.

'None,' Weasel responded tersely.

'Jesus, Mary and Joseph, what is he up to?'

As if in answer, the dark congealed to a shape that passed within a half-mile of the *Anne-Marie*. For no reason that he could fathom, Noel O'Neill felt suddenly cold. Like many another seaman, he had seen his share of odd sights: ball-lightning skipping playfully from wave to wave, green fire on the mast. Once he had seen his own father, lost three months before, scanning a chart in the wheelhouse while his bereaved son stared in horror through the glass door; and, though he was an inveterate storyteller, no amount of plied Guinness had ever wrung that vision from his lips. But this lightless ship sent tremors through his large frame.

A rumble from the hatch and a cloud of smoke shook him from his reverie. The deck shuddered beneath his feet as the old engine coughed apologetically, fired and held. O'Neill turned to Weasel, all foreboding flushed away by the steady hum.

'I always said Jerry was a genius. Let's go fishing.'

31

The Priest's House

MICHAEL AWOKE. ONLY his eyelids moved, his body remaining inert in the tangled bed. *A nightmare? No, a sound.* There it was again – a faint groan. *Christ!* He kicked free from the bed, pulling on his trousers and sweater, and slid stealthily to Mack's door. The idea that his old mentor might be drunk surfaced in his mind. He paused, his hand almost on the door handle. A long, gurgling sigh decided him.

'Mack, you OK?'

The bare bulb momentarily scalded his eyes, but the face of the old man hunched on the bed shocked him into focus. He took the pyjamaed shoulders in a strong grip. Dear God in Heaven, he thought, he's skin and bone. 'Mack,' he asked again, more gently. 'What is it?'

'The dresser, Michael.' The words came through clenched teeth. 'Envelope… tablets.'

Swiftly, Michael ran his hands through the litter on the dresser, knocking the heavy breviary – *bean chéile an tsagairt*, the old people called it, 'the priest's wife' – to the floor. Finally, his hand rattled the contents of an envelope. Hastily, he swept a glass of water from the bedside locker. 'How many, Mack?' he asked urgently, spilling the pills in a fold of the coverlet.

'Two.' Mack's lips were white; globules of sweat welled up beneath his hairline. With infinite care, Michael prised open the lips, deposited a tablet and held the glass to the old man's mouth.

'Easy now,' he murmured as if to a child, his free hand sliding to the back of Mack's head. Mam did this for me, he thought suddenly. *Take it gently, dear…* When he was satisfied that the second tablet had gone down smoothly, he pressed Mack back on the pillows, moving his hand to the wrist that felt weightless, feeling the pulse flutter at his fingertips like a plucked butterfly.

After a while, he felt the drugs take hold in the loosening of the fist. He tucked the coverlet on either side of Mack and sat to keep vigil.

'Michael?' Something approaching normalcy had crept back into the voice.

'Here, Mack. I'm right here.'

'A terrible thing to find a priest afraid of death.' A wraith of a smile flickered over Mack's face, but his eyes, open now, were thoughtful rather than pained.

'Only the good die young, Mack,' Michael whispered, struggling to steady his voice. It was a feeble attempt at either levity or denial, and the old man pressed on as if he hadn't heard.

'Are you happy, Michael?' He spoke softly, but his grip was firm, brooking no evasion.

'To be honest, I don't think about it, Mack' Michael sighed, searching for words. 'The work is—'

'The work,' the old man grunted with surprising force, 'is the great seducer, Michael. It gives us the illusion of living and deserts us in the end, leaving nothing but a longing for more.'

Michael searched for some words that might offer rebuttal or consolation, but came up dry.

'Thank you,' Mack smiled.

'For what?'

'For not having an answer. Oh, how I loved the work, God knows. I threw myself into it, always doing, doing. It was my pride, Michael, and my shield. Who would venture near that furnace?'

He coughed suddenly, a wracking cough that made the bedclothes shudder. Michael lifted his head from the pillow until the spasm passed. The old eyes sought his own.

'Your father, the Master, has been my friend... oh, about forever. But your mother saw through me.'

'Eileen,' Michael whispered involuntarily.

'Eileen,' Mack echoed, 'though I never called her that, in all our time. It was always "Mrs Flaherty" and "Father Mack"; but she... she told me once that I tried too hard.' He gave a small laugh of such sadness that Michael could hardly look at him. '"Jesus was at his best in Bethany," she said straight out.'

'With Mary and Martha,' Michael murmured automatically.

'Yes.' The old head nodded heavily. 'Amongst women, Michael, who were too full of ordinary living to be impressed by saviours. She was the only woman I ever allowed myself to be... myself with.' His voice trailed off, his eyes closed. 'Did I wrong you, Michael?'

'Never,' Michael answered vehemently. 'You opened up the world to me. You were always there, Mack, especially after...' But he could not continue, and Mack completed his sentence.

'After Eileen died. I remember your face at my

door, the day we put her in the ground. I thought you'd pine away and follow her. So I built up a world of words and ideas to keep you safe, to give you hope.'

He was exhausted; that and the medication were combining to take him down to sleep. He struggled against it, the burden heavy in his voice. 'But there was selfishness too, Michael. I took such pride in your mind, and you were all I had left of Eileen. Maybe my need deprived you. Women understand such things. Perhaps Kate was right after all.'

'Kate?' Michael could hardly breathe. With a huge effort, he controlled himself, aware that he had tightened his grip on the frail hand. 'Kate, Mack? What did Kate say?'

But the old priest was asleep at last.

32

New York

MAL DID AN undignified toe-heel shuffle across the street to the Bronx Park, ignoring the curious stares of passers-by, intent on ridding his shoe of its burden. As he scraped his shoe savagely on the grass verge, his attention was drawn to a familiar tableau, and the sight restored his equilibrium. An elderly Hasidic Jew, complete with black hat and long side-curls, sat at a park table over an inlaid chessboard; his opponent was a mirror image of himself, give or take fifty years. Mal often loitered as a spectator at these highly charged games, marvelling at the blend of skill and passion.

The old man spoke without turning from the board. 'Mr Policeman, come, make an arrest and rid me of this *meshuggus*.'

'Aw, Granddad,' the young doppelgänger protested, his round, sallow face flushing under the broad-brimmed hat.

'Come sit. I need a witness.'

Good-humouredly, Mal eased himself onto the bench, carefully extending the offending shoe on the brown stubble masquerading as grass. It was a perfect evening, he thought, dog shit notwithstanding. Here and there, young couples walked hand in hand or pushed strollers along the paths under the trees. From the far end of the park, he could hear the thock of bat and ball and the shouts of young voices. 'You got a nice set,' he said, squinting at the chess pieces.

The old man plucked the queen from her protective position before her stolid spouse. 'With your permission,' he said to the boy, who rolled his eyes and sighed dramatically.

'You see this piece? What is it made of? Tell me.' Again, the acolyte's body language semaphored boredom. He knew the answer.

'Is it ivory?' Mal said.

'Good guess, but no cigar.' He placed the piece delicately on Mal's palm. 'Bone, Mr Policeman, human bone. I won't bore you with the details.'

The young man relaxed and hunched forward.

'Enough to say it came from Kiev, from the collection of a policeman. How did he come by such a thing? He's not telling, on account of he's very dead.'

'Dead a long time, Granddad,' the boy corrected.

'That counts as very dead, no?' the old man said equably. 'So, from the *shetl* in Kiev to the parlour of a policeman to an old Jew in New York, and now to the hand of a policeman again. What a world. Look at it closely,' he commanded. As Mal bent forward, the old man continued in a softer voice, 'Someone is watching you. No, continue to admire the queen... The same person has passed the gate twice. Even grandmasters like myself are not so fascinating.'

He plucked the piece from Mal's palm, raising his voice to address his grandson. 'You shall never have her. I would rather she were taken by this gentile.'

His other hand squeezed Mal's arm, fleetingly. 'Play chess,' he roared at his opponent; 'you will be dead a long time, very dead.'

Mal sauntered casually towards the exit, pausing occasionally to scrape his clean shoe with feigned exasperation, taking the opportunity to scan the sidewalk beyond the park railings.

Nothing. He shrugged his overcoat higher on his shoulders, digging his hands deep in his pockets as if aware of a chill in the balmy air, and pressed a button on his cellphone. The fingers of his right hand sought the grip and guard of his handgun, flicking the safety with practised ease.

'Hide in plain sight.' Siren remembered the Major's mantra and smiled. 'Stealth and shadows excite suspicion. Be invisible in the open.'

A jogger, cloaked with the anonymity of hood and sweatsuit, was the most familiar of sights in the city, and therefore as unremarkable as a fire hydrant or yellow cab. As if to confirm her cover, the quarry panned the street right and left before crossing, never exhibiting a hint of interest in her.

Mentally, Mal raced through his checklist. The guy sitting on the stoop of the brownstone, practising Zen on the brown bottle between his feet – Academy Award material or lush? *Lush.* The old lady at the corner of the Chinese laundry with a squatting dog – *maybe.* A dog had already winged him today. *Concentrate. You can't pass your entrance; too suspicious. Concentrate.*

She began to lope in pursuit, moving lithely on her toes, head bowed in the hood, homing in. The target was maybe thirty yards ahead, still moving slowly, his broad back looming larger. Without breaking stride, she swept her right hand inside her top.

Jogger! Even as the thought struck him, Mal was swivelling on his feet, seeing her weapon swing up. Sorry, Hanny, he thought. Sorry, Hanny.

She registered the look of resignation on his broad face. Something in her peripheral vision clamoured for attention, but she was all hunter now, her attention focused on where she willed the bullet to strike.

Mal was aware of a powerful engine screaming in sudden acceleration from behind, and turned to see the black sedan bearing down on him, the rear passenger window sliding open, the metal finger extending. Double hit, he thought numbly, bracing for the impact. It hits before you hear, his mind registered. Then the high-calibre boom battered his ears.

The blow spun her sideways into the stoop of a brownstone, dislodging a bottle that teetered with agonising slowness and smashed into foam. 'Shit!' the man exclaimed. She felt no pain; shock sent endorphins flooding through her system. She rolled left, away from the numbness in her right side, and sighted. The quarry was already tumbling for the cover of a stoop when she squeezed the trigger and the shoulder of his overcoat erupted. *Winged or dead? No time to find out. Abort and report.* She was on her feet again, staggering and weaving, placing the round-mouthed old woman at the laundry corner between herself and her attackers, cutting away towards the raised subway station.

Mal, turning painfully on the steps, saw the sedan canted on the kerb, Sal's hooded eyes gazing implacably at him.

'You OK?'

'Yeah, I'll live.'

'Don Alfonso wipes his own shoe,' Sal said, and the sedan squealed away.

The top of Mal's shoulder burned. *OK, remember the manual.* Pulling a huge white handkerchief from his pocket, he wadded it between coat and shoulder. He felt a little light-headed and lay back to admire the September sky, all high cirrus and contrails with a backing of siren.

Tony smashed up on the kerb, rolling out before the car had come to rest, his weapon held double-handed. 'Mal! Mal,' he called, scanning left and right, edging across the sidewalk.

'You took your own sweet time,' Mal said, and passed out, a serene expression on his upturned face.

She squatted on the hard seat nearest the door of the train, her weapon held across her lap, hidden by the outsized sweatshirt, ready for pursuers. Black is good, she thought, blood won't show. She dipped her fingers to the blazing furnace in her right side and struggled to control her breathing. Joggers pant, she thought. No sweat. Blood, lots of it, reached warmly down her leg, leaching her consciousness. She dug her fingers into the wound, arching her neck, clenching her teeth to stifle a scream. She was lucid again, agonisingly so.

'Sure takes it out of you, don't it?' a young man offered pleasantly as he passed to the exit. A tall guy, with a blond Mormon bob and a trim suit, unaware that he had met his death on the road to Samara and survived. She counted the station stops. Every sway of the rusty, squealing train worried at her wound, shaking her mercilessly like a dog shaking a rat. 'One more stop,' she gasped, and the blue-haired lady seated in front of her smiled confirmation.

'Move the pain outside yourself, child. See the bright red ball of it before you,' her old Zen master counselled gently, sitting cross-legged in the filthy aisle. 'Free the mind, child,' he added, and vanished. *Off. Now.* She stood upright on splayed feet and dragged herself to the door, aware of the deflating sphere that was her mind; aware that her right shoe squelched. This is the city of ghosts, she thought as she shambled towards her apartment. You want to slouch? So slouch. You want to run yourself into an early grave? So go for it, and have a nice day; who cares?

Whimpering, she jabbed the code on the lock, calling the numbers aloud, and slid along her hallway, leaving a scarlet swathe on the tasteful paintwork. *Phone, numbers, numbers.* She huddled over the glass-topped coffee table, her reflection dissolving in a spreading crimson pool.

'Yes.' A voice.

'Mal! Mal!'

Hanny's anxious face swam into focus and Mal started, his eyes widening. 'You're home, hero,' she said, holding his face firmly in her hands. He relaxed.

Tony's face surfaced like a worried moon behind her shoulder. 'Doc's almost here, Mal. Everything's fine.'

The moon disappeared as he heard the apartment door open; a flurry of voices, a new face. *Shit, why do doctors have to look so young?* 'Lucky, lucky,' the child-man murmured. 'No call for the ER; this I can fix here.' Was there just a hint of disappointment? As the doctor probed and prodded, Mal turned for relief to Hanny. Her face was inscrutable. *Later*, her eyes promised, and he groaned. The doctor tweaked and tucked, peering through his bright new grown-up glasses, and was gone, shepherded by Tony. He's ours, Mal thought contentedly: no paperwork, nada. *Shooting? Nah, ma'am. Backfire. Some old guy's heart couldn't take it. Move along, now.*

Tony loomed again, full of unctuous charm. 'I'd just love a cup of coffee, ma'am.'

Mal closed his eyes, anticipating Hanny's reaction. Surprisingly, she disappeared meekly to the kitchen. Bad omen.

Tony hitched up a chair, so close that Mal couldn't break eye contact without betraying something. 'Hey, Mal, how're you feeling?' No '*hombre*', no '*compadre*'.

'I've felt better.'

Tony's face was thoughtful; only his voice betrayed his hurt. Story time, Mal thought, and held his gaze.

'I got your signal, Mal, loud and clear – good move. So…' He stretched the word to breaking point. 'I'm on my way over and I call for back-up – you know, routine stuff.'

The voice was deceptively calm, but Mal knew

what was coming and wished with all his heart it could be otherwise. Tony shrugged the tension from his shoulders and continued.

'Long delay, Mal. Me, I'm banging the dash, screaming a blue streak, and finally this guy – Ivy League voice – says, "Hey, *hombre*, you just mosey on down to the OK Corral and bring old Earp back to base, dead or alive. And *hombre* – none of this happened, you get me?" So I say, "What is this shit? We got a brother officer under fire; where the hell is the cavalry?" But old Ivy League just lets me rant, Mal.'

'And then he told you,' Mal said softly.

'Yeah. Not so I could ever write it in my memoirs or nothing. But I got the message. Stupid I ain't, Mal.' There was accusation and betrayal in his voice.

'Stupid you never were, Tony. You understand I—'

Tony raised his palm, putting the air before his face. 'No need, Mal, OK?' He got to his feet tiredly.

'I'm sorry, Tony. Need-to-know, old buddy.'

'Sure, Mal. No sweat.'

And Tony left, passing a surprised Hanny in the doorway.

'Well,' she said, replacing him in the chair, 'Clint Eastwood looks like someone ate his horse.'

'I think I should sleep for a while.'

'You'll be dead for a very long time,' she said evenly.

'Very dead,' Mal answered automatically.

Hanny's eyes narrowed, searching his for any trace of sarcasm. 'We need to talk, old man.'

'Ah, Hanny, for the love of—'

'Mal.'

He looked at her stern expression and capitulated. 'So talk.'

'OK,' she said pleasantly. 'I talk, you nod. Think you can manage that?'

'Hanny…'

'Good. So…' She gathered her thoughts. 'The story so far. The retired cop collects his citation from the great and the good. Big day, big deal. The cop's wife… current wife,' she corrected herself, lifting an imperious hand to stall his protests, 'she buys new togs for the photographs and gets slobbered over by the mayor in City Hall.'

Hanny's accent was slipping from Bronx to Ballina, and Mal closed his eyes. 'Don't die just yet, old man,' she snapped. 'I haven't finished. So, la-di-da, lots of Guinness with the lads and home to live happily ever after. And I'm thinking to myself, I married this flatfoot for better or for worse, but not for lunch. He'll be under my feet, wanting to help around the house – wanting to cook, for

God's sake… But no. He's busier than ever: reunions, funerals of old comrades, widows' and orphans' committees, even *golf*.' Mal had always known that 'golf' was a four-letter word, but in Hanny's mouth it was way beyond expletive. 'So I ask myself, who is she?'

'Hanny.'

'Nah, I said. He's not the sharpest chisel in the toolbox, but he's not suicidal either. You can sing now, Blue Eyes,' she concluded sweetly.

'They wanted some help, Hanny,' Mal said heavily. 'Gee, my shoulder hurts like crazy.'

'Good,' she said equably. 'If it was gangrene, you wouldn't feel it.'

'Anyway,' he continued tiredly, 'I got called in to give a hand, and that's the holy all of it.'

Hanny was inches from his face, all levity flown. 'It was all smoke, Mal. You didn't move out; you moved up. And that's why little fat man won't be calling again: because he didn't know.'

'Yes.'

'Because you didn't tell him.'

'Yes again.'

'And you didn't tell me, Mal. I think there's lots of things you didn't tell me – and you'd better sing, birdie, or you'll have this cosy nest all to yourself.'

'OK,' he said finally. 'What do you want to know?'

'You can start with Michael.'

Mal settled his head back in the chair and sighed. Silently, Hanny went to pull the drapes, so that the night noises of the street were muted. Shadows softened the angles in the kitchen as she resumed her place.

'I need to go back a bit,' he said eventually. 'Some time ago, the White House decided it needed a war. Most of the better-known enemies were already in self-destruct, so it came down to drugs. Vietnam all over again, Hanny, and just as unwinnable. So they moved it off the streets and south of the border. And now it had to be a secret war so the president could say "What war?" if he was asked. Are you with me so far?'

'Where else?'

'So we got phantom generals, most of them in seersucker suits, and phantom armies, made up of guys with a talent for killing; guys who were an embarrassment and a liability in peacetime. And we had a dirty war, funded with dirty dollars confiscated from runners and pushers. Irony wasn't a word any of them could even spell. Then some bright spark smells an *opportunity*.' Mal hit the word hard, as if spitting in distaste. 'Turn the suppliers against each other, and set up your own warehouse. The competition kill each other, the flood dries up and the canal opens for traffic. So, this person, or persons, unknown sends in a rogue unit, right into the heart of Smackland, to do just that. Murder and mayhem, no Queensberry Rules or Geneva Convention; whatever it takes.'

Somewhere, a siren whooped uncertainly and was still again.

'But it gets out of hand and comes to the notice of someone who isn't in on the secret, and this white hat sends in a regular unit to clean the neighbour's kitchen before the smell spreads. The regular unit was all killed, Hanny, except one.'

'Michael,' she breathed.

'Yeah, Michael. He got himself wounded, but he made it back. He got out as soon as his tour was up and Army Intelligence had wrung him dry of everything he knew. He was Special Forces, and they were in a blind about letting him back into the real world. Had he told them all he knew? Would he tell anyone else? And what would happen if the badasses ever found out there was a witness? And that's where I came in.'

'I'm not going to like this, am I?'

'No, Hanny,' Mal said very quietly, 'you're not. Somewhere, there's a computer that just eats information all day long; and when they punched a button... it made a connection between Michael and me. So there I was, sitting in Pennsylvania

Avenue with guys who can hardly stand up straight with all the brass they were wearing, and these guys were mouthing about protective custody and witness relocation…' He shook his head at the memory. 'I've seen them, Hanny, the witnesses in those programmes. They're birds in gilded cages – five-star all the way, but it's still Sing Sing. Living with shadows. So I made the brass an offer.'

'You'd be his shadow?'

'Yeah, I'd be his shadow. They figured the rogue unit had to have authorisation from someone high up, someone who had the muscle to finagle the records so that they would never officially exist, just disappear. The same someone would stand to make a truckload of money from their drug dealings. He's the guy they want, Hanny.'

'What has this to do with Michael?'

'Michael was bait, Hanny.'

'Bait?'

'They figured there was a chance the badasses would find out that Michael had survived in South America and come looking for him. Then Michael comes up with the cockamamie idea of going to a seminary. Well, what do I know? Some guys miss the army life and go looking for something similar. I asked around. Can't do him any harm, they said; it might even help him get it together. So Michael did his time, and afterwards I asked the cardinal if he could come and stay with us. I thought it would keep him out of circulation, keep him safe.'

'You asked the cardinal?'

'Yeah, with a little help from Washington.'

She thought he had finished, but he hushed her with a wave of his good hand.

'We've been tracking that rogue unit all over the world, Hanny. Some of them had the decency to die in a plane crash, but the rest are still out there, doing what they do. And now we have the leader's name.'

'What kind of man is this fella?'

'Profiles say he's the worst kind of crazy, Hanny. They want whoever's with him for information, but him they want in a body bag. Michael called me today, asking if I could check out a few names. This guy's was one of them. I called Michael back – and wham, bam, here I am. Someone listened, so someone knows Michael knows.'

'Where is this fella, Mal?' Hanny asked, her voice hoarse with premonition.

'He's on the Island, Hanny.'

'What will you do?'

'Whatever I can.'

He could hear her tears, and he stretched his hand to find hers.

'I thought I'd got used to not having kids,' she said brokenly.

'I know, my love, I know.'

She sniffed loudly. 'You know you're on probation, old man?'

'I know that too, Hanny.'

33

The Island

BY THE PRICKING of my thumbs, something wicked this way comes. The Major swung to face the door, all surprise planed from his face.

'Sergeant?'

Wordlessly, Skald placed a sheaf of papers before him. The Major carefully shifted his glass of red Esparão and donned his glasses.

'The music, Sergeant.'

Debussy clicked off abruptly.

'Our master, Sergeant Skald,' the Major sighed as he scanned the top sheet, 'gazes into the abyss and his heart faileth.' He was on his feet, pacing the

room, his voice rising in a parody of funda-
mentalist preaching. 'Yea, verily, now shall they hie
to their bunkers. Now shall there be a shredding of
documents and a calling to mind of Swiss bank-
account numbers. Now shall they dread the knock
at the door and the emissaries with shaded eyes.
They shall protest, "We know not the man, nor
were we party to his deeds. Let him be cast out."'
A single drop of sweat trembled on his upper lip.

'Sir?'

'In short, Sergeant Skald,' he continued calmly,
'the General wishes to take off his uniform and
mingle with the crowd. As for the enlisted men…'
The Major slumped in his chair and swung it to
the window. 'Place not your trust in princes.'

Savagely, he snatched the ringing phone. 'Yes!'

No voice answered, but he could hear Bach
swell in the background.

'Siren?'

'Major.'

Her voice was a wraith in the ether, and he
pressed the receiver to his ear. 'I'm here, Siren.'

'I'm sorry, Major. I was expected.' She groaned,
and his entire body clenched.

'Siren, are you hurt? You must seek help.'

A long silence, as Bach warmed to his dark
theme.

'Siren, listen to me. You know who to call.'

'Thank you, Major, but no. There were too many of them. Sorry.'

'Susan Wang Tao,' he said gently, 'you have been a dutiful daughter.'

He heard the telephone crash to the floor, then only Bach. In a rage he swept the papers from the table, oblivious to the flying glass and the wine that splashed his hands. Skald watched him carefully, but the moment passed and he was granite again.

'Is there more, Sergeant?' The Major gestured at the strewn papers.

'Yes, sir; one thing more.'

Carefully avoiding the broken glass, Skald sifted through the papers, found the page he wanted and brought it, half-sodden, to the desk. The Major read the final paragraph with a humourless smile.

'Even the dead don't stay dead, Sergeant Skald.'

He handed the page to his aide, steepling his fingers.

'You see, Sergeant, some people need killing twice. The priest survived and, I think, remembers you – I wondered about his reaction when you spoke. It may well be time we packed our bags and stole away into the night. I say "we", but you are free to find your own way. Consider the offer. You have two minutes.' He smiled wearily.

'I'm with you, Major.'

The Major nodded. 'Then we must tie up loose ends, Sergeant Skald. This shipment is our last. I give you personal charge of the matter. Mr D'Arcy, I believe, has a grievance that irks him. I shall offer him surcease, which leaves you short a pilot.'

'I am considering someone, sir.'

'Willing and able?'

'He could be persuaded, sir,' Skald answered. 'His name is Brian Quinn.'

'Ah... leave him to me,' the Major said. 'I think it's time we repaid in some small measure the hospitality we have enjoyed here.'

Skald listened stonily to his instructions. When the Major left the room, Skald bent to retrieve the sodden papers from the floor. He squeezed them in his massive fist, and let the bright-red drops ran between his fingers.

34

The Church

MICHAEL AND FATHER Mack were divesting in the sacristy. By tacit agreement, neither had spoken of the night before, and Father Mack folded the vestments into the drawer with studied care.

'Ah, the damn thing is stuck again. The damp gets in everywhere.'

'Here, I'll do it.'

As Michael moved up beside him, Father Mack said quietly, 'I think there's someone to see me. I'll be in the confessional for a while. I'll be back later.'

When Michael emerged, he saw Fi chatting with an old lady near the gate.

'Father?' an English voice said, behind him.

He extended his hand. The woman was small, almost dainty, and appeared nervous. The tall man standing a pace behind her had a soldier's bearing, despite the stick.

'Could we have a word?'

'Of course, let's go in the house. Father Mack is engaged for a bit; we'll have it to ourselves. Why don't I just say goodbye to some people? The door is on the push. You'll find the sitting room on the right; go ahead in and make yourselves comfortable.'

The woman's intelligent face registered his effort at protecting their privacy. Impulsively, she gripped Michael's arm, and he was startled by the strength of her grip.

'It's about your brother.'

Despite the intensity of his gaze, her eyes held his, and with a sinking heart he read pity in them. Gently, he covered her hand with his. 'Then I'd like to bring my sister, if that's OK with you?'

She nodded.

The confessional was dark, and smelled of damp and old incense. Father Mack eschewed the 'lights on' practice of many younger priests, believing that the shadows encouraged a burdened heart. He was in a place where the language had no word for privacy; he knew the supplicants' voices, and they knew that he knew, but it was best to observe the formalities. As some people have a gift for divining, Mack had developed the gift of knowing when someone was seeking him, and he pushed back the slide in readiness for the one he knew would come.

The side door creaked, and he heard the familiar thud of knees on the *prie-dieu*. Automatically, he kissed the embroidered cross on the slim purple stole before looping it over his shoulders. 'You're welcome,' he said gently, hunching his elbows on his knees, chin bowed in his cupped hands, ready to share the burden.

Michael wound his way through the mass-goers, pausing to shake hands, nodding at the efforts of some to sustain his hopes for Gabriel, returning the hand pressure of the silent ones who knew better. At last, the old lady departed and he had Fi to himself.

'I suppose you were up drinking whiskey till all hours,' she said, attempting a levity her pale face belied.

'Fi, there's a couple – I think they're English. They want to talk to me about Gabriel. I thought you should be there.'

For a moment she turned her head sideways, looking out over the water, and he was struck by the memory of how she would raise her chin as a child whenever something frightened her.

'Are you afraid, Fi?'

She nodded, unable to speak, tears beading her lashes. 'I don't… I don't want…'

Michael wrapped his arm around her shoulders, and both of them looked sightlessly into the distance.

''Tis only the dark, love,' he whispered, as he had in answer to her childhood night terrors. 'There's nothing there to harm you.'

But she could not be comforted. He heard her sniff and felt her shoulders straighten under his arm. 'We'd better go in, so,' she said in a small voice.

35

Major Devane's House

THE ROBIN BOBBED sympathetically at the woman through the window of her cage, pecked the cable between its feet, then flew off to the business of survival. Deirdre smiled. 'Just a few pounds heavier, bird,' she murmured, 'and Mama Lybe would be basting you for lunch.'

There had been no call. Yet. She did not actually hope that Carlo would sober up, straighten out, become the man she'd thought she'd married and pick up the goddamn phone. How could he? He had never existed, except as a projection of her need to find a man who was strong, authoritative, yet gentle and kindly – Daddy and not Daddy. She really knew who Carlo was. There was flash Carlo, with the immaculate suits and manicured hands; Carlo the bountiful, with a bulging wallet and immediate access to the best tables at the right restaurants; closed Carlo, who disappeared on business at all hours; Pavlovian Carlo, who barked dutifully whenever the cellphone beeped. But under the range of masks was nothing, an enormous zero. Deirdre had danced the masked ball herself, she reminded herself ruefully, played all the parts – slave, slut, dutiful Italian housewife, trophy wife – trying to be whatever he wanted her to be, to be accepted... like Mommy and not Mommy. And would she too take an army-issue .45 to blow all the masks to hell in one last bloody effort at being real?

'A penny for them?'

Lybe's quiet voice smoothed the ever-widening whirlpool that threatened to pull her down.

'Bad bargain, Lybe,' she answered.

She was mildly surprised when Lybe sat down at the table. Somewhere in Lybe's genetic make-up, there was a 'move' command that kept her in constant motion.

'Child.'

The tremor in Lybe's voice drew her attention. 'Something wrong?'

Lybe hesitated, as if weighing her anxiety against some notion of loyalty, and then pressed on. 'The Major says we are to pack – essentials only.'

'Pack? Why?'

'There is no why, there is never why. Only pack and be ready to go.'

'Where is he now?' Deirdre asked, rising.

Lybe's hand kept her effortlessly in the chair. 'He is gone, somewhere… I don't know.'

'And Skald?'

'That man, he is at the factory. The other one, D'Arcy, is also gone. Miss Deirdre, I'm afraid.'

The beep of the cellphone startled both of them. Lybe rose automatically, moving to the cooker. Comfort zones, Deirdre thought, pushing Receive.

'Yes.'

'Miss Devane, are you alone?'

The voice sounded like two pieces of sandpaper rasped together, and goosebumps stippled her arms.

'Who the hell is this?'

'Miss Devane, please.' The man paused. 'I am Alfonso Vespucci, your husband's uncle.'

Deirdre's brain whirred. 'Oh.'

'Yes, indeed.' She sensed a hint of warmth in the gravel tone. 'In private, please.'

Waving a distracted hand at Lybe, she hurried to her room and closed the door. Sitting on the bed, she breathed deeply and fixed her eyes on the ocean before speaking.

'Signor Vespucci.'

'You remember?'

'I remember.'

She remembered the dying stages of the wedding reception: a queue of beefy men, country builds in city suits, kissing her formally on both cheeks and pressing envelopes into her hand. She remembered Alfonso, small and frail, leaning on a cane, and his throat. She had had to drag her eyes upwards to his pale, intense gaze. There had been no envelope, no kisses, but he had a presence that had brought the big men to stillness. 'You are family,' he had said, and she could not distinguish between warmth and sympathy in his voice. 'If ever you should need, I am here.' And he had gone, the big men trailing sheepishly in his wake.

'I bring you sad news of my nephew Carlo. You will pardon me being…' he paused, as if searching for the correct English word, 'direct,' he said finally. 'Carlo is dead. I have a concern for your safety.'

Deirdre combed a hand through her hair, catching it in a tight, painful knot at the nape. *Look at the water*, she commanded herself, to still the rising panic within her. 'What happened?'

'He was murdered, *cara*. I am sorry.'

She clung to the affectionate '*cara*', as if it was a lifeline to sanity, as the darkness loomed again.

'I am concerned for your safety.'

'I… I am in my father's house, *signor*. I'm safe here.'

'Perhaps not, Miss Devane. Find a safe place. At once. My number is on your cellphone. *Va bene*.'

Deirdre deliberately placed the cellphone at arm's length on the coverlet, as if it was contaminated. The sea showed intermittent flecks of white, like a child's colouring that didn't quite meet the lines; the top third of the window moved steadily to the left as the clouds passed in and out of frame. She moved her left hand along the coverlet – cool. Somewhere in the air there was a hint of lavender. The breath through her dilated nostrils was cold, warm, cold, warm, and this mantra thawed her mind. *Carlo is dead*.

In one swift movement, she was off the bed and striding to the kitchen. Lybe, turning from her pots, mirrored her own shock.

'Miss Deirdre,' she gasped, dropping the teacloth and extending her arms.

'No, no. Don't hold me, Lybe.'

Lybe shrank back, her face a map of puzzlement and apprehension.

'I need to think,' Deirdre said, almost to herself. 'You say my fa— the Major is away, and Skald is in the factory?'

'Yes, a ship comes to take cargo from the factory, but—'

'The door to his room – is it locked?' She was surprised at the metallic quality of her own voice and aware of how Lybe matched her formal tone.

'Yes, Miss Deirdre.'

'Do you have a key?'

'No.' Lybe's hands fluttered before her breasts.

'Lybe, I need—'

'No.'

Deirdre's temper flared. 'Oh, for Christ's sake, Lybe – the Major doesn't own you!'

Lybe's head flinched backwards as if she had been struck. She took a moment to regain her composure before speaking. 'Miss Deirdre, there are many things you do not know… many things.'

She lapsed into a silence that Deirdre could barely endure.

'Many years ago, my husband Fernando is a poor man where we live in Negros. He works for the plantation boss, who lives in a hacienda with white walls and a red-tiled roof. Me, I work in the cane also, like my mother and sister, like everybody. We want to marry, Fernando and me, but there is no hope. Many reasons. The priest, a missionary – I think he is Irish; he has, you know, spots on his face…'

'Freckles,' Deirdre offered quickly, trying to accelerate the story.

'Freckles, yes. He says he will get us to the American base in Subic, and his friend, also a priest, will get us visas to the US. It is like a dream to us, and so we go. When we come to Subic, we hear that our priest in Negros has been shot. No reason. Many people are shot all the time. There is no one waiting for us, Miss Deirdre. Someone says the other priest has been sent away by the bishop, somewhere else. There is a camp there beside the base. Lots of soldiers. It is Marcos' time, and people like us from Negros are called rebels. In this camp, they have… interrogation. Fernando they beat with bamboo on the bottoms of his feet; and me, a soldier puts a cloth over my face and they pour water so that I can't breathe. And then he comes.'

'The Major,' Deirdre whispered bleakly.

'He says he can get us out if we work for him. Fernando to be his… agent, to collect information on people in the mountains and the missionaries. And me to be housekeeper. He says, "You have two minutes." This, I remember.'

'Oh, Lybe.'

'Miss Deirdre, there is more. The ship that

comes, my son is captain of that ship. So, yes, Miss Deirdre, the Major owns us.'

The misery in the older woman's face shamed her. 'I'm sorry, Mama Lybe, truly sorry.' Daddy's web, she thought bitterly; yet another to be trussed and toyed with, and eaten.

Lybe was back at her pots. As she stirred, she spoke in a low voice. 'I told Fernando what the Major says: you must lock all doors and arm the system.' She spoke as if by rote, a child feeding back the instructions of an adult; but then her voice changed to something nearer her own. 'But Fernando you can tell ten times and he forget. I tell him, in the library – always put the key in the library, in the same place. Men!'

Deirdre bent to kiss the back of her neck, then raced from the room. The library was a short, book-lined corridor; books bought at auction by the yard leaned disdainfully away from one another on grey metal shelves. Feverishly, she scanned the titles. The encyclopaedia section she dismissed instantly as fillers, a stab at pseudo-gravitas. *Technical tomes? No. Lives of great men? Possibly. Tennyson, Shakespeare, Walt Whitman... Shakespeare! Oh God, yes: always a quote from the goddamn Bard.* She heaved the entire corpus to the floor. *Bingo.*

She was in, awed into immobility by the

massive glass wall and the fretful water beyond. The winking console drew her like a magnet to the computer; its screensaver, floating across the monitor from left to right, read 'ENDGAME'. *No going back now. Daddy's little girl is right up to her buns in the Rubicon.* She breathed, flexed her fingers. She avoided the chair, his chair, nudging it aside in a token of filial impiety, and knelt in supplication before the keys.

PASSWORD? *Only one try, Deirdre, only one, and you've got two minutes.* 'DEIRDRE,' she typed. A pause. *Come on, come on, you lousy lump of silicon...*

ACCESS GRANTED. She tapped at the main menu, and the screen blossomed into titles, mostly meaningless... 'SIREN'? She hit Show.

She scanned quickly as the pages rolled up before her. It was all there, in precise military language: 'ETA', 'TARGET' and 'TERMINATE' pinged her eyes until she flinched, but she kept reading. And there it was. 'VESPUCCI, CARLO, WITH EXTREME PREJUDICE' – a terse epitaph for his daughter's husband.

In a daze, she clicked the file closed, trawling the main menu again. 'PISCES'. *Fish?* She hit Show. In the cold wash of the screen, her face was gaunt, shadows stretching back from cheekbones and pooling to a smudge beneath her nose, the cleft between the lower lip and chin a cave. She sat back on her heels, head bowed, rubbing her hands for warmth. Pandora had lifted the lid and it could not be resealed. The cold of the metal desk was soothing to her forehead.

When she raised her eyes again, they held a glint of determination. *You want endgame? You got it.* From memory, she tapped in the e-mail address of her newspaper editor in New York. The message was terse. 'Harry, this is a hell of a chain letter… pass it on. D.' Momentarily, her fingers trembled over the keys. Send, one finger instructed, and coiled back to the fist for comfort. 'Done,' she whispered, and the red light beneath the console blinked black.

Lybe and Fernando sat at the table in the kitchen, their eyes huge with anticipation.

'Miss Deirdre?'

'Lybe, Fernando, listen to me. We have to go now. I have friends who will hide us.'

'There is no hiding from him,' Lybe responded fatalistically, and her husband nodded his assent. But Deirdre was a dervish, whirling them up and out and down the path between the brooding sensors, prodding and cajoling them to move,

move, deaf to their protestations. *Where can we go? To Fi? To Anne? No.*

'We'll go to the priest,' she told them. 'Priest' was the magic word that gave the couple solace. This time, the priest would be waiting.

36

The Church

'BLESS ME, FATHER, for I have sinned.'

How many hours had he spent in this box, Father Mack wondered, sifting the wheat from the chaff that blew around his ears, monitoring the timbre of voices often redolent of the drink that gave the penitent Dutch courage?

'It is…'

He knew it had been a long time since Sarah Dolan had graced the confessional and hurried to cover her hesitancy. 'You're here now,' he said quickly; 'that's all that matters. Just you and me and the God who wants what's best for you. Tell your story.'

'I'm pregnant, Father.' The revelation came in an explosion of air. He expected the tears, and heard her sniffing in the dark.

'It took courage to come with that burden. Don't lose it now,' he said firmly. 'Listen to me: this is no place for shame or condemnation. Do you hear me?'

'Yes, Father.'

He went on, more gently, 'Have you family who will help you?'

'No, Father.' She said it with a finality he could not counter.

'Very well, then. We'll sort it out ourselves. I know a family in Dublin – good people, helped me out many's the time before. You could go there.'

'But what'll I say when people ask, Father?'

'Say Father Mack got you a job. When your time comes, you can decide what to do. I'll give you all the help I can. The man – will he stand by you?'

Relieved of her secret, Sarah gave vent to her anger. Father Mack sat back against the hard timber, pressing his hand to the growing knot in his stomach, willing his pain to wait until hers was assuaged.

'Man! He's no man. That Leo is nothing but a mammy's boy. He's had his way, and now he'll go back to his three meals a day and his job in the factory. I should have seen through him, God knows. The night we were up the headland by the old lighthouse, he was all bluster, but the Yank knocked the *teaspai* out of him, all right.'

'Yank?'

'Yes, Father – you know that odd fella works for the Major. He was up there, sure Leo nearly lost his life hiding in the heather when young Flaherty went by; and then he was nearly caught by the Yank. God, when the screaming started—'

'Girl.' The old priest's voice had an edge of pain and horror that stopped her narrative abruptly. 'Tell… tell me what happened.'

Delighted with the attention, and the opportunity to blacken Leo in the eyes of her new champion, she told him. As she spoke, the pain twisted inside him, squeezing sweat from his pores; tears freckled his purple stole. He welcomed the agony as an offering against the awfulness of Gabriel's fate, reading his butchery in the relentless, blaming voice of Sarah Dolan.

With enormous effort, he raised his hand in benediction. '*Ego te absolvo*, I absolve you from all your sins…' And who will shrive *me*? he wondered. Me, who shut his ears to any voice that dared to question his great accomplishment, his abiding monument. Me, who said, 'I do not know the man', turning my back while they took a boy as sacrifice.

'Father, are you all right?'

'Yes...' It was a gasp from the core of his tormented soul. 'Yes,' he said, more evenly, gathering his last resources in an effort at control. 'You'll come to the house tomorrow and we'll make the arrangements.'

'I will. And God bless you, Father Mack.'

Sarah was gone. In the darkness, Father Mack stretched out his hands in supplication. '*Eli, Eli, lama sabacthani...* My God, my God, why have you forsaken me?' He heard no answering voice, nothing but a dying wind moaning for succour in the empty church. Nothing but the dull drumming in his belly and the darkness that welled up to coat his face and hands and clog his throat, like ashes. His head sank to his knees. 'There will be no blessing for me,' he groaned, 'no blessing for me.'

On the other side of the screen, the red light faded.

37

The Nurse's House

KATE DUMPED THE heavy medical bag on the kitchen table. Ruefully, she pondered the cracked leather and fraying handles. The lock had given up the ghost some months before, succumbing to the corrosive salt in the Island air. Instinctively, she brushed her fingers over the seams beside her eyes and on up into her coarse raven hair.

'Off out again?' Brian's voice, roughened by the alcohol of the night before, rubbed her raw.

'It's what I do,' she replied tersely.

'Oh yes, I know what you do, all right.'

Oh God, she thought wearily, I don't need this,

not now. There's a baby due in O'Toole's that hasn't a notion of turning, a long queue of ingrown toenails and arthritis and a plethora of pains and aches that'll only respond to an hour's chat by the fire and the inevitable cup of strong tea. And there's Father Mack, with a crab gnawing his insides, probably offering it up for someone like me.

Brian loomed into view. He is in as much pain as any of them, Kate thought, and incapable of cure. She felt drained, and turned for relief to the ritual of packing the drugs, consciously replacing the analgesics with something stronger for Father Mack.

'You'll be calling to see the priest, I suppose?'

For a moment, she stood stunned. Confidentiality on the Island was as sacred for the nurse as for the priest. A secret, she believed, was something known to one person. Had she innocently given a clue to anyone in casual conversation? Surely she couldn't have mentioned it to Brian, of all people. Then it struck her who he was really referring to, and she turned to ice.

'Nothing to say to that, now, have you?' he goaded. She snatched her coat from the back of the chair, but he was between her and the door, his face suffused with blood.

'Like a bitch in heat, you are.'

'Stand out of my way.'

There were flecks of spittle at the corners of his mouth. 'If you were a man…'

'If I was a man,' she said calmly, 'I'd be the only man here.'

She thought he would strike her. For a moment, he teetered on the verge of madness; then he tore the door open.

'Go, then,' he shouted, 'and don't come back. I won't have another man's leavings.'

She was through the door and on the path, intent on putting one foot ahead of the other, making distance between herself and the agony that bellowed from behind.

Another man's leavings, spoiled goods. Stríopach. Whore. The word rattled in Kate's skull like a cruel-edged stone. It's what I am, she thought grimly, to have sold myself to a man I didn't love, for the sake of my child. Oh, Father Mack had been sweet sanity itself. 'You can go to Dublin, Kate, to a family I know – good people. You can have the child and do your training like you want to. I'll see you right for the money.' Isn't that what whores do, she thought fiercely, take someone else's money? 'You wouldn't want to wreck another life, Kate.' And when she returned, holding a child by the hand, Father Mack had been waiting for her, staring down the starers, bringing the both of them to his own house, despite the whispers.

Father Mack, always Father Mack. 'You'll want to settle, Kate, forget what's done and gone and make a life for yourself. For the child's sake, Kate. A boy needs a man in his life.' And she had let him erode her grip on hope, given herself to the current and been swept away.

'Ah, Nurse Quinn.' The Major blocked her path. 'Is the man above in the house?' he asked, affecting the half-mocking toora-loora voice he used with islanders.

'No,' Kate answered, as if to herself, 'there is no man there.' And she was past him, striding resolutely away from a charade she would never again be part of.

So the shrew was not for taming, the Major mused, making his way to the open door. Brian was slumped at the table, his head sunk on his chest, the light from the cottage window cruelly exposing the puffiness around his eyes.

'The door was open,' the Major said, but the big man showed no reaction, as if he were in a trance. Unperturbed, the Major pulled a fallen chair upright and straddled it opposite the inert figure.

'Mr Quinn, self-pity is a drug for the weak,' he remarked affably.

The big head rose slowly, the eyes straining to focus. There were still enough embers of madness

to fire him into fury again, so the Major leaned
closer. 'No, Mr Quinn. No. Despite the fact that
you are a younger man, you know that I am quite
capable of dislocating each of your limbs and
leaving you pissing blood on your kitchen floor, and
I doubt very much if your little nurse will come
running to your assistance, now or ever again.'

For a moment, the eyes flared; then they died.
The head began to sink.

'Look at me, man. Look at me.'

His command, like a slapping palm, stung
Brian Quinn upright before him.

'Listen to me carefully, Mr Quinn, because I do
not repeat myself and I have little patience for
explanations. You will wait until I have finished and
not interrupt. Do you understand?'

After a slight hesitation, Brian bobbed his head
robotically, a flicker of unease in his eyes. The
Major leaned closer still, his voice dropping to a
lulling whisper.

'You have trouble, Mr Quinn. Look at me,' he
snapped as the man began to avert his gaze.
Reluctantly, Brian dragged his eyes back to the
intensity of the other's. 'You have been cruelly
used, Mr Quinn. I take no pleasure in saying this,
but it is the truth. *Used* to take another man's
woman and another man's bastard into your
home.'

Quinn flinched, but could not pull away.

'*Used* to bind yourself to a woman who would never share your bed, who never gave you anything but her contempt, who would not lower herself to you – you, who put a roof over her head and food in her bastard's mouth. Are you hearing me, Mr Quinn?'

Dumbly, Brian nodded, and the Major pressed on in that same merciless whisper. '*Used*, Mr Quinn. And you know why, don't you?'

Before Brian could answer, the Major was on his feet, towering over him, his voice cracking like a flaying whip. 'To cover another man's shame. To cover the fact that he took easily what you were never given. To make you the laughing stock of every other man on this spiteful island. I know, Mr Quinn. I know.'

He was pacing, circling the man at the table. 'I have eyes and ears everywhere, Mr Quinn. In Finnegan's. I see them whisper behind their hands when you pass and sneer as you search your pockets for the price of a drink, and laugh out loud when you stagger out to piss it all away against the wall. Ah, yes, the men with steady jobs and willing wives, men with boats of their own – men who dismiss the hard hours you give on their boats and toss you a few pounds, like a bone to a dog. I know how you debased yourself before men like that –

men who will never be the boatman you are – and for what? For a woman who gave you no word of thanks and who goes back to the one she always wanted. And now, the laughs and sneers and whispers will grow louder and louder.'

His voice rose, manic with hollow laughter, so that Brian pressed his hands to his ears. 'Wasn't Quinn the right fool, all the same? Mooning after someone else's woman – a woman who took all he had and spat in his face.'

The big hands clenched on the table, trembling.

'Oh, there's more, Mr Quinn.' His voice dropping, the Major resumed his seat. 'There's a man beyond in Galway who has a little note-book, a long memory and no patience. Do you remember him, Mr Quinn?'

The head signalled assent, the eyes a study in misery.

'One of these days he's planning on making a visit – and not on his own, oh no. And his friends will take what's due to him, and no one will raise a hand to stop them – not Finnegan, not O'Toole nor Dowd nor any of the friends you bought with beer. You have nothing and nobody, Mr Quinn… but me.'

Brian clenched his face in a grimace of mute despair, bringing his hands to his head like twisted claws as if he would gouge himself. When the spasm passed, his head drooped all the way to the tabletop.

The Major resumed soothingly, 'All that is behind you, Mr Quinn. You can wipe the slate clean and start again.'

A snort of disbelief escaped the cradled head.

'Oh, doubt no longer, Mr Quinn, but believe,' the Major intoned. 'The money you owed is already paid.'

The head rose fractionally.

'I think Mr Joyce was disappointed somewhat. I gather he was rather looking forward to having you chastised; but no matter, he has been paid with interest and owns no part of you now.'

With seeming indifference, the Major tossed a much-thumbed notebook on the table. Brian snatched it up, feverishly fumbling to the last page.

'Paid in full?' he croaked.

'Yes,' the Major replied calmly.

'Why?'

'Why? To get you off your knees, Mr Quinn. Whether or not you stand up straight, like a man, depends on how you respond to my offer.'

'What offer?'

The Major tracked the twin currents of avarice and wariness in the dull eyes.

'I need a pilot for my boat, Mr Quinn, a master. I have an important order to deliver to a ship offshore. No, no questions; I haven't finished. This will be my final shipment. The factory closes today. Oh yes,' he continued in response to the shock on Brian's face. 'There'll be no time for whispers or sneers or winks after today, no time for laughing at "poor Quinn" left high and dry by his woman, because today the easy ride stops for all of them… except you. After today, I will have no further use for my boat. It's yours.'

'What—'

'It's what you wanted, isn't it – a boat of your own?'

'Yes, yes.'

'Then consider my offer and give me your answer. You have two minutes.'

38

Leo's House

LEO FOUND HIMSELF standing on the headland, ankle deep in heather, wrestling a reluctant pair of jeans from knees to waist. A woman's voice taunted him from behind, but he could not turn; if he did, the shadow would devour him. The shadow was hunting other prey, but he knew, in the depth of his bowels, that if he proved an impediment, he would be trodden down, dispatched without thought or feeling. The woman's voice grew shriller in his head and, to preserve his sanity, he clutched a brass button, like a talisman.

'Will you stay the day in that bed? Get up, you *amadán*, and go to your work. It's been light for hours.'

Leo opened his eyes to the tangle of his room and squinted resentfully at the light from the window. 'Jesus,' he groaned, and, having started his day in heartfelt prayer, swung his white feet to the cold floor. His head bowed forward between his bent knees as the residue of the night before coursed through his memory.

Sarah had been all coy and beguiling, leading him unsteadily to the dark at the far end of Finnegan's yard. God, the air had smelled good after the fug inside; but, as his senses aligned, he had begun to understand the import of her words. She had raced on, her words tripping over themselves: 'Finnegan's sure to keep me on – after, like. Sure, he has no head for the books at all. And my mother's doddering; she won't say anything when you move in—'

'What?'

He had heard her tone change to a lower, fiercer register, snapping at him from every angle like a collie worrying a sheep to the pen. God, she sounded just like his mother. And then, harried by her hurry, he had said it. He had felt like a man in deep water, grasping at any splinter of the wreck that might keep him afloat; he knew he should have

let her rant away and gone home and let his brain
settle, but no, he had opened his big mouth.
'There's no knowing whose baby it might be.'

At that moment, a man weaving out of the pub
door to relieve himself had probably saved Leo's
life. Sarah had disappeared back inside, leaving
him light-headed in the dark.

'Soft night,' the man had said.

''Tis that.'

'God, I'm bursting... Aah, there's nothing like
it.'

Leo climbed into his work clothes, lacing his
boots with the exaggerated care of the still
inebriated, then clumped his way to the kitchen,
holding to the scent of frying bacon. As usual, his
mother was hunched and black before the range,
antagonising the spitting pan. His father sat side-
on to the fire, his swollen feet extended on the
cold flags for ease.

'What time did you fall in last night?' Leo's
mother asked. It was a regular ritual, and he had
the responses by rote.

'Late.'

'Finnegan's, I suppose.'

It was a statement and required no answer. He
speared a slice of bread from the board. 'You'll lose
your good job in the factory, so you will, and what
will you have then? Nothing, that's what. And you

needn't think my brother will take you back on his boat, after you tangling his pots because of the drink.'

'Good job,' the old man sneered, tilting back his toes for inspection.

Jesus, Mary and Joseph, Leo thought, it's a two-hander this morning. He looked at his father out of the corner of his eye: a man who had never broken sweat in his life, who knew every grant and handout available to the idle, who played the system like a fiddle and spent his evenings penning begging letters to a far-flung brood in Canada and the States. Whether because of guilt or what, Leo didn't know, but the eejits sent it home to finance the father's only exercise: the walk to Finnegan's to buy his round, slapping the crisp notes on the bar with relish. Suddenly, Leo felt weary of the lot of them. He had half a mind to write a note himself, asking for the fare to… anywhere.

'And there's that young strap beyond in Finnegan's telling the whole parish how you're her fella, and you without two brass farthings to your name.' His mother tossed the bacon on his plate. 'Eat it up and go to work, or I'll have you lying beyond in the bed the whole day, like himself, and me a skivvy to the pair of ye.'

'Work,' the old man echoed. 'Work, hah.'

'More than you ever had, old man,' Leo

muttered around the bread and bacon in his mouth.

'What's that? Mind your manners, boy. You're not too old yet for my belt.'

'Those days are over, old man,' Leo growled ominously, and felt a glow of satisfaction as the old man subsided into the chair.

Suddenly, he was ashamed and sick of it all. Sometimes he wanted to scream at them to be quiet, to stop the useless mad rigmarole that bound them all inside themselves. At that moment, he hated his brothers and sisters – hated their freedom far away, hated their wives and children who came back the odd summer to smiles and admiration. He heaved himself out of the chair, dragging his jacket from the back of the door.

'When will you be home?'

'Late.'

He leaned his back against the slammed door, breathing in the salt air, letting the rhythmic collapse of water on sand dissolve the hard knot in his head. There must be something better than this, he thought. One of these days...

He took the cliff walk to shorten his journey. A lark rose before him, vaulting up and up, its song full of boasting at its accomplishment. 'Easy for you,' he said aloud, and smiled, the rancour of the kitchen already erased. The sea sparkled to his left, and he lengthened his stride. Below him, the flat rocks stretched out to the white rim of the turning tide. Long-legged birds staggered in the sea-wrack; far above it all, a hunting gannet spread its wings and scythed down from the sky to strike a fish in a tiny, silent splash. Leo had never grown used to the wreck, forlorn and rusting where the big wind of '84 had berthed it. He didn't think of it as a blot on the landscape, but as something noble and tragic, something made for another life and now becalmed, decaying slowly into the Island. 'Something like me,' he muttered aloud, and laughed. 'Jaysus, you're in great form this morning,' he told himself, and walked on, his step a little lighter.

Something in his peripheral vision snagged his attention and he stood still on the path, turning his eyes seawards. There was always the chance of dolphins, sewing the surface with flashing leaps, or the lazy flick of a basking shark. Once, he had caught a salute from the rising fluke of a whale. That had kept him late for work too. *Work...* The thought was beginning to tug his head forward when he saw the boy. He knew immediately it had to be the nurse's boy. Who else would be abroad on the rocks at that hour, and who else could move with such grace over the broken surface? The boy held his hands aloft as he ran; what looked like ribbons streamed from his fingers. For a long

moment Leo stood there, shading his eyes, drawn
into the exhilaration of the small dancing figure.
Somewhere in his own heart, another boy grieved
for lost innocence.

A cold prickling in the hairs above his collar
made him stiffen and look away, searching the
landscape for the source of his sudden unease.
Among the piled rocks, nearer the shore, a figure
stepped out of shadow. Leo, automatically crouching on the path, watched the squat figure pack
binoculars into a case slung around his neck and
move, with long, loping strides, in the direction of
the factory. He shivered involuntarily, crouching
even lower on the path, though the man was
almost out of sight. *Why would he be watching the
boy? Should he mention it to the nurse, or to Quinn?
Christ, not Quinn. That one's as likely to bite the
hand of friend as foe these days.*

Leo's dilemma was resolved by an overriding
consideration. He was late for work, again, and the
Yank would be there before him unless he took a
short cut and shifted himself.

39

The Fish Factory

LEO WAS CONGRATULATING himself on slipping unnoticed into the holding yard and on having had the foresight to give his clocking-in card to Whelan the night before in Finnegan's – Whelan would always oblige in exchange for a free pint – when the foreman stepped into his path from behind a tower of empty crates.

'Are you on a half-day or what?'

O'Toole – typical bloody boatman, simmering with discontent on dry land – took every opportunity to harass the younger men. 'I was a bit delayed, Mr O'Toole,' Leo blurted, hating his own schoolboy tone.

'You'll be delayed on the Day of Judgment,' O'Toole growled. 'O'Brien called in sick, again, so you can get your arse into the forklift and start shifting. We have a big order going out to the ship today.'

Relieved, Leo circled around the big man. 'Yes, Mr O'Toole, straightaway,' he mumbled. 'And may you blacken your arse and slide backwards up a rainbow,' he added to himself as he made his escape.

'Ah, finally. Big night last night, hah? Big bump in the blankets this morning!' He ran the cheerful gauntlet of the other men as he made his way to the forklift at the rear of the store. 'Better keep your heads down, lads. Top Gun is taking her up,' he shouted as he fired the engines.

For the next hour, he scooped pallets laden with fish from the yard and ferried them to the Holy of Holies, as the workers called it – the closed area at the rear that led to the huge freezing unit, where he stopped to stack and reverse. Everyone knew the drill: it was a no-go area for any employee except the forklift operator, who was forbidden to alight there for any reason. Skald had imparted this injunction to every new worker on his first day, in a tone that brooked no exceptions and encouraged no enquiries. Maybe O'Brien will be out for a few weeks, Leo thought as he loaded the last pallets, shoving the gears forward, negotiating the slalom of piled pallets with increasing confidence, and I'll get a toe in doing this job. It beats working.

Jesus! His concentration snapped back to the job as his load bumped the corner of the pallet nearest the fridge. No, he thought dully, as the pile swayed in agonising slow motion and crashed to the floor. *Ah, fuck...* There were fish everywhere. Without thinking, Leo was out of the bucket seat and scrabbling on the floor, hunting slipping salmon back to their bed of ice. An especially fine specimen slipped from his grip as if alive, until he cornered it and held it steady under his knee. Its mouth gaped open, and something emerged. Intrigued, Leo poked two fingers between the dead jaws and prised out a cellophane pack of white powder.

'What the loving...?'

The tips of his fingers were already numb from the dead fish, and that feeling spread throughout his crouched body as he sensed a presence behind him.

Skald, his mind registered, before everything dissolved into bright light.

40

The Priest's House

AS THEY MADE their way to the priest's house, Fiona saw a couple standing uncertainly beside the gate.

'It's Anne,' she said to Michael.

'Who?' But she was already striding forwards to hug the young woman.

When Michael drew abreast, Fiona made the introductions, obvious pleasure in her voice. 'Anne, this is my wayward brother Michael – turned out a priest, for God's sake.'

He registered the lack of recognition in the woman's eyes. 'You don't remember me, Anne?'

'Ah, indeed I do, Michael Flaherty,' she answered, smiling. 'I just don't see you.'

For a moment, he was puzzled; then realisation dawned. 'I'm sorry, Anne. I didn't know.'

'No need to be,' she said simply. 'Sure, who could ever forget Michael the book-boy? Do you remember, Fi, how we would go into his room and get up to all sorts of capers?'

'Yes.' Fiona laughed at the memory. 'And we'd have bets on how long it would take him to notice us.'

'Oh, excuse me,' Anne said. 'This fella hanging out of my arm is Mario; says he's a photo-journalist.'

'Aren't you the sly one, Anne,' Fiona remarked, appraising Mario with a frank stare. 'This is my brother, Michael.'

'We've met,' Michael said shortly.

'Yeah, on the ferry,' Mario replied as they locked eyes.

'You don't have your bag with you today, Mario?'

'In a safe place, Father,' the young man responded easily.

There was an awkward silence.

'You two really *do* know each other,' Anne said thoughtfully, and added lightly, 'Imagine, two enigmas on the one small island.'

'We were just going inside to meet the English couple,' Fiona explained. 'They want to talk to us about Gabriel.'

'Would you mind if we joined you?' Anne asked. 'We'd like to help.'

'Why, of course,' Fiona answered, and Michael's heart tightened at the hope in her voice.

'Here,' Anne said, disentangling her arm from Mario's, 'you can tow this one inside, Fi.' She extended her hand in Michael's direction. 'It's been a long time, Michael.'

He took her hand in his, tucking her arm under his own. As they followed Mario and Fiona, she slowed her pace until a gap grew between the couples.

'So who's the young Lothario, Anne?' Michael asked casually as they walked.

'Lothario?' she laughed. 'Oh, my God – he told me he was seventy and single and had a huge sheep farm in Virginia.'

Michael was reflecting that Mario probably did have some connection with Virginia when Anne stopped walking and leaned close.

'*Ni mar a shitear, biteur,*' she whispered, adding the translation out of courtesy – 'nothing is as it seems here, Michael.' She squeezed his arm. 'Walk carefully.'

Daphne and her husband seemed unfazed as

the group filed in. She was sitting, very upright, in
a hard, green-topped chair – a porcelain doll in the
mayhem of Mack's sitting room, Michael thought.
Her husband managed to look erect in one of the
priest's devouring armchairs. After Fiona had made
the introductions, Michael spoke directly to
Daphne.

'You have something to tell us about our
brother?'

She nodded, then paused to collect her
thoughts. He was impressed by the strength of
character in such a delicate face.

'Some weeks ago,' she began slowly, 'I went for
a walk. My husband can give you dates and times,
if you wish. He's rather good at that sort of thing.'
The tall man smiled faintly at the compliment. 'As
I turned the corner of the path near our home, a
young man appeared. I believe that man was… is
your brother.'

Her face tightened at the correction, but
Michael nodded encouragement. 'Can you
describe him, please, Mrs Bentham?'

'Daphne, please,' she said firmly. 'He was not as
tall as you are, Father, and his hair was not as red
as yours, Miss Flaherty; but, now that I see you
both, I have no doubt at all that he was your
brother. He seemed… agitated.'

Michael knew she meant 'afraid' and willed his
face to remain impassive.

'Before I could greet him, he just leapt over the wall, in the direction of the sea.'

Brother and sister nodded: Gabriel would always turn to the sea. Daphne's face seemed to wrestle with some memory, and her husband leaned forward, patting her hand gently. 'Continue, dear,' he said calmly, and she seemed to take courage from his touch. Michael was moved by the small intimacy. Grow old along with me, he thought, the best is yet to be.

'Shortly afterwards,' she continued, a trace of tension still riding her voice, 'I encountered a second man.' She stopped speaking, and the silence lengthened.

'Did you feel frightened?' Anne prompted gently.

'Oh yes, dear.' Daphne turned to her with relief and something like shame. 'Very frightened.'

'You had every reason to be,' Michael said firmly. 'Please go on.'

'This man was... huge. Not tall, but squat – almost square. He had an air of menace about him, and his voice...' She paused again and reached for a handkerchief. 'I do beg your pardon; I'm not at all a fanciful person. He asked if I had seen anyone on the path, and I lied. I never lie,' she added simply. 'Because of – well, other things. I could see he didn't believe me, but he just looked at me and passed on.'

'You mentioned his voice, Daphne.' Michael was surprised to hear Mario speaking. 'Did he have a particular accent?'

'Yes. It was a peculiar mix of American and Middle European, I would say. But the tone was so flat, almost like one of those talking machines – devoid of any feeling; quite unlike anything I have ever heard before.'

Her husband coughed gently into his hand and leaned forward. 'I made some enquiries among acquaintances here. My wife's description seems to fit a man called Skald. I understand he works for that American Major.'

He addressed himself directly to Michael, and so he was the only witness to his reaction. 'You know this man, Father?'

'I know him.'

Again, a pall of silence draped the room, punctuated only by the dead tock of the clock.

'I guess everyone could use a cup of tea at this point,' Mario suggested breezily, and they looked at him in astonishment. 'You just point me to the kitchen, Father Flaherty, and I'll set it up.'

'What?'

'Why don't you do that, Michael?' Anne added quickly. 'I'm sure Daphne and her husband would love a cup.'

Mario held the door of the kitchen for Michael

and closed it carefully behind him, pressing his back to it.

'You know this guy Skald.' It was a statement.

Michael regarded him steadily. 'Him I know; you I don't.'

'Whatever happened to faith, Father?'

'Not without reason, my son.'

'OK…' Mario exhaled slowly. 'Flaherty, Michael Joseph, Caucasian male, six three, two hundred and forty pounds, initial induction at Bronx Recruitment Centre 159. Boot camp in Georgia; top of the class, except in water. Headhunted to Fort Bragg in North Carolina. Proficient in demolition, extreme survival, hand-to-hand, various weapons. Special Forces in various theatres of war… Off-the-record rumours mention a special unit in South America, all members lost in combat…'

'Enough.'

'But the dead aren't dead,' Mario pressed on implacably. 'You lost your dog tags and found a dog collar. No,' he said sharply as Michael bristled. 'Between us we know maybe two dozen ways of killing each other, so let's not go there, OK?'

The moment of tension passed. Mario dropped his hands to his sides and spoke urgently. 'Michael, your brother is dead. Listen to me. I'm sorry, but he's dead. These guys don't leave witnesses, except one, a long time ago. *Capisce?*'

'Why are you here?'

'He thought you might ask that,' Mario sighed. 'Your file also says "recalcitrant". Jesus, what kind of word is that? Why not say "dumb-ass stubborn"? Same difference. Anyways, he said I was to say Genesis 12:4 to 12:7. Said you'd know what it meant.'

Michael sat down slowly in a kitchen chair. He recalled long hours of argument over Liam's death; his own sense of guilt, and Mal's repetition of the line, 'Am I my brother's keeper?' The mosaic began to form; angular pieces, seemingly incompatible, eased into congruence to form a whole.

PTS, they had called it in the place where Michael had been sent, afterwards. Post-Traumatic Stress – the great catch-all term that had replaced 'cowardice' and 'malingering', a term that hadn't come in time to save Sassoon or any of the legions of poets, farmers, servant boys and sons of gentlemen who had borne the badge of trench foot in Passchendaele and wandered back to the world 'changed, changed utterly'. 'The world' – that was what the hard drinkers on their forays out of Bragg to the town called it. Those sons of Iron Mike, that colossal metal icon of the

all-American hero which bestrode the base; hard
men who wore no insignia into combat but their
tattoos of a sword crossed with three bolts of
lightning. And there was lightning in their most
casual moves: at the pool table, around their wary
kids and tiptoeing wives. They were heroes, home
from the dirtiest wars, honed to kill and castrated
by normality.

'Normality,' the young doctor had intoned in
the bare room with one reflective glass wall.
'Normality is a country you can't go back to,
Michael.' Earnest Jewish kid, his skullcap bobbing
with sincerity. 'Not now, not ever. You must make
a new normality.' This had been his favourite
mantra, recited day in, day out, and always there
had been the one-way glass and the watcher
behind. Mal. The Board, that array of clean-cut
hard faces, had walked Michael through the jungle
to the killing zone time and time again, until his
hospital gown darkened with sweat and his
shoulder screamed and the young doctor
intervened They had asked Michael to wait
outside, and as he sat in the ante room with a bored
orderly, he heard another door open and someone
else enter the conclave to plead his case. Mal. He
had been brought back before the Sanhedrin:
'honourable discharge', 'pension rights', 'chance at
a new life'... It had seemed to comfort them,

except the young, skullcapped doctor, who couldn't meet his eyes. And when Michael had broached the idea of the seminary, who was it, who knew a guy, who knew a guy who knew the monsignor? Mal. Mal the watcher, Mal the advocate, Mal the fixer. My keeper, Michael thought bitterly. And so he had reached the prison, and the students in the university, and come home in the evening to Mal the ubiquitous. *Does Hanny know?* Somehow Michael was sure she didn't. Oh, Mal, he thought without humour, if Hanny ever hears of this, prepare for squalls.

'So,' he said, returning to the shabby kitchen and the young man who watched him quizzically from the door. 'So, Uncle Sam sent you?'

'Yeah.'

'I hope you won't take this amiss, Mario,' Michael said wearily, 'but you and what army?'

'I got you, hero.'

'No. That's all over,' Michael said flatly. 'I'm a priest.'

'Oh, that's right,' Mario said, his voice all mock-understanding. 'A priest. So run it by me, Father: when the black hats toddle off into the bright blue yonder, what will the priest do? Comfort the afflicted, raise the dead? How about calling Gabriel forth from the tomb? Boy, that would be a sight to—'

He never even saw Michael move. He felt the crushing pressure of the forearm across his throat, grinding him into the door, and the flat, lethal palm poised before his face to strike. And he saw the eyes.

'OK, OK,' he wheezed.

After the longest moment, he saw the madness dissolve and felt the air return to his lungs. 'Wow,' he said shakily. 'Gandhi gets vicious.'

Michael resumed his seat, his chest heaving. Mario shrugged his broad shoulders and came closer, dropping his voice to a whisper.

'You have choices to make, Michael. I respect that. What you don't have is time. It all goes down today. I need to know if—'

The knock on the door dispelled the moment. Father Mack opened the door tentatively, and Michael was shocked to see how quickly he had deteriorated.

'Michael?' he quavered. 'Oh, I'm sorry; you have company.' He started to close the door, but Michael took him gently by the arm into the hallway, closing the kitchen door behind him.

'Fi and I brought some people back, Mack. Is that OK?'

'Yes, yes, of course.'

'Would you like to meet them?'

'No, no. I thought I'd just lie down for a bit.'

'You OK?'

'Yes, yes. I have an anniversary mass later for…
Anyway, I'll just lie down.'

Michael looked at the grey face and trembling
hands. 'I'll walk up with you.'

'No, not at all. You have visitors.'

'They'll be fine.'

He put his arm around the old shoulders,
careful not to exert too much pressure. In the bedroom, he lowered Father Mack onto the bed and
slipped off the old man's shoes. Father Mack
seemed to be instantly asleep. Michael was turning
the door handle carefully when he spoke. It was no
more than a whisper.

'There is a time for everything,' he said.
'Source, boy?'

'Ecclesiastes,' Michael answered softly. 'One of
the books of the Wisdom literature in the Old
Testament. Probably a handbook for aspiring civil
servants.'

'Easy on the conjecture,' Father Mack
whispered, a faint smile on his face. 'A time to be
born and a time to die…' His voice was a slender
thread. 'A time to choose. You hear that, Michael?
Always a time to choose: to speak up or to be
silent, to act or to endure? With Gabriel,
Michael…' His voice was almost choked with
tears.

Michael knelt quickly at the side of the bed, covering the frail hand with his own. 'It's OK, Mack.'

But the old priest went on. 'I thought he would let it go. I begged him, Michael. I chose the lesser of two evils, as I saw it… and, for evil to thrive, it is enough that good men do nothing.'

Tenderly, Michael brushed the tears from Father Mack's face with the tips of his fingers. He rummaged in the core of his heart for some words of consolation, but he knew instinctively that Father Mack was beyond consoling, and he was relieved to discover that the old man had fallen asleep.

41

Due West of the Island

RAIMUNDO SCANNED THE sky for the tenth time in as many minutes. *There is nothing there to merit your attention*, his brain signalled wearily, but something in his belly overrode the cerebral cortex and he continued to twist his head skywards until his neck hurt. Fleecy cumulus, grazing over the skyscape; apart from that, nothing, except maybe that light band of haze that blurred the horizon. His belly gurgled.

'Belly', the old fishermen had called him when he was a boy, when he was all angular arms and legs and had no discernible belly. Belly, because he could feel trouble coming on the most innocent sea, could predict the sudden storms that pounced in from the China Sea to savage the outrigger boats. Belly, because, inexplicably, he had changed course one velvet night in the lee of Negros, hissing his crew to silence, just as Marcos' US-gifted gunboats converged on where his fishing smack had been. He remembered his belly gurgling ominously as his crew held their collective breath, the Kalashnikovs sweating oil in the hold below.

'Hey, Skipper, what you looking at?' Pepe's anxious face peered from the porthole of the mess, jaws masticating automatically, despite the concern in his voice.

'Nothing, brother, just the sky.'

Pepe's face digested this and devolved into relief. 'Radio call,' he said, as an afterthought.

'Call sign?'

'Golem.'

'Oh, shit and double shit,' Raimundo muttered, swinging away from the handrail, scooting his spare frame up the steps to the wheelhouse. He didn't duck in the doorway; Norwegian-built, it could have accommodated him with Pepe on his shoulders. Pepe gave an expansive, mocking bow towards the transmitter. Fucking dopehead, Raimundo fumed. *Hope to Christ he didn't talk on the open line.* The Major was serious about such things – no, not just serious: deadly.

'Mother to Golem. Over.'

Even the hiss of static couldn't soften the voice on the other end, and Raimundo held the receiver a little from his ear, nodding to Pepe to go outside.

'Mother, are you on scrambler? Over.'

Quickly, he checked that Pepe had pulled the switch. Happily, and miraculously, he had. 'Affirmative. Over.'

'Mother, children and baggage coming home this p.m. Is all in readiness? Over.'

Children? Holy Virgin, they're pulling out. Why? The question popped sweat between Raimundo's shoulders. He reached back to chafe the prickle with his hand. 'All OK. Over.'

'Over and out.' Click.

The deckhouse was suddenly airless. Raimundo made his way back to his original vantage point, breathing deeply, drinking the cool Atlantic air into his lungs until he shivered and felt clean again. His ship lay swinging lazily on her anchor in calm water, riding high above the plimsoll line on an empty hold. That would change later – the elderly crane would swing a cargo of dreams from the laden launch into the darkness below, and they would weigh anchor and be gone. The thought gave him no satisfaction. At that moment, he would have swapped his vessel for any of the flimsy craft that plied a faraway turquoise sea. 'This is the last time, Major,' he vowed. *The Major always said, 'This is the last time, kid; just one more trip.' The Major, always the Major, from way back.*

Raimundo's earliest memories were a mix of light and dark: playing with the other kids on the bridge outside the base, diving into the fetid canal water for coins tossed by the Joes, marines carrying the madness of war to the brothels of Olongapo; serving tables with the other scrawny kids as the Joes roared to the rhythm of a gyrating girl, herself a dream-seeker from any one of seven hundred islands, lured into being a 'hostess' for the troops. Young, way too young, he had known 'hostess' translated into 'whore'.

Each month, the whores – young dreamers hoping that some blue-eyed GI Joe would marry them and bring them home to Mom and Pop and happy ever after – sent money home, a place they could never go again with honour. But for Raimundo it was all an adventure – straddling the umbilical bridge between Subic and Olongapo, diving for dimes during the day, rolling the drunks in alleyways at night to the beat of 'shit-kicking music' from the bars. Smoking and drinking the dollars in a corrugated hut perched on bamboo legs above the bay, watching the ships go by. One

day, he thought through the haze, and his belly
growled. It was a small and lethal step to the white
powder that took you away, away from all of it.

The priest just blended with the scene – not
like the priests on base, with pips on one
shoulder, a cross on the other and an attitude
between. This one spoke Tagalog like a native.
This one called the girls by name; and, if they
wanted, he got them out. 'Little brother, the
powder is not your friend. It will steal your
strength. When you are ready, I am here.'

The centre clung to a scrub hill outside the
town; the site had been provided by the council,
under pressure from the missionaries and the
military. It was a safe place. Good food, no drugs;
rattan furniture, destined for homes in Boston and
Alabama, to weave from the sunlight of a quiet
workshop every day. And when the demons came,
the priest stepped from one writhing boy to
another, swabbing their faces clean of sweat and
snot with a soft towel, letting them scream the
horrors they had seen. 'It will pass, little brother.
One day soon, it will pass.'

Raimundo remembered the day he had looked
in the mirror for the spectre and had seen himself.

'You are well, Raimundo. Can you stay to help
the others?'

'Yes, Father.'

And then the Major had come, shadowed by the one who smelled of death. Raimundo's mother, Lybe, sat in the jeep outside, anxious and ashamed and wearing her good dress.

'Load him up,' the Major had said. The silent journey to the house on base; a room without a door or window.

And then, the girl. The girl had white hair, white as powder, and long, lean limbs tanned brown. 'Want to catch fish?'

'No.'

'Want to play ball?'

'Go away, little Yankee girl.' He had pushed her – a push that ended with him ass-over-backwards in the yard. 'Try that again, I'll break your goddamn arm.'

Deirdre. Deirdre who jumped from the bridge, a look of pure, mad joy in her eyes. Fearless Deirdre who punched above her weight when things got rough. Deirdre, who stood between her father and Raimundo, defying him to strike. The Major.

'Time you worked for your keep, boy.'

Dark nights in rough seas, waiting for a swimmer, cargo, men with wild eyes, dope, guns, whatever. Working harder than the older ones, fighting with a flick so he would be feared, respected. Swimming naked underwater to the gunboat, to set the charge, lungs bursting in the boiling sea. The Major.

'You have a talent, kid.'

'Please, sir, what is a talent?'

'Something I can use, kid.' Use and own.

'The police are searching for you, kid. Maybe they'll find your mama and papa. Take them back to the camp.'

Owned by the Major. The Major who knew everything.

'You go back to the priest and he is a dead man. You have only me. I want you to skipper my boat; you have a talent. You have two minutes.'

Two minutes had become two years, four years, more. I am a man and no man. *His man.*

'Never again,' Raimundo said vehemently, his breath clouding in the cold Atlantic air.

'What did you say?'

Pepe was at his elbow, with anxious eyes. Raimundo flicked his head to the horizon and his belly grumbled.

'Storm, Pepe,' he said, and Pepe was torn between fear of the storm and wonder at his skipper's smile.

42

The Fish Factory

SKALD NEVER SMILED, never had. 'Even when a baby,' his mother had boasted to her neighbours on the summer stoop; black crows in the swelter of a New York August, knitting, always knitting, never still.

'Never smile. Maybe a changeling, no?'

'A changeling, my boy? No. He is serious boy. No beer, no girls. He will be doctor.'

And the women had smiled, lancing their wool to knit and purl, knit and purl.

'You laugh now, but you will see.'

Skald did not smile now, even though satisfaction coursed buzzing through his veins. He had done a deed for the Major; another awaited, and then one more. After that, all would be complete. He would have fulfilled his orders, and purged himself of the lapse of leaving one man alive so many years before. He glanced up to the mirror from the basin, nodding to his reflection. He did not smile. Sometimes the Major smiled, but Skald had learned that was a sign of danger, a portent of death and destruction, and so he excused him.

The men were lounging on upturned crates, their task completed. They talked – always they talked – and smiled. The chill preceded Skald into the shed and stiffened them to stand, a few surreptitiously stubbing butts on the concrete floor. As one, they turned to face him, and again he felt a surge at their passivity. Few could look him in the face; their eyes were roaming randomly or downcast.

'Is the order loaded?'

'Yes,' replied O'Toole, the big man who fancied himself a leader.

Skald nodded. 'This is the last delivery. Today the factory closes.'

He watched their faces: shock flowing into disbelief, and then despair.

'What?' O'Toole, as expected. The seaman who

had sold the sea to pack dead fish in ice; O'Toole, who hurried to the pub in search of manhood, then wandered home to the new fridge and cooker and all the things that were replacements for his soul. 'What?'

'You heard.'

Skald could see the anger rising in the man, his face suffused, his fingers bloodless and coiling into fists. 'You wish to say something?' Instinctively Skald readied his body, hands flexed at his sides.

O'Toole wrestled with his anger, his face contorting as he tried to form the words. 'We worked hard,' he managed.

'You were paid.'

The man shook his head, as if slapped, and came back for more. 'But what will I... what will we do now?'

'Mr O'Toole, I think you mistake me for someone who gives a fuck.'

'You bloody monster—' O'Toole began, but Skald was in his face, his voice a dull club that battered remorselessly.

'You want me? I am here. But I am not a boy to be kicked behind a pub by a man who thinks drink is courage. You did what you were told, Mr O'Toole: carry a message, bring back a story, whatever. You were paid – well paid, Mr O'Toole – to be the Major's man.' Calmly, Skald took a roll of banknotes from his pocket and peeled a few bills free. 'A little tip from the Major,' he said. 'For services rendered.'

He dropped them on the floor, then turned his back on the broken man and walked away, in a final gesture of contempt.

Skald sat at the computer in the office overlooking the shed. From the fly-specked window, he had already seen O'Toole beached on an island of cold concrete, the other men ebbing away from him into animated groups. O'Toole sat on an upturned crate, staring vacantly at his hands, a marionette whose strings had been summarily sheared.

With great deliberation, Skald single-fingered 'ENDGAME' on the keyboard and read the scrolling file, his lips moving silently. Finally, he slotted home a disc and keyed it to wipe the computer clean. *Collect the dog tags, Sergeant. Count the bodies. No witnesses.* Savagely, he shoved that thought from his mind, swinging away from the desk to a metal box ensconced in the wall. The open door revealed a stubby red metal lever, angled at nine o'clock. Skald took two small silver keys from his pocket and twisted them simultaneously clockwise until they clicked, then snapped the lever up to noon before relocking the box.

Done, he thought. But not completely. The

typewriter ribbon that had eluded him flapped at his ease of mind, his sense of completeness. Now, at last, he knew where it was and who had it. The boy. *No loose ends, Sergeant.*

He eased open the side door to the outside fire escape and padded softly down the metal steps, counting in his head to avoid the squeaking number seven. Then a ground-eating stride brought him to where he had been earlier in the day. The shadows of the rocks had moved and lengthened, and he burrowed into their dark.

The boy was there. Tired of flight, he was folded into a crouch, perched above a rock pool in the lee of the wreck. Skald's eye marked the scribble of ribbon, black against the humped green of the weed around the boy's feet.

He froze. The boy's head had jerked up as if he was surfacing from a smothering dream; he turned to the land, halting momentarily on the rock pile before returning to his meditation. Skald relaxed, checking his clothing for loosened zips, spare coins, anything that might snag or jingle and betray him to his prey. Satisfied, he eased his right hand to his trouser pocket and brought something out. His broad, flat thumb pressed down. The steel blade sprang to attention before his eyes.

Now.

43

The Cliff Path

MATTHEW O'DOWD, FOR once without his doppelgänger, folded his soutane and surplice, bedding them carefully in the small battered suitcase his mother had given the twins when they had started as altar boys. 'A plastic bag just isn't right,' she had said. Not everybody – particularly not some of the bigger boys at school – had shared her pride in her boys flanking Father Mack at mass. The twins had turned up in the sacristy a few times with identical puffed eyes and cracked lips, until Father Mack had rounded on them.

'Today, boys,' he had said sternly, 'is the Feast of

All Saints, and I celebrated it with two martyrs. 'Can I ask who is the perpetrat— who's doing this to ye?'

Silence.

'Fair enough. *Omertà* is a long-standing Island tradition.' He had smiled slightly. 'Listen to me now,' he had said in his most commanding voice, stripping and folding his vestments as he talked. 'Jesus had four Evangelists. Who were they?'

'Matthew, Mark, Luke and John,' the twins chorused dutifully.

'Correct,' Father Mack replied, coiling the cincture around his fist. 'John was the beloved disciple, because he was young and a dreamer. Luke was a handy man to have around, because he was a doctor; if anyone got hurt, he'd fix them up in jig-time. But the other two were different. Matthew was a tax collector,' he had said darkly. Noting their lack of interest, he'd put it in context: 'Like the excise man.' Immediately, both boys had nodded their understanding. Excise men were not held in high regard on the Island, where a degree of smuggling traditionally supplemented family incomes. 'His job was taking money from people, hard-earned money. Did they like that?'

'No, Father.'

'Did they like him?'

'No, Father.'

'And, of course, Matthew and Mark were small men. Did I mention that?'

'No, Father.'

'And the other fellas were huge. But Matthew and Mark had a secret weapon.'

'What was that, Father?'

'They might lose a fight,' Father Mack said triumphantly, 'but they were never beaten. Are you with me, boys?'

'No, Father.'

'All right, all right, listen to me now. If they were up against a bigger fella, they would take a box in the eye, get up and lay a kick on him, or run around and punch him behind the knee. Every time they got hit, they bounced back and did some damage.'

The boys had been mesmerised, watching the old priest duck and jab in the centre of the sacristy floor.

'And do ye know what happened, boys?'

'They got slaughtered, Father,' they had chorused promptly.

Father Mack had suddenly been convulsed with a fit of coughing.

'No, no, boys. They were *dreaded*,' he had pronounced darkly, when he had recovered his breath. 'How can you beat men who won't lie down, who keep snapping at you from all angles?

And the crowd would begin to change its tune.
"Fight someone your own size," they'd shout at the
big fella. And by that time the big fella wouldn't
know where the next kick would come from, and
he'd walk away and never bother them again. Are
ye with me now, boys?'

'Yes, Father,' the twins had said loudly, sliding
down from the bench. 'We'll be off, so, Father.'

'Away with ye, then, desperadoes,' he'd called
cheerfully in benediction. And it had worked.

Matthew O'Dowd was proud to be an altar
boy. It meant that he was released from school
without question to attend church services and
could return late without excuses. Like today, he
thought contentedly. The old wreck lured his
attention, as always – a rusting mystery, a catalyst
for all sorts of imaginings. He was well into his
reverie when he noticed the boy.

The boy was another mystery, and a source of
envy. He didn't go to school. 'It isn't right,' the
twins' mammy always said, 'a boy running wild like
that. What can Kate Quinn be thinking?'

'Now, now,' their father would counter, mellow
after a night in Finnegan's, 'isn't the child a *duine le
Dia*.'

Matthew knew the words meant 'a person with
God', but he wasn't sure what that said about the
boy. Mammy had filled the gap, pressing on over

the interruption. 'He's simple in the head, man; he should be away where they could manage him – in a special school, like.'

'Away from the Island?' their father had asked incredulously. 'Away, over there?' He'd stabbed his pipe stem dismissively in the general direction of Ireland. 'Lumped in with children like himself – and for what? So he can learn how to count money and cross the road and go to the shop. Would anyone swap this island for that, Mary O'Dowd? Is that what we'd want for one of our own, woman?' He had puffed at his pipe, making the kitchen blue with indignation.

'Well, still,' the twins' mother had repeated, 'it isn't right', and Matthew had heard the hesitation in her voice.

One of the bigger boys at school had called the boy a name once, within earshot of Father Mack, and had got a stinging ear of his own for his pains. 'On this island we respect God's angels,' the priest had thundered.

Matthew watched the angel watching the rock pools, and time passed. The thought of Miss Flaherty's sharp tongue was tugging his head towards the path when he saw the man. Something in the stillness of him shrivelled Matthew's heart. He jerked his eyes back to the boy, willing him to look up; and, miraculously, he did, scanning, his eyes passing over the spot where the man was lurking. Then he turned back to the pool. *No,* Matthew wanted to shout. *No, by the rocks, look!* But his fear strangled the voice in his throat. 'It isn't right,' Mammy always said, and Matthew O'Dowd sensed deep down in his fluttering chest that something about the scene was wrong.

The man moved in such a way that Matthew started back and raced away.

44

The Island

ROSE O'TOOLE'S EYES welled up with relief when Kate opened the door. 'Nurse,' she said, trying to control the fear in her voice for the sake of the children, 'I think it's time.'

Kate placed her bag on the kitchen table, shrugging her coat to the back of a chair. 'Sheila,' she said firmly to the eldest girl, 'you've done a great job minding Mammy. Now, will you take the little ones outside for a while so we can chat?' The girl reddened at the compliment, her expression struggling between pleasure at the praise and annoyance at her exclusion. She did as she was bid, clucking the little brood to the garden outside.

'How do you feel, Rose?'

'I... I think there's something wrong, Nurse.'

Kate rinsed her hands in the sink, huffed on the stethoscope and rubbed it on her blouse for warmth before applying it to Rose's distended abdomen. Rose scanned the nurse's face for signs of unease but failed to find anything there except quiet strength. She felt her panic loosen under the sure touch of Kate's hands.

'And is himself at work?' Kate asked casually, folding the stethoscope back into the bag.

'He is, Nurse. There's a big order going out today. He said he'd be late home.'

'Right, then; I'll just check on the young ones. I won't be a minute.'

Stepping outside, Kate was struck by the beauty of Sheila's hair, streaming in the wind – not as hectic as Fiona's, but a paler, softer gold. Automatically, she checked the sea and noted how the white horsemen had marshalled out there even since her arrival. 'Sheila, away with you, love, to the factory, and bring your father home.'

The young girl started like a colt and was off with the same alacrity.

'Are you Tom?' Kate asked the bigger of the boys.

'I am.'

'Go to the priest's house and ask him to send someone.'

The boy nodded with self-importance and fright, and was over the wall before Kate turned to the little ones.

'Now what would the nurse have in her bag for good children?'

The children followed her into the kitchen, their noses running from the heat of the range. Colouring books and assorted markers from Kate's bag soon absorbed them, so they were unperturbed when she returned to their mother.

'The baby will need help, Rose,' she said simply. 'We'll manage fine between us. Let's get you to the bed now.'

A window rattled angrily as Michael made his way back down the stairs from Father Mack's room. In his absence, Mario had done the honours with the tea. Fiona and the English couple formed a triangle, with Daphne as focal point, while Mario and Anne sat in companionable silence. Michael was standing in the doorway, reflecting on the normality of the scene, when the banging started at the front door. He was about to close the parlour door behind him, but Mario eased through; he took up a position in a corner of the hallway, where the open door would conceal him, and nodded to Michael to open the door.

The three figures were pushed into the hallway by the force of the wind, and Michael instinctively caught Deirdre Devane in his arms. Mario quickly closed the door behind them and put his back to it, alertness radiating from him.

Deirdre was the first to break the sudden silence. 'Father Flaherty, we just can't go on meeting like this,' she said mischievously.

Abashed, Michael stepped back and surveyed the others. 'You know Lybe,' Deirdre continued, more seriously, 'and this is her husband Fernando. It probably sounds too Hollywood for words, but we came for sanctuary.'

'You're welcome. Please come inside,' Michael replied.

Lybe and Fernando smiled with relief. Deirdre turned to Mario. 'And who might you...?' Her voice faltered as he stepped into the light. 'I should have known,' she said tersely. 'It was only a matter of time.'

'Ma'am?'

'I'm an army brat, soldier. I can smell one of you guys at fifty paces.'

As she went into the parlour, Mario shot Michael a look behind her back. 'You can really pick them, Father,' he whispered slyly.

Michael followed them into the parlour and

waited while the new arrivals were introduced and made welcome.

'Devane is leaving,' he said abruptly.

Surprise registered on every face except one.

'Your father is leaving, Deirdre. Isn't that so?'

'Yes.'

'Where will he go?'

'He'll think and plan for number one first, he always has. He'll have a boat or a chopper stashed away somewhere on call.'

'And what of the others?'

'Skald he'll send to the ship with the drugs. D'Arcy is surplus to requirements. Oh, and there's one other thing. He's a lousy loser. If he can't win he'll wreck the game.'

'What are you saying?'

'I'm saying he'll do as much damage as possible. He doesn't like to leave traces or witnesses. Let him go to hell.'

'I can't do that.'

For a moment, Michael's inner conflict surfaced in his tone, and two of the group stood upright: Fiona, her face full of hesitation, and Mario, taut-bodied and ready for orders. Someone banged at the outer door. 'It's a child, Michael,' Anne said hurriedly.

The wind lifted the boy into the lighted hallway, his wind-flattened hair dark with sweat, his breath rasping as he tried to speak. Kneeling, Michael placed the flat of his palm to the boy's chest. 'Easy, *a mhic*,' he said gently. 'Easy, easy,' as the pulsing beneath his hand slowed to the rhythm of his voice.

'The baby, Father,' the boy stuttered. 'Nurse said come.'

His duty done, he began to cry. Michael swept him into his arms. 'Whose son are you, boy?'

'O'Toole's,' the boy managed, before his tears consumed him.

'Fi, he's soaked through. Put him to the fire.'

Automatically, his sister took the burden, crooning comfort.

'Mario, Mr Bentham – a word, please.' The command in Michael's voice straightened the old soldier.

'Dear?' Daphne said uncertainly.

'Nothing to worry about, my love. Drink your tea.' The light in Ron Bentham's eye did nothing to dampen his wife's anxiety.

The three men huddled in the hallway, the wind beneath the door poking cold fingers at their legs.

'He's leaving,' Michael said, keeping his voice just above a whisper. It was a flat statement, inviting no discussion, and the others nodded. 'And he won't go quietly. Mario, go to the headland and watch the ship. I take it you have friends offshore so take your bag and keep them informed.'

He turned to Ron Bentham. 'Which branch of the armed forces did you serve in?'

'Bomb disposal,' Ron answered promptly, surprised to find his spine stiffening.

'I'd be obliged if you could monitor the situation at the Major's house. Mario, give him a headset.'

'Yes, sir,' Mario smiled.

Michael's face did not lighten. 'I'll meet you at the headland later. Listen up, both of you,' he added as they turned to go. 'No engagement, understood? There's been enough killing.'

They nodded, but he was already through the door and into the howling wind.

45

The Fish Factory

THE WIND HAD driven the men to find shelter in the factory, leaving O'Toole alone outside, unaware of the buffeting wind, swaying his body.

'Is your man gone?' someone asked.

'Who?'

'The Yank, for Jaysus' sake.'

'I think so.'

'Good.' A match flared, and the sweet tobacco smoke swirled crazily in the draught beneath the double doors.

'Where's Leo?'

'Skiving off, where else?'

'We'd better find him and tell him.'

'Ah, let him sleep. He'll know soon enough.'

'Are you coming?'

Fitz and Doyle detached themselves from the gloom of the group, relieved to have something to do. Gradually they eliminated all the likely hiding places until they met before the no-entry area.

'He was on the forklift.'

Tentatively they stepped inside, scanning the broken boxes and the empty cab.

'He had an accident, surely. Is he under it?'

'No. You go left, OK? Call out if you find the daft hoor.'

Fitz felt sick. The stench of fish and diesel, usually imperceptible, seemed enhanced by the acid of disappointment in his stomach. He kicked the litter of boxes from his path. 'Where are you hiding, you *amadán*? I'll put my boot in—'

'Fitz.'

Something in his companion's voice congealed Fitz's blood so that he stood immobile.

'Fitz – Fitz…'

'I'm coming,' he blurted, shaking off his lethargy, trying to calm the hysteria in the voice that kept calling, 'Fitz, Fitz, Fitz…'

He found Doyle bent forward on his knees, his forehead touching the cool-room wall. Above his head, the small observation window radiated a glow of neon from within. When Doyle turned, his face made Fitz's stride falter.

'What is it?'

'Fitz.'

'What in the name of—'

Doyle gestured weakly to the window, flapping his palm at it as if trying to repel something. Reluctantly, Fitz turned and looked inside. He struggled with his breath. His tears blurred the sight of the figure, seemingly carved from marble, hanging by its collar from a metal hook.

'Oh, Leo,' he gasped. 'Oh, poor lad – poor lad.'

He was oblivious to Doyle's departure and the subsequent shouting. Placing the tips of his fingers to the ghostly glass, he began to pray. 'Eternal rest grant unto him, O Lord, and may perpetual light shine upon him…'

By the time he had concluded the short prayer, the others were jostling to view the murdered man. The room hummed with their fury.

46

The Island

MICHAEL HAD NO time to anticipate the impact of their meeting; his concentration was focused on making good time over the uneven path. He was dimly aware of the white horses pounding lines from the horizon. At the door, he readied himself before entering, but to no avail: the sight of Kate struck him like a blow, so that he stood rooted, his hand still holding the door handle in a drowning grip. She had her back to him, running water in the kitchen sink, scrubbing her hands vigorously with a small brush. Perhaps it was the influx of cold air that straightened her.

She turned, her streaming hands held up before her.

Always, in his dreams, the sleeping or waking dreams, her eyes had been blank. He could project her hair, the pallor of her skin, the shape of her neck, her profile against firelight; but never the eyes. He dreaded their revelation, but the eyes that looked into his revealed a soul without bitterness. There was pain and exhaustion, but not hate.

'Michael,' she said simply, 'I need your help.'

Dumbly he nodded.

'The baby is the wrong way round,' she explained, as if to a child. 'I think I can manage if you could hold Rose for me.'

Again, he nodded, and she led him into the bedroom.

Rose O'Toole's eyes widened even more when she saw him. 'Father...' she began, modesty and fear warring on her face.

'Ah, Rose Clancy,' Michael said easily, maintaining eye contact while stepping closer to the bed.

'You remember my maiden name?'

'Indeed I do, Rose, and I remember the hair colour you had that time in school.'

'Ah, Michael, don't be reminding me – that damned sachet.'

Kate moved between them. 'For the love of

God, you two, could we leave Memory Lane and get this baby into the world?'

Before the fear could reclaim Rose's face, Michael slipped his arm under her shoulders, holding her right hand in a firm grip.

'Look here to me, Rose Clancy,' he said softly, 'and breathe with me.'

Lena lifted her head and listened. She padded to the office door and put her ear to the surface. Nothing but the keening wind.

'They've gone away, Mother,' she whispered, in a small voice breathy with excitement.

Good. Bloody shower of wasters, morning and night, chasing whatever they can get for nothing. Come on over here, love, and sing me a little song.

Lena moved across to the mirror on the dresser, smiling at the woman who smiled back. 'What'll I sing, Mother?'

Sing 'Shortening Bread'. I do love that one.

'Mammy's little baby loves...' she began, and was pleased to see her mother mouth the words along with her.

Mammy's having her baby and there's something wrong, Sheila thought as she timed the snapping gate with the surety of experience, catching it on the in-swing and trapping it with her hip while she tugged at her father. Another child might have run for help to a neighbour when confronted with the dazed man on the upturned crate, but Sheila was made of sterner stuff. Anyway, she was damned if he would be the talk of Finnegan's. The shouting, milling men had frightened her, but she had held his hand firmly, pressing her mouth to his ear.

'We'll be away home now, Daddy.'

Docilely, the big man had stumbled home behind his daughter. The sight of the young priest washing his hands at the kitchen sink was more than he could comprehend; he stood staring until Sheila pressed him into the chair.

'I'll see to the small ones,' she said, and left them.

Michael moved to the chair before O'Toole and sat in silence, waiting for his eyes to engage.

'What's happening in the factory?' he asked quietly.

O'Toole's mouth worked before the word emerged. 'Finished.'

'And the Americans?'

Again, the spasms racked his face. 'Gone.'

'Gone where?'

'Don't know.'

Michael stretched across and slapped him, open-palmed. O'Toole rocked back in the chair and struggled to right himself. The dullness had gone from his eyes. 'You dare to hit me in my own home? Priest or not, I'll—'

'You'll what, Mr O'Toole?' Michael grabbed the front of the man's coat and dragged him across the table. 'Look closely, man. This is not the boy behind the pub, and you have no other drunks to cheer you on. Now answer me: where are they?'

'I don't know.' Michael hit him again. O'Toole's head rolled on his shoulders with the force of the blow.

'Michael!' Kate was behind him, wrapping her arms around him and holding his wrists. 'What in God's name are you doing?'

'This man beat my brother. Him and other vermin like him.'

She leaned into his face. 'Michael, look at me – look at me!'

With enormous effort, he turned his gaze from O'Toole.

'Let him go, Michael, please. His child is born and Rose needs him. Please, Michael.'

For a moment, Michael's grip tightened on O'Toole, raising him from the chair. Then he opened his hands and the man slumped back.

'Go in to your wife,' Kate told him hurriedly, and, slack-limbed, he left the room. Then she sat in the vacant chair and rested her elbows on the table, watching the pallor of Michael's face return to something less cadaverous.

'She had a boy,' she said gently. 'She said she'll call him Michael.'

'No.'

'What?'

'No.' He looked up. 'Please tell her I thank her, but I would be grateful if she called him Gabriel. For my brother,' he added with difficulty.

Her hand moved instinctively towards his face and stopped short. She brought it back to her own face.

'Kate.'

She shook her head fiercely. 'You went away, Michael.'

'I had to go.'

'Yes. But you left me here.'

Michael's face contorted in pain. 'Kate, I wrote. I asked you to come. I sent the fare. You didn't answer – never, not even to say no. And then Father Mack wrote to say you... you were married...'

She gazed at the agony in his eyes, and knew. He had sent his letters to the same person she had entrusted with her own. She was about to speak, but she stopped, bowing her head over the table, chasing a strand of blue-black hair from her eyes with a tired hand. He has so little left, she thought. I'll not take it from him.

'Excuse me, Nurse.' The girl spoke shyly from the door to the parlour, her troubled eyes going from one to the other.

Kate said quietly, never taking her eyes from the bent head before her, 'Your Mammy has a new baby to show you, Sheila.'

Something in her voice and the sit of her made Sheila wrap her arms across her barely budding breasts. 'Nurse,' she said again, 'there's a boy running on the path.'

Kate was up and out the door before Michael was upright. He caught up with her at the gate.

'It's one of the O'Dowds,' he said.

Kate's face was stark with apprehension. The boy was running blind when Michael caught him. He struggled frantically for a moment, his fists flailing at Michael's shoulders.

'The Yank's after him,' he gasped.

'After who?' Michael asked, cupping Matthew's face close to his ear.

'The boy, Father. The boy beyond in the wreck,' Matthew whispered, his eyes focusing on the nurse behind them.

47

The Wreck

SKALD HAD PACED the wreck from stem to stern and back again, making no attempt to muffle his steps, but the boy did not panic into flight.

'Softly, softly, catchee monkee,' Skald said aloud. He slipped off his shoes and socks. The open-hatched hold gaped darkly, a flight of rusting steps descending to deeper dark, and the shadows swallowed his descending shape.

Michael was hardly aware of the wind in his ears. Instinctively, his body tacked to the gusts as his feet pounded the path over the headland. It was only when he topped the crest that he was enveloped in the thunder of the sea, which drowned the rasp of his own breath. The wreck nestled on the flat rocks beneath, ruddy and remote. Out beyond, white foam vaulted to escape a bilious green sky. For a moment, Michael's legs buckled and he hunkered down, cradling his head in his hands. Familiar nightmares surged up to claim his mind.

Slowly, he stood upright and began to run again, loping down the cliff path, focusing his mind to rid it of sea and sky and all that might distract him from the task at hand. He was a hunter again.

In a pool of comparative quiet under the bulk of the dead ship, he pressed his face to the metal skin and closed his eyes to boost his hearing. A faint protest of metal under pressure, filtering through the hull and the ambient sound, stiffened him upright.

As he swung up to the canted deck, his breath caught in his throat. The shoes, neatly aligned, were tokens of madness and deadly intent. There was no ingress to the ship other than the gaping hatch. With a savage fling, Michael arced the shoes high out over the rotted handrail, smiling grimly as the wind pummeled them across the rocky plateau.

The boy had no vocabulary of prow or stern, fore or aft, but he knew exactly where the man was. This forlorn hulk was his sanctuary, and those half-lit catacombs, hazardous with jagged rusted spurs and outcrops, had mapped themselves into his mind, so that he knew instinctively where the wind found access in the battered hull. And where the man was now – paused on the long, latticed gangway, directly overhead.

The boy stood submerged in water to his chin, the man's vague shape mediated through the metal mesh above. Something in the man's tone signalled beast, a hunter capable of taking prey without thought. The boy wrapped his arms around his thin frame and then relaxed. The man was beast, and not beast: he had not sensed the boy's fear. His eyes shifted sideways as the shape floated off from where he was hiding and stopped further along the walkway. *Why?*

Someone else had reached the bottom of the ladder from the hatch – someone who had planted his foot in the water that puddled there and instinctively withdrawn it, making that faint sucking sound. The beast moved farther into the shadows and became still. The boy sniffed tentatively, filtering out the all-pervasive stink of stagnant sea water laced with rust and gasoline. He found the beast-smell, the high, salty tang of a creature coiled.

Michael swung his head from left to right until shapes began to form around him. He moved slowly, inching a foot before him, his weight always on the back foot, all the while straining his ears. Nothing. Then a hand tightened on his ankle.

Always, in times of crisis, he had turned to the cold, cerebral part of himself for balance. Now, even as his nerve endings flashed panic through his system, that detached command centre overrode the adrenaline kick to his reflexes. *No threat. No threat.* Head buzzing, he bent cautiously and peered under the walkway. The boy was featureless in the gloom, but his hands wove a message of the dark: *Stop. Danger. There.* Cautiously, Michael turned his head in the direction indicated; but whatever light existed where he now stood was absent farther along. Again, he looked down at the boy and saw him gesture. *Come.*

Skald waited. Standing in the dark alcove, he
sucked the shadow from the space and wrapped it
round him, drawing long, slow draughts until it
suffused him. He closed his eyes, leaned his back
to the bulkhead and listened. A few moments
before, he had paused on the walkway, puzzled. A
fox will run a stone wall, a hare circle in its own
track, a man will run in water, but there is still a
faint scent afterwards, some indentations at the
ingress and egress points, something; but the boy
had disappeared from his radar. Even the dark
ferrets of taunt and threat he had whispered loose
in the warren of the ship's hold had brought no
panicked flight, not even a twitch. And yet he knew
the boy was here.

A slight tremor through the bulkhead from
above tingled in his shoulder. Old ships complain,
he thought. No. It was the sound a handrail makes
when it takes someone's weight. It flexes, and the
hunter hears.

Skald scanned the dark passageway, tensing as
the shadows distilled into a form – a form that
diminished and disappeared. He began to slide,
instinctively flexing his feet for silence, his left
hand splayed before him, his right hand curved
behind, the scorpion-sting extending from his fist.

The cold of the water shocked Michael, and he struggled to suppress a gasp. Even more shocking was the texture of oil and detritus sliming his skin. He forced himself lower until the water greased his chin, focusing on the dark mass of the boy's head before him. He felt a hand find his hair, pressing him gently down. The boy submerged.

Skald halted. This was the spot, his senses told him, as if his body was occupying a space recently warmed by another. Slowly, he reversed his stance, left hand moving behind for balance, the knife-hand swinging up and out, until, like some malevolent divining rod, it tilted down.

The voice surfaced immediately, his brother's terrible, despairing voice wailing over the roar of water in his ears, 'Michael, Michael.' Unbidden, his hand stretched out and grasped another hand, a small hand that trembled in his grasp until the voice subsided. Michael opened his eyes, sensing the eyes of the boy on him.

The rat was no more than a sinuous blur, weaving through the water above their clasping hands.

Skald struck.

Something flexed in the shadows beneath him, and the blade darted. A quiver travelled from the shaft to his wrist, and instinctively he jerked back. The thrashing rat, pierced through the hind-quarters, arched and struck. Skald stumbled back, clanging on the walkway, slamming his arm against the bulkhead.

The boy tugged upwards and they emerged, exhaling silently, drawing in the fetid air gratefully. The boy tugged again and Michael followed his angel unhesitatingly through the dark. He could hear the frantic thrashing behind him fading as he tracked the boy through a labyrinth of darkness. The light stung his eyes as he stepped through a hole in the hull. The boy was already moving, beckoning him to make silent haste, flowing effortlessly around boulders and through fissures until he suddenly disappeared.

Tentatively Michael stepped into the shadowed defile where he had last seen the boy, and waited. From a screen of hanging weed on the face of the cliff, a hand emerged, the fingers curling into invi-tation. He stepped warily into the dark beyond. Slowly, his eyes adjusted to the greenish gloom and the boy materialised, sitting solemnly on a boulder glinting with quartz. Like a photographic plate, the cave rose into detail. All around the dripping wall, nestling in niches, were the boy's treasures: shells; stones; a glass float, truant from some fishing boat; a pencil stub; a rough-carved wooden dolphin arcing out of a wooden sea.

Standing in his sodden shoes, Michael remembered. *This was where we came.*

She was sitting on the wall at the bend beyond Father Mack's. 'Is this yoke any good?'

'What? Oh, *The Great Gatsby.* Yeah – well, it's good enough, I suppose.'

'Good enough for what?'

His explanation took the length of the beach.

Another day. 'What? It's a conch. I can't hear anything, Michael.'

It was like someone else's name in her mouth, and he tugged the hair on the crown of his head to stop himself floating away. 'Let me hold it for you, Kate. Now do you hear it?'

She listened as the world wheeled for the longest time.

'Yes.'

The stile was sturdy and she was an Island girl, yet she steadied herself on his shoulder, her palm burning through his shirt, filling his chest with smoke. And there was that day on the headland, when she had turned from the sea to face him, the wind at her back, her eyes playing hide-and-seek with her flying hair.

'Will we step off the edge of the world, Michael Flaherty?' she asked, and, without waiting for an answer, took his hand. They stepped through the heather to the hidden flue and climbed down to the dark, to this place. Their place. He had waited for the dark to lighten, but it didn't, because she stood before him, so close her breath was moist-warm on his face.

Michael closed his eyes, but the darkness plunged him into nightmare.

He had come to consciousness in the battling currach, the dull throb in his skull punctuating the screaming gale. 'Liam?' He started to rise, but something weighed him to the ribbed floor. Liam. His brother's body rocked fitfully with the rhythm of the boat. 'Lost you, lost you, Liam. Sorry,' he whispered, smoothing the salt-stiffened hair from the pallid forehead. The sea towered over them, slavering slabs of green water. The faces of the men at the oars were flayed fleshless, masks of rigid concentration, their bodies bowing to the oars. One man's lips moved ceaselessly, perhaps in prayer, his words whipping away in the madness. Michael sat in the belly of the boat, his legs braced against the cross-struts, his brother's body cradled in his lap; Liam's face wore a lost small-boy expression, his head lolling with the sway of the boat as if in disbelief. A white-veined wall of water bore them up, and Michael glimpsed the shore. Strong arms took the dead boy beyond the thwarted waves, the pool of islanders parting before them so that they could lay him at the feet of his father. The ululations of the keening women threatened the seams of Michael's skull so that he sank to his knees. The Master's large hand stroked the dead boy's face, trying to erase the puzzlement in his son's eyes. 'I'm sorry, Eileen,' he repeated over and over in a strangled voice. 'I lost Liam, our boy.' Then his eyes rose and fastened on Michael's. He saw them waver from relief to loss before they dropped guiltily to the corpse again.

I am dead too, Dada, he thought. I am dead too. And, ghost that he was, he stumbled unseeing and unseen from the murmur of their prayers. He was oblivious to the gale that buffeted and the salt-sting of the spray and the numbness that spread through him; he wanted only to be away. And here, where the sea was just an echo, he fell to the sandy floor, cold beyond feeling. This was where he had come and lain down, because the dead should lie down. He closed his eyes, and when his brother's face surfaced behind his eyelids, his own scream shattered him awake. His eyes, gummed shut with salt, would not open, and he spasmed with cold and fear.

'Michael.' Someone clasped his head in steady hands, thumbing his eyelids clear. 'Kate,' he cried,

his rattling teeth tearing her name to rags. 'Kate.'
Her fierce gaze held his as she peeled him out of
the sea-drowned clothes and wrapped him in a
sleeping bag. 'Cold, Kate, so cold.'

'Michael, Michael, wake up. Don't sleep.' She
prised his eyes open, slapping his cheeks.
'Michael.'

'Dead, Kate.'

'No,' she shouted. 'I won't lose you.'

Frantically, she stripped and climbed into the
sleeping bag, her warmth an agony to his frozen
skin. He remembered his limbs on fire, the
urgency of her mouth on his, and how he had been
lost in her.

Her face dissolved into that of the boy, the boy
with the sallow skin and solemn oval face. The boy,
holding a tattered manila envelope in one hand
and a coil of black ribbon in the other.

'Gabriel?' Michael breathed.

The boy's face contorted with effort, his lips
stretching as his tongue rose to the roof of his
mouth. 'Liam,' he said with infinite slowness, in a
small voice rusty with disuse. 'My name is Liam.'

Skald held the dead rat suspended by its tail. His
right forearm flamed. He could feel slick blood

trickle down his fist to the blade. They were gone. Reflexively, he smashed the rat against the bulkhead one last time and dropped it to the floor.

Outside, on the wind-raked rocks, he plunged his arm into a rock pool. He held it there for an agonising minute, gritting his teeth; then he ripped his shirtsleeve and formed a rough bandage around the wound. He broke into a steady trot, a mantra keeping time in his mind. 'Some men need killing twice.' Failure burned like acid in his gut. Warily, he circled the factory, but it was deserted, the door of the large shed banging disconsolately in the wind.

Quinn was waiting at the appointed place, shifting from one foot to the other, a circle of cigarette stubs testimony to his unease. 'God, man, you took your bloody time.'

'Quiet.'

The single word smacked him into wary silence. Skald gestured and Quinn shambled after him, breathing heavily at the unaccustomed exertion, until they came to the slipway.

'You can pilot this boat?'

'Jaysus,' Quinn breathed, all else forgotten as he ran his eyes over the sleek craft. 'With one hand behind my back and one eye closed.'

'Do it.'

48

The Devil's Finger

AS THEY CLEARED the shelter of the slip, the sea mounted and battered the craft so that Skald clung to the handrail in the stern, feet splayed for balance. Quinn stood at the wheel behind the glass window, his smile revealed with every swish of the wipers, nosing her out to the mouth of the harbour. Then Skald felt the sudden loss of thrust as the boat wallowed. He edged to the wheelhouse and wrenched the door open. 'What?'

'Look out there, man.' Quinn gestured.

Skald pressed his face to the glass. A line of black shapes stretched in a dotted line a few hundred yards before them, stitching the harbour mouth closed.

'Bastards,' Quinn growled. 'A bloody blockade.'

'Full speed ahead, Mr Quinn,' Skald said angrily, his breath dulling the glass before him.

'Are you mad, man?'

Skald's gun quivered an inch from Quinn's nose. 'Full speed, Mr Quinn,' he spat, and Quinn's belly turned queasy at the madness in his eyes.

'They'll...' His voice steadied. 'They'll have nets spread between them under the water. We can break through all right, but they'll foul the propellers.'

For a moment the madness flared white-hot, and involuntarily Quinn closed his eyes. When he opened them, the rage had retreated, the soldier returned.

'Another way?'

'Only one, over there.'

Skald swung his gaze to the Devil's Finger and the sliver of white between the rocks and the headland. Quinn felt a surge of satisfaction as a flicker of indecision registered in the awful eyes, but he kept his expression neutral.

'You can do this?'

'I can. You stand in the prow and signal left or right.' A note of authority had crept into Quinn's voice, and Skald looked at him quizzically. 'You can start by taking that fucking gun out of my face so I can see where I'm going.'

The trigger finger tightened, and the huge hole of the gun barrel gaped to devour him. Then, abruptly, Skald swung it away.

'Do it,' he muttered.

Quinn waited for the door to bang behind him before he buckled at the wheel. Finally, he dragged himself upright, a terrible exultation in his eyes.

'Watch this, boys,' he shouted at the currachs in the distance. 'Watch this and remember.'

Savagely, he swung the wheel, slamming the engines to full thrust. The boat bucked wildly, a thoroughbred under rough rein. 'C'mon, you bloody bitch,' he screamed, straining with every ounce of strength, sweat running in his eyes like spray. Slowly, the boat submitted to his will, arrowing for the maelstrom ahead.

Skald braced in the prow like some blunt figurehead. Quinn shook his head fiercely to clear his vision. He rolled on the balls of his feet, twitching the wheel, his shouting muted to a whisper as the boom of the water shook the cabin. 'Holy Mary, Mother of God; Holy Mary, Mother of God,' the mantra rasped from his mouth as the channel boiled up before them.

Skald's right hand spread out from his body, and Quinn bore down hard on the wheel. They were in the passage; there was only blackness in his peripheral vision, his eyes were bursting from their sockets to catch the signs. 'Holy Mary, Mother of God…' The treacherous currents wrestled with the wheel in his sweat-slick grip, and the boat yawed violently. He was aware of Skald frantically signalling right.

He boosted the massive engines, and a rock loomed dead ahead. Skald cowered in the prow as it rushed to meet them. Then the wave Quinn had anticipated flung them to the right. He hauled hard on the wheel, and they were through.

'Now who's a man?' Quinn roared, over and over, until his breath failed him.

Skald could see green water stretching out before him and the hump of the ship in the distance. He eased his hold on the handrail, his fingers still clawed with tension. The engines stopped.

Quinn saw him turn in surprise as the throbbing ended. He reached behind and turned the key in the cabin door, then leaned on the wheel and stared at the sea.

'Mr Quinn?' The small voice from the prow barely pierced the silence of the cabin. Skald was running, sliding from side to side as the boat bucked. 'Mr Quinn,' the face at the glass screamed, 'we are drifting back. Start the engines.' Quinn stared fixedly ahead as he lifted the gun. 'Mr Quinn!'

'Kate,' Quinn whispered, just before Skald fired.

Skald was dimly aware of the figure punched back against the door of the cabin, but he was already moving. The boat swung side-on to the waves and rocked violently as the rocky mouth sucked them back. Lunging, he grasped the door handle, his slippery hand fighting for purchase. It was locked. Frantically, he turned it again; then the gun boomed, and he flung his weight against the door. Quinn's lifeless body yielded a small gap.

Skald was gathering his strength for a fresh assault when the boat struck the rock. A high, metallic scream chilled him. He turned his head as the sea lifted the boat disdainfully and smashed it down. Skald fired repeatedly at the wall of rock that rushed to claim him.

49

Major Devane's House

RON BENTHAM PAUSED outside the priest's door, filling his lungs with salted air. I'm too old for this, he thought, and smiled. Jauntily, he pressed up the winding lane, filled with such a sense of purpose that he almost bowled the small man over on the first bend.

'Beg pardon.'

'That's OK. Where the hell is everybody?'

'It's rather a long story, and I really wouldn't expect you to believe the half of it.'

The other man's eyes held his. *Try me*, they invited. Ron scanned the figure before him, noting the compact body, the close-cropped hair and workman's hands.

'May I ask, did you ever serve in the US Army?'

'Sure.'

'What exactly did you do?' Ron asked delicately.

The man's gaze didn't waver. 'Whatever needed doing.'

'Thank God,' Ron breathed in relief. 'I would appreciate your help.'

'You're the only show in town,' the man said, and smiled.

As the limping Ron and his new-found ally hiked together, Ron recounted as much of the story as his failing breath would allow. At the entrance to the Major's compound, he halted suddenly. 'Mr... I'm sorry, what do I call you?'

'Call me Jake.'

'Thank you, Jake. I'm Ron, Royal Engineers, retired – actually, propelled into retirement by a few pounds of Semtex.' He tapped the stick to his leg. 'Don't want to lose the other one, now do I?' he mused aloud, glancing at the path to the door. 'Daphne would not be amused. Shall we reconnoitre?'

Warily, the two men skirted the fence, Ron occasionally crouching low for a worm's-eye view. At last he straightened painfully. 'I suspect that our host had more pressing matters on his mind than the defence of the perimeter. Or perhaps he thought the natives sufficiently cowed.'

'We ain't natives,' Jake observed laconically.

Gingerly, they went to the door.

'I suppose it would be too much to expect...' Ron said quietly, pushing gently with the tips of his fingers. The door swung open.

'I feel rather like the fly that got the invitation to the parlour. Step warily, Jake.'

Feet sliding sideways in the dark, Ron felt forward with questing fingers. He felt the barest kiss of metal, and the room filled with the sound of a canister rocking itself horizontal. Carefully, he located it in the dark and held it to his nose. 'Polish,' he declared with satisfaction. 'I think we might be sufficiently far from outside eyes to try the light switch.'

Holding the can at arm's length, he sprayed high into the room. 'As I thought, no beams – well, none activated, anyway.'

'No beams is good beams,' Jake said with a straight face.

The signs of flight were everywhere: spilled papers, jutting drawers, all the internal doors ajar. 'Don't close anything open, Jake, there's a good fellow.'

Their shuffling footsteps brought them to a

short corridor lined with bookshelves, and to a door that resisted Ron's tentative pressure.

'The Major's lair, I imagine,' he murmured. 'You don't look like a fellow who carries a complete set of locksmith's tools... No. I suppose a hairpin would be out of the question?' Ron ran his hand across his forehead and seemed surprised at the sweat-sheen on his fingers.

Click.

'What?'

'MasterCard, Ron,' Jake smiled. 'I never leave home without it.' He gestured broadly to the open door.

'Deirdre Devane was rather certain the Major wouldn't leave any traces behind, so I'm afraid we must presume a bomb on a timer,' Ron said. He spent two precious minutes standing quite still in the study before dragging a chair to the side of the desk. Awkwardly, he stood on the chair and prised open a small box set in the wall. He scanned the device inside with an expert eye. In the top right-hand corner, a digital clock silently subtracted seconds.

'Are we in shit or what?' Jake enquired equably as Ron pored over the device.

'The former, I'm afraid,' Ron said absently. 'It's all new to me. Been away too long.'

The silence gathered.

'What does the clock say?'

'Soon.'

'Can we make it back outside?'

'You can.'

'Nah. The enlisted men vote to stay. So, you're the officer, strut your stuff.'

'Thank you.'

'You're welcome.'

Ron inhaled a long breath, held it and let it go. His fingers were rock steady when he held them up before his face. He flexed them once and let them fall gently into the innards of the timer, like a concert pianist. His face remained impassive as his fingers worked away, pulling at wires.

'Done,' he said abruptly, dropping his hands to his sides.

There was a moment of sudden stillness, and then another.

Slowly, the two men backed away from the box until they reached the corridor, where they broke into a frantic dash for the light outside.

Ron slumped down on a moss-cushioned stone.

'You OK?' Jake asked.

'Yes. I think so. You?'

'Yeah.'

They sat there in companionable silence.

'That was some job of work you did in there,' Jake said finally. 'How'd you figure what to do?'

'Oh, I just trusted in the old touch, you know?' Ron said airily.

'This would be the old touch that gave you a tin leg, right? You know you're full of it, don't you?'

'Yes, I believe I am rather,' Ron said, and began to laugh.

'Up to the brim,' Jake said and joined him.

50

The Church

MARK O'DOWD WAS wise to the effects of drink. He and his brother were often designated to nudge their father home from the pub, chivvying him like miniature tugs until he was safely berthed at his own fireside. Happily, he was never anything but maudlin in his cups.

Mark felt no unease as he watched the old priest negotiate the sacristy door. Too careful, Mark concluded, as Father Mack proceeded wordlessly to the vesting bench. *No talk today. Afraid I'd smell it on his breath or hear it in his voice.* He watched Father Mack flounder in the

folds of the long white alb, search behind for the
elusive loop of cincture and tighten it savagely in
an effort to straighten from his stoop. Finally, he
draped the stole askew across his shoulders and
nodded perfunctorily at the door. Mark stood his
ground and waited for the rheumy eyes to settle
on him.

'What?' There was a hint of petulance in the
hoarse voice. Mark inclined his head and nodded
at the vesting bench.

'What? Oh!' The chasuble curled over Father
Mack's head and unrolled behind. 'Satisfied?'

Mark nodded, watching the priest concentrate
on moving in a straight line to the door. He
adopted the same deliberate gait as they emerged
on the altar, hoping to deceive any sharp-eyed
worshipper with their shambling synchronicity. He
needn't have worried. The sparse congregation
half-rose to greet them and subsided almost
immediately into their accustomed postures.
Fleetingly, Mark noticed his mother, alone in a seat
beside the confessional, and remembered her
saying something about a mass for Nana's
anniversary. Father Mack bent to kiss the altar
stone and intoned the opening responses.

When the door to the church crashed open,
Mark darted to the priest's side, convinced he had
upturned the chalice. He was tall enough that his

head cleared the altar table and so he alone of the congregation had a perfect view of the young woman who was advancing up the central aisle. Mark knew her name was Sarah and that she served behind the bar in Finnegan's, but something in her expression sent a surge of anxiety through his stomach, and unconsciously he reached out his left hand and grasped the priest's trailing cincture.

'He's dead,' Sarah said, in a voice so controlled that Mark tightened his grip on the cincture.

'Who?' Father Mack had both palms on the altar and was squinting in her direction. 'What are you talking about, girl? Who's dead?'

'Leo,' she shouted, and there were gasps of disapproval and horror from the congregation. Mark saw his mother rise and make her way sideways along her pew towards the girl. She placed a hand on the girl's arm, but Sarah shook it off and pointed at the priest.

'You and me were the only ones to know. I told you about Leo seeing the Yank chasing young Flaherty to the lighthouse. He made me promise to tell no one, but I told you, Father, and now the Yank has killed Leo. Hung him up like a beast in the factory.' Her voice cracked, and Mrs O'Dowd made another attempt to hold her. 'I'll have my say,' Sarah screamed, shaking her off. 'It was only

me and you, Father, in the confession box. On my
solemn oath, I told no one else.'

Father Mack recoiled as if struck. 'You don't
know what you're saying, girl,' he said, almost in a
whisper.

'Oh, but I do, Father, and I thought I knew who
I was saying it to when I told you. Who did you
tell?' Sarah screamed, and a knot of worshippers
half-dragged her away from the altar. 'Who did
you tell?' she wailed, before the door swung
mercifully closed behind her.

Those left inside the church were standing now,
looking uncertainly at Father Mack. 'I told no one!'
he shouted. 'The secrecy of the confessional is
total. I would never breathe a word of anyone's
business.'

But his voice slurred on the last word and he
leaned his hands on the altar for support, shaking
his head from side to side in agony. Then, with a
huge effort, he lurched from the altar to the con
fessional, with Mark still in tow, and wrenched
open the confessional door. 'For forty years I have
sat here in the dark and listened to the sins of this
island's people. Forty years. And for all that time,
what was said in the dark has stayed in the dark.'
Tugging the penitents' door open, he exposed the
shabby kneeler and the small grille through which
they spoke. 'Those who had burdens brought

them here,' he thundered, 'and they left here unburdened, and I carried them nowhere, except here.' Father Mack thumped his chest, his voice cracking. 'And now—'

'Father?'

With a dazed look, the priest registered the small voice. 'What?'

'Father, what's that?' Mark dropped the cincture and bent into the box, scrabbling beneath the kneeler. Then he straightened, holding in his hands a rectangular metal box. A dull red eye glared in the object's cold face.

'Oh, my sweet Jesus,' Father Mack breathed, and slumped sideways into a pew.

'What is it, Father?' Mark asked. When Father Mack raised his gaze, there was a wildness in his eyes that made him start back.

'It is an abomination,' he said harshly, his lips flecked white with spittle. 'It is the ear of the Devil, and it heard every word, boy. Every sacred word.'

Slowly, the pool of people ebbed to the door and outside. 'Mark,' Mrs O'Dowd called quietly, 'come away home now. Come home, *a ghrá*.' Mark could read pity warring with fear on her face, but he shook his head stubbornly. His mother, about to argue, thought better of it and stepped quickly out of the church, her footsteps loud in the sudden silence.

Mark sat on the bench facing the old priest. After what seemed an age, Father Mack raised his eyes, and the boy's heart contracted at the pain in his face.

'Will you also go away?' he whispered.

'I will not, Father. Amn't I your altar boy?'

Tears welled up in the old man's eyes. 'You are that, Mark O'Dowd,' he said softly, laying a shaking hand on the boy's head. 'You and your brother. The finest I ever knew in all my years. Gunslingers,' he added, with false strength, 'real desperadoes. And now, Mark O'Dowd, I free you from your vow. Go on home to your mammy.'

'I will not, Father.'

'Go home when I tell you,' Father Mack said fiercely. 'There's nothing for you here.'

Blinded by his own tears, Mark stumbled to the door. He raced for the cliff path, holding the soutane up from his knees. At the top of the path, he turned away behind a big boulder and curled into a ball in the lee of the sheltering stone.

51

The Cliff Top

THE SEAL RAISED its sleek head and snuffled, then settled back indolently on the rock as the boy coughed softly. At a cave in the headland, the boy paused; his head jerked upwards, and Michael nodded. The rock face was slick with running water, but he mimicked every move the boy made, matching hand- and foot-holds until they popped through a clump of heather. Michael recognised the spot. It was where the boy had duelled with the lark before the earth had swallowed him.

Away to his left, he saw a dotted line of currachs skimming high in the water, making for the Devil's

Finger. The oars flashed in the struggling sunlight and Michael realised the wind was tiring. Why would they go there? he wondered. 'This way,' he called, zigzagging down the headland towards the cliff edge. He paused and scanned the hillside, conscious of the boy's eyes on him. Then, almost within touching distance, a clump of gorse parted and Mario struggled free.

'What's happened, Mario?'

'It seems,' Mario said grimly, plucking gorse spines from his jacket, 'that your countrymen rediscovered their backbones. They strung a blockade on the mouth of the harbour, so the bad guys sailed thataway.'

Michael followed the pointing finger with his eyes. 'The Devil's Finger,' he said in disbelief. 'Impossible.'

'Not only possible but successful. Then the damnedest thing happened. Their engine cut out on the other side. The sea's been spitting wreckage ever since. See for yourself.'

Michael took the binoculars and scanned the white water. Flotsam bobbed on the angry surface wherever he looked.

'Michael.'

Something in Mario's tone tensed him. Lowering the glasses, he turned slowly. He saw the gun and stepped before the boy. D'Arcy lounged almost nonchalantly against a boulder, his back to the sea, but the gun was rock steady. 'Not so clever this time, Padre. There's no damsel to get the hots when loverboy comes on all gallant.'

Michael saw Mario drift in his peripheral vision, and the muzzle swung lazily in that direction.

'Tsk, tsk,' D'Arcy said, shaking his head in mock surprise. 'The Major said to kill, not maim, but suit yourself.'

The gunshot was masked by the massive boom from the other side of the headland as the factory detonated. The ground shook beneath Michael's feet, and he was rolling through heather and gorse, the startled boy wrapped in his arms.

The same boom shocked Mark O'Dowd out of his misery. He stumbled to his feet, wiping his eyes with the white surplice. He saw a man stumble upright from where he had fallen; he saw his hand rise and the gun waver from left to right. Mark backed away. He began to run. 'Father Mack,' he gasped as he ran towards the church. 'Father Mack, Father Mack...' His words hammered in his throat, keeping time with his flying feet.

Michael laid his finger to his lips. The boy blinked and curled into a protective ball. Soundlessly Michael began to edge sideways through the cover, away from the boy's lair.

Mario had felt the punch before the earth swung around and hit him between the shoulders. His surprised gaze took in the canopy of yellow gorse above him. *Hit*, his mind registered calmly. Somewhere a bell began to ring.

'You hear that?' Michael shouted, and immediately rolled to his left. Where he had been lying, a bullet shredded a tall fern. From his new vantage point he could see D'Arcy's gun searching for a target. Carefully, Michael plucked a stone from beneath him and skimmed it far to his right, then immediately burrowed left, smiling grimly in satisfaction as the shot echoed the stone's fall. He found himself in deep gorse, and listened. The bell was an insistent atonal sound in the background.

'Michael.' It was no more than a whisper. Cautiously, he crawled towards its source. Mario was lying prone on his back, his left hand pressed above the bullet wound in his thigh that was soaking his trouser leg with blood. Michael scanned the wound anxiously, and was relieved to find that the blood was not arterial and that there were no flecks of bone at the entry site. Hastily, he pulled off Mario's belt and looped it above the wound in a makeshift tourniquet, putting the loose end in Mario's fingers.

'Michael.' Mario's eyes fluttered open.

Michael lay beside him, his mouth close to his ear. 'Mario, listen to me. I need your gun.' As if to emphasise the urgency in his voice, a bullet snarled through the undergrowth close by.

'No,' Mario said between gritted teeth. He turned, agonisingly slowly, until their faces were just inches apart.

'Give me the goddamn gun.'

'No,' Mario repeated. 'You won't kill him, Padre.' He smiled wanly on the last word, but his eyes held Michael's in a steady gaze. 'I got the gun, you got the legs,' he gasped. 'Move and taunt, Michael. Use him up.' His breath began to come more rapidly as the pain overrode the shock. 'I got one good shot in me. Don't fool around, OK?' He smiled weakly.

'Loosen the belt every few minutes,' Michael whispered.

'Yeah, yeah, I know the drill. Go!'

The rock Michael found was just over two heads high, if one head was glued to the ground. Needs must, he thought, rolling on his back in its meagre shelter.

'Hey, buddy,' he shouted. 'The officers are all gone AWOL, and guess who's the patsy?' The rock bucked with the impact of the bullet, stinging his face with flying shards.

'Hey, Padre,' he heard D'Arcy shout. 'Want to

know something? Right here is where your brother took a dive. Yeah, he wouldn't talk, so he flew.'

He laughed insanely, and Michael struggled to remain calm. Then he rose slowly from cover. 'Skald is dead,' he said evenly.

The man flinched as if struck. 'Fucking liar.'

'And guess whose sad ass gets left behind?' Michael was closing the distance between them in slow strides.

'That's far en—'

'And guess who gets extradited to the good old US of A to have his fat ass fried in the chair?' He was shouting, coming closer, ever closer.

'Motherfu—' The gun swung up wildly.

'Stop.' The voice froze them where they stood.

D'Arcy's eyes widened in confusion and disbelief as Father Mack crested the brow of the path, an Old Testament prophet in full flight, his face afire. 'Dare you point that damned thing at one of my people?' he roared. 'You cowardly cur!' He strode across the cliff as if oblivious of the gun that swung erratically from him to Michael. He circled between Michael and the gunman, his finger pointing to the rage of the Devil's Finger.

'Look out there, man,' he bellowed. 'Out there, the crabs are already eating the eyes of another gunman. For the wages of murder is death

everlasting.' D'Arcy's eyes shifted to the sea, and
Michael saw Mario rising to a crouch. The priest
had backed a confused D'Arcy nearer the cliff
edge. The gun swayed back to the priest, bobbing
up and down as if to wave him back.

'You want to shoot someone?' Mack said
fiercely. 'Shoot me, then.' He flung his arms wide.
'And go back to the hell that spawned you.'

Michael saw Mario's arm rise, his other hand
sweep up to clasp his wrist in the classic firing
posture.

The two shots were a single crack. Michael saw
the surprise on D'Arcy's face and the blossoming
black hole beneath his hairline before his body
arced out over the lip of the cliff as the bullet
punched him back. In the same instant, he saw
Mack clutch his chest. 'Jesus no,' he whispered as
Mack began to crumple and roll.

Michael dived full length and slithered, his
hand outstretched, grasping at Mack's wrist as he
disappeared over the edge. Desperately, he spread
his legs and dug his toes into the turf as his upper
body inched towards the abyss. He felt Mario's
weight thump down on his legs, halting his slide. 'I
got you,' Mario gasped.

'Mack, Mack!' Michael shouted. 'Mack, reach
up your other hand. Mack.'

Father Mack's eyes fluttered open. 'Michael.' It

was a drowning voice, and Michael groaned in horror at the blood on his mouth.

'I won't let you go, Mack,' he screamed. 'Just reach up to me, please.'

'Michael, Michael, my son...' Father Mack's eyes fluttered closed again.

'Mack,' he sobbed, 'just reach up a little.'

'Let me go, boy,' Father Mack wheezed, and fresh blood spurted at the effort.

'No, Mack, no,' Michael wailed in agony, reaching despairingly with his free hand.

'Michael...' The old voice strengthened to something like its former self. 'Michael,' he repeated with infinite tenderness, 'if you ever loved me, let me go.'

For a long moment, their eyes held.

'I love you, Mack,' Michael whispered, and let him go.

The helicopter boomed over the headland, pushing flat the gorse and heather as it passed out to sea.

'Sonofabitch,' Mario growled. He turned painfully on his back and emptied his magazine after the fleeing craft. Michael lay where he had fallen, his hand still stretched beyond the lip of land. The boy was coiled around him, his hand gently stroking Michael's hair. 'Sonofabitch.' Mario fumbled in the pocket of his jacket and dragged the radio to his ear. Savagely he stabbed in a code. 'Seal to Poseidon. Do you read? Over.'

The static crackled and cleared. 'We read you loud and clear, Seal,' came the voice from the submarine. 'Over.'

'Chopper heading east. Do you register? Over.'

'We register chopper,' came the metallic reply. 'Over.'

'Terminate. Over,' Mario said grimly.

'We copy. Over.'

'Poseidon, one last thing. Patch me through to target. Over.'

There was a static-filled pause before the submarine answered. 'Make it brief, Seal. Over.'

Mario lurched upright and limped to the edge of the cliff where Michael was lying. He raised the radio again.

'You know the drill,' the Major said curtly as the helicopter swooped over open water.

'Absolutely, sir,' the pilot responded, tilting his head to the neck mike. The Major settled his earphones more comfortably, his eyes speeding over the water beneath, tracking their shadow as it moved like a Leviathan through the deep. He liked the image, and closed his eyes to savour it.

Retreat and regroup, he thought, mentally tallying his options. Find new conduits. Next year's crop would come in, as it always did. A given. He would nurture new contacts; already he was formulating a list in his head of the finest people money could buy, all the way from Colombia to Capitol Hill.

Deirdre. His train of thought bucked on the name and almost derailed. Almost. She had made her choice, he concluded. His duty was done.

And Skald... Their flight path had taken them over the Devil's Finger, hugging the Island coastline before turning due east over the sea. The wreckage was everywhere, and for a brief moment the Major had gazed from on high, remembering his trusty right hand. The world is awash with men of his calibre, he argued with himself. And yet, men so devoid of human feeling are a precious rarity. Like me, he concluded, and settled back in the padded seat. 'Well, goodbye to all that,' he muttered.

The radio crackled into life. 'Devane.'

'Who the hell is that?' the Major shouted at the startled pilot.

'Devane, I send you a quote.'

There was a pause, and then the voice continued. '"If you prick us, do we not bleed? If you tickle us, do we not laugh? If you poison us, do we not die?"'

Another pause. 'Finish the quote, Major. You got two minutes.'

'What the—?' the pilot muttered, staring at the radio, but the Major sat immobile, apart from a tiny tic pulsing in his left eyelid.

Suddenly, he raised his head and said, '"And if you wrong us, shall we not revenge?"' His eyes widened with awareness and shock. 'Take evasive action now,' he snapped.

Abruptly, he turned his attention to the sea before them, where a patch of water boiled white for an instant. A finger of light pulsed through the surface and began to climb the sky. The Major watched it arc towards him, growing ever larger, filling his empty eyes.

Raimundo stood in his appointed place at the rail, head cocked. His stomach told him the storm had moved on. Pepe hovered anxiously at his right shoulder. 'Captain,' he said at last. 'What's happening?'

Raimundo, dragged from his reverie, turned to face his old comrade. 'Time to let go,' he said simply

Pepe's face contorted as he digested that morsel. 'You mean like cast off and get the hell out of here?'

'No,' Raimundo replied. 'Just time to stop.' His shoulders sagged and he turned back to the rail. 'Get the crew on deck, Pepe.'

She was a corvette, the greyhound of the sea, and even at this distance Raimundo knew from her bow-wave that he couldn't outrun her. He sensed the huddle of men at his back and turned.

'It's over,' he said, so quietly that those at the back had to lean forward to hear him. 'I am tired of running.' He nodded to his left, and their eyes swivelled to the lean grey shape cutting towards them.

'Arms and ammunition to be dumped on the other side. Do it.'

Slowly, some of the men detached themselves from the group and faded into the superstructure.

'What happens to us?' Pepe asked tentatively.

'You know nothing, understand? We have an empty hold and our documents are in order. You know nothing. I'll... I'll tell them everything – I'm the captain, it's my responsibility. They'll question

and question; it doesn't matter. You are innocent
seamen, you expected to take a cargo of fish – end
of story. OK?'

They looked at one another uncertainly.
Finally, Pepe spoke. 'But what will happen to you,
Captain? They'll put you in prison, no?'

'Yes, Pepe.' Raimundo smiled. 'No sweat. I've
been there a long time.' He turned as the corvette
loomed across their bows. 'And Pepe…'

'Yes, Captain?'

'You know something? My stomach, it ain't
gurgling no more.'

52

The Priest's House

MICHAEL SAT IN Mack's armchair sorting through the happenings of the day before. The fishermen had found Mack's body. He would be buried today. Lybe's son Raimundo had been arrested on the Major's ship, to the relief of his parents, who planned to live with Deirdre Devane in America. Everybody was intent on creating a new normality after the malevolence of the Major.

A knock on the porch door interrupted Michael's reverie. He felt the cold draught as the door creaked, and footsteps echoed in the hallway. Michael judged the priest framed in the living-room door to be somewhere in his mid-thirties. His head was lichened with a cap of red hair – not Fi's red; Fi's hair was lava, whereas this man's had cooled to basalt.

'Father Flaherty?' The voice was elocuted and pitched lower, Michael suspected, than its natural register – whether in deference to the bereaved or for some deeper reason, he couldn't fathom. He nodded.

The priest approached, hand extended. 'I wish to commiserate with you, Father, on the loss of Father Mack. I understand you were, eh, close.'

After a long moment, Michael rose and shook his hand. 'Thank you, Father…?'

'Oh, I do beg your pardon.' Under the pressure of embarrassment, the voice slipped almost to falsetto and the priest blushed. 'Father Gerard Hynes.'

It would always be Gerard, Michael concluded, never Gerry or Ger; and it would always be Father. He gestured to the armchair. 'Won't you sit down, Father?'

Gerard folded himself on the edge of the cushion, smoothing the tail of his black crombie to avoid creasing. 'I am the bishop's secretary, and His Lordship appointed me administrator of Father Mack's estate.' He couldn't quite mask the expression of dismay as his eyes wandered over the rumpled room. Michael suppressed a smile. 'Father Mack left a rather terse will.' He gave a small sigh at the irregularity of it all.

'Then it won't tax you unduly, will it, Father?'

Michael instantly regretted the ice in his tone. The man before him flushed and bowed his head. He had known more than his fair share of bullies, Michael guessed: the lads, that messy brotherhood bound too close for comfort by their exclusion from the normal life, vent their angst on their own, always eager to assert their masculinity on a Gerard with pale eyes and an arching voice.

'I'm wound a little tightly today, Gerard,' Michael confessed softly. The absolution and gratitude in the other man's eyes burned him.

'Father Mack had very little to leave but memories,' Gerard continued, as if he hadn't heard. 'I... I didn't know him very well, I must confess. I did occasionally meet him in the the course of my duties; but we didn't... we didn't quite hit it off, as they say.'

'Mack didn't always get it right, Gerard,' Michael said, adding quickly as a defence against any further expression of gratitude, 'so what can I do for you?'

'You might advise me, Michael. May I call you Michael?'

'Michael it is.'

'Thank you. There is the matter of his books. He has… had quite a collection. Actually, he left them to you.'

Michael looked around at the stacked shelves, the ramparts of his youth. 'I think I'd like the school to have them,' he said finally.

'Quite. Eh, there is one other matter. I hope you don't mind; I was here a little earlier. Didn't wish to disturb you after… after all that's happened. I had to make a list, you see. Rather a futile exercise. I came across this in a bedside locker.'

He held out a package wrapped in brown paper, secured with string. 'Your name is written on it, so I presumed it was meant for you.'

Numbly, Michael took the package and laid it gingerly on the table. 'Thank you, Gerard.'

'Oh, not at all. I read somewhere once that St Thomas More left the Chancellorship of England with less than he had before his appointment. There is something rather special about a priest who leaves only his books and two small packages.'

'Two?'

Gerard was flustered. 'A slip of the tongue, Michael, I assure you. I wouldn't like you to think that I am other than discreet.'

'No, I would never think that of you, Gerard.'

Gerard seemed assured of the sincerity of his reply. 'Thank you.' He paused, as if weighing his words in his head. 'I suppose it wouldn't be improper of me to mention that there was an identical package for a lady. She was his nurse, of course; I imagine it was some token of thanks for her ministrations.' He stopped suddenly, a crimson flush rising from the horizon of his collar to flame in his face. 'Well,' he concluded hurriedly, 'I mustn't detain you.' He stood up, his hand extended. 'God bless you, Michael. Really,' he added with a small smile.

'Thanks, Gerard. And take care, eh?'

'Yes, and you.'

Michael sat in the silence after Gerard's departure. Absently, his hand strayed to the twine that bound his bequest, but he didn't open it. Sufficient to the day, he thought, and placed it gently on the coffee table.

'Michael.' Fiona breezed into the room, tossing her windcheater on the vacated chair. 'I just met a real priest on the path.'

'Mormon haircut, outsize Roman collar, black all the way down to the boots, "Good morning, dear"?'

'Yes. How did you…?'

'That would be Father Gerard Hynes.'

'Is he for real?'

'Sometimes. When it's safe. He's OK.'

'And?' She looked at him quizzically.

'And, Ms Headmistress, all you see stacked around here is yours.'

Fiona turned slowly around the room. 'All the books?'

'All of them.'

'I thought he'd leave them to you.'

'He did.'

'Thanks, Michael.'

He nodded.

'You're sitting in his chair.'

He nodded again.

Fiona went and sat in his lap, as unself-consciously as a little girl, laying her head on his shoulder. His arms closed protectively around her.

'He'll get a great send-off, Michael,' she said quietly. 'People are coming from all the islands. Tommy Coyle will sing 'Chualainn' and Dan Twomey will probably play the pipes. His grave is right beside Mam's, you know. I was talking to Mr Twomey earlier and he said the sea is taking the cemetery.' Her voice faltered. 'Before long they'll all be with Gabriel.' She shivered. 'I wish... I wish we could have put Gabriel in holy ground, Michael.'

Gently he stroked her hair.

'The ground isn't holy, Fi,' he said slowly. 'It's the body makes it holy. I remember Mack at a funeral when we were kids. There was a huge crowd packing out the church and no body. Never found. I remember he quoted from Shakespeare – didn't he always?' He smiled crookedly. 'Ariel's song from *The Tempest*:

Full fathom five thy father lies;
Of his bones are coral made;
Those are pearls that were his eyes:
Nothing of him that doth fade
But doth suffer a sea-change
Into something rich and strange.
Sea-nymphs hourly ring his knell:
Hark now I hear the ding dong bell.

Mack would sell his soul for a quote.'

'You loved him, didn't you, Michael?'

'I let him go, Fi.'

'Because you loved him.'

'Yes.'

'Don't let me go, Michael.'

He held her tightly as the old clock ticked away the silence.

'What will happen here now, Fi? Without the factory, I mean?'

She sat up and ran her fingers through her flaming hair. 'Can I let you into a little secret, Michael?'

He nodded, intrigued at the hint of laughter in her eyes.

She lowered her voice conspiratorially. 'This island is awash with drugs.'

'What?'

'Yep. There's stacks of neat white plastic packages under every rick of turf and flagstone floor. I swear,' she said, highly amused at the expression of disbelief on Michael's face. 'We have enough drugs on this little island of ours to keep the half of Europe happy for a very long time.'

'But... but that's unbelievable, Fi.'

'It's salvage, Michael, that's what it is,' Fiona said mock-solemnly. 'To be handed over in good time for a fat finder's fee. The income per head on this island is about to become the envy of the world. They're already talking about new trawlers, big ones that will go farther, and a factory ship.'

She eased up from his lap and swished aside the curtain. 'I was talking to Kate,' she said in a matter-of-fact voice. 'She said I could come up to the house and do a bit of work with the boy... with Liam,' she corrected herself.

When Michael made no reply, she turned from the window to face him. 'You know you could stay, Michael. God knows we could do with you, and—'

'Fi.'

'What?'

'It isn't as simple as that, love. I went away.'

Fiona walked away from the window and sat on the floor with her back to his chair.

'So, you're going back, then?' she asked sadly.

'Yes.'

'I was thinking I'd like to see America,' she said bravely. 'Maybe I might come out next summer for a while?'

'I'd like that, Fi.'

'Michael?' She knelt and faced him. 'Don't just disappear this time.'

He nodded.

'I love you, Michael.'

'I love you too, Fi.'

'Would you like a cup of tea?'

He began to laugh, a long, slow laugh that built up from his belly, but the breath hitched in his chest, contorting his face. Fiona reached up her palm and wiped his cheeks.

'You've cried enough, brother,' she said firmly. He laid his head on hers, his tears dropping silently into the furnace of her hair.

53

The Flahertys' House

THE MASTER SAT upright in the winged chair before the fire, the flickering flame kinder to his face than the cruel sunshine slanting from the window on the other side. Michael drew the curtain closed and sat on the small stool before him, head bowed. He felt bone-weary and empty. The warmth of the fire lulled him, and he closed his eyes to remember.

'A violet by a mossy stone,
Half hidden from the eye!
Fair as a star, when only one
Is shining in the sky.'

The Master's voice floated from near the classroom window. He always stood there to recite poetry, his eyes lost in the seascape. 'Brian Quinn! Maybe you'd explain that to us.'

Quinn, whose eyes were also on the sea, started.

'Eh, he hadn't much time for her, Master.' The suppressed laughter in the seats pleased him, and he looked around with a smile.

'And how do you determine that from the text, Brian?'

'Well, if there's just the one star, like, there's nothing much to match her with, Master.'

'Very astute, Brian, very astute,' the Master murmured. 'Now, whose is that boat you've been watching?'

'Brown's, Master,' Brian answered promptly.

The laughter flowed freely and the Master smiled. 'Indeed it is, Brian. And if Mr Brown was abroad on the Atlantic in the black of night, without a compass, and with fog all around, how might he view that one star then, Brian?'

'Through the bottom of a bottle, Master.'

Michael was oblivious to the gales of laughter and the sight of the Master stifling his own smile. His eyes had found Kate, palm to chin, lost in her own thoughts. She tensed under his gaze and turned her head, the wing of her hair swinging down over her eye.

'It means that, when it's dark, a single star can be the most wonderful sight in the world,' Michael said aloud. The shock in Kate's eyes startled him back to reality. The class had fallen still, watching the Master's reaction.

The Master closed his book gently, placed it on the desk and gazed at his son. 'Yes, it can indeed, *a mhic*,' he said finally, and left the room. Michael found his eyes straying back to Kate, and glowed when she smiled. The others were already battling with books and bags, happy at the premature parole – all except Brian Quinn, who tore his eyes from the pair of them and looked fiercely at Brown's boat, bucking into the westerly wind.

'Michael.'

'Yes, Master,' he answered automatically, before he realised he was in the present and his father had spoken.

'Michael.' The old man's face was contorted with concentration.

'Yes, Dada.'

The Master gestured, and Michael moved to sit on the floor at his feet. He saw the fire waver and the eyes begin to glaze.

'Dada,' he whispered urgently, and his father focused.

'Your mother, Eileen,' he whispered. 'She was

longing for a girl. I thought maybe God had given us more than our share of blessings in the boys.'

Again the eyes clouded, and his lips worked soundlessly.

'Three boys I had, Father,' he said suddenly. 'Three boys, and a little princess. She was the stamp of her mother – so much her image that, after Eileen died, it hurt me to hold her. God forgive me, Father, I held back. I became her teacher, feeding her mind and starving her heart. I hardened my heart against my own flesh, Father, for fear God would notice her too. If it wasn't for Michael, she might have been lost to us.'

Again, he fell silent, nodding to some inner dialogue.

'The boys,' he continued, in a voice so diminished that Michael leaned towards him. 'I should have been stronger... Lost in myself I went back to what I was before.., before Eileen. Liam drowned, and Gabriel fell in love with the sea. Two boys lost to the water.'

'And Michael?' his son prompted gently.

'Gone,' the old man replied. 'Gone a long time. Father Mack took him in... made a home for him. He was doing what I couldn't do, and I paid him back with envy. Isn't that a terrible thing? But' – his voice strengthened again – 'there was one day, Father. The day my wife... I put her in the stern and looked at them – the men. And only one man joined me. I don't judge them for it; they had wives and children themselves. On that day there was only Father Mack and Michael.'

Michael sat as if carved from stone as the dormant memory broke over him.

'Dada! I'll come, Dada.'

'Mind Gabriel for me, Michael.'

The rough hands prising his fingers from the gunwale as he wailed into the wind, 'I'll come, Dada. Take me, take me.'

Sobbing on the beach as the men lent weight to the stern and the prow lifted to the green wall of water. Someone's hand on his head: the solemn-faced girl with the raven hair.

'Come away up home, Kate. Do you hear me?'

'I'll be up by and by,' she had answered fearlessly, staring her sharp-faced mother into capitulation.

His father's agony burst in upon Michael's reverie. 'I didn't take him because I wanted to spare his life, to save his life, my poor, lost boy. Will you bless me, Father?'

He was weeping, the silent, awful crying of an old man.

Michael took his head in his hands. 'I love you, Dada,' he crooned, 'I love you, Dada.'

But already his father had returned to another time. He was calm again.

'Eileen will be in soon from the school,' he said quietly. 'Will you not stay for the tea, Father?'

Michael looked into the old man's face. 'Your children were blessed in you, Master,' he said softly, and, having kissed his father for the first and last time, he left.

54

New York

'AND THAT'S IT, Hanny, soup to nuts.'

'And Michael?'

'You're doddering, old woman,' Mal said in exasperation. 'I just told you: he's A-OK, right as rain. What more can I tell you?'

'Tell me he's coming back, Mal.'

The longing in her voice ached at his heart. 'He's coming back, Hanny.'

'But?'

'But I can't say if he's coming back to us.'

Hanny pondered his answer, stacking sugar

cubes in the bowl with trembling fingers. 'Can't say or don't know?'

'Hanny…'

'I've got two good arms, Mal, remember that.'

'Don't know, Hanny,' he sighed. 'Fiona didn't say, and I didn't ask her.'

She tapped the sugar pyramid experimentally with her finger to see if it would topple. It held. 'There's a message for you from them.'

'Them? Did Mata Hari and James Bond turn up at the door?'

'It's from the spooks you've been canoodling with.'

'You read it?'

'Nah, but the delivery boy had "spook" written all over him – short hair, fidgety eyes, bulge under the open coat… you get the picture?'

'You should've been a cop, Hanny.'

'So should you, Mal,' she said without humour.

'Could I have the message, please?'

'It's on the dresser. It's your arm that's been shot, not your legs.'

'Charming.'

Mal opened the envelope one-handed, with much theatrical grunting, and slumped back in the kitchen chair.

'Well, I'll be damned.'

'Probably,' Hanny retorted sharply, but he could tell her interest was piqued.

'I have to go to Washington.'

'When?'

'Today.'

'Business or pleasure?'

'Both,' Mal answered, his blue eyes shining.

55

The Devil's Finger

THE BLACK-BACKED GULL dipped a wing and swung in a wide arc above the littered water. It had come late to this particular feast and couldn't hope to compete with the screaming kittiwakes that scavenged the surface. With the slightest twitching of wingtips, it rode the wind and scanned the flat shelf above the tide line. Something moved in the shadows and the gull dived, flaring its wings at the last second to drop and waddle to its prey.

Skald opened his eyes. Almost comically, the bird flapped backwards, clawing up the sky,

screaming in fear and frustration. Skald flexed his
limbs, groaning in pain at the arm that hung
limply by his side. His good hand found the lump
at the base of his skull. He pressed it and the
agony focused his mind. The wave had slammed
him into a crevice, knocking him unconscious.
The left side of his face stung savagely and his
fingers came away red from where the rock had
abraded his flesh.

He thought of the priest and anger coursed
through his body, shaking him upright on the flat
ledge. The water was calmer now, bobbing with
pieces of wreckage. It took him three agonising
hours to reach the Island, his upper body
supported on a buoyancy cushion liberated from a
tangle of wreckage. As his feet touched the sandy
beach, he turned and spat into the sea.

Under cover of darkness, he made his way to
the deserted pier, sniffing in satisfaction as he
passed the outline of the charred factory. In the
deeper dark, against the pier wall, he nested in a
coil of rope to catch his breath.

With his good hand, he did a trawl of his
pockets. A pallid moon raced in a clear space
between scudding clouds and Skald held up his
knife to the light. His thumb pressed a switch and
a silver gleam appeared in the gloom. He had
unfinished business with Michael Flaherty. He

knew there was only one way the priest could leave the Island and he was content to wait. This time his quarry would not escape. He would do his duty. The moon darted for refuge in a cloud and it was dark again. In the darkness, Skald made his way to the ferry boat.

56

Flight AA66, New York to Washington

MAL WAS WELL into the complimentary glass of champagne when Tony loomed in the aisle, checking his ticket stub against the seat numbers.

'Lay it right here, *hombre*,' Mal said amiably, patting the seat beside him with his good hand. Tony threw his jacket into the overhead locker and slammed the lid before lowering his bulk into the soft seat.

'So what is this, Mal? You an air marshal as well as everything else?'

'Me?' Mal said innocently, holding the glass before his face as if to admire the winking bubbles.

'Nah, not me. Him.' He shifted his eyes fractionally to the right behind the cover of the glass.

Nonchalantly, Tony flexed his neck, sweeping his gaze in the direction indicated. 'You gotta be joking,' he muttered, bending to select a magazine from the net pocket. 'We are talking about the ageing Caucasian hippie with the earphones, bopping to some different drummer, right?'

'The very one,' Mal said smugly. 'Aisle seat near the front, one foot tapping in the aisle, head scanning – that's him. He's got reflectors on the inside of his shades, and his headset isn't plugged in. No distractions, Tony.'

'Top marks, Columbo,' Tony said sourly. 'You gonna tell me what this little charade is all about?'

'"Charade" is good, Tony, very good. Now lift up your magazine, lean back, and listen.'

Tony did as he was bid.

'Do you remember Deirdre Devane?' Mal started.

'Devane? Yeah, she was married to that Vespucci guy. The tunnel guy with the scary uncle.'

'Right, same lady. Seems she hacked into Daddy's computer and downloaded the whole shebang to her newspaper editor Stateside. She knew he couldn't print it, but he accidentally sent it to the Pentagon.'

'Your friends must have been pleased, Mal.'

'Touché, Tony. I got a message this morning. In among all the drugs and dead bodies, the computer had a little file on the guy who pulled the strings to send Devane into South America. This guy had the clout to make sure they got out and stayed operative and invisible. He's also the guy ultimately responsible for planting a Special Forces unit in unmarked graves. All except one. It turns out this guy was in the clubhouse all the time, one of their own, a goddamn general.'

'So we're going to read him his rights?'

'No, not exactly. You know the ancient Romans gave a failed general a choice. He could go to trial and be shamed before the people…'

'Or?'

'Or he could sit in a warm bath and slit his wrists.'

'Gives a whole new meaning to "taking a bath", Mal.'

'That it does, Tony,' Mal replied and smiled mirthlessly.

The suits on the tarmac waved them to the limo parked on the blind side of the plane, away from the gaze of any curious passengers. For the next half-

hour, they watched Washington unroll through
tinted windows, Tony craning as the landmarks slid
by, Mal looking but not seeing. Finally they left the
freeway and wound their way through suburbs that
grew ever more salubrious, until the limo eased to a
halt before the blueprint for the all-American
home. It was straight from the Rockwell catalogue,
all shingled roof and fluttering flag on the lawn. The
nearest neighbours were a good acre away, behind
tall hedges and a scattering of mature trees.

'Here?' Tony asked tensely.

'Here,' Mal replied calmly. He had his hand on
Tony's sleeve. 'You don't have to be party to this,
Tony,' he said gently. 'You can just sit it out in the
car.' But Tony was already angling his large frame
to the sidewalk.

On the second ring, a Hispanic maid opened
the door. '*Buenos días, señora,*' Mal said easily. Her
face set in a look of resignation.

'Relax, ma'am,' Mal added. 'We're not immi-
gration, our business is with the General.'

'Maria?' a young woman's voice called from
inside. 'Who's at the door?' The woman who
appeared behind the maid was dressed for riding,
carrying a quirt in her left hand. Mal removed his
hat and made the introductions, flashing his badge
one-handed. After a moment, Tony did likewise.

'How can I help you, gentlemen?'

'I believe you're on your way to an appointment, ma'am,' Mal continued smoothly, glancing
at the jodhpurs. 'It wouldn't do to keep the
gentleman waiting. We need to consult with your
husband. Perhaps Maria here would be kind
enough to show us in. We needn't detain you.'

He held her gaze as he spoke and saw her eyes
shift from outrage to calculation.

'See to it, Maria,' she said evenly, and brushed
by them. Mal and Tony stepped into the hallway,
Tony nudging the door closed behind him.

'Maria,' Mal turned to the frightened maid.
'Mrs Fox forgot to tell you to take the rest of the
day at home.'

The woman looked startled and uncertain.
'*Señor*,' she began querulously, her hands balling
her white apron.

'*Por favor, señora*,' Mal added courteously,
stilling her panic.

She nodded and opened a closet in the hallway,
retrieving her coat.

'Tony.'

'Huh? Oh, yeah…' Tony plucked the coat from
her trembling fingers and helped her into it, then
ushered her through the door.

In answer to their knock, a testy voice boomed
from inside. 'Maria, I told you distinctly, I didn't
want any breakfast. I'm working. Jesus God.'

The door swung open and General Vincent J. Fox froze momentarily. Will he bluster or blubber? Mal wondered, watching his face intently.

'Who the hell let you two bozos saunter in here?' *Bluster.* Mal sighed. 'Maria, goddammit, you come here right this minute!'

'General Fox,' Mal said firmly, and the man closed his mouth with an audible click, the use of his rank straightening his spine. 'Maria and your wife had to step out for a while.' He raised his badge chest high. 'A word sir, if you will, in private.'

The General tensed as if he might bar the door, then seemed to think better of it. The study was strewn with papers; a shredder whined hungrily from a low table near the window. Mal ushered the General to his seat behind the desk as Tony silenced the shredder. Then both cops sat formally facing the man. Mal read from a prepared text, careful not to inject any inflection into the long list of capital crimes of which the General stood accused.

The General seemed dazed. Occasionally, as Mal spoke, he leaned forward to realign the blotter with the desk edge; sometimes he steepled his fingers before his face as if in prayer. Mal finished, and folded the document.

At length, the General stirred, drawing himself erect, his face composed. 'And the deal?'

Mal gazed stoically at the flag to the right of the desk. 'I am instructed to tell you that the United States does not do deals with those who murder its citizens.'

'Ah, I see.' For a moment the General struggled with his composure. Then he quoted softly:

'"*And that which should accompany old age,*

As honour, love, obedience, troops of friends,

I must not hope to have."'

'*Macbeth*, General?'

'Why, yes.' The General looked sharply at Mal, as if seeing him for the first time. 'You know the play?'

'Yeah, a bit, sir,' Mal replied calmly, never shifting his eyes from the flag. 'As I recall, Macbeth has already betrayed his country and murdered his own countrymen. But he missed one, sir: Banquo's son. I think his name was Fleance.'

'"We have scotched the snake, not killed it,"' the General quoted almost inaudibly.

'We'll be outside in the car, sir.' Mal rose to his feet, surprising Tony, whose head had twitched from one to the other during their exchange.

In the car, Mal said, 'Driver, would you mind cracking the window open?' The smell of new-mown grass filled the interior.

'Mal, what the —?'

Mal stopped Tony with a raised hand. The

gunshot was a just a dull thud, probably unidenti-
fiable by a gardening neighbour or a casual passer-
by. Mal waited a few moments and then took his
cellphone from his pocket.

'It's done,' he said simply, and hung up. 'Driver,
we're all done here.'

They drove to the airport in silence.

'Mal?' Tony said on the flight back to New York.

'Yeah.'

'Why you?'

'It was part of the deal I made. If they ever got
the guy, I wanted to be there. You remember I
mentioned a survivor back there?'

Tony nodded.

'He's someone I care about, and I guess he
thinks I jerked him around some. I owe it to him.'

Tony digested this for a time, his large brow
furrowed. 'And why me, Mal?'

'Same answer, Tony.'

They didn't speak again until Tony had his rust
bucket leaning against the kerb outside Mal's
brownstone. As Mal straightened gratefully on the
pavement, Tony called, 'Hey, *hombre*, we got us
some loose threads hanging in Dodge City. You
know how it is? The guys in the black hats never
take a holiday. Maybe you could mosey down
sometime? Do some real police work, Mal. Make a
nice change.' Tony smiled.

'Maybe I could do just that,' Mal replied, fixing his hat at a jaunty angle.

'Hey, pilgrim, thanks. OK?'

'*De nada, hijo*,' Mal threw over his shoulder, and went home.

57

Anne O'Connor's House

'WHO IS IT?'

'It's Mario Ricci, ma'am. I'm an American.'

'You'd better come in, Mario Ricci of New York City.'

Anne went to the little kitchen and snapped the percolator to life. Mario stood at the coffee table, watching her load the small tray and wondering at the grace of her movement, how her little finger found and snagged a spoon. Carefully, she placed the tray on the table between them and sat back in her own chair, swinging her legs up beneath her as he had known she would. 'Sit down, man,' she said quietly.

Awkwardly, he lowered himself into the low chair.

'You're still hurting?' she said.

'I'm OK. The nurse says I'll mend.' He sat forward in the chair. 'Anne, I had to —'

'You did what you had to do, Mario,' she interrupted softly. 'It's done now, and you'll be off. And we'll...' She bent forward and located her coffee mug, cupping it for warmth. 'We'll think about the wave that washed over us. Why it took some and left others. Then we'll move on.'

'I have to go back, Anne.'

'I know. It was very nice meeting you, Mario Ricci of New York City,' Anne said quietly.

'I have a little R and R owing,' Mario said. 'I was thinking I might come back and recuperate here. On the Island, I mean.'

'You could finish that article on the far-flung isles.'

'Yeah, that too.'

'That would be nice.'

'Please tell me that 'nice' is an Irish euphemism for great, fantastic, wow.'

'"Nice" will do for now.'

'Nice it is then, Miss O'Connor,' Mario said, and took her in his arms.

58

The Island

MICHAEL PULLED GABRIEL'S sweater over his head, inhaling the salt smell. The windcheater was Mack's, the only thing Michael had of him. It was glossy with age and use in all weathers, yet he put it on like a vestment, pulling up the zip gently. Now there was just his small bag and the brown paper package. He tucked the package inside the windcheater, where it nestled beside his heart. He knew he had to go now, before the ghosts in the room possessed him.

Michael trudged the path between the silent houses. From the church in the distance, the muted swell of singing voices called to him but he would not, could not, go there. He had said his goodbye to Mack on the cliff top and, at the memory, his right hand clenched painfully. Standing before the closed door of the cottage, he relaxed his right hand and held it sideways.

'You can come out now, Liam.'

The name came strangled from his throat. The boy vaulted from his hiding place behind the stone wall and took his hand. He nudged the door open and tugged Michael into the warmth of the kitchen. Without releasing his hand, he led him to a chair at the cloth-covered table and sat beside him. The boy gazed at Michael's face, then his gaze shifted and softened and Michael knew she was there.

Kate moved to the other end of the table and sat. 'Will you go on out and play, Liam, or I might have to find a few jobs for you?'

Reluctantly, the boy released Michael's hand and left.

'I'm sorry about Father Mack, Michael,' she said finally.

'I know that, Kate.'

'And Gabriel.'

His brother's name exploded in his chest and he shuddered.

'They killed him, Kate,' he said bleakly.

'I know.'

She looked at his bowed head for a moment

'Michael, listen to me. You didn't kill, Liam. You know that.'

'I didn't save him. I let him go, like Mack.'

In his agony, he raised his clenched right hand. Kate moved to the chair beside him and took his fist between her hands. 'Not everyone can be saved,' she said. 'Even if a boat does come, it's not always the one of our choosing. I know that.'

He tried to speak but she hushed him with a raised finger.

'When you didn't come and didn't... when your letters didn't arrive, if I hadn't had Liam, I...' She shook her head and continued. 'My mother... well, she's dead since, so I won't speak ill of her. Father Mack took us in, gave us a roof over our heads, but there was a price.'

Michael raised his head and saw the pain and weariness in her eyes.

'The man who married me was Brian Quinn,' she said, holding his gaze. 'He went down with the Major's boat, they're still looking for the body.'

'I... I'm sorry, Kate.'

'You can be sorry for him, Michael, not for me. He might have been a different man with someone else. He got nothing from me and it withered whatever good was in him. I didn't save him, Michael, but I didn't kill him either.'

The silence lengthened.

'Is Liam my son, Kate?'

'He's your child, Michael. He's my son. Whether he'll ever be your son is a matter for the both of you.'

'And what about us, Kate? We were…'

'We were children, Michael, and we walked off the edge of the world. Remember?'

He nodded and his tears dropped on their clasped hands.

'And then the world turned,' she continued, 'and we went separate ways. Whatever you have to sort out is over there. It's here for me.'

'Kate, I…'

'No. You always had words at will. So no words and no promises. Let the world turn, and we'll see.'

'And Liam?'

'Liam is well minded. He has me and the Island and what he never had he'll not miss. Liam doesn't need a father. I'm sorry if that hurts you, I don't intend it to. I just think that need and obligation are a poor basis for… well, anything really. Write if you want to but no envelopes with dollars, Michael, and no big Yankee presents at Christmas. I couldn't compete.'

She smiled to soften her words. Slowly, she raised her hand to his head and tugged a lock of his hair upright.

'You'll be taking the ferry today.'

'I will.'

'Go safely then, Michael Flaherty,' she said firmly and kissed him on the cheek.

He paused outside the door. 'I'm off now, Liam,' he called.

The boy did not come.

Michael took a mazy, roundabout route that brought him along the side of the gutted factory. He stopped to cross himself, then walked out the pier to the ferry. From the other side of the breakwater, he could hear the murmur of men's voices. He knew they would be sitting on upturned lobster pots, unravelling the recent happenings in low voices, leaving long pauses so that they could watch the water.

Tess Duggan stood in the prow of her boat curling a rope, looping it expertly between thumb and elbow. Michael stood for a moment admiring the grace of the movement.

'I was waiting for you, Michael,' she called without turning her head.

'Thanks, Tess.'

She turned to face him as he stepped onto the boat. 'I'm sorry about Father Mack, Michael. Ye were close.'

'We were, Tess,' he replied. 'Thanks.'

She busied herself with the mooring lines while he walked aft and settled himself on the bench at the stern, his bag resting between his feet. The deck shook itself awake like an old dog as the engine coughed and fired, and the ferry nudged away from the wall.

He glanced to his left, towards the beach, as they cleared the lee of the harbour. The men's heads rose to track their passage and the talk drifted into silence. A man stood, and then another and another, rising up from their nets until the entire body of men stood erect, all eyes on the figure in the stern of the ferry. Glancing up over their heads, Michael saw a straggle of people silhouetted on the headland, watching. He thought he recognised a woman holding a boy by the hand, and when the little figure of the boy broke free and waved, he turned his blinded eyes back to the sea.

The boat rocked once, and stalled. Michael wiped his sleeve across his eyes and saw Skald.

He was standing between Michael and the wheelhouse, feet splayed for balance. One side of his face was flayed raw and his left arm hung uselessly, but his right hand was extended before him, and there was a glint between the fingers of his closed fist. Slowly, Michael stood up as he approached.

'Some men need killing twice,' Skald said, and lunged. The force of the blow to his chest knocked Michael back on the seat, but he felt no pain. A look of surprise twitched what remained of the assassin's face into a hideous mask. Slowly, Michael put his hand inside the windcheater and withdrew the parcel. The brown paper cover was pierced through, revealing a torn envelope and a fragment of the letter inside. He recognised the writing. Turning it slowly, he saw the small bloom of blood, like a wax seal on the bottom of the package. Carefully, he nestled it back inside the windcheater, over his heart, and stood.

'Three strikes and you're out, Skald,' he said calmly, and hit him. He struck him again and again, straight-arm jabs that rocked Skald back, sending a spray of spittle flying with every impact. They stood panting, the first flurry of violence spent.

Skald swayed, fresh blood from his nose making a red delta to his chin. Michael heard the hiss of indrawn breath, and he was already moving as Skald lunged again, the knife hand arcing deep and up. Turning from the blade, Michael caught Skald's wrist and, back to back with his attacker, bent suddenly forward. There was an audible crack and Skald screamed. Michael switched his grip, dragging the broken arm up behind and wrapping his free arm across Skald's throat. He could hear the men shouting on the beach, see some of them already bouncing boats onto the water. He tightened his forearm across the man's windpipe and leaned in close. Skald's strangled breathing pulsed in his ears. The shouts of the men in the currachs, the screams of the gulls, the groaning of the wallowing boat fused to a white noise that filled Michael's brain. He began to drag his forearm tighter.

A thin thread of sound trembled across the water and snagged him back to himself. Liam stood on the headland, head tilted back; a high keening, part exultation, part anguish, came from him. Abruptly, Michael pushed the gasping man away, locking his gaze on the boy, sucking a measure of peace into his raging heart from the small, still figure.

He sensed, rather than saw, the wave gathering and surging towards the rolling boat to smash it broadside on. Michael shifted his stance to ride the roll. Skald tottered at the impact, trying vainly to raise his arms for balance. He stumbled back on the canted deck, his feet scrabbling ever faster for purchase, an expression of surprise on his ruined face. The stern rail struck him from behind and, almost in slow motion, toppled him up and over. The water seemed to rise for him, and he disappeared. Almost immediately, he bobbed back to the surface, working his legs and leaning back for buoyancy.

A terrible animal sound rose from the pursuing boats, a baying that belled over the water. Michael stood in the stern, watching the bobbing shape recede; watching until the hunting currachs circled Skald like sleek, cutting fins, the oars rising and falling, clubbing their prey until the water turned red beneath them.

He slumped in his seat, his back to the scene.

'Michael. Are you hurt?'

Tess's anxious face sported a red weal, already beginning to plump up, by her right eye. 'I was checking the chart,' she muttered. 'He was just there, and he thumped me. I —'

'It's all right, Tess,' Michael said. 'He's gone now.'

She lifted her gaze over his shoulder and shuddered. Then she took a deep breath and faced him. 'Will we head on, so?'

'Yes,' Michael replied. 'It's over.'

Acknowledgements

I owe a debt of gratitude to Breda Purdue of Hodder Headline Ireland, who took a chance on a first-time novelist, and to Claire Rourke, my editor, whose wise counsel and attention to detail was invaluable. Jonathan Williams, my literary agent has been a staunch ally and the gentlest of critics.

By the same author

The Joseph Coat and Other Patches
A collection of poems published by Gilbert Dalton, Dublin.

Out Foreign and Back
A collection of poems published by Gilbert Dalton, Dublin.

Strings and Things
A collection of poems for children
published by Paulist Press, USA.

Miracles and Me
A collection of poems for children
published by Paulist Press, USA.

Maura's Boy... A Cork Childhood
published by Mercier Press, Cork.

The New Curate
published by Mercier Press, Cork.

Life after Loss
A handbook on bereavement
published by Mercier Press, Cork.

Christy Kenneally is also a scriptwriter and presenter of the
television series *Heaven on Earth* and *The Lost Gods*.